Peter Macdonald was in the British Army for thirty-two years. He has written six novels and seven works of non-fiction: a book about bomb disposal, a short history of the world, the highly acclaimed biography of General Vo Nguyen Giap (the man who defeated the French and the Americans in Vietnam), three books about Bristol and this autobiography.

CORNERS OF MY MIND

Here, Peter Macdonald recounts many of the highlights of his interesting life. He had a successful career in the British Army for thirty-two years and attained the rank of Brigadier. His speciality was ammunition and explosives and, latterly, all forms of Army ordnance. It is a thought-provoking book, full of humour and anecdotes, and gives forthright opinions on a number of controversial issues of the day.

PETER MACDONALD

CORNERS OF MY MIND

Complete and Unabridged

ULVERSCROFT
Leicester

First published in Great Britain in 1998

First Large Print Edition
published 2002

The moral right of the author has been asserted

British Library CIP Data

Macdonald, Peter, *1957* –
    Corners of my mind: his story.—Large print ed.—
Ulverscroft large print series: non-fiction
1. Macdonald, Peter. *1957* –
2. Great Britain. Army 3. Soldiers—Great Britain—
Biography 4. Large type books
I. Title
355′.0092

ISBN 0–7089–4654–2

Published by
F. A. Thorpe (Publishing)
Anstey, Leicestershire

Set by Words & Graphics Ltd.
Anstey, Leicestershire
Printed and bound in Great Britain by
T. J. International Ltd., Padstow, Cornwall

This book is printed on acid-free paper

'Memories, light the corners of my mind,
Misty water-coloured memories,
of the way we were.'

(A. & M. Bergmann)

1

Mac, Bet and Tia Jean

Ask a man in the November of his life to tell you what the high points of it were and the odds are that he will think first of the things that are most visually memorable. Then he might try to isolate the happiest days. Then he might tell you what the turning points have been.

Ask me, and I think first of sunshine. At the beginning of my life, in a high town in the Andes, the sun casts dark shadows from grey stone buildings in the dusty shelter of which shabby women wearing bowler hats and shawls squat as a mangy dog pads by, his tongue lolling. Next, I see sunshine sparkling on the water of the Pacific, shimmering along a golden shore where waves smash down and hiss away. Years later the sun's rays are soaking into my back on a Welsh hillside in the Spring: I am lying face down, with my arms stretched out as far as they will reach, my fingers clawing at the grass, those of my right hand almost touching the blue speckled eggs I have stolen from birds' nests in the blackthorn hedgerows bordering the field in which I lie. For a moment I imagine I can feel the earth lifting as it drifts endlessly through the void of heaven. (To me, then, in my early teens, it seemed that my life's journey would also go on forever.) In my strong youth, sunshine beats down through the thin cotton of my khaki shirt and burns my neck and the skin that shows between my khaki shorts and stockings; puttees, wrapped tightly around my ankles, cover the tops of steel-studded boots that ring hard on the rocky paths of the Troodos Mountains in Cyprus. Years later, sunshine saturates the North German Plain, which rolls past smoothly underneath the perspex bubble of a lilting helicopter; great fields of ripening golden corn, dotted here and there with villages and the bright blue of garden swimming pools. Germany is a big country, with wide horizons that go on and on and on. (Northern Europe is almost dead flat for hundreds of miles. It is said that if it were not for the curvature of the Earth, from Holland, on a clear day, it would be possible to see the domes of the Kremlin.) Decades later I am flying low over the Mekong river, seeing it greyly snaking out the border between Laos and Cambodia.

Visual impacts, then, mark some of the high points of my life: strong light, white walls, sparkling water, parched earth, green fields, jungle. (It is no wonder, is it, that van Gogh went mad, seeing things the way he did, with such extraordinary vividness?) For my part attending grand opera was blighted on two occasions, in Berlin and Vienna, because never once did the stage lights go up. In deference to the need to inject what the directors regarded as modernity (another way of saying that they were desperately trying to make a name for themselves by doing something different) the singers blundered about as gloom shrouded Beethoven's massive chords and Mozart's lilting arpeggios. I walked out of Fidelio at the interval but couldn't get past a sleeping Japanese as Don Giovanni slid ludicrously off an upended table into an even blacker hole in the middle of the stage.

The happiest days? Ah, well, there were some, of course. On reflection, quite a lot, many of them given to me by women. Not just by the ecstasy of sexual contact, though there was that too, naturally, but more because the touch of a hand, or laughter shared, gave me a sense of completeness not otherwise attainable; as if the man, almost but not quite whole in himself, was rounded off by the presence of a woman. Other than when I shared companionship with women the happiest times for me were for the most part when I was overseas, living with different people in different cultures. And when I was with animals.

Turning points? For the most part they were not of my doing. They came about because of other people's decisions or because I allowed myself to be carried along by situations I failed to control — or couldn't see the consequences of.

★   ★   ★

These are the memoirs of a man who was born between the two world wars and who, for a long time, felt himself to be part of the generation that took the greatest part in shaping the 20th Century. Now I am not sure that we did, or indeed that anyone was, or is, shaping it: it becomes more evident, day by day, that for all the words spoken by men in their quest for a better way to order things, human nature goes on as it has always done: defying good nature. As for me, in my late sixties, I feel that I am becoming more distant from events, like a comet whose orbit is swinging out into space, further and further away from the centre, until in the end I too will spin out into the blackness from whence I came — and woke in all that sunshine.

I have never kept a diary — a fact I regret, in so much as it would have helped me to be more accurate about the timing and sequence of events. Since recall will inevitably fade even more, I feel I should make a record now, for my own benefit and for my sons'.

And, too, that I had best get on with it.

★　★　★

My birth, for instance. I don't remember a thing about it! My parents never mentioned it; perhaps it was too painful an experience.

The place where I made my entrance was certainly unusual for someone of my pedigree: not as one might expect in a house in Aberdeen or a hospital in Glasgow but in a villa in a town seven thousand feet up in the Andes overlooked by a snow-capped extinct volcano named, with no great flight of the imagination, El Misti — not far from Lake Titicaca on the Bolivian altiplano, where the Inca civilisation probably originated. The time was July 1928, not quite ten years after the end of the First World War and a bit more than that from the beginning of the second. That fixes me firmly in terms of European history, though 1928 was neither here nor there as far as Peruvian history is concerned: the way along El Sendero Luminoso, The Shining Path, was not yet beckoning.

How was it that I was born in Peru, of all places?

My father was a Scot, Andrew Macdonald, who was born in Aberdeen in February 1882. That means he was forty-five years old when I was conceived, elderly for a father by today's standards, and in consequence I knew him only as a middle-aged and then an old man. A fit man, a hearty eater, a sound sleeper, an energetic walker — until he was nearly eighty, when he suddenly faded, took to his bed, trembling and spindle-shanked, and point-blank refused to leave it until he died. After two very long years of that existence he left us like a candle guttering out, one of his nicely-shaped hands clutching my brother Brian's.

Andrew was not tall, or small. He was about five-feet-seven inches in height, and in appearance remarkably like the older Picasso; only he always had a moustache, clipped so short that I sometimes wondered why he bothered with it at all. He was a straight hard-working and well-meaning man with absolutely no spite who liked the simple things in life — his food, reading the newspaper from cover to cover, listening to the wireless and, later, watching football on the television.

Of my father's family I knew very little until recently, when I asked a man in Edinburgh who does these things to find out something about them. It turns out they were all, from the end of the 18th Century, which was as far back as he could go, Aberdonians, except for one, Christian, the daughter of James Murray, a Sheriff's Officer of Stonehaven, who married John McDonald, a labourer, in June 1831 — the same year as the Bristol riots, about which I was to write much, much later. Andrew's ancestors on his father's side were James, John, Archibald, and on the female side Christina, Christian, Helen. (Learning the names, in a strange way, brought these distant people fleetingly back to life.) On his mother's they were James, David, John, and Margaret and Jean. The men were labourers and farm hands, street porters and tailors and shoemakers. (The street porter died in Aberdeen of Asiatic Cholera, for God's sake, in 1866.) In Archibald's time people like that were paid about two shillings and sixpence a day, and yet they managed to raise a family and, I imagine, to be staid, God-fearing and upright people. (Though no doubt there was a rogue or two among them.) Despite their poverty,

Scots of that ilk were literate, if only to be able to read the Bible, which they did with great diligence every day.

Brothers, Andrew had, and sisters, many of them, ten in all. Where they all went, and why, I do not know. I have a sepia photograph of his mother and father, a typical Victorian pair: a stout, forbidding-looking woman, Christian by name, nee Hunter, standing panelled in bombazine and staring apprehensively at the camera from under a sort of truncated black silk bonnet; sitting beside her is James, a solid, bearded, hairier version of my father, posed and stiff in his Sunday-best frock-coat. He was a merchant tailor, so my father's birth certificate says, but what that means is open to wide interpretation. Was he employed in a clothier's shop in Aberdeen, measuring males: chest, elbow, waist, inside-leg? (Yes, surr; certainly, surr; fitting on Thursday in the morning convenient to you, surr?) or did he cut cloth and sew, crouched over a big table? Or, even, imagine it, sit cross-legged under a hissing gas jet wondering, as he tried to thread a needle, how he was going to earn enough to feed his bawling brood? Or did he, maybe, glory of glories, own the shop?

Macdonalds (with a small 'd') come from the Western Isles or the Highlands and for years I was aware of, and proud of, the distinction. (some of the 'small Ds' think themselves superior to those who spell it with a big 'D' or McD. In time I was to meet Ranald Macdonald of Macdonald, clan chief of that sept, who asked me how I spelt my name and when I told him said 'Oh good, you're not one of the Jocks, then.') but as the Edinburgh man discovered when looking into the records the spelling was quite arbitrary in years gone by. Whatever, one of my father's forebears must have moved east into the granite city. Perhaps a half-starved clansman dragging a bandaged leg limped into Aberdeen soon after the battle of Culloden rather than risk being captured by the patrolling redcoats of Cumberland's army who, in 1745, harried the beaten Highlanders through the glens on behalf of his father, the King of England, and stamped out, once and for all (or at least until 1997) Scottish rebellion. One hundred and fifty years on a bewhiskered descendant had achieved enough well-being to be able to afford a decent suit, a starched collar and high-buttoned boots — and the cost of a posh portrait taken on a new-fangled machine. Shades of Mr Polly.

My father Andrew wore spats, quaint relics of Victoriana, long after the 1939/45 war, until they became so archaic that my mother told him he had to give way to the march of time and consign them to the bin. Grey suede, they were, with little fasteners that had to be fiddlingly eased into their holes with a button hook. They made him feel warm and comfortable, he said. In South America, he sometimes wore an equally old-fashioned solar topee, which no doubt made him feel cool and comfortable; I have a photo of him, so hatted, standing beside a car that had been converted to run on railway lines. And another, wearing a Homburg hat, standing beside the Prince of Wales and the Duke of Kent in the late 1920s in the shade of a large high-wing monoplane that looks as if it had been cobbled together from sheets of galvanised iron, on an airfield on a high plateau in the Andes. My father used to speak of a man called Dan Tobin who in those days flew the first passenger-carrying aircraft up and down the long spine of South America; and of hair-raising flights with him over the mountains. That really was flying, he used to say. I believe him. Now, Pan American Airways have vanished from the scene, and so too has Dan Tobin, long since.

How was it that this middle-class Scotsman came to be standing beside the Prince of Wales, the future King Edward VIII, in Peru?

The prince was on a world tour with his brother, smiling palely at oceans of eager faces and charming the ladies — as he continued to do for another ten years or so until he bolted with one of them. Andrew had sailed away in his Twenties, as had so many others like him, to find fame and fortune, which were hard to come by in Scotland. Twenty years later, by then British Vice-Consul in Arequipa, he stood respectfully beside a scion of the House of Hanover, against which his forefathers had rebelled so bravely but futilely.

Andrew went first, a few years into the new century, to Tiera del Fuego, the Land of Fire, in Patagonia, in Chile, on the southernmost tip of South America, to farm sheep. I don't know what possessed him to go to such an outlandish place but it was a prescient thing to do for otherwise he might have been one of the millions killed in the Great War. It is a sad fact that in his rather dour way he did not volunteer information about himself or his family and I, self-absorbed, disinterested, as young people tend to be about the past and the lives of their elders, never thought to ask. Well, hardly ever. When I did the answers did not encourage further questions. Whatever the motivation, he ended up in the back of beyond managing a huge sheep farm that took days to circumnavigate on horseback. I have a photo of him astride a large nag, both of them apparently full of energy.

What he did with all that energy in his spare time is not recorded, except that he and a few like-minded scattered European friends introduced Association Football to that part of the world, from where it migrated to Brazil — with disastrous consequences, in years to come, for European hopes in the World Cup. I suppose he has a lot to answer for. Other than that it seems he lived a solitary life, far away from other people, with few amenities or diversions: no hotels, clubs, pubs or female company. In the Far East in those days planters found solace in the arms of beautiful Tamil or Malay girls. Today, Punta Arenas is said to have more brothels per head of the population (and more alcoholics) than any other place in Latin America, but it is hard to imagine any attractions for a Scot in the ugly, squat, sour-smelling females who are native to Patagonia. Maybe my father played patience, as I do, to while away hours that would be better spent doing something productive. He must have tired of loneliness after a while, though, because he came home to Scotland to find a wife.

The happy outcome of a marriage is an extraordinarily chancy business, made even chancier in the Western world by the largely Hollywood-invented chimera of 'love'. An arranged marriage between Pakistanis is as likely to prove happy as is a modern British one entered into by people conditioned to expect an unendingly romantic union. Yet what could it have been that persuaded a pretty, genteel Scottish girl to set sail for Patagomia if it was not 'love'? She must have been beguiled by his personality and promises — monosyllabic at that, no doubt, more implied than specified. Or perhaps just for once in his life his tongue was untied. But, too, she had a great sense of adventure. Whatever the reasons, Elizabeth Michael Smith became a Macdonald. Twice.

Elizabeth had two sisters and a brother, and a mother who was a Stewart and came from Perth. Her father, Samuel, was part-Irish, with a trace of Spanish somewhere; maybe a long link with a sailor from the Armada who, wrecked on the Irish shore by the gales that saved England in 1588, managed somehow to find the words to woo a wife and make a new life. Sam's mother was a McMichael. He it was who brought an arty, slightly raffish touch to the family. Musical, with a fine baritone voice, he had the confidence and charm to circulate in the upstream pools of Glasgow. Photographs of him show a face with a long aristocratic nose on which pince-nez are perched, through which gleams high intelligence; under it an Imperial beard; on the head, a jauntily-cocked Homburg hat. He has the look of a man who enjoyed life and found humour in it, but, of course, he had a temper, the Irish and Latin ancestry coming out. His daughter, known as Bet, inherited the temper, the good-looks and the intelligence. And enterprise: during the Great War she drove a motor ambulance, vehicles that could only have existed for a year or two, wheezing and clattering through the streets. And wore a scarf around her hat to keep it on — which is more than the policeman did who bounced off her front bumper one day when he was on point duty at an intersection in central Glasgow: she put her foot down and sped around the corner as he got up off the ground and reached for his notebook to take her number. (She would tell the tale with a giggle and no sign of contrition because, she said, he must have been all right; he was waving his fist in the air.) When she sailed away on her long journey with her new husband she was a pretty woman, nine years his junior. (It turns out that one of her McMichael ancestors was a policeman in Londonderry, a fact I did not know when I used to fly over the place in a

14

helicopter in the 1970s.)

Elizabeth was to give Andrew three sons, two of them born in Punta Arenas (Sandy Point) — Basil Andrew Stewart and Brian Michael — and the third, me, in Arequipa, whence they had moved in stages via Santiago and Antofagasta in Chile, the source of income changing from sheep farming to importing and exporting on behalf of a Scottish firm, Balfour Williamson. Peru was a far cry from the Glasgow Orpheus Choir — in which her father had sung — and from Jack Buchanan, a popular musical comedy star whom she knew and whose career she followed from afar over the years. I have the feeling that as time passed she hankered for what might have been; came to feel that she had married badly and could have done better for herself. In fact the plain Scot, Andrew, at first did well by her, for in Peru they lived very comfortably, socialising a lot, employing a cook, maids and a garden boy — indeed, living a life very similar to that lived by the British in the colonies, cheap labour providing a far better standard of existence than that which they might have expected at home.

My earliest memories are of servants. There was a Peruvian nursemaid, predictably called Maria, who was my constant companion, so much so that I spoke Spanish before I could properly speak English. I remember her being sharply reprimanded for some lack of attention to me and weeping loudly. And I recall her leading me by the hand into the sea at a place called Mollendo, whence we had travelled in a big, shiny, maroon-coloured Packard, and having a chunk bitten out of one of her legs by a baby shark. You may imagine the consternation: the wails and the shrieks; the blood staining the sparkling blue water; the panic as other bathers thrashed their way to the shore. From then on I was not allowed to enter the sea at all and instead pottered about wearing sandals, a smart miniature one-piece belted bathing costume and a floppy white linen hat. On another occasion I stood enthralled watching a huge white fish with a jagged dorsal fin slicing through the water, rolling over and over and splashing foam against the blue sky.

Sunshine, dusty roads, priests, bell-towers, donkeys, llamas, alpacas, women plodding along on bare feet carrying heavy loads, chickens scratching in the dust, big earthenware pots brimming with exotic-looking fruit, excited, jabbering voices, my mother opening my bedroom door late at night after she had returned home from a party to see if I was all right — these are some of my early recollections. And asses' milk.

As a child I was often sickly because of the heat and the height. Inevitably, I contracted enteric-type illnesses and because it was bland I was prescribed asses' milk. Water, full of microbes, could be lethal and my father never drank it, unboiled, for years; never drank it at all if he could help it, preferring bottled soda water, either straight or diluted with a wee whisky. Many years later, for the same reason, I too avoided water when I was in Vietnam, relying on Coca Cola or tinned Heineken beer. (Heineken? In Hanoi? Ja!)

I remember very clearly the first contact I had with music — Bocherini's Minuet, recorded on a little red floppy disc (not a bit like the floppy disc in the computer I am now using) and disseminating, via a punishingly destructive steel needle, its lilting, catchy melody through the tinny playing head of a toy, wind-up gramophone bought in Selfridges, Oxford Street, London, by an aunt, Jane, known as Jean, and sent all the way to Peru. It was no bad way for a small boy to hear music for the first time — apart from church bells, that is, which rang through the mountain air morning, noon and night.

Roman Catholicism permeated life in Arequipa. The Corpus Christi processions winding through the streets, spindly-legged, dark-skinned men staggering along bearing tons of imagery on their sore shoulders; misty-eyed women genuflecting and grovelling on their knees in the dust as the cortège passed; incense smoke lying like a pall over the heads of the moaning crowds lining the streets — these were the first great human spectacles I saw.

The comfort and hope of religion was absolutely essential to those simple people, every spark of Inca energy and intelligence bred out of them by centuries of poor diet and dull life. (It is astonishing to think that the illiterate Pizzaro achieved his conquest of their million ancestors with just a few dozen soldiers, is it not? Actually, it was his thirty-seven horses that did it. The Peruvians were scared stiff of them, never having seen such creatures.)

Scots Presbyterian probity looked down upon all this idolatrous nonsense with mild contempt and wondered at the wealth of the church; at the jewels encrusting the Madonnas in contrast to the terrible poverty of her worshippers. In later years my parents drifted into the Church of England, by default, really, as so many people do, so as to have somewhere to go for christenings, weddings and funerals, but religion, in the sense of a sure belief and faith, was never a significant factor in their lives. For me, there was to be a passing phase of intense commitment as a boy, and another as a young army officer.

Arequipa is an Inca city, enlarged by the Spanish hundreds of years before I opened my eyes there. In it there was a small coterie of society consisting of Spaniards (that is to say, Peruvians who claimed descent from the Conquistadores and their migrant successors) who held themselves aloof from the native peasantry, and Americans and Europeans who largely ran the show: the bankers, merchants, lawyers and administrators who managed the commercial life of the place. A sizeable town it was, with a 17th Century cathedral, indeed a city, the capital of the southern part of the country, in those days mainly concerned with tanning and textiles.

By the time they had reached Arequipa a big problem had arisen for my parents. My eldest brother, Basil, was eight years older than I and the middle one, Brian, five. As they reached prep-school age the decision had to be taken whether to send them home to be educated. If they stayed in Peru they would grow up Spanish-speaking, and would almost certainly settle there and eventually change their nationality, so it was decided to send them home to a boarding school in England, in the care of Aunt Jean during holiday times. It meant long periods of separation, for in those days a ship took weeks to cross the Atlantic. Time and cost made it out of the question to bring the boys back to Peru for the holidays, or for us to go to see them, except at very long intervals. (On one of the rare visits to England I became ill with diphtheria on board ship and had to be taken off at New York, where I stayed with my mother for a few weeks until I recovered. I regret to say that I remember nothing at all about that interlude: New York, to me, is the vicious, noisy, dirty place depicted in Cagney's and Lacey's constant battles against anarchic mayhem.)

I was too young to understand, or care, about the problems of education, and furthermore it was something I was spared, for there was no kindergarten for me to attend. But somebody, I do not remember who, taught me to read, in English, when I was five or six. Apart from those enforced periods of study, day after day I pottered about in the sunshine, sometimes riding a donkey, or, later, a pony. (Since then I have never been astride an equine back, a fact that I don't know whether to deplore or to be thankful for. As a peer of the realm, then a lieutenant-colonel in the Coldstream Guards, once said to me, only half-joking, languidly holding a very large glass of port in his right hand and tapping his knee with the fingers of his left, 'Horses are dangerous at both ends and uncomfortable in the middle.' Harvey Smith, great show-rider of the 1960's and '70's, thinks ninety per cent of them are evil. He should know. Mind, visually I think they are the most beautiful animals in creation. It is looking into that unfathomable depth in their black eyes and seeing wisdom but no recognition that confuses me.)

We travelled to Southampton or Liverpool on German liners, the *Bremen* and the *Europa* of Norddeutscher-Lloyd, because they were good value for money and comfortable. (Forty-five years later I was walking through the grounds of the Villa Hugel in Essen, the home of the Krupp family, who made a vast fortune out of making guns for Kaiser Wilhelm's, and then Hitler's, armies, and there on a plinth was one of the gigantic propellers from the *Europa*, kept as a memento of other, more peaceful endeavours. Not long after that I used to go into a pub in Bremerhaven, the *Europa*'s home port, on the walls of which were several photographs of the ship. Often in my life loops have closed in this way.)

By the early Thirties my father was well off, with a salary of over £1,000 a year, which in

21

those days was a lot of money, but as he had to pay for his sons' education, and for maintaining them in England, his financial worries began. The need for money is, of course, relative to one's expectations: to some people we would have been 'comfortable', to some disgustingly affluent, to others pitifully deprived. Looking back, we seemed always to be trying to do too much with too little, to be stretching the available funds. And schooling was to remain the basic cause of the problem. From that point on, Andrew began a slow descent into penury.

My brothers went first to a preparatory school called Homewood House, near Colchester (it still exists) where the headmaster (a Mr Duggan) and his wife kindly looked after them during some holidays when they were not with Jean. Later Basil went to Clayesmore, a school near Blandford in Dorset (where my son Alexander regularly played tennis in the early-1990s: another closed loop) and Brian to Woodbridge in Suffolk, where one of his classmates was Edward Du Cann, one-time multimillionaire Chairman of the Conservative Party but now, too, in sore financial straits. (Relatively.)

Our stretched family existence inevitably became untenable and in 1936 we sailed from Callao, Lima's port, for the last time. I remember Sambo, a negro houseboy who was gentle with me and good-humoured — and immensely strong: when we came to leave he man-handled huge crates quite alone, lifting them up like empty cardboard boxes high above his head, his muscles bulging and his sweaty body wafting sour smells. I remember, too, going through the quite new (1914) Panama Canal, though of course I had no idea of the price in lives, sweat and sickness that had been paid to carve it through those mosquito-ridden swamps and jungles.

On arrival in England we stayed in London with Aunt Jean, who ran a small hotel in Torrington Square, near the British Museum. She was a woman of delightful charm, blue-eyed, blonde, warm, generous and full of fun — in appearance and demeanour resembling Dr Hilda Bracket of Hinge and Bracket fame. She was bandy-legged (Jean, not 'Hilda') though whether she had always been like that or only became like that in later life I do not know. Bandy-legged or not, she could charm the opposite sex, unfortunately.

When her father died my father had undertaken to look after her interests, a responsibility which, like all those he entered into, he took very seriously. Consequently, he was furious when on her way to Peru for a holiday visit Jean stopped off en route in

Buenos Aires and sent him a cable announcing that she had been married aboard ship. And to a Greek at that! Her starry-eyed state of matrimony lasted about two weeks, for after a lone shopping expedition she returned to the hotel bedroom to find her new husband closely cloistered with a chambermaid.

In those days divorce from a man whose whereabouts were not known (and still are not, for that matter, though he must be long dead) was very difficult, and when enough time had elapsed for her to qualify she did not bother, and hung on to her outlandish surname. It gave her a kick, I think, to go into Fortnums or Fullers in London loaded with furs and jewellery and 'put on dog', as the Scots say, loudly announcing that she was Mrs Roussiano and demanding to know, in a nice, smiley way, which table had been reserved for her. Perhaps she thought that the maître might take her for a Balkan princess: she certainly looked the part, and had the clothes and presence to fool them. Though her affluence was skin deep, birthdays, Christmas and outings were the occasions for the donation of lovely gifts.

Though Tia Jean never married again ('Tia' is Spanish for Aunt. She liked to be called that because it maintained a tenuous

24

link to her visit to Peru) she lived for years first with Walter Cortis-Stanford, known for propriety's sake as Uncle Wattie — it was years before this dawned on me: I really thought he was an uncle — and later with Jim Elcock, his brother-in-law. Jean and Wattie had moved from Torrington Square to a much nicer hotel, Ivy House, in Hampton Court, which had a huge mulberry tree in the garden that dripped scarlet juice in the height of summer. On a Sunday they would go to the chapel royal in the palace, where she would put on dog again, in high style and never allowing, for a moment, the fact that she was living in sin impinge on the situation and dull the fawning reception with which she was received by the ushers as they bowed her into her pew.

In his Sixties, Wattie, poor man, suddenly became very ill and died, demented, and Jean sold up the hotel and became companion help to his sister in Bournemouth, a lady who had lived for most of her life in Assam and could not bear the thought of having to make tea in the morning. It was the worst thing she ever did, for her husband fell in love with Jean and she with him, and after a few months they decamped and set up home together. A mile away.

Until then I had naïvely assumed that

people changed immeasurably as they grew older; that the ageing process altered the person inwardly as well as outwardly; that the handsome young man in cavalry uniform with chain mail epaulettes was only very distantly related to the handsome old man who drove a sky-blue Humber Hawk at a snail's pace along the roads of Canford Cliffs in the 1950s — largely because he was half blind. Jean would lean towards him and say 'Take care, Jim! We're approaching traffic lights,' or 'Look out for that woman on the pedestrian crossing, Jim dear . . . ' It came as a big surprise to me to find that, subject to minor adjustments, the boy is still alive and kicking in the old gentleman — and the romantic girl in the starry-eyed elderly lady. The two were like young lovers and must often have rued the fact that they had not met in their Twenties.

In those days, as now, there was a law that a person who made money over to another in his or her lifetime had to live for several years after making the gift in order to escape what were then called Death Duties. On the morning before the due date Jim Elcock came down to breakfast, sat down, poured milk over his cereal, commented that it was a beautiful morning and then paused for a moment. 'My God, Jean,' he said, 'do you realise that I've only got twenty-four hours to go?' The thought was so stunning that he had a stroke, fell forward into his cornflakes and died.

I have more than once wished that Aunt Jean had propped him up in front of an open oven door and kept him warm for a day, or had gone to visit relatives overnight, subsequently disclaiming knowledge of the actual time of death. As it was, the Inland Revenue descended like vultures and picked off the fat, removing most of the remainder of the flesh when, eventually, she too died.

★   ★   ★

After we had lived for a few weeks in Torrington Square my father rented Gainsborough's House in Sudbury, Suffolk, which was then a hotel. He thought that if Jean could run one, he could, but in that he was very much mistaken. He may have been an efficient merchant in faraway places but had no experience of dealing with English tradespeople — or complaining English customers, come to that — so the project did not last long. However, it left me many memories, one of which was the first time I was allowed to go on an errand by myself: to the nearby ironmongers to get a replacement radio battery. It was in a glass box, in which could be seen the lead plates and the electrolyte, and had to be charged up at fairly short intervals; handed in, another was issued in its place. Another, is of church bells. My bedroom was a small one at the back of the house, overlooking a lovely walled garden and a tennis court. It was approached, as I remembered, by a narrow, creaking, curving, oak-panelled staircase, at the side of which was a cupboard in which, I was quite sure, something nasty lurked. On practice-night the bells in the nearby church rang out beautifully but now, perhaps not surprisingly, the sound of people ringing the changes in another nearby church inspires melancholy in me.

The tennis court was the scene of the only occasion when I saw my father completely lose his temper and resort to violence. He had a man whose job it was to rake and roller the red gravel of the tennis court, a thankless and unending task largely due to the exuberance of a vivacious, leggy, blonde girl whose idea of expertise was to demonstrate just how far she could skid on a good day. (I wonder what she looks like now, that lissom, sexy female? On second thoughts, better not to think about it.) This roller-man clobbered me one day, hard, and sent me sprawling, causing a bloody scrape on my elbow, the scar of which I still have. I must have cheeked him, no doubt, and probably deserved a clout but my father, appearing in response to my shrieks of pain, grabbed the man by the scruff of the neck, bellowed at him like the proverbial enraged bull and literally booted him off the premises.

Recently, I returned to Gainsborough's House, now a museum dedicated to the genius of that superb 18th Century artist. The public rooms have become galleries, the garden has been truncated, the tennis court has gone, the dreaded staircase turned out to be four steps high, its panelling is now painted white and the cupboard wouldn't hold a self-respecting garden gnome, let alone a giant ogre.

While living in Sudbury I joined my brothers in Homewood House and became known as Mac 3. Like my mother I had a short fuse, and made a name for myself on my first day there by pushing the headmaster's son through the glass of a french window. While this did nothing for my reputation with the owners of the establishment it had a salutory effect on the other pupils, who approached me cautiously from then on; there was no question of ever having to endure bullying, and it was a lesson well learnt.

Having made a poor show of running a hostelry, my father bought a business in Felixstowe, where he did no better. Basil had to leave Clayesmore and take a job as a clerk in Marriage's flour mills. Brian stayed on at Woodbridge for a while. I left Homewood House and did not go to school at all — a situation that these days would not be tenable. My memories of that unsettled time are very fragmented: a bad-tempered and very vocal macaw that sat on its perch outside a nearby shop and did its best to amputate the fingers of the silly people who tried to prod it, while whitewashing their shoes to boot; outings to the pier pavilion to hear Yunckman's Czardas Band on a Saturday evening in the summer when East Anglian men wearing Hungarian costume leapt around the stage banging tambourines, or twanged balalaikas like crazy; swimming in icy water off a stoney beach and marvelling at a black labrador dog that ate every pebble tossed for it and rattled when it ran; a place called Bawdsey, further up the coast, where we hired a beach hut and crouched over a spirit stove in our bathing costumes and towels while the East wind off the North Sea howled outside and lashed sand into the sandwiches. We still managed to live, you see, middle-class fashion, even though the bawbees were in short supply, optimism triumphing over common sense.

In those pre-National Health Service days my father's financial troubles were much compounded by the fact that my mother was seldom well — though not as ill as she thought she was. That is not to say that all was gloom. Oh, no, she had a keen sense of humour, read voraciously, loved companion-ship, and cared deeply about the welfare of her children. And she could cook like an angel — always assuming that such beings have culinary skills, which I doubt; she was a 'natural', disdaining cookery books and relying on sure instinct: a spoonful of this, half a cup of that, a pinch of the other producing a scalloped edge on a rich pie crust, lovely dumplings, stews, cakes and puddings. The trouble was, she was bored. She needed a mentally stimulating man beside her, while he wanted only peace and quiet.

I have said that Elizabeth twice became a Macdonald. On the twenty-first of June 1915 she married Andrew, known to many as 'Mac' (which is what she called him) both of Mount Florida, Glasgow, in the Gorbals Registry Office. His age was given as 33 and hers as

24. Four years later, on the twenty-ninth of June 1919, she married him again, at the Scotch (sic) Church in the parish of Kingston, Jamaica. Their ages are given as 33 and 24. It is a mystery that I have never unravelled, and probably never will, now, since I came into possession of the marriage certificates only after the two of them were dead, as are all the other people who might have shed any light on the matter.

* * *

As the 1930s drew to a close things were not looking good for the Macdonalds: my father's ambitions had been shattered, my mother's health was poor, my brothers' education had been interrupted and I remained happily missing from any school register.

As war loomed many young men joined the Territorial Army, Basil among them, becoming a gunner in the Royal Artillery. Catching the martial spirit I often led a gang of embryonic soldiers, shrilly shouting orders, up and down what I remembered as wooded cliffs but which on recent inspection turn out to be a grassy bank with a few bushes growing on it behind the Great War memorial on the promenade. On the more recent, 1939 – 45, additions to it the name of B.A.S.

Macdonald is carved on a stone slab.

The saving grace for me was that I loved reading, and had found the road to adventure. I could stumble through the Wild Wood with Ratty or Mole, or charge the Saracens at the head of a host of Knights Hospitaller, or win the VC in a last-ditch stand against the enemy.

2

Not much peace

I was eleven years old when the Second World War began and remember quite clearly the tone if not the content of Neville Chamberlain's broadcast telling the nation it was at war — the measured, apologetic, slightly quavering voice I have since heard repeated many times on radio and TV programmes. And the fact that about an hour later the air-raid warning sirens sounded.

We were living in a house called Green Gap at the time, the back garden of which bordered one of the fairways of the golf links. I used to make pocket money by poking around in the hedge with a stick and finding lost golf balls, which I then sold for a penny or two to the next daft golfer who came poking about on the other side of the hedge after slicing his ball off the tee. Many of those I found had been hit only once and to this day I find the appearance and feel of a brand-new golf ball pleasing — though what I contrived to do with such things in later years was very disappointing.

When the sirens went off on the 3rd September 1939 — the first time they had all sounded since Armistice Day in 1918 — there was a concerted rush for the loo. We all thought that we were going to be blown to smithereens any minute, the bombing of Guernica during the Spanish Civil War having given a lot of people a totally erroneous idea, as it proved, that aerial bombardment would quickly end any conflict. (Incidentally, I have always loathed Picasso's painting which, like most of his output as far as I am concerned, is the product of a sick mind. In a speech made in 1952 he himself said 'I cannot regard myself as an artist, in the strict sense of the word. I am only a joker who understood his epoch and has extracted all he possibly could from the stupidity, greed and vanity of his contemporaries.' No-one, it seems, took him at his word and as a result his deadly virus has infected all modern art. Art based on hate, Kenneth Clark called it, and said he thought it couldn't last. Unfortunately, he seems to have got that wrong.)

Within days Basil was called up, then spent several weeks doing practically nothing in the local Drill Hall. Mac 2 left school and began a badly-paid job somewhere but like millions of other people my father found that war had

35

its compensations, for suddenly his ability to read and write Spanish fluently became a saleable commodity. The government had decided that every single letter and parcel entering and leaving the country had to be censored, and in consequence an army of readers of foreign languages had to be recruited. To house one of the biggest branches of the Censorship the Littlewoods Pools building, at Edge Hill, near Liverpool, was requisitioned, and so it was that in 1940 we found ourselves in that city.

My impressions of Scouseland were then, and remain, generally bad. Mile upon boring mile of dingy streets lined with little semis interspersed with clusters of poky little shops interrupted here and there by the would-be imposing art-nouveau façades of red-brick cinemas — most of which are now bingo halls; a flat, slate- and brick-coloured hinterland that spread out, street after street north of Scotland Road and T.J. Hughes' department store. In the city centre were trolley buses, St George's Hall and Lime Street Station — and a couple of theatres. Nearby, were the Anglican Cathedral, Bold Street — then the posh shopping mecca — and the unfinished Roman Catholic cathedral. And, too, there was the Adelphi Hotel, of which my father spoke almost with awe, for before the war it had been the overnight stopping place for people waiting in the greatest luxury to board the Cunard liners that would take them across the Atlantic; a place of unattainable luxury as far as he was concerned. (Forty years later I stayed there on my way to meet Lord Derby at Knowsley Hall. During my interview with him strange noises emanated from behind the desk which I put down to an embarrassing ailment that afflicted the unfortunate peer but all was revealed when, on my departure, an ancient grey-jowled Labrador emerged, wagging his tail, and came forward to say goodbye. I found the Adelphi run-down and tatty, its bars full of whores, but I believe it is now much improved.) Further south were the Liver Building, with its two golden phoenix atop the domes, big ships, and the Ferry, on which people 'crossda Mairzee to Dew Brighdon and Burken'ead.' Once or twice we took the 'fairy', too, just for a giggle, really, because Burken'ead was even worse than Liverpewl, though the scene on the river when going back and forth was very impressive.

People say that poverty exists in this country today — and indeed there are people who sit begging on the pavements of most cities with a dog at their feet, poor beast (for which they get an increment to their dole) in between visits to the Benefits Office — but it is nothing compared to the dire penury that existed in the 1940s. Around the slum areas of Scotland Road it was commonplace to see barefoot children in rags holding on to a woman wearing a shawl standing outside a down-at-heel terraced house with crumbling walls, broken windows and unpainted doors. There was real destitution then. But the poor did not beg . . .

An uncle of mine, Peter Garioch, the Godfather after whom I was named, spent many years of his life carving stone for the new Roman Catholic cathedral (somewhere in my family's genes there must be a carving chip of DNA). I don't think we saw Peter very often and for the life of me I can't think why my parents were so misguided as to lumber me with such an awkward middle name. The 'och' part of it is pronounced in the same way as the Scottish word 'loch' which, when it has to be written down, immediately calls for an explanation as to its spelling. The writer's pen stops dead as soon as I get past the G-A-R part. Sighs and frowns of annoyance, and a close look to see if I am some sort of a foreigner, are the usual follow-up, then I have to start again, and proceed very slowly. Consequently, I have cursed the name of that small town near Aberdeen. (It was only recently that I found that Garioch is pronounced Garry by the people who live in and around Aberdeen.)

We stayed in Liverpool until, like St George's Hall, we were bombed out, going from one lot of crumby digs to another and leading a very peripatetic existence. The three of us, my parents and I, began, full of hope, in Wavertree. There, one May evening, out for a stroll in the Spring air, we happened to pass the railway station as a hospital train full of wounded soldiers who had been evacuated from Dunkirk, hundreds of them, was being unloaded: the stretchers had been brought out and lined up on the forecourt to await the arrival of ambulances that would take the occupants to local hositals. Some of the soldiers were joking, others had legs that looked like blood-stained, amputated logs. One young man's skull had been almost entirely replaced by a chromium-plated dome; he was still breathing — gurgling would be a better word — but I cannot believe that he continued to do so for long.

Because of our frequent moves my education continued to be a problem. I spent a few months at a Roman Catholic school where, because I was a Protestant, in the mornings I was made to stand alone in the corridor, head-down, embarrassed, bored and shuffling my feet, an outcast, while the rest of the school assembled and said their prayers. I believe that they prayed for me while they were at it, willing me to become one of them. What a damned cheek! And they could not have gone about it in a worse way, could they? They must have had some influence, though, because it was about this time that I entered the first of my two frantic religious phases.

As a young teenager I worked out a sequence of prayer that had to be observed as punctiliously as a Buddhist's: if I got it wrong I had to start all over again. Furthermore, if I got it wrong I was doomed, and so were my nearest and dearest, so night after night I knelt before an icon — a small cross hanging on a nail above my bed — and desperately went through a long ritual, shivering in my pyjamas while dreading the arrival of a bolt of lightning from heaven if a syllable was misplaced. If I heard my mother's approach on the stairs I quickly abandoned God and ducked under the bedclothes, then after she had gone, profusely apologised to Him, genuflected, and began the litany all over again. Mercifully, this weird phobia did not last long, and instead I took to reading novels under the bedclothes with a torch, a much more rewarding occupation.

Mac 1 was at this time stationed in Sevenoaks in Kent and Mac 2 had joined the Royal Navy. Up in Liverpool we moved to Newsham Park, a once-posh place that someone had spoiled by building a monstrosity of a power station in the middle of the green bit. At first we had a top-floor flat with nice views towards the cooling towers but we left that after my mother had a flaming row with the landlady about her morals — the landlady's, I mean, obviously. This rather blowsy blonde had a husband away at the war but fairly early on, I imagine, had decided that she might never see him again and did not intend to waste the bed years of her sex life on the off chance that she might. In any case, how would he ever know what she had been up to? (And what was he up to, come to that?) Anyway, judging from the outraged comments that my mother heaped, sotto voce, upon my poor father's nodding head behind his newspaper, the woman led a very active love life. We departed in high dudgeon to the other side of the park, to a semi-basement flat where I received lessons from a deadbeat old man who was trying to eke out a miserable pension by doing private tuition.

41

I think this possessor of dirty shirt cuffs finally packed it in because he came to the conclusion that the pennies my father paid him were entirely inadequate recompense for the task of trying to drive snippets of history and geography into the idle brain of a disinterested little brat. For my part, I only heard one word in three, being mesmerised by the trickle of saliva that continually issued from the corners of his thin lips and ran down his deeply creased cheeks into the stubble on his chin, from which he would occasionally wipe it off with a grey handker-chief. My tutor, poor fellow, was a truly revolting sight, though someone, somewhere must have loved him — before he grew long black hairs on the end of his nose, that is. (Or then, again, maybe not.) My father would have aided the educative process greatly if he had only bought the old fellow a razor blade and a shaving brush, but he wasn't to know that. So ended another attempt to extend my knowledge.

Air-raids became a nightly occurrence and stirrup pumps, wardens, whistles and tin hats part of daily life. One evening, returning home from one of those sunset perambula-tions, anti-aircraft guns opened up without warning and as we raced, panting, for shelter the pavements around us were splattered with red-hot fragments of jagged shrapnel; the next day I went back and collected a pocketful of these trophies.

Sometimes when the sirens sounded and it seemed that we were in for a bad time the young couple who lived in the top-floor flat would be invited to come down to the basement for greater safety. On one occasion the father, a rather pudgy, self-conscious, fair-haired young man brought his baby daughter to the top of the stairs in a carry-cot and contrived to let go of one of the handles. The unfortunate bundle tipped out and bounced down the stairs, bump, bump, bump, accompanied by the shrieks and shouts of the onlookers — except me: I was too taken aback to open my mouth and stood awaiting the outcome with interest. The mother was sobbing and wailing as the baby came to rest at the bottom of the stairs, opened her eyes and smiled up at her.

Not many days later a German plane dropped a stick of bombs right across Newsham Park. The first demolished one of the outbuildings of the power station (so justifying, if you stretch it a bit, this loosing-off of war weaponry on the civilian population); the last landed a few yards outside our front windows and blew the whole lot, frames and all, into the middle of the room, and the coals in the fireplace on to the sofa. We were crouching in a hole under the stairs at the time. So ended our tenancy.

My mother announced, not unreasonably, that she had had enough of Merseyside and she and I took off for North Wales, where we lived for a few idyllic weeks in a little village called Llanfair Talhairn. It was Spring, and I diligently searched the warm hedgerows, collecting single tribute from wrens, thrushes, finches and blackbirds. I had nothing else to do, you see, being unable to communicate with the natives, bach, so I indulged as much as I have ever been able to do in my whole life the pleasures of solitude and the countryside. Looking back, it is astonishing to think that as I dawdled along or lay in the peaceful fields sucking the juice out of long-stemmed grasses while staring up at clouds drifting along high above me, not too many miles away unspeakable things were being done to human beings in places like Auschwitz and Buchenwald.

While I had been loafing around my father had been looking for somewhere for us to live and in due course we were summoned to a place called Frodsham, in Cheshire, from whence, six days a week, he caught a train to Edge Hill, about fifteen miles away. (Yes, everyone worked on a Saturday morning in those days.) Frodsham, with its prominent, grassy mound that rises high above the town, was where we began another spate of two-month stands, moving from one temporary home to another, mostly due to the acid tongue of my mother, who was unable to keep the peace with anyone for long. In one of these crappy residences we lived next door to the Bandmaster of the Lancashire Fusiliers, whose son amazed me one day by saying that he lusted after his mother — Oedipus incarnate. (She had banana-shaped legs, I remember, which have never appealed to me since.)

Whether it was the influence of that would-be mother-fucker or just a natural development I do not know, but around this time I became interested in girls. I experienced the act of kissing for the first time (an event that caused, to my astonishment, great poundings of the heart) when a tall, dark, pretty girl called Rhonda did it for a bet in the nearby co-ed secondary school to which I had been urgently sent. In her excitement she pushed me perilously close to a flaming bunsen burner, which might have added to the excitement.

The bet was all part of the collective baiting of this peculiar little twit who spoke with a posh accent — which must have been acquired at Homewood House, for both my parents spoke with a Scottish accent. Having lived in Peru, Suffolk and Liverpool I suppose they all cancelled each other out and I ended up with 'standard' English, which was enough to goad the Frodsham lads into sneering contempt. Thus I quickly learned one of the basic principles on which human beings operate: that you must conform to local norms or face penalties. I resisted until I was threatened with the cane by my teachers for being disruptive, then gave in, whereupon I was beaten-up by my persecutors. However, remembering the french-window incident I kept on fighting and eventually was first ignored and then accepted. In fact the possession of such an accent was to prove a godsend in years to come because, as we all know, to the English an accent is an instant indicator of status and education — and, by inference, intelligence: to many people someone with a thick Geordie, Brum, Scouse or Cockney accent must be, by definition, a moron.

An English accent places a person in a clearly-defined pecking order, whereas the possession of a Scots, Welsh or Irish accent does not have quite the same connotations. Indeed in Scotland it can be the reverse: I have known officers in Highland regiments who insisted on sending their sons to school in Scotland, however inconvenient it might have been geographically when they were serving in far-flung stations, in order to ensure that they acquired a Scottish accent. (Not a Glaswegian one, mind.)

While in Frodsham I persuaded my parents that I should be allowed to become a Boy Scout, and became very proud of my navy-blue shorts, dark-green shirt and light-blue neckerchief; my side-drum, toggle and the few proficiency badges I was awarded. The scoutmaster resembled, and acted, like Bruce Forsyth and so, as you may imagine, looked a bit of a charlie when on parade wearing that big wide-brimmed hat and long shorts in front of his diminutive flag-bearers, drummers, buglers and rank and file. I feel a bit guilty, these days, that I don't enjoy Armistice Day parades, and put it down to standing shivering, with blue, knocking kneecaps, behind the Home Guard contingent, many of whom must have caught pneumonia and died. (Actually, there is a bit more to my dislike of Armistice Days than that, as will presently become apparent.) The Girl Guides lined up behind us — and quite right and proper, too.

At about this time my parents persuaded me to become a choir boy, and in my cassock and surplice I would file into the stalls with my fellow choristers, sing a hymn or two — some people would doubt the accuracy of that statement — whisper rude comments to my neighbours about the organist and the sopranos, and get terribly bored during the sermons. Once or twice I had to pump the organ with a long handle, making sure my attention did not wander, for if it did shortage of air would bring about a descending groan from its innards and hissed, angry admonitions from the organist.

While gracing this church with my presence I was confirmed into the Church of England by the Bishop of Chester. I had reluctantly learned my catechism but nevertheless expected a physical and mental transformation when the bishop laid his hands upon my head: somehow, I would feel sanctified, glorified, see a great light. When nothing happened and I filed out feeling the same as I had when I went in I felt very let down. (The sight of my pimply, rather smelly school chums kneeling beside me with their eyes popping might well have had something to do with it.)

An activity I entered into for a very short time was learning to play the piano. I was given three or four lessons but then developed a whitlow on a finger and had to desist. When it got better, we had moved yet again, and piano lessons became history. (The finger was treated by a makey-learney nurse who taped it up the wrong way, leaving me for life with an unsightly blob on the end of it. This was the first occasion, but was not to be the last, when I felt that the medical profession were doing something wrong but desisted from saying so because I thought they must know what they were doing.)

Frodsham has a broad main street which in those days had, on one side of it, a strip of sandy grit lined with trees. (Today, inevitably, it has been metaled and turned into car-parking spaces.) I used to bicycle like a lunatic up and down this chicane, trying to prove something, I know not what, and stopping for breath every now and then. On one such occasion I was importuned by a dirty old man who offered me a shilling if I would go around the corner with him. Having no idea what the old bugger wanted I smiled politely in a puzzled sort of way and declined — thank the Lord.

Beside that strip of road lived my best friend, Alastair Wilson, who had a shock of bright red hair and a cavalier attitude to life. One of the few things that had caught my interest in the chemistry class was the recipe for making gunpowder. With our pocket money we bought two of the ingredients from a chemist's shop and made the third by charring some wood and scraping off the black bits. We mixed these together in the right proportions, stuffed them down a pipe with a blocked-off end, added some rusty nails, hammered wood into the other end to seal it, then laid it on an open fire in Alastair's back yard to see what would happen. We got better at this as time went by, managing eventually to pepper the bank manager's back gate with grapeshot at fifty feet, but had to desist when people became alarmed — not for our welfare, I may say, but for that of their property.

The Scouting, singing and experimenting came to an end when my father purchased, for a ridiculously small amount of money, a very large house in the next-door town, Helsby, which also has a large but rocky hill looming over the landscape.

Orchard Croft, it was, a massive, three-storey Victorian property with a double garage (once a coach-house), many outbuildings, a very large greenhouse and garden, and an orchard with seventy fruit trees in it — I counted them one day. It was half-timbered, here and there, and from the main rooms there were lovely views across the valley towards the nether slopes of Frodsham hill.

The house had been requisitioned by the army for a time and used as a recuperation centre for medical cases and when we moved in there were still notices on the walls saying Disinfectants, Bandages and so on. There was dry rot, too, brought on by the Army, who had stupidly piled sandbags around the walls and left them there to moulder, though the chance of a German bomb landing anywhere near must have been as remote as getting BSE from eating beef on the bone or winning the lottery. We lost the floor of the billiards room as a result, and it had to be concreted. The rooms upstairs were high-ceilinged and big and it was a long time before we acquired enough furniture to fill them; but it was all ours, dry rot and all, a home in which the family could, at last, settle down.

Once there I began the only continuous schooling I ever had; at the County Grammar School at Runcorn, about ten miles away, where I was put into a class a year behind the pupils I should properly have been with — which is not surprising, when you come to think of it. Even there, though, I did not really try, being much influenced by a British characteristic that has become ever more evident with the passing of the years: namely, that you are winning if by some means you

51

contrive to do as little as possible. Accordingly, I horsed around in the back row, despised our local swot — a bright little lad by the name of Gandy, who has no doubt since made a pile of money — played noughts and crosses and flicked ink pellets at the unprepossessing specimens of girlhood who by no stretch of the imagination graced the class. (Except, that is, for little Ivy Worrell, a bright little raver who made a — probably quite unjustified, you know how people love to talk — name for herself behind the bicycle sheds.)

Of history, taught by a gaunt old gorgon with lank grey hair, I remember very little, though strangely enough I clearly recollect being told about Baldwin, the 12th Century leper king of Jerusalem about whom, thirty years on, I was to write my first book, *The Hope of Glory*.

During the early summer months of 1183, when Saladin was besieging Aleppo, Baldwin was at Acre with his court.

Though for some weeks he had been spared the recurrent fevers that struck him down, death was near. He was blind; one eye had rolled upwards so that the iris was nearly hidden, the other was glazed and empty. His fingers and toes had shrivelled and worn away. The bridge of his nose had collapsed, merging his features into the lion's face of a lepper. But for a while his body rallied.

When, in June, Aleppo surrendered, Baldwin ordered the mobilisation of the feudal levies that were pledged to come to his aid in time of danger. They, and the Hospitallers, the Templars and his own soldiers came together under his command near Nazareth, the biggest force that had ever been raised in defence of the realm: fifteen-hundred knights, fifteen-hundred mounted sergeants, fifteen-thousand infantrymen. When they had all assembled they passed in revue before him for the last time.

He had led them for nine years, sometimes defensively against Saladin's incursions from Egypt, sometimes offensively against Nur ed-Din in Syria. Sometimes successfully as at Ramla, sometimes disastrously, as at the Meadow of Springs. Always, though, bravely and confidently. Now, sitting under the awning of a tent, veiled in his darkness, he raised a mangled hand as they rode past him shouting greetings. But within two days he was struck down by a raging fever; was near to death again and knew it. Taken to the palace in Jerusalem he was laid in a curtained room.

He was wooden in his darkness — no light touch of gentle sensitivity in his body, no movement of fingers and toes, tactile and perceptive. Only an unfeeling weightiness of movement at the end of his limbs.

He heard, still. Dully, as if through a blanket: his life thumping on his ears, a caged bird singing in the courtyard, the hollow heaviness of a horse's hoof on stone, the rasp of metal where a soldier honed a dagger. And distant voices, speaking quietly.

He felt. Numbly. Heat, his clothes damp with sweat, the sheet covering him; if it slipped off he had to try to grip it with his spadelike fists or pull at it with his teeth, or cry out for help like a small child. And like a child he was sometimes overwhelmed with fear and sadness.

One night he awoke, twitching convulsively and mumbling incoherently, then as dawn came slipped into a coma, breathing with a curious penetrating hiss that gently faded as the morning wore on. At midday he died, aged twenty-three, released at last from the ugly mangled husk that had tormented him for so long.

The Hospitallers and the Templars took

his body to rest beside the other kings of Jerusalem in the Holy Sepulchre. 'He was the most holy and gallant of them all,' they said; 'His was a valiant spirit.'

Of French I remember even less, though the same cannot be said of the teacher, pretty, red-haired Miss Sarah Richards, a very sexy-looking young woman who had long, shapely legs. When she crossed them about six feet in front of my narrowed eyes they caught my attention and imagination much more than her French verbs did. I cannot remember the names of any of the other teachers except Mr Bamberger and Mr Cross.

Bamberger was an irascible, bald-headed gentleman of Teutonic origins. (Aeons later I was to spend a delightful weekend in lovely Bamberg, near the Austrian border, during the weekend in 1989 when crowds took to the streets demanding the downfall of the Communist regime in East Germany. I sat up in bed watching with total disbelief the torchlight processions in Leipzig and Dresden and Berlin broadcast live on television). Mr Bamberger ruled his class with a T-square of iron; though he imparted little knowledge about art he undoubtedly ran the tightest ship in the school: no snigger or whispered aside ever escaped the lips of his scribbling pupils.

Cross was very hairy and had a beard. Bamberger never mentioned the existence of Toulouse-Lautrec but if he had, that was who Mr Cross would have reminded me of, he too having a limp as well as a beard. Perhaps he *had* heard of Henri.

Science, including maths, escaped me entirely, until several years later.

★ ★ ★

The war was, to me, just a distant background to a fairly normal process of growing up. Each day I cycled a mile to the railway station, during the half-hour journey made a stab at the homework I should have done the night before, then walked down the brick-lined hill to the school, which stood near the Transporter Bridge over the Manchester Ship Canal, both marvels, we were told, of Victorian engineering. Which was more than could be said for the school itself, a tall, draughty, ugly building in the front office of which lurked, like a caged tarantula, the large, grey-haired headmaster. The only direct contact pupils had with him was transmitted down the length of a cane; otherwise he was only seen at assembly,

56

where he uttered a monosyllable or two before striding back to his lair, his long black cloak billowing out behind him.

After school I trudged, nattering, back up the hill and caught the train home. As a form of release from the enormous pressures generated by trying hard to do absolutely nothing all day the boys and girls used to fool around and damage each other and the rolling stock of the London, Midland and Scottish Railway. Light bulbs were screwed out of the ceilings, filled with red ink and then hurled out of windows; other removables were removed and stolen, or vandalised; girls were grabbed in tunnels and interfered with, and so on. But it was quite mild stuff, really. Not vicious, just mischievous.

Basil, who in appearance resembled the young Doctor Christian Barnard, was now serving as a bombardier in charge of a gun in a Medium Regiment, the 50th, of the Eighth Army, firing 4.5″ shells at Rommel's Afrika Corps — or, perhaps, being Gunners (known as 'The Drop-Shorts' in the rest of the Army) into the sand. As the battlefield moved back and forth across what is now Gaddafi's kingdom (if we had only known what would happen in the years to come I doubt if we would have bothered to shed blood for it) my father avidly followed the news bulletins on the radio. My mother's knitting needles would stop clicking whenever Sidi Barani or Benghazi were mentioned, but all that came to an end when Basil was captured at Tobruk. He disappeared from sight for a while, then emerged in a prisoner-of-war camp in Italy. Bet hoped her firstborn was safe for the duration of the war and concentrated her attention on her second son, who was now an officer.

Brian was one of the 'wavy navy' — so called because as reserve officers they wore wave-like gold rings on their sleeves to indicate their rank instead of the straight rings of the 'pusser', regular officers. He looked smart, clean-cut and handsome in his doe-skin best uniform, and was much taken with it. (As a wartime junior officer he spoke with awe about 'four-ringer' Captains RN, though when I got to know some of them well in later years they turned out to be fairly normal human beings.) At first he served in Atlantic convoys as an Ordinary Seaman in HMS *Clare*, one of the fifty ancient, clapped-out, four-funnelled destroyers that President Roosevelt had so kindly let the British have in exchange for long leases on defence installations in British Caribbean islands. He, my brother, stayed soaked through for weeks on end, sleeping on sacks of rotten potatoes up in the sharp end of the ship next the 'heads', as the navy call the latrines. (Why are they not at the blunt end, I ask myself? Would that not be more sensible? I suppose there must be a good reason. Oh yes, of course, that's where the captain has his cabin, isn't it, at the stern?) After being commissioned at HMS *Raleigh* he became the First Lieutenant of a tank landing craft, and in due course the captain of another. In fact he had a relatively dangerous war, taking part in the North Africa Operation Torch landings and later sailing with the armada that assaulted Festung *Europa*; after dropping its ramp his ship was holed below the water-line by a mine tied to a steel pole inserted into the shingle and was left high and dry on Juno Beach, where it was strafed from time to time by what remained of the Luftwaffe. And once by the RAF!

Brian was given another ship, and then another — they got bigger as time went on — but by then the impetus of the war had moved to the land battle. I am not sure whether the highlight of the war for him was the moment when, five hours after H-Hour on D-Day, his troops rolled their tanks off his ship on to the Normandy beach or whether it was the pink-gins and Wrens that he and his fellow officers consumed while they were at anchor off Falmouth. I like to think it was the latter. Either way, I have a feeling that for him, as for millions of other people, nothing in the future ever matched the excitement and interest of those days.

★ ★ ★

I, meanwhile, was pedalling around Cheshire on my bike. There was no petrol available for pleasure motoring so the roads were almost empty, and I thought nothing of riding twenty or thirty miles in a day, usually alone but sometimes with a crony. I was strong and fit, but then caught pneumonia and very nearly died from tobogganing too enthusiastically and for too long down the hill behind our house.

Those were pre-penicillin days and I was treated with a new substance known as M & B 693 (which made me feel very peculiar) by our small, admirable and smiling GP. He was a fine doctor who died prematurely from the cumulative effects of treating his many patients with no assistance during all hours of the day and night with hardly ever a break from duty. A lot of doctors these days, so I have heard, kill themselves or take to the bottle, but I don't think many of them die from overwork. And not many of them smile either, come to that. There must be a moral in it, somewhere.

After we had been in Orchard Croft for a while my father decided that we could have a dog. He called in at the Liverpool dog pound — which happened to be at Edge Hill — and earmarked a pooch, and one evening I was despatched on a train, clutching two pound notes, to fetch it.

Roger (I cannot for the life of me think why we called him that, but it turned out to be quite appropriate) was a Blue Roan Cocker Spaniel with a touch of Springer in him: he had the colouring of a Blue Roan but the bone structure of a Springer. He was a splendid-looking animal but was a bit short on brains and not amenable to discipline: to get his attention it was necessary to hit him over the head with a cricket bat. However, he loved the walks on Helsby Hill and many was the happy hour I spent up there with him. Not infrequently, he would disappear down a rabbit hole and not come up again; I would go off in disgust and he would reappear hours later with his nose covered in mud and his stubby tail wagging the rest of him.

One memorable afternoon Roger plunged into some bracken and flushed a couple who were approaching the climax of a very intimate performance indeed. I watched the show for a stunned moment, averted my eyes, walked on a bit, decided I would like to see a bit more of the action and returned to satisfy my curiosity, only to find that they had satisfied theirs and were now sitting up looking, to my amazement, as if nothing had happened: she was replacing her hairpins and he, bald and beefy (good grief, did pretty women let ugly old men like him do such things to them?) was adjusting his dress before leaving, as the signs in public lavatories used to say.

★　★　★

It was in the summer of 1944 that I and a group of schoolmates went camping near Goosetree, in Cheshire, assisting the war effort by providing free labour on local farms.

I loved it — sleeping in a bell-tent, feet towards the centre pole, eating in the open air, not washing — and was annoyed when I was taken aside and quietly told that I had to return home immediately. I thought that maybe, and not for the first time, my mother had imagined another grave medical crisis and had summoned me to be beside her in her last moments on earth, but when I arrived home it was to be told that my eldest brother was dead.

When the Italians surrendered, the Germans, rather than free their prisoners-of-war took them across the Alps into Germany. (Most of them walked all the way.) We didn't know what was going on, and were surprised, but relieved, when we heard that Basil was in Stalag VIIIB in Silesia. Things settled down again and my mother sent him parcels of clothes — mittens, a balaclava helmet, a leather waistcoat (which, extraordinarily, eventually came back to England) that sort of thing. Then we heard that he had been moved east into Poland, and communication became more sporadic. It was just after D-Day, when all thoughts were of Brian, that the shattering news came.

It transpired that British soldiers had been working as labourers in a mine near Katowice. (Under the Geneva Convention those of the rank of bombardier (corporal) and above were not obliged to work; however, if they offered to do so the Germans gave them extra rations, an incentive that in the circumstances ensured that most of them did, though it was a mistake: any energy they derived from the extra food was quickly eaten away by their exertions.) A small tipper truck had run away down an incline, gathered speed, swung round a corner and smashed one of my brother's legs against another truck. It was not serious (in other circumstances treatment would have ensured his survival), no bones were broken, but he was badly bruised. He was put to bed in the camp medical centre but died a few days later, aged twenty-three, when a blood clot travelled through a vein up into the entrance to his heart, blocked it and stopped it. He was buried with full military honours in the British Military Cemetery in Crakow, where he lies in good company.

My mother's anguish was beyond belief and she nearly went mad, literally, with grief. My father was deeply hurt, he had loved his eldest son, but he took it with typical Scots calm and stoicism. Brian, too, felt the loss keenly: he and Basil had been inseparable for years, and very reliant on one another. I hardly knew him — what with our separation while I was in South America and he was away at school and, later, in the army — but life was never the same again, for me or anyone else in the family. Gloom hung around as my mother self-indulgently imposed her grief on everyone. All light-heartedness was banished; all pleasures were momentary because, inevitably, a frown and a tear would appear, indicating that we were all still in deep mourning — how could we be so callous? Years later my mother told me that 'all that' stopped when Basil died: my father was to go on living actively for another twenty years. (In fact, it was only after he died that she decided that she had mourned Basil enough, though I hesitate to draw any conclusions from that.) Despite the tragedy of Basil's death, life had to go on; fruit had to be picked, grass had to be cut, letters had to be censored.

Andrew was now sixty-two but still set off to walk, rain or shine, to the station every morning, and trudge back up the hill every evening, winter and summer. Once he said to me 'I think I must be cracking up; as I came up the road I staggered.' He was much relieved to read in the newspaper the next morning that there had been a very minor earthquake in the north of England, which, it seems, had momentarily unbalanced him. (Another time, at precisely the same spot, I watched for some minutes what in future years would become known as a flying saucer: a cigar-shaped, bright object that hovered on the horizon in the direction of Liverpool then sped quickly away — for which it can hardly be blamed. There must have been a rational explanation — a 'floater' in the eye, perhaps.) I am not so sure about the ghost.

Orchard Croft was alleged to be haunted. I scoffed, but it was a big house and in some rooms there was definitely an odd atmosphere. I never saw anything, but twice, in my bedroom at the top of the stairs, I heard someone, in the dead of night, come up the stairs and walk past my door. The following mornings when I asked my parents if they had been prowling during the night they said no, they hadn't. Roger, because of his anti-social habits, slept in a big straw-filled box in one of the outhouses, so it wasn't him. There seemed to be no explanation. I mentioned it to our very part-time gardener, a villainous-looking but delightful southern-Irishman, and he confirmed that it was a ghost all right, no doubt about it.

Martin Foy was the most cut-throat-looking character I have ever seen in my life. He was small, gnarled, one-eyed, had a slit ear, thinning black hair and didn't wash too often, but he was a lovely fellow with a dazzling smile. I was very fond of him and we used to cheer each other up no end: I loved his stories and he loved to have an excuse to lean on his spade and tell them. He was one of a gang of Irish labourers who worked on the marshes between Ellesmere Port and Helsby, draining them and making roads — which have now been turned into a motorway. They all lived in a hostel not far from our house and drank to excess, would you believe.

One evening when I was walking past The Railway Inn two of them burst out of the door of the saloon bar, grappling, followed by about a dozen cronies, all cheering loudly. Then, in front of my appalled eyes, one of them pulled a knife from his belt and stuck it in the other fella's guts. It was the first time I had seen human blood spilt in quantity. Once, in Liverpool, I had seen a spaniel run over by a car which broke both its back legs; the poor beast dragged itself into the gutter and was promptly set upon by every dog in the vicinity, who appeared as if by magic, snarling and snapping and trying viciously to put an end to it and satisfy a primeval instinct that called for the despatch of a wounded member of the pack. I felt much sorrier for that dog than I did for the Irishman, who was carted off and dumped in the car park to await an ambulance. (Since his death was not reported I presume he survived to tell his grandchildren how he got the scar: 'Look at this, will ya! Yule never guess how I got it . . . A German came at me one night when I was . . . ')

The grammar school had no playing fields, so there was no opportunity for team sports. Not that it worried me: I have always been quite hopeless at trying to keep track of a moving ball, and not much better trying to hit a stationary one, either. When I tried to play cricket in the army I always swiped and missed; when I scrummed down in a rugby pack the only thing I hooked was scarred shins. However, I was quite good at gymnastics, and also learned to swim in the town's ancient pool, though not very well.

In those days I was reading a lot, but with no plan or discipline. One of the first books to make a deep impression on me was the Story of San Michele, by Axel Munthe — me and about a hundred million other people. I read Walpole, Galsworthy, Conrad, Cronin, Defoe and Dickens; and a very good book, by an author whose name I have forgotten, called War, Wine and Women. (What a title!) Today, the accounts it gave of the Great War, and of the author's encounters with the other two subjects, would be thought very tame but in those days they were verging on the pornographic — which is no doubt one reason why it appealed to me. But also the book began a lifelong interest in the Great War.

If I believed in reincarnation I would swear that the last time I was here was when I trudged up a sunny hill towards Mametz Wood on the 1st July 1916 wearing the uniform of the Second Battalion of the Gordon Highlanders. I went back there on the fiftieth anniversary of the beginning of the Battle of the Somme and walked the same ground.

The wood was ringed with barbed wire and skull-and-crossbones danger notices but I clambered in, started to pick my way through the trees — which have regenerated themselves over the years in almost the same area as they were originally, before they were pulverised by shell fire — then realised that the Germans had made deep dug-outs in the clay which have never been filled in: if I disappeared into one of them no-one would know where to start looking, so I retraced my steps, picking up the odd trophy on the way — a cartridge clip, a spent bullet, that sort of thing. Then I walked quietly along the rows of dead highlanders in the little cemetery nearby.

If you buy a War Graves Commission map you will find the front line precisely delineated by hundreds of war cemeteries that were created where the Battalion Aid Posts had been: the men died or were carried there from the trenches and were then buried in batches during a lull, usually at night. Eventually, the whole ghastly mess was tidied up, walled, and graced with a tall stone cross with a steel sword inverted on its face.

If you go down the road to Thiepval, the place near where the Gordons massed before making their attack, you will see Lutyen's magnificent memorial to the fifty thousand men who died in the battle but who were never dug out of the mud and identified. A short distance down the road, near Arras, there is a German cemetery with fifty thousand bodies in it where, until time took away the loved ones, tattered, windblown black remembrance ribbons hung from crosses which bore names like Hans, Wilhelm, Franz-Joseph. What an unbelievably stupid waste of life it all was.

★   ★   ★

Music was beginning to be of interest to me. We had a beautiful rosewood piano that I played by ear: boogie-woogie at first then, after a blinding flash of revelation, wrongly constructed bits of Tchaikovsky's First Piano Concerto and Rachmaninov's Second. The former, the cause of the blinding flash, had featured in a film in which Mark Hamburg played the part of a down-and-out pianist who banged out those magnificent opening chords on a broken-down upright on wheels in a street in the pouring rain: up-market busking. Ludicrous though it was, the scene could not dull the impact of the music, which would lead me, as time passed, through Beethoven, Mozart, Brahms, Puccini and Sibelius to Mahler and Richard Strauss: which is as far as I can go. Or want to. Schoenberg, Bartok and the like leave me cold; discords scraped on a violin or offnotes blown through a bassoon are for musicians who want to play scramble on their keys, not for the listening ear. It is the emotional, lyrical stuff that appeals to me: the incredibly beautiful trio in the last act of Der Rosenkavalier; the slow movement from Mozart's Clarinet Concerto; Elgar's First Symphony, Mahler's Fourth; the Sibelius Violin Concerto, that sort of thing. The tinkling, clinical stuff, Bach, Vivaldi, Haydn etc, generally speaking does not ring many bells for me either. (The piano played all sorts of music if you loaded paper rolls into the machinery behind its sliding front door, pulled out the pedals and pumped air into the system with your feet. It had little levers that controlled operations and was a truly magnificent instrument, the like of which must be very rare today. Where is it now, I wonder?)

Aged about seven I picked out the notes of the national anthem on a piano and was promptly hailed as a musical genius by my mother, who eagerly showed me a picture of the infant Handel sitting at a harpsichord in his nightgown with his astonished parents in theirs standing holding a candle by the door and staring at him with their mouths open. (How he had played without any illumination before they arrived on the scene was not apparent.) The fact that she enthused so much made me realise early on that art is important.

Music moves me emotionally more than any other art form. Painting is a very rare gift that can bring colour and insight into life. I am not at all sure about sculpture: I can reproduce a good likeness of a face in clay and cast it so that it lasts, a matter of coordinating hand and eye, but I think that some artistic talent is like being born with big lungs and being able to run fast: the mind is not greatly engaged. Good sculptors are even rarer than good painters. I am not convinced that Elizabeth Frink's goggle-eyed men will be visible in the light of history. I do hope not.

Drama enthralls, and acting entertains, but it is the playwrights who are the true creators, not the actors, however pretty or proficient they are. As to writing, I have had more pleasure from it than I have from music, painting or sculpture, both performing or received. D.H. Lawrence said that 'The novel is the bright book of life, which can make the man alive tremble; which is more than philosophy, science or any other book-tremulation can do.' A bit ponderous and pedantic, but I know what he means.

As to fine art, I was aware, and could draw a little. My bad performance at school indicated that I would never achieve anything much academically, so when the chance of a scholarship to the Chester College of Art came along my father entered me for it. It must have been a bad year for them — there must have been few applicants and they wanted to keep the show on the road — because I got it, and in 1945 began to learn to be an artist. I travelled east every day instead of west and entered a different world.

★   ★   ★

The art school in Chester was not very big and shared the same building as the City Museum. The tempo of work suited me — that is to say, it was very slow — the teachers and fellow pupils were congenial and Chester was then a delightful place. (Today, like so many other towns, it has been ruined by too much traffic, too many people and the ubiquitous presence of mass-market designs and logos that obliterate the individuality of shop fronts. Only the Rows, quite unique, save Chester from being unidentifiable from everywhere else.) On summer days we would go down to the River Dee and paint landscapes, or if we had a penny or two to spare, take a rowing boat out and splash around on the excuse that we could get a better view or achieve a more artistic atmosphere by doing so.

In 1945 there was a three-year course of study, starting with the antique (drawing and painting from statues of classical figures) design, then painting in gouache, then water colours. Not until later did a student graduate to the life class and oil paints. Along the way, if so inclined, he or she could divert into modelling in clay or sculpting in stone or carving in wood. These days there is little or no structure, and students are allowed to 'do their own thing.' How anyone can do their own thing, or anything else, when they have never been taught the fundamentals of it — in this case perspective, colour values, the correct use of materials, and so on — I do not understand.

Sometimes, because I found it infinitely absorbing, I played truant and visited Chester

Assizes, almost next door in the Castle. I sat in the public gallery and watched a murder trial, presided over by Mr Justice Croom-Johnson; a rape, a grievous bodily harm or two, and some divorce cases, the latter rattled through in double-quick time by bored counsel, someone's personal disaster dealt with in two minutes. I was struck by the way in which great human drama was reduced to desiccated, boring facts by the barristers, who hung on to their lapels, droned away and leafed slowly through piles of paper. All the same, I sat with my chin on my fist taking in every word.

★   ★   ★

The war ended with no perceptible difference to our lives except that it made it even more difficult to accept the fact that Mac 1 would not be coming home. Mac 2 was to stay in the navy for another year or so. I had grown up while it lasted, after a fashion; I was still incredibly ignorant and naïve but as is the way with young people thought I knew it all. The future, as far as I could see, would consist of going into commercial art — nobody could make a living painting or sculpting, I was told.

One day we students visited the Jacqmar

factory in Macclesfield and watched good artists doing boring work on silk scarves. They broke someone else's design down into its basic colour components then prepared a screen (silk, stretched on to a wooden frame) for each colour. In the printing room with its long tables the screens were laid on top of silk squares one after the other and the appropriate colour applied through the part of the design that was not blanked off by varnish, merging it with the other colours underneath until the desired effect was achieved. The prospect of doing this for the rest of my life did not enthral me, but what was the alternative?

Then it was announced that National Service would continue for the foreseeable future because of Britain's many world-wide military commitments. Suddenly, I was faced with the fact that I was going to be conscripted.

I do not remember being alarmed at the prospect, or even thinking about it much, but the day came when I had to go for a medical examination. My mother was quite upset when I returned and announced that I had not got curvature of the spine or flat feet or anything else that would have excused me from service: whether she liked it or not, I was going to be a soldier.

In the summer of 1946 I sculpted (modelled and then cast in plaster) a bust of my father in an attic room in Orchard Croft. I have a photograph taken at that time of a bird-like, gawky young man wearing a badly-cut Utility suit and a slightly whimsical smile. That was me, just eighteen and about to embark on the great adventure of life.

3

Happy Days

On the 26th August 1946 I began to work for the monarch.

I left Orchard Croft with a railway warrant folded carefully in one of the pockets of the Utility suit and clutching a cardboard suitcase. I changed trains in Liverpool and arrived at midday at Carlisle, where I reported to the Castle. Having answered my name when a sergeant shouted it out from a nominal roll I was told to get fed in the cook-house and then get lost.

Much to my surprise, I spent my first afternoon in the army strolling around a park, after which I went to a cinema. That evening, after being offered another plateful of sausage and mash, I and four hundred and ninety-eight other young men (one had not turned up) still in civilian clothes, entrained for Stranraer, in Scotland. On arrival there we were formed up into a shapeless column of humanity which then straggled a mile or two up the road to receive our third free meal of — you've guessed it, sausages, only this time with chips and an egg. Having washed it down with a pint of strong tea we sullenly shambled all the way back — and then a bit further, to the docks. In the moonlight people kept falling out of the line of march, if you could call it that, and noisily peeing up against people's front gates. (I should have thought the owners had a strong case for a reduction in the rates, since this was a regular occurrence. Furthermore, their dogs must have had a nightmarish existence trying to figure out what all the new smells were every few days.) The unruly mob, which resembled a mini retreat from Moscow, was in due course shovelled on to a small ship, which crossed the Irish Sea to Larne. There, we were herded around more, given another meal and a 'haversack ration' — two Spam sandwiches — and told to get on a train. This we did, of course, and then sat there for hours and hours as it solemnly puffed south, then north-west, then south again, then east, sometimes going forwards and sometimes backwards. It was my first exposure to what in the army came to be known as 'the Irish Dimension', i.e. something illogical, unexpected and totally inexplicable. And bloody stupid. Eventually I found myself sitting on the lower half of a creaking, rickety, wooden double-bunk in a barrack room in one of the

Belisha blocks in Ballykinlar Camp, County Down. (Hore Belisha had been War Minister when the barrack blocks were built.)

The camp was a Primary Training Centre, through which something like twenty-five thousand soldiers were processed every year. It was commanded by a colonel, ex Brigade of Guards, assisted by a Guards regimental sergeant-major and assorted infantry officers, warrant officers and non-commissioned officers. My platoon commander was a very slim, tall good-looking Scots Guards lieutenant by the name of Godsal, who was a great deal tougher than his appearance, courteous manners and languid demeanour suggested.

One day Godsal took us all to the top of Slieve Donard, the highest of the Mountains of Mourne, and with his long legs soon had us all panting along behind him. I can still see him now, holding a stout walking stick and stepping carefully over the streams of peat water that cascaded down the mountain; another example of the Irish Dimension, for who ever heard of water that flows in a torrent nearly three thousand feet above sea level? Where on earth does it come from? Typically, when we reached the summit it was shrouded in mist, though Godsal assured us that on a good day we would have been able to see five countries: Scotland, England, the

Isle of Man, Southern and Northern Ireland. (And a sixth, The Kingdom of Heaven, he might have added, had he been Irish.) Godsal gave me the impression of regarding us, in a kindly if slightly puzzled way, as a very odd group of people whom fate, with a weird sense of humour, obliged him to put up with.

We certainly were a disparate group, verging on the desperate. The barrack room contained twenty-four young men who all had two things in common: all our names began with 'M' and we were all born in July 1928. Other than that, I don't think we had anything in common at all: we were the sons of Liverpool dockers, Lancashire mill workers, Cheshire farmers. Of bus drivers, businessmen, civil servants and slaughter. Friendships and antagonisms formed quickly, and cliques developed — one corner of the barrack room, one side, adjacent bunks. It was an enlightening example of people's clannishness, of the need they have for mutual support.

Our platoon was ruled over by a corporal in the Hampshire Regiment, as bright as his cap badge and seemingly hard enough to walk through a brick wall. He demanded, and got, instant obedience, and contrived somehow to make us accept without question the infantile nonsenses that were perpetrated, in those days, in the name of good order and military discipline. Our kit was scrubbed, ironed, boned, blancoed and burnished for hour upon hour; our straw-filled palliasses and bolsters were stiffened, with great difficulty, into sharp-edged shapes. For two days before the room competition we walked on stockinged feet for fear of dulling the highly polished floor with our boots — in the process polishing it even more; the night before the inspection we slept on it, on a blanket. In between these frantic spasms of manic bullshit we marched on the barrack square, did gymnastics, fired rifles, threw grenades, dismantled and remantled machine guns, crawled, snake fashion, through thick undergrowth and ran, screeching, towards large swinging sacks of sawdust into which we thrust our bayonets. As light relief we could buy for a shilling (5p) in the Sandys Home sausage, bacon, egg and chips, a slice of bread and butter and a mug of tea. (Our pay was 7 shillings a day.)

Having begun life with the Indian Army, Sandys Homes then existed in Ballykinlar and Catterick, endowed by the generosity of someone who had admired the army. The feeling was reciprocated. There was a religious undertone in it somewhere but it was not made to intrude. Unlike the shock effect of our first Padre's Hour.

It had been explained to us that Padre's Hours were part of military life, that they were good for our souls and could only be avoided by those who were not Christians, or were unbelievers. A few cheeky souls said they were Buddhists or Moslems (they were not, really, this was long before the United Kingdom became a multi-religious society) and sloped off somewhere out of sight to have a fag. The rest of us Christians of various denominations, a large proportion of whom had never been near a church in their lives, clumped into a hut in our ammunition boots (regulation 13 studs in the soles, steel heel- and toe-plates) and sat down to await events. The padre strode in, the NCO shouted, we all stood up, he shouted again, we all sat down. Then the Man of God picked up a piece of chalk and before our protruding eyes, and without uttering a word, proceeded to draw a massive erect penis on the blackboard, taking some time and care over it. (I'll say this for him, it was a sure way to get our attention.) When he had finished he turned around, glared at us and then delivered fifteen filthy minutes' worth on the subject of venereal disease, at the end of which he made a run for it. He clearly believed in original sin, but God was not mentioned.

While in Ballykinlar, for the cost of my bacon and eggs in the Sandys Home, or a shilling, I drew some pencil portraits of my fellow inmates in the barrack room. Vanity being what it is, they tried hard to see a likeness where little existed and proudly stuffed the sketches into their kit-bags — or even sent them home to Mum who, seeing the drawn features of their loved ones, must have had their worst fears of army life confirmed. In fact, for the first time ever most of the young conscripts ate regular, good meals, spent hours in the fresh air every day and took hard physical exercise. They were so transformed physically that sometimes their mothers failed to recognise them when they reappeared. (A few years later I was to become part of another sausage-machine system that turned a civilian into the makings of a soldier, and I could see the difference in a matter of days. Bearing had something to do with it. And the self-respect that grew with achieving things that had been thought far beyond the individual's capabilities.)

Of course, thousands of young men loathed nearly all aspects of army life and literally counted the days until they were allowed to become civilians again (the 'Demob calendar', with each day thankfully crossed off, was a common feature of the conscript army) but

I was not one of them. I loved it, mainly due to the sudden release from the constraints of an over-protected home life. Also, I was part of a vigorous and efficient organisation: if someone said something was going to happen, it did. And, too, there was the glamour, for such it is, of military uniforms, bands and ceremonial.

Already, pride in a regiment was being fostered. Though it bonds people closely and thus strengthens a unit, especially in times of stress, it has its dark side. The first time I became aware of it was when the recruits were told where they were going when they left Ballykinlar. One strong, pleasant but rather dim young man almost wept when he was told he was going to be a 'Chunky' in the Royal Pioneer Corps, and had to be comforted by his buddies. 'It's all right, Joe,' he was assured, 'you could become an assault Pioneer. They don't all just hump ammunition around all day, you know.' But Joe was not to be comforted or convinced, and I expect that in the end he was proved right and spent the next two years lifting bales, boxes and gravity runway.

It is a pity that the pride of some is the cause of shame in others, an aspect of army life that was to irritate and dog me for years. In the Royal Navy and the RAF, although there are seamen and specialists, and aircrew and ground-crew, the demarcation is not as sharp. In the army the Household Cavalry think they are a cut above the rest of the cavalry and refer to the infantry of the Foot Guards as the Mud Guards. People in the cavalry regiments look down on the mechanics of the Royal Tank Regiment; together, they all look down on foot soldiers. Within the Brigade of Guards the Grenadiers and the Coldstream look down their aristocratic noses at the Scots, Irish and Welsh, and all of them on the Infantry of the Line, within which each regiment thinks it rates better than those that have more Feet than it has (the 1st of Foot, the Royal Scots, must, by definition, be superior to the Argylls, who have more than 90, poor things.) And so it goes on, right down through the Army List. Two corps think themselves aloof from all such mundane matters: the Royal Engineers are ubiquitous and frightfully clever fellows and the Royal Artillery, with no great justification, look down on everyone — though the Royal Horse Artillery think themselves superior to non-horsed Gunners. It is all very childish. Within the army as a whole there is, of course, enormous camaraderie and plenty of mutual respect, but the undercurrent of regimental snobbery is pervasive, and people should not be encouraged to take it beyond the bounds of common sense.

Apart from giving us basic military instruction, the job of the Training Centre was to sort people out into various categories so that they could be usefully employed in the army. We were given intelligence and aptitude tests and then interviewed by a man known as the PSO, the Personnel Selection Officer. I have not the faintest idea who mine was but I owe more to him than to any other single person I have ever met in my whole life, for in the short space of about five minutes he completely reshaped my future. Having successfully assembled a bicycle pump in the allotted time I was ushered in to see him. He asked me which regiment I wanted to serve in and, mindful of my brother and not wishing to be too energetic, suggested the Royal Artillery, please. He nodded, wrote that down then looked up and asked if I wanted to be an officer. An officer? Wot me, an officer? I begged his pardon and he repeated the question. After the moment or two it took me to decide he was being serious I said yes, please. Sir. He nodded again and scribbled again.

I'll say this for him, he was a good judge of character, though on what basis he made his assessment I do not know: it could not have been academic prowess, and still less my appearance, wearing as I was those boots, an ill-fitting itchy battledress and one of those cow-pat shaped khaki berets they saw fit to issue at that time. Maybe he was psychic. More probably he just had a quota to fill. Whatever the reason, I came out of his office a potential officer and pointing in a very different direction than if I had been labelled a trainee gunner. (These days, with my lack of academic qualifications, I would not even have been considered.)

★　★　★

When my platoon had finished panting around the Irish countryside a batch of us were sent to begin our training as artillery-men. I arrived in Tonfanau, in North Wales, in the late autumn of 1946, just in time for the worst winter of this century. We began each day by marching to the gun park and it is no exaggeration to say that sometimes it was possible to actually lean into the wind without dropping. We then fought with numb fingers a venomous lump of iron known as a Mark 1 Bofors anti-aircraft gun. It was a very efficient Swedish design that was to stay in service, with electronic improvements, until the 1970s but this particular version must be indelibly imprinted in the memories of everyone who fought with it — and not against the enemy, either.

The problem was that in order to fire accurately it had to be lowered from its wheels on to the ground, thus giving it a 'stable platform'. To do this the crew had to deploy fore and aft, undo a couple of large clips and then lift steel bars at each end of the gun until they got past top-dead-centre, whereupon the weight of the gun took over, it pivoted around on its wheels and then dropped with a mighty crash onto its pads. Quite often an unfortunate gunner's foot would be under a pad, in which case he would be carried away, bawling, to the Medical Centre; or else he might be catapulted through the air by a steel bar. Despite what you might think, it is quite possible to loathe an inanimate object.

Apart from the dreaded gun park there were other aspects of army life to be introduced to. The gymnasium, staffed by PTIs (Physical Training Instructors), muscular NCOs who swaggered around wearing black pumps, tight black trousers and black-and-red horizontally-striped jumpers. The cook-house, staffed by ATS girls who clattered around in the steam wearing clogs, a khaki overall and a bandana, mostly gravy-stained. The NAAFI, where foul tea was dispensed by bad-tempered women dressed like Lyons Corner House waitresses: a blue overall and a ducky little cap atop what were usually granite-like features. The Education Centre, staffed by intense, academically qualified young NCOs, mostly bespectacled, who had failed the officer selection board and therefore had a huge chip on their shoulders. (They taught a subject called British Ways and Purpose and through its syllabus, so it is said, had been largely responsible for the Labour landslide in the 1945 General Election, the Education Corps having been much infiltrated by the Left.)

The opportunity for sex did not exist for ninety per cent of the inhabitants of Tonfanau (that probably applied to the Welsh, too, though I was referring to the soldiery) so any mention of it brought drooling lips and sparkling eyes. One day a Lance-Corporal ATS kitchen hand, a cheeky, bright-eyed, wise-cracking little Scouse, was seen to have been reduced to the ranks, the reason being, it quickly became known, that she had been caught red-handed grasping a gasping, red-faced PTI in the gymnasium, where her curiosity about his rippling torso had proved too much for her. Instantly, she became the recipient of more wisecracks, and a lot of lecherous looks.

I do not remember any of the officers in Tonfanau, not one, so presumably they must have been crouched around the fire in the mess most of the time, keeping out of the wind. Our troop sergeant, who looked like William Hartnell (who often took such parts in films before he became Doctor Who) announced his presence every morning at reveille by banging with a pick helve on the big iron fuel box beside the door of the hut. If your feet did not touch the ground in ten seconds he enthusiastically strode forward and tipped your bed over. Not a good way to start the day.

As winter clamped down we withdrew more and more into our barrack hut. It had two coke-burning stoves which were lit at five p.m. and then kept roaring until lights-out at ten, their chimney stacks glowing red-hot. By morning all the heat had dissipated and the inside temperature in the hut had dropped to well below freezing; tea dregs in a mug would be frozen solid, and the iron studs of our ammunition boots were stuck to the floorboards. I contracted whooping cough and at night lay barking and retching for hours on end. The trouble was that when I reported sick and was told to cough by the Medical

Officer all I could summon up was a short, sharp yap. The doctor would give me a disbelieving look and a bottle of linctus. Sometimes, doubling to the gun park in the freezing air I would start to whoop, and end up hanging on to the gun-shield, wheezing and choking. 'Report sick, lad,' the sergeant would say to me. 'Have done, sergeant,' I would gasp. 'Well, go again. Do as you're told!' he would retort. I drank so many bottles of Veno's Lightning Cough Cure that I almost anaesthetised myself on its chloroform content, and staggered around in a daze. Eventually it wore off; the cough and the daze.

One fine day I climbed up Cader Idris and marvelled at the view and my blisters. Some Saturdays I went to Barmouth, had tea in a bun shop and then went to the cinema. Otherwise, light relief in Tonfanau consisted of sitting crouched around a red-hot stove, on the offside of the steaming boots and clothes that ringed it. Because it was so cold and fuel was heavily rationed, from time to time we burnt some of the furniture — for which we had to pay eventually, of course: barrack damages, they were called. One evening we were raided by the occupants of the next-door hut, who climbed on the roof and poured a bucket of water down the chimney stack: the stove exploded, filling the hut with

92

steam, carbon monoxide and lumps of red-hot coke. Another time a lad got a large piece of four-by-two (inches, of cloth, flannel, cleaning barrels for) stuck in his rifle — his was four-by-ten — and in order to dislodge it, on the considered advice of his mates heated a poker until it was white-hot and stuffed it down the orifice, thereby playing havoc with the rifling. He was put on a charge, given jankers — confined to barracks, as if that was any hardship, considering there was no alternative — and made to pay for a new one. (If I remember rightly, they cost around £8 in those days.)

Another time I read in Part I Orders (the routine orders of the day) that I had been given 28 days detention in the cells, which came as something of a surprise. It turned out to be another MacDonald, a dwarf-like Glasgow keelie who had once returned from a Rangers and Celtic match with half an ear missing. When I asked him how this had happened he fingered the dirty piece of sticking plaster that was folded over the remains of his lug, gave me a sharp look and said 'Och, a fella hit me wi' a broken bawtle. It's nothin'.' When he came out of his 28 days in the moosh he bought me a beer on the strength of the mistake made in the regimental office.

One of my most vivid memories of Tonfanau is of that awful GWR journey through Machynlleth and Wrexham to Chester. Or, to be more accurate, the return trip on a Sunday night after a civilised weekend at Orchard Croft, standing with my shoulders hunched up and my hands stuffed into my pockets for two bitterly cold hours on Machynlleth station platform in the dead of night waiting for the connection. I suppose there are worse places, like the Gulag Archipelago, but I have yet to come across them. The sense of despair and desolation was overwhelming, and a bacon butty and a mug of tea on arrival in camp made even that benighted place seem homely.

Another memory is of a young conscript called Bieber. I would like to meet him again, for I am sure he is now a very wealthy man — could Bieber have become Biba, perhaps? Within a couple of days of our arrival in that ghastly hut he began what became a thriving business: for a penny he would blanco and polish your belt, for tuppence belt and gaiters, for sixpence the small pack as well, and for a shilling the whole boiling lot — Field Service Marching Order, as it was called; acres of webbing and dozens of brass buckles. A lot of his hut-mates willingly handed over their pennies and sloped off to the NAAFI for a beer or a char and wad, and soon men from neighbouring huts came in to ask if they, too, could avail themselves of this service. By the time I left North Wales, in his off-duty hours Bieber was surrounded by piles of webbing and had two Liverpudlian assistants, all blancoing and polishing like mad. People made nasty cracks about Jew-boys but Bieber just smiled and took their pennies. I admired him, for his enterprise and for his disregard for Gentile contempt; after all, he was coining it and we were not. I went on Christmas leave, after which I was ordered to report to Larkhill, the country home of the Gunners. (Their town house was at Woolwich.)

At Larkhill the object of the exercise was to learn to drive before going on to an Officer Cadet School. The winter of 1946/47 was exceptionally grim, not only because of the fierce cold but because, just after the war, there were shortages of most things, including coal. I spent two or three weeks driving around Salisbury Plain in the back of an open fifteen-hundred-weight truck, a Chevrolet, blowing on my hands and stamping my feet on the boards. Once, morning and afternoon, each learner-driver got half an hour at the wheel. Pneumonia wagons, the Chevs were called: they had no windscreen, just a couple of plates of glass in front of the driver and the instructor, and webbing 'doors' that could be clamped into place beside you if you felt so inclined, though there wasn't much point. I did not catch pneumonia, mostly due to the frequent stops at roadside 'catts', where we thawed out. Chevs were good vehicles on which to learn to drive: there was no synchromesh, so you had to match engine revs to road speed in order to make your gear change; they had a 'gate' gearbox and heavy controls, so they made the subsequent driving of light cars easy and the transition to 3- and 10-ton trucks not too difficult.

From the window above my bed in the spider block in which I lived (wooden huts with a dormitory at each end and the ablutions in the middle, hence 'spider') I could look across the bleak countryside to Stonehenge on the horizon. As an American woman once said when gazing at it 'It sure mustabeen a hellava place to heat,' but I doubt if it was much colder than the inside of our hut. Anyway, I passed the driving test and was duly given a pink slip of paper which has since authorised me to drive more than half a million miles.

While at Larkhill I attended the War Office Selection Board at Horsham, where, in the snow and mud, I slithered and skated around trying to display, despite all the evidence to the contrary, that I had 'officer qualities'. I think I got good marks for trying; for the first time in my life people were making me work and offering me an incentive to do so, so I did my best — and passed, so justifying that Personnel Selection Officer's judgement.

The next stop was Aldershot, where I stayed for eight weeks at Mons Officer Cadet School. This was presided over — there is no other appropriate word — by Regimental-Sergeant-Major Ronald Brittain of the Coldstream Guards, a gigantic figure of a man with a voice to match. On parade he would have something like a thousand cadets responding instantly to his words of command, and succeeded in licking them into a degree of smartness they would never have believed possible. In this he was assisted by Company Sergeant Majors who strutted around the ranks like fighting cocks, their heads thrust forward snarling encouragement sotto voce, their pace sticks clamped under their left arms. Handel's Scipio, played by a military band, has meant a lot to me ever since. (Brittain died in 1981 aged 81. They don't build them like that these days.)

During one exceptionally long-drawn-out parade one of the sergeant-majors (he was in the Somerset Light Infantry) saw a cadet who looked as if he was going to pass out and fall flat on the tarmac. He stood beside him, grabbed his belt at the back and held him up, hissing 'Stand up, sir. Stand up straight!' The boy braced up and in due course marched off the parade ground with his head held high. Nearly thirty years later I was talking to a group of Barrack Officers — Ordnance officers commissioned from the ranks who are responsible for the furnishing of barracks and army quarters — in Osnabruck when something about one of them, a major, reminded me of the incident. I asked him if he had ever been a young Somerset's CSM at Mons and he confirmed that he had, before transferring from the infantry. It gave me a great kick to meet him again, after all those years.

While at Mons we were sent to Okehampton, on Dartmoor, to the Battle Camp, where we were subjected to much indignity. Live ammunition was fired over our heads, we were driven across wind-swept hills like herded cattle, we were made to lie in bogs while other people used us as duckboards and detonated loud things in close proximity to our heads. In the aftermath of the blizzards the moor was littered with dead sheep and the smell of them added another dimension of realism that would not have been there normally. The next major item on the agenda was our Passing Out parade, when some would be commissioned and others would go on to specialised cadet schools for further training — in my case, to the Royal Artillery school at Deepcut.

In contrast to Mons, the RA OCTU was dominated by the officers. The Commandant was a full colonel — nicknamed by an irreverent cadet (Angus Arnold Thomas, who played the battered piano in the cadet's club rather nicely) Madame Arcati, after Noel Coward's Blithe Spirit character as portrayed by Margaret Rutherford in the film of that name; the colonel (Matthews) had the same jutting jaw and slurping way of speech. Physical stamina was the dominating theme at Deepcut and Matthews was mad about 'Gutch'. 'Gutch,' he would say with Churchillian intonation, 'that's what I want to see, gentlemen, plenty of gutch.' Thus we were made to 'bash' ten miles in full kit in an absurdly short length of time, then go over an assault course, then fire ten rounds on the thirty-yards range. Some of us came nearer to dying than others. (A few months later one of the cadets did. What a way to lose a son.) Mind you, I have never been so fit in my life — or so near to ending it.

Boxing was another thing that everyone

had to do. Milling, it was called: three three-minute rounds during which the cadets were required to bash their opponent as hard as possible — there was no question of a scientific approach to the matter. The inter-battery matches were like a Roman Carnival: the officers wore their mess-kit uniforms and their wives got all tarted up and came and sat at the ringside, with disdainfully raised eyebrows watching some mother's son spitting teeth out onto the canvas. If you back-pedalled around the ring you were on your way back to your unit on an early train the next morning, so, not wishing to do that I got through the qualifying rounds by, in sheer desperation, quickly raining blows on my adversary. He had no time to bounce around waving his gloves in the air trying to size me up: before he had reached the middle of the ring he was already at a severe disadvantage. This worked well during the elimination rounds but in the finals I came up against a Scot called Fleming, who had boxed for Glasgow University — and was also one of my best friends. That did not deter him, however, and he knocked me out. As I looked down at my blood dripping on to the canvas my sincerest wish was never again to have anything to do with boxing but in later years

I qualified as a boxing judge and then, as a brigadier, was chairman of the British Army of the Rhine Boxing Association. At least I knew what it felt like to take a leathering. I think amateur boxing, properly run, as it is in the army, gives a man pride in having overcome his natural fear of physical punishment, keeps him fit and helps to develop a good spirit in a unit; boxing professionally is another matter, since constant sparring and jarring must, in the end, damage brain cells.

Amongst many other activities the cadets had two or three sessions when we sat on the Hogs Back above Godalming drawing 'panoramas', sketches of the countryside on which we annotated items of interest, such as church steeples and railway lines. The point of the exercise was, as an embryonic Forward Observation Officer, to plot the compass bearing to the steeple, or whatever, and estimate its distance, that information then being quickly available when identifying targets for guns at a later stage. Beside one of the steeples was a rectory, in whose garden, many years hence, I would attend a summer cocktail party given by its occupant, a major-general who would one day become the Chief of the General Staff and then Chief of the Defence Staff — Michael Carver. But that was a long way away on the other side of the horizon.

J.P. de E. Skipwith was my battery commander (who died in 1980) and a nice man by the name of Pat McConchie was my troop commander. He it was who was responsible for instructing us in gunnery, including learning how to handle 25-pounder field artillery pieces. When we had done that we fired them on the ranges at Sennybridge, in South Wales. In turn each cadet had to act as F-O-O, directing the fire of the guns that were manned by the other cadets in his troop. Once in a while an unfortunate chap would make a mess of it, get hopelessly lost while ranging and have to give up before the guns ran out of ammunition, but more often than not he would make five or six corrections at about 6,000 yards range (guns-to-target) and then order Fire For Effect, which meant he had bracketed the target with one gun and the rest of the troop could fire at it on the same elevation and bearing. When my turn came I found myself lying on the forward slope of a hill peering disbelievingly at a map which indicated, unless I was much mistaken, that the target was extremely close: only about a thousand yards from the guns and two hundred yards in front of me. 'Well, what are you waiting for?' Skipwith demanded at my side. I picked up the radio handset and gave the orders loudly, so that he could not be in any doubt, and waited for him to pounce. He said nothing, and after about thirty seconds a shell whistled over a few feet above our heads and crumped down on to the slope in front. I gulped, gave a correction and another shell bracketed the target, a clump of gorse bushes. I went to fire-for-effect immediately, with my fingers crossed and my head withdrawn into my shoulders. The hillside erupted. When it was all over Skipwith grunted and then said: 'By the way, never set up your OP on a forward slope: what would happen if you desperately needed a shit in full view of the enemy?' I took it as a rhetorical question, nodded, got up, saluted and departed hurriedly.

I must have been extremely fortunate at Deepcut — that, or they were getting short on their quota again — for on another occasion I led a full troop of guns (four 'Quads' — the 4 x 4 wheeled towing vehicle — four ammunition limbers behind them, and four guns behind them, all joined up, each entity some forty feet in length) up a cul-de-sac near Ash Vale. In order to get them out everything had to be unhooked, man-handled around and hooked up again, amidst much roaring of engines and cursing. I was not popular with my fellow cadets. Another time I kept everyone waiting when I could not get my motor-bike to start (that was another thing we learned to do, to ride motor-cycles) when acting as Battery Sergeant Major, the man who leads the guns from one position to another. The Norton 500, I concluded, was first cousin to a 40mm Bofors. However, generally those were good days for me. One of the officers was an old-Etonian and he arranged for the cadets to have the use of the school's boats on the Thames at Windsor. I coxed in the fours — I weighed a skinny 9 stones for years, until I got married — and with my crew got a little medal for being runners-up in the inter-battery competition. Not having the faintest idea what I was doing I screamed encouragement at them when less shouting and greater expertise would have achieved better results. Still, it was fun. The Senior Under Officer of our troop was also an old-Etonian, by the name of John Maltby. He was the son of an Air Vice-Marshal, was a handsome young man and had an acute brain. He had everything going for him, as people would say these days, and not long ago I read that, predictably, he was chairman of a large company, Burmah Oil. We were a happy lot, all young and full of beans, and the thought never entered our heads that one day we would grow old and grey. No, not us. On the 12th October 1947 I marched across the parade ground to the strains of The British Grenadiers, wearing my new Service Dress uniform, a shiny Sam Browne belt and a rather pleased look on my face, no doubt. Even if I did not betray my feelings, I was pleased: I had a single pip gleaming on each shoulder and thought myself no end of a lucky dog. In less than fourteen months I had grown up very quickly.

4

Contrasts

On more than one occasion my arrival at a new place has been attended by an element of farce. On the morning I joined for duty at Stoneleigh Park near Leamington Spa, a wartime, nissen-hutted camp, I had left Orchard Croft early and had had nothing to eat when I arrived there. At noon, I and another two newly-joined subalterns, chinless Haywood and gormless Morris, formed up in front of the adjutant of the 62nd Light Anti-Aircraft Regiment, to which we had been posted. Tiny Morton, who stood six-feet five-inches in his socks and was a Scot from the Isle of Arran — to which he later returned as postmaster — possessed a large Alsatian dog, which was lying under his desk. His office was one-tenth of a nissen-hut and one of those coke stoves was burning in the corner, red-hot two feet up its pipe as usual. I filed in first and ended up next to it.

Morton had a thick handlebar moustache. He glared at us, the dog growled, and he then introduced himself: 'My name is Morrrton,' he announced threateningly, 'and my middle name's barrstard. Yoo play fair by me, and I'll play fair by . . . ' He stopped dead in his tracks as I collapsed in a heap on top of the dog. When I came to, he was slapping my face anxiously and loudly urging me to wake up. I could not, really, have made a worse start in a new regiment.

Stoneleigh Camp, on the site of what is now the Royal Agricultural Society's showground, was in lovely parkland on Lord Leigh's estate. It housed two anti-aircraft regiments — one Light (with 40mm Bofors) and one Heavy (with 3.7″ calibre guns) — and a Brigade Headquarters, commanded by a cheerful ginny fellow called Stewie Ross. I spent more than two years there, converting to a 3-year Short Service commission and serving in both regiments.

The 62nd LAA Regiment was put into suspended animation, a sort of Gunner limbo, after I had been with it for a few months, part of the general run-down and retrenchment of the Army and in particular Anti-Aircraft Command. (Aged 20, I was made its adjutant during the run-down period.) When it had been put to bed I moved across to the other, the 50th HAA — which was, by strange coincidence, the same regiment that Basil had been captured with in Tobruk five years before, only then it was a Medium Regiment. I was, in turn, troop commander and Assistant Adjutant in both regiments, both of which were shambolic. But I enjoyed life because I was young, busy, paid sixteen shillings a day, and because I liked being with soldiers. As I didn't know any better, I thought this was the usual standard in Gunner regiments.

There were a number of reasons why the regiments were in a bad state: like post-war turbulence, which resulted in a lot of unprofessional officers and warrant officers hanging around; like the fact that a lot of people were on the fiddle; like the fact that a lot of people were absent a lot of the time. The bad side of National Service was responsible, in part, for this situation because after men had been trained it was difficult to keep them occupied and interested; in those days Adventure Training, which is challenging and educational, had not been thought of. But the main reason, as is always the case, in the army or anywhere else, including politics, was the incompetence of the man at the top.

My first commanding officer was a plump old fellow — he couldn't have been forty-five, but he looked seventy — called (Daddy) Sheehan, who beamed benignly at everyone but hadn't got a clue. My second was an ex-German POW (Robin Scott-Moncrieff) who had a pleasant wife, shattered nerves and a neck that would go red like a turkey's wattle when he was angry, which was quite often. (I used to stand behind him as adjutant, my silver-topped swagger stick under my left arm, when he was taking 'orders' — when men who were accused of a disciplinary offence were brought before him — and wait for the predictable explosion, which was preceded by a sudden reddening of the said neck.) He was a good man, a pre-war Woolwich Academy cadet, but the regiment folded before he could get a grip on it. My third (Elliot) was a gentleman, and very conscious of it. He was frightfully nice but innately incapable of exercising his authority. Battery Commanders, trying desperately to impose some sort of order would refer malefactors to him for punishment only to have the case dismissed. (Once when I was present he told a repeated absentee that over and over again he had given him a chance and over and over the man had let him down: Why? The soldier thought a for a moment and then replied: 'Well, sir, it's like this: I tells myself I shouldn't, but after a while I just gets fed up, an' I jus' 'as to fuck orf. Sir') Nothing was ever achieved because we spent most of our time sorting out yesterday's cock-up.

The situation was put right with the arrival of an Australian by the name of (Digger) Chessels, who had joined the British Army during the war. He looked very much like President Eisenhower but was a stronger character. On his first day in command he told the assembled officers that we were 'a complete bloody shower' and that he was not going to put up with it. For a start, all subalterns would do three-quarters of an hour sword drill under the RSM every morning before breakfast. Within twenty-four hours everyone, even the soldiers in the cells — especially the soldiers in the cells — knew he had arrived. He had rules which he applied rigidly: if a man came before him he got the maximum punishment he could give: 28 days detention; if he reappeared, he was Court Martialled, which meant a longer sentence; if he was an NCO and he could bust him, he busted him: if not, he was Court Martialled.

I had spent many hours in the unit acting as the Prosecuting or Defending Officer at Courts Martial and had been kept very busy, but soon there was just a trickle of work. It was a lesson I never forgot. The unit was transformed not, as some might think, into cowed dejection, but into one full of optimism — and much more efficient. People knew what they had to do and got on with it, with a minimum of embuggerance from the cussed members of the community whose chief delight it was (and is) to draw attention to themselves by trying to snarl up the works. (Nowadays, such people are drawn as if by a magnet to the small screen, where they are encouraged by ambitious interviewers to explain at length and in whining tones why they are justified in messing things up.)

★   ★   ★

Chessels was aided in his crusade by a splendid RSM by the name of Cullen, who at one time had been in the Royal Marines. He was enormous, similar in size to Brittain but more rugged-looking, like a heavy-weight wrestler. He was bald and bull-necked, and standing behind him it was possible to see the tips of his moustaches sticking out on either side of his face. A fearsome figure, he had a young, rather toothy but attractive wife, whom he thought the world of, and a small daughter, and ran a very well-ordered Sergeants' Mess, where of an evening he would quaff great quantities of beer and eat half a dozen pork pies smothered in mustard. His way of life, indeed, ended it; also I think he was a good deal older than his pay book said he was.

One day when I was walking up a gentle hill I saw him stop to draw breath in front of me. As I approached he turned, tucked his pace stick under his arm, cracked up a splendid salute and his grey face tried to break into a smile. 'It's nothing, sir' he replied in answer to my inquiry as to his health, 'just a touch of indigestion.' A couple of weeks later, in the middle of the night, he had a massive heart attack and died.

We gave him a tremendous send-off. After a service in the Roman Catholic church his coffin, draped in the Union flag (Mick Cullen was a Southern Irishman, but proud to serve) was put on a gun carriage. With a band playing the Dead March from Saul the whole regiment slow-marched with arms reversed down to the Parade in Leamington Spa, past the Pump Rooms and on to the cemetery. There, three volleys were fired over his grave and the Last Post was sounded by a bugler whose lips were so dry in the heat that he messed up a note or two. I expect it was only my imagination but I thought I heard an angry thumping coming from inside the coffin.

In those days the army was about half a million strong and British troops were serving in Hong Kong, Singapore, Malaya, the Gulf, Aden, Egypt, Cyprus, Malta,

Gibraltar, the British Army of the Rhine and the West Indies, amongst other places. It was still in India, but about to depart with unseemly haste: yes, there was agitation to get us out but, as always, it emanated mostly from the intelligentsia; the ordinary peasant was content to try to make ends meet and happy to live in peace with his neighbours, Hindu or Moslem. Here, the Welfare State had arrived and signalled the beginning of the end for Britain as a world power: as a nation we became totally self-centred. In future, the wealth generated by the minority was to be siphoned off for the benefit of an element of the population who took much more than they gave. (Though nobody should be miserable for the lack of adequate food, shelter or medical attention, if they contribute nothing to society then in my opinion society is under no obligation to give them a free ride.) The army was still very much a part of the life of the nation, not least because of National Service. Today it would be quite inconceivable to have a public military funeral such RSM Cullen's. People would be ringing up their local TV station to complain that the traffic had been held up for three minutes.

★ ★ ★

One of the effects of the Partition of India on Stoneleigh Park was that we had an influx of ex-Indian Army majors; that is, British officers who had been serving with the Indian Army. They were offered the choice of transferring to the British Army or taking retirement. A few stayed, but most left; and seeing what the Gunners were like at Stoneleigh it is not surprising. In the regiment we had a Dogra, a Punjabi and a Rajputani. After spending years of his life in hot climates one of them carried a hand-warmer in his pocket to help counter the effects of a British winter. The Dogra, Peter Denman, stuck the course and ended up as a brigadier, but the others took the pill and left. Twenty years later I glimpsed one of them, Peter Adams, an ex-Japanese POW with a twitch, poor man, and not surprising, in a crowded Tube train in London. For many years the British army used words of Hindi and Urdu in daily usage, brought back by men who had served on the subcontinent.

Like a lot of subalterns in those days I wore my rank uncomfortably and was a bit of a martinet. I could not see that I could get better results by disciplined persuasion than I could by sharp coercion, so I flung my weight

114

about. But I was not alone: one of my fellow subalterns, Lehman by name, had a white bull terrier. He cultivated a pugnacious, threatening look (the dog already had it) and aided by a bristling moustache, steel-rimmed glasses and an unlovely countenance struck terror into the hearts of his unfortunate troops. He would walk down the ranks on parade, his silver-knobbed swagger stuck under his arm, thrust his angry, pop-eyed face about four inches away from a soldier's and bark a question. Since the man's mind had turned to jelly at his approach it was a rare occasion when the right answer was forthcoming. To add to the fun he would then nudge the bull terrier bitch, which he kept on a choke lead, and make it lunge forward, snarling. If the man moved so much as an inch he was berated to the point of near lunacy. I doubt if many of Mike Lehman's National Servicemen signed on as regular soldiers.

In an attempt to revert to pre-war standards the Senior-Subaltern system was instituted in the regiment. This gentleman was supposed to rule over the Junior officers, assisted by a touch on the tiller by the Adjutant if the need arose. If he was a good man a newly-joined subaltern would be helped to find his feet; if he was a bully, the boy's life could be made very unpleasant. We had one, Gerry Mott by name, whose great joy was to make the novice bare his private parts amidst drunken howls of derision during his first regimental dinner night, long after the senior officers had wisely called it a day and gone to bed. I regret that I did not have the guts to protest, and sneaking to anyone in authority about it was out of the question.

To this day I detest bawdy songs and the inebriated cavortings that go on under the name of high spirits. There was a time when it was thought manly to get blind drunk during a Dinner Night and indulge in violent and destructive horseplay. It was alleged that it proved a man's worth and let off steam but in my experience when all inhibitions are released someone, usually the weakest and most easily put-upon, suffers. Thirteen years later I chanced to meet a nice man, married to a pretty wife, whom I had once seen so humiliated, standing near to tears on a table with his pants down. I don't know if he knew I knew, but we both pretended we didn't.

★ ★ ★

Another character I remember in Stoneleigh was the second padre I came across in the army. He was a short, plump, round-faced, amiable little man who was as bent as a corkscrew. In those days I didn't know what the phrase meant but I sensed that something was not quite right, for he was much given to patting his parishioners on the bum and suggesting solitary outings together. The padre dwelt in the same hut as the Educators, who were led by a little moustached man by the name of Sanctuary. 'Yes I would like a drink, Sanctuary much. Very kind of you. A double gin and tonic,' he would say in the mess, grinning and jumping from one foot to the other. (He died in 1997, much mourned by his family, it seemed, judging from the obituary notice.)

As to our profession, we trained to fire those guns and once a year went back to Tonfanau to do so, Oh, my God. Once we went to Sennybridge in South Wales with the 3.7 inch guns, where we fired them in the ground role — because they had a very high muzzle velocity they could penetrate the armour of a tank — like the German 88mm that did so much damage to Allied tanks: it, too, was originally an anti-aircraft gun. On this occasion we went in winter-time, towing these monsters with 10-ton Matadors. The convoy was being led by a despatch rider who became so cold that he eventually fell off his motor-bike. The engine of the Matador was housed in a large metal box in the centre of the cab and in order to thaw him out the Don-R was laid on top of one. As the truck was being driven round a bend in the road the driver suddenly saw a gun standing stationary in front of him; he braked sharply but the barrel crashed through the front of the radiator and crushed the despatch rider where he lay, killing him instantly.

The guns were capable of sending a shell up to more than 30,000 feet; the problem was to get it to arrive at the same time as the aircraft it was aimed at. The death knell of anti-aircraft command could be heard in the sonic boom of planes that flew faster and faster though muzzle velocities had been pushed as far as they would go. Forty years on, rocketry has redressed the balance to some extent but in the late 1940s and '50s we were giving the kiss of life to a dodo. The radar sets and 'predictors' that controlled the guns (looked after by an alcoholic captain by the name of John Boughey) were the electronic equivalents of Stephenson's rocket, and would make today's microchip men curl up in hysterics.

For light relief I and other young officers would go of an evening to Leamington Spa — then a rather genteel place, now a dormitory suburb of the Midlands industrial conurbation — often on a Friday night to the Town Hall dance. We were allowed to drive a Tilly (an Austin utility van) on repayment; people still did not have private cars, you see. Sometimes, for a change, we went to Coventry. Indeed there was an outstation of Stoneleigh at a place called Binley, in the shadow of a slag heap, where I lived for a while with the 62nd. Bagginton airfield was not far away and I would occasionally see a strange object called a flying wing wobbling through the sky. It was almost uncontrollable, but someone had a point to prove. Failing to do so, the flying wing was consigned to the scrap heap. It went at about the same time that I left Warwickshire on posting to a posher place.

★   ★   ★

The Royal Artillery Training Brigade at Oswestry consisted of four regiments and a Brigade Headquarters, commanded by Peter Gregson (who had two brothers, also Gunners who, between them, had five DSOs). In it there were two Selection Regiments, which took fortnightly intakes from civilian life, and two Field Regiments, which taught young soldiers to fire

25-pounders. I went to the 67th Selection Regiment, the sausage-machine to which I have already referred, commanded by Lieutenant-colonel David Burnaby, a stout, snobbish, pompous man whose main interest was athletics. To give him his due, he succeeded in having a fine running track built on which a fellow subaltern, Christopher Chataway, did some useful training before he left the army to become an Olympic medallist, an MP and eventually a Junior Minister. (Physically, his lungs were far bigger than most people's, enabling him to suck in great quantities of air and transform them into the oxygen which fed his muscles. The same must, presumably, apply to all long and middle-distance runners.) He was a nice, unassuming man; perhaps a shade too nice for Westminster.

There were two officers' messes at Parkhall Camp, each shared by a Selection Regiment and a Field Regiment, the members of which seldom spoke to one another, congregating as a rule at opposite ends of the ante room. The Field gunners thought themselves infinitely superior to the Selectors, a strange attitude when one's presence in one or the other depended largely on the whim of an overworked junior officer in the Artillery postings branch. But the two regiments were trying hard to get back to pre-war standards, so such small things mattered,

One of the symbols of Gunner superiority was to hunt the fox but since those animals were in fairly short supply around Oswestry the next best thing was to hunt the aniseed trail. Thus on a Saturday morning fat, red-faced, bucolic officers would energetically pursue a smelly bundle of rags dragged at a horse's tail across the Shropshire countryside, later clumping into the mess spattered with mud and breathing heavily after a long chase on a spavined nag. If one 'hunted' one was definitely In, and marked out for a bright future (perhaps I should have seriously considered mounting a horse again, after all) but strangely enough none of those who thought so highly of themselves achieved high rank as the years went by — except, perhaps, a man called Jasper Browell, who became, I think, a colonel. Technology had a lot to do with it: willy-nilly officers had to have the brains to be proficient with ever-more complicated systems; it was no longer enough just to play games or hunt.

In Oswestry I made friends with a doctor by the name of Tony Dalzell, doing his National Service, who regarded most of the Army's customs as totally laughable. With hindsight he was probably right about some of them, but at the time I felt that such things must have been of value or people would not attach such importance to them. Since then most of the things he found infantile or ridiculous, such as the inordinate amount of bullshit, have passed into history. There was a joke that went the rounds: if it moved, salute it, if it didn't, paint it. There was some truth in that. Tony encouraged me to read a wider range of literature, and so it was that I came across Ulysses, by James Joyce. Not that that did me a lot of good but it did open the way to new means of expression that I have used in my books; stream-of-consciousness writing for one thing, the place of sex as a driving force in life for another. And it was through Tony that I met Sheila Fell and L.S. Lowry.

When he was demobilised Tony decided to practice in Aspatria, in Cumberland. He bought a gaunt Victorian villa and there, with his wife Kathleen, also a doctor, put his brass plate on the gate and waited for his first customer. After a day or two an old lady tottered in and was prescribed a placebo. She was the first of many — customers, not placebo imbibers — but no thanks to the local doctors, who much resented his unnegotiated presence there. I visited Tony and Kathleen there twice, in the before-and-after situation. 'Before', there were gas jets on the walls and dark red flock wallpaper; 'after', there was central heating and Sanderson prints and a warm house with children living in it.

On the second occasion Tony asked me if I would give a girl a lift in my car to Carlisle Station. She turned out to be a Miss Fell, who painted and was quite soon to become a Royal Academician. A year or two later she had a one-woman show in Middlesborough and I went to the preview. The walls were covered with large, grim landscapes, stark and sombre: windswept, cloud-covered hills in which crouched, if one looked closely, battered human habitations and flocks of starving sheep. They were tremendously powerful and disturbing pictures yet they were created by a pretty, feminine, bright-eyed waif-like girl who was wearing fishnet stockings, a black velvet skirt and jacket and a frilly lace blouse that frothed out at the neck and wrists. No paint-stained, grimy lank-haired arty type was Sheila.

At the preview she introduced me to her friend LS Lowry — he of the famous stick men — who had travelled from Manchester to see her pictures. He was very tall, warm and simple — and called me 'sir' because I was a major and he had been a private in the Great War! What a strange world it is. I saw

Sheila again a few times and on one occasion asked her why she did not go to the Mediterranean and paint those fantastic colours that had inspired Cezanne and van Gogh. She said that only the rolling hills of Cumberland inspired her. It was with real regret that I was to read that she died, very prematurely, in 1980.

★ ★ ★

Another young doctor at Oswestry was John Deakin, who was terribly shocked when one weekend a young soldier died on him. There had been an outbreak of influenza and two barrack rooms had been set aside as wards. One of the men was running a very high temperature but instead of responding to treatment as the rest of them did he went over the top, so to speak, and died. It was that particular doctor's introduction to the grim fallibility of human life.

★ ★ ★

It was at Oswestry that I bought my first car, a clapped-out 1937 Morris Eight Tourer which I obtained from a REME corporal — who did me. I used to drive along anxiously eyeing the oil-pressure gauge to see if it fell below five pounds, which was as much as the rattling big-ends allowed it to achieve. With its canvas hood and perspex side windows it was like piloting an open biplane but not withstanding that I sometimes drove up into the lovely Welsh hills, muffled up against the winter chill. Soon I cut my losses and sold it to an even bigger fool than I. (He was a garage owner, so I thought he was fair game.)

* * *

The Assistant Adjutant of my regiment was a red-haired, red-moustached man called Hudson, who was sent to Korea and was killed by a Chinese shell soon after he got there, a long way from Parkhall Camp, where we continued to receive our fortnightly intake of recruits. Hundreds of faces passed before my eyes — by the time I ended my army career it must have been tens of thousands. Life revolved around intakes and troop competitions and the men were just ciphers: bodies to be measured up, weighed, kitted out and churned out. It was a rotten system, for the men were not with us long enough for the officers or NCOs to get to know them. (The only few instances of systematic bullying I ever came across or heard about during my many years in the Army took place at recruit training centres, where the NCOs could take advantage of the insecurity and ignorance of young men, but at Parkhall they were not there long enough for that to happen, which was about the only good thing to be said for it.)

After a while I too was churned out, and sent to Bristol, which as far as the Gunners were concerned was like being put into suspended animation. The army, and the Royal Artillery in particular, was shrinking. Anti-Aircraft Command, which comprised half the Gunners, was at the end of the line; Coastal Artillery, which had protected such places as Gibraltar and Malta, had already sunk. But the crucial thing for me was, I think, the lack of a proper education and the necessary certificates to prove it. (Or it could have been that I had jokingly told an officer in Parkhall Camp that I had once shot a fox.) Anyway, I found myself in a Fire Command Troop commanded by a little fisherman called Arthur Turney who disappeared on his motorbike to Devon or Cornwall as often as possible to try to catch anything.

Horfield Barracks had a Brigade Head-quarters in it, commanded by a nice man called Jock Stewart. It was an ancient place and the Other Rank married quarters jammed within the walls were of Crimean vintage, built above what had been stable blocks. There was no question of swinging a cat in those little apartments or anything else. Talk about communal living! It was there that I made the second of my farcical entrances.

On the day I arrived I was escorted up the stairs in the mess to be shown my bedroom by a small, bespectacled, rather intellectual lieutenant. He flung open the door and ushered me in. I duly looked around approvingly while he stood watching me and then suddenly, for no apparent reason, the light bulb under which I was standing fell out of its holder, and the shade with it. The bulb bounced off my head on to the floor without breaking and the shade rolled away into a corner. Why, I ask myself?

★   ★   ★

The Task of the 25th Fire Command Troop was to plot enemy aircraft movements and control the fire of anti-aircraft guns, which we did with the help of Territorial Army WRAC girls whose tight skirts would stretch out over the plotting table below the dais on which I sat, making it extremely hard for me to concentrate on waves of imaginary Russian bombers that were supposedly making a beeline for Bristol (yes, by then the enemy was firmly Russian).

It was while I was in Bristol that there was a major fire at Avonmouth Dock. Two men had climbed on to the top of an empty oil storage tank to clean it when suddenly there was a flash and it began to burn. By the time evening came several of its neighbours were also on fire and the army was asked to send troops to assist. We mustered two or three lorry loads and set off, and on arrival found that fire brigades from all over the area had been called out; there were dozens of appliances parked around the compound in which the tanks were blazing.

Not surprisingly the whole fire-fighting operation had developed piecemeal. In order to get anywhere near the blaze as more and more vehicles arrived they had to run over hose that was already laid. The result was that by the time we got there everyone was working in a thick cloud of spray that was coming out of the punctured hoses. Water pressure had been lost to such an extent that at the sharp end the firemen were holding nozzles from which came only a trickle: there was a great deal of activity and a lot of effort but not much effect. The soldiery worked hard, shifting equipment, laying out reels, puncturing cans of ox blood which they then poured in to canvas tanks full of water — when it was sucked out by the pumps the water and ox blood were mixed to create foam, which was then directed on to the tanks.

Fortunately, the flaming oil that spilled out of the tanks was contained by the low walls built around the group that were blazing, and prevented the fire from spreading all over the tank farm. Even so, seventeen of them brewed up. The heat was intense and the sight breathtaking as flames gushed high into the sky out of a red and orange inferno and billowing black smoke. By dawn the fire had almost burnt itself out and we all went home. The remains of the two oil workers were never found.

On another occasion my soldiers were called upon to assist in quite a different way; by the Festival Ballet, who were performing at the Bristol Hippodrome. They phoned to ask if we could provide some extras and I took a group of eager volunteers to act as warriors in Scheherazade, starring Tamara Touvanova, Anton Dolin and John Gilpin. On the night Bill Bloggs, Bert Bumsted and their pals were plastered with grease paint and decked out in tawdry finery: large turbans, wide-sleeved tunics, baggy pants, and boots with long, pointed toes. Armed with wooden scimitars they chased with unconcealed relish the rather effeminate male ballet dancers around the stage, prodding protruding posteriors a little too impolitely.

At the Colston Hall, which many years later I would attend in an official capacity as the Lord Mayor of Bristol's Secretary, and the City Swordbearer, I went to hear Kirsten Flagstadt singing Schubert, Brahms and Wagner. Also many years later Geraint Evans told me that the first time he sang with Flagstadt he went in to her dressing room and found her drinking a glass of Guinness and knitting.

* * *

My exit from Horfield Barracks was not farcical but rather sad. The time had come to decide whether to leave the army or not. I was interested in politics and went for an interview in Smith Square with a view to becoming a Tory Party agent but was not encouraged to learn that if I stayed with them for twenty years I would end up earning £1,200 a year. And, too, I looked out of my bedroom window in the mess one day on to the square and the soldiers on parade there and decided that I did not want to say goodbye.

I had been in the army five and a half years, was now twenty-three years old and had learned a lot, the most salutary thing being that many people are not nice to know.

One thing that had appealed to me so much about Axel Munthe's book was his sincere belief in the innate goodness of human beings; the Little Sisters of the Poor selflessly giving and caring; the humanity of the rescuers in Naples after the earthquake; the nobility of the moujiks stricken with rabies in the infirmary in Paris. Well, either he was a much nicer person than I am, which is more than likely, or he was very naïve, for in my experience most people can overcome their selfish, aggressive and critical impulses only by making a tremendous effort.

For me, by 1952, the bright innocence and the hopeful expectancy of youth had gone. I had learned some of the hard facts of life.

And I had reached another major turning point in my life.

5

Big Bangs

As I walked into the Officers' Mess of the Central Ammunition Depot at Corsham no halberd fell off the wall and hit me on the head, no suit of armour swayed and toppled as I approached. I gazed around at the lovely oak staircase and the panelled walls and, since I have always had a feeling of well-being in such surroundings, immediately took to the place. There was even a grand piano in the ante room. It was not until much later that I discovered that the house had once belonged to Isambard Kingdom Brunel, whose ageless and beautiful Clifton Suspension Bridge I had marvelled at when I was in Bristol. The house was built near the entrance to Box Tunnel, and was Brunel's base while he was supervising the construction of the Great Western Railway.

If, the next time you take the train from Paddington to Temple Meads, you look to the right as you enter Box Tunnel you will see a branch-line disappearing into the rock. If you were able to go along it you would find yourself in a hidden world: a maze of subterranean tunnels, eleven miles of them in all, which in 1952 contained a quarter of a million tons of ammunition.

In Georgian times the mellow stone that was quarried (mined would be a better word) in that part of Wiltshire was used to build Bath and other lovely places. Men would work and sleep in the tunnels for days at a time, their 'snap' brought to them in cloth bundles by their wives or little children. The men would slice a deep cleft into the rock along each wall with a long-handled pick and then, lying on their side on the ground, make a deep undercut linking the two sides. Holes would be drilled at the top, gunpowder would be tamped in and then the miners would retire to a safe distance. When the charge was exploded it broke off and released the suspended block of stone, letting it drop, as a seven-foot cube, on to wooden rollers that had been pushed into the undercut. Next, horses would be brought to the rock face and harnessed with chains and iron hooks to these great chunks of stone, which would then be rolled out into the daylight, to be sawn and chipped into workable pieces. The result was that the hillside became a honeycomb of tunnels nearly two hundred feet below the innocent surface of the ground.

The mine lay there like a giant boomerang on its side. The top and bottom of the boomerang were known as the North and South Drifts. Between them were eleven major connecting tunnels, and many lesser ones formerly used by men and horses to get to the working faces. Some had been enlarged so as to become sizeable long vaults and before and during the Second World War these had been converted into underground storage for ammunition. In some of them lay millions of projectiles, ranging in size from the huge 15″ monsters, shaped like gigantic green turds, that the defunct Coastal Artillery had once used, down to 20mm Oerlikon cannon shells that were the size of a jumbo pencil; in other vaults were acre upon acre of boxed cordite, stretching as far as the eye could see. Up near the surface a giant 'paddle wheel' turned, grabbing air out of the sky and pushing it down a ventilation shaft, from whence pumps and air-locks circulated it through the system. Beside the wheel, lifts took men down into the fluorescent glare of the shafts. At one end of the boomerang, accommodation for two or three hundred men had been built: dormitories, cooking and washing facilities, the lot. It was only infrequently used but was available for other, unspecified, purposes if needed.

If appointed as duty officer on a Saturday morning one's task was to take an enormous bunch of keys and, entirely alone, solemnly walk through specified tunnels from one end of the boomerang to the other, unlocking, opening, closing and then locking every door at each end of every tunnel. The object of the exercise was never satisfactorily explained to me but allegedly we were supposed to scan the walls and electrical conduits as we trudged through and 'keep an eye on things'. It was an eerie task, as you may imagine, and in the smaller, dimly-lit tunnels I often expected to find the dusty, uniformed skeleton of a long-lost Ordnance Officer who had mislaid a crucial key, and whom nobody had missed, not even his wife.

In addition to Tunnel, as it was called, there were two outstations, similar but smaller, on which little money had been spent. One was full of rusting aircraft bombs; its ceilings dripped little stalactites and its walls were covered in green slime. In the other was an agglomeration of cobwebbed stuff that nobody could identify with certainty: was it Saxon? Or even Ancient Brit? Standing at the entrance to these caverns, looking down the long stairs that disappeared into the gloom — there were no lifts, it was a matter of descending reluctantly and ascending eagerly, but ever more slowly — was like looking into the mouth of Hades. These two places were soon to be progressively emptied and their contents dumped into the Irish Sea — where, I suspect, they have been giving the fish palpitations ever since.

Tunnel, though, was another matter. It was a highly efficient depot, with mile upon mile of rubberised conveyer belting. A box of ammunition removed from a railway wagon at the underground siding could travel miles to its pre-planned destination untouched by the 'uman 'and — though booted in a different direction now and then at intersections by a disgruntled Chunky. Its destination depended on a safety scheme worked out upstairs which would ensure, in theory, that should an explosion occur there would be no chain reaction from one tunnel to the next. Fortunately, it was never put to the test.

One Sunday I returned to my room after a walk in the parkland that adjoined the house to find a brassed-off Scottish officer by the name of Killin lounging on the second, until-then-unoccupied, bed. He had just returned from a spell of duty in Aqaba, which, in the considered opinion of those who knew about such things, is a dreadful place. The Persian Gulf, so they said, was the arsehole of the world, and Aqaba was a hundred miles up it. Luckily, I was never required to make a judgement about the matter but Howard had done so, and agreed whole-heartedly. It was bad enough having had to put up with the rotten place for years but the reason that he was really cheesed off was that he had asked the Ordnance postings branch if he could be sent to Scotland so that he could be near his future wife, Eilleen, but with their usual helpful response to such requests they had posted him to Corsham, which, other than Penzance, was about as far from Edinburgh as they could possibly have put him. Howard was to become my oldest pal in the army.

I stayed in Corsham only a matter of weeks and the place lasted only a matter of years. In the early Sixties it was shut because it cost too much to heat, light and ventilate but in its way it was a marvel: perhaps a portent of what life might be like in years to come if human beings have to retreat from the after-effects of a nuclear war.

★ ★ ★

I next started upon a series of courses of instruction. I had already, as a young officer, been taught the basics of being an infantryman and a gunner, and also attended courses on Pay and Accounts, Military Law, how to supervise the feeding of a regiment, and the mysteries of keeping Mechanical Transport on the road. By the time I finished my army service I would have learned Industrial Management, Warehousing and Distribution, Stock Control and Procurement, how to ensure the safety and serviceability of munitions and missiles, how to deploy an all-arms battle group in the attack, defence and withdrawal, how to use armed force in aid of the civil power, how to co-ordinate the activities of the three services in Combined Operations, the principles of the deployment and use of nuclear weapons, the integration of the logistic support of NATO armies and air forces. And along the way I would also become an expert on bomb disposal. I never stopped learning in the army.

In all, I spent about one-seventh of my service learning new things. (That seems a lot, but in fact it was less time than a Soviet officer on the other side of the Iron Curtain spent learning his profession.) I attended some very imposing places of instruction — the Royal Military College of Science at Shrivenham, the Army Staff College at Camberley, the Joint Services Staff College at

Latimer, but the most beautiful setting of all was, without a doubt, the NATO School at Oberammergau in the Bavarian Alps, where the classrooms nestled under the towering, snow-capped pinnacle of the Kochel — from which crazy people would sometimes launch themselves to para-glide to the valley floor. (I also attended some rather threadbare establishments where the students sat on wooden benches in draughty wooden huts being taught by people with wooden minds.) Much of what I learned was good for all time but some things were overtaken by the march of time; for example, the replacement of some types of artillery by rockets. It was not possible to stand still.

After Corsham, I was sent to Deepcut again, which had become the depot, training battalion and school of the Ordnance Corps. There, with a number of other officers who were still wearing their original cap badges — Royal Engineers, infantry and so on — I learned about army logistics. Having passed the course we were re-badged and sent on our way to various units.

It was around this time that I used to go to the Nuffield Officers' Club in Eaton Square in London, a place endowed by that worthy man Mr Morris and very attractive to impecunious subalterns because it cost so little to stay there. It is amazing just how much we could get for our pound-a-day pay in the early 1950s; bed and board and a free ticket to a West End production, supplied again by the generosity of the maker of motor cars.

One day as I walked towards Eaton Place I found myself witnessing the making of part of the film *The Million Pound Note* — the bit at the beginning where two old gentlemen offer someone that amount of money for a bet: namely, that he will live like a lord on tick because nobody will be able to change the note. Hansom cabs were bowling along the street, a soldier wearing a pillbox hat was walking along the pavement with a girl in Victorian dress on one arm and a swagger stick under the other, an old man led a dog past them, a delivery-van driver off-loaded trays of pastries out of the back of his little horse-drawn vehicle, Wilfred Hyde-White opened an upstairs window, leaned out and beckoned to Gregory Peck, who was supposed to be an American down on his luck in London: 'Young man! I say, young man! Could you come up here for a moment? Yes, you.' I watched three or four takes — everyone had to go back to square one and start again, the cabs, the people, the dog, the pastry van — and then left them to it.

Because I knew a little about fuzes and projectiles I opted for another course that would make me a specialist in munitions, and after a few weeks found myself at Shrivenham. Science, which had been a closed book to me, became interesting and understandable because there was an obvious application to what I was being taught. We students could photograph a bullet in flight, test to destruction the tensile strength of a piece of steel, X-ray the mechanism of a clockwork fuze, measure the rate of expansion of an explosive gas. And even, with great care, make gun cotton and nitroglycerine in the laboratories.

I had some very happy days at the college, and bought my second car, a 1929 Austin Seven. Its engine was the size of a shoe box, it had a gravity-feed petrol tank under the bonnet, a hand throttle and an advance/retard lever on the steering column. Its registration number was NG 2029 — which in my still-childish mind stood for Nitroglycerine 2029. I could make Flora dance on the road by twitching her steering wheel, much to the consternation of passengers. Her cruising speed was 38 mph but on a good day, with the wind behind her, she could attain 40. She was a gem in brown and black, with green leather upholstery, but I am very much afraid that by now she must have gone to the Great Car Park in the Sky.

Two incidents stand out from the ammunition course, both connected with dinner nights. The first involved a major in the Pakistan Army, one Mubarak, who made the mistake of going to bed early after dinner. The boys decided that this was not good enough and that on no account must he miss the fun, so they called upon the half-Nissen hut in which he slept. (This was while we were at the School of Ammunition, at Bramley, near Basingstoke.) Mubarak awoke with a start, thought the shouting and banging at the door indicated the presence of a lynching mob, took off out of the back entrance and legged it down the road wearing only a white nightgown. He ended up perched on someone's porch with the British officers whooping and dancing gleefully around it. Though no harm was done — in fact, he was carried home shoulder high in triumph — it was some weeks before he could be convinced that we were not harbouring a grudge from the time of the Indian Mutiny.

The second incident took place after we had arrived at Shrivenham and were living in Roberts Hall, one of the huge messes there. Our lab assistant was a studious-looking, serious young man whose father was a parson, in consequence of which this lad had never touched a drop in his life. At a party someone mixed him an innocent looking 'squash' which had been laced with just about everything on the bar shelf, including lighter fuel. He drank this down with relish, turned green and was carted off to his bedroom, where his collar was loosened and he was laid gently on his side — to ensure that he did not choke — before the light was turned out and we left him in peace. He had, of course, a frightful hangover the next morning but the interesting thing is that from then on he could not stay out of the bar, and was to be found there every evening on the stroke of six with his tongue hanging out. (He never thanked his rescuers, presumably because he did not remember having been rescued.)

Shrivenham was run by a Major-General, with a professor as his deputy. The staff was civilian and military and the students came from all the three services and from overseas. Some were taking science degrees, some were specialising, as we were. The place lies beneath the downs in Wiltshire in a lovely setting, and has its own 9-hole golf course. Like many other military establishments it contributed a great deal to the general betterment of the nation — especially during

National Service. The RMCS created science graduates. The army as a whole produced thousands of mechanics, cooks, clerks, drivers and technicians — tradesmen whose skills were very valuable. (Many many years later I was to spend weekends there with the Commandant, Edmund Burton, a Gunner, and his wife Angela. But in 1952 how could I have known that? They lived in a beautiful old mansion beside the church, in a lovely garden, one of the perks that came to some senior officers and their wives out of the blue, never to be repeated.)

One day Field-Marshal Montgomery came to the college to speak to us. In honour of his visit we had put on uniform, a rare event but, typically, he turned up wearing mufti. He climbed up on to the stage, told everyone that there was to be no smoking and that he would allow no time for questions — since everything he was going to say would be perfectly clear, there would be no need for questions — and then asked for a billiards cue. In a panic one was found, and using it as a pointer he began with Japan and then worked his way westwards across a gigantic map of the world that hung at the back of the stage, giving a brilliant extempore summary of the world politico/military situation. His perceptive comments were bejewelled with cutting witticisms about world figures, such as Eisenhower and Franco. ('I sent Ike a Christmas card last year but didn't get one back: I expect he's a bit miffed because I said in my memoirs that he wasn't much of a general.' And: 'I saw General Franco last week. He offered me seven Spanish divisions for NATO but I declined: I would not be at all happy having seven Spanish divisions swanning about in Germany — Oh, I should have asked: are there any Spanish officers in the audience?') At the end of this astounding tour-de-force, which lasted for an hour without his drawing breath, he handed the cue to the Commandant, beamed at us, bade us a polite good-day and strutted out of the hall like the cocky little bantam that he was.

★   ★   ★

After the course ended I was posted as a captain to another large ammunition depot, at Kineton, in Warwickshire. It was on the site of the Battle of Edgehill where, after the gory hand-to-hand combat in 1643 more than four thousand corpses were buried in a mass grave — which, incidentally, has never been located. (Some of the officers, those who were identified, lie in the parish churchyard at Kineton.) Perhaps the bones of all those

Roundheads and Cavaliers lie under one of the two-hundred-and-fifty big brick sheds that were built during the Second World War, all linked together by a rail network.

Kineton is not one of my better memories. Times have changed, but in those days it was a dump, in more ways than one. The Commandant was a hopeless administrator, totally out of his depth as the boss of a big organisation. His Chief Clerk, a Warrant Officer, came near to a complete mental breakdown because important files, Secret, or even Top Secret, would go missing. The Commandant would flatly deny ever having seen them when the clerk tried to retrieve them, and the poor man would go out of the office wringing his hands and feeling, with a touch of panic, that he was going out of his mind, or that he was the victim of a deadly conspiracy. However, the mystery was solved when the colonel left on retirement and his successor inherited the keys of the safe for there, locked away from sight, thought and anxiety, were the missing files. (Which proves something I have long suspected: namely, that if you do nothing, eventually problems resolve themselves; are overtaken by events or someone else makes a decision — though not necessarily the right one, of course.)

Apart from this lack of direction from the

top, Kineton had other inherent difficulties. It was spread over a vast area and men had to walk to work in all weathers — along the railway lines, since there were no roads. On arrival at their sub-depot headquarters they were allocated to tasks in specific sheds, but after they had sloped off into the mist there was no way of ensuring that they went where they were supposed to go, or worked if they did. Several times 'nests' were found in the middle of block-stacks of explosives where Pioneers had hollowed out a small room, safe from prying eyes, where they could smoke and play cards on top of a box of gelignite in order to while away the long, cold and boring hours. Smoking was, of course, verboten, and men were supposed to hand in all contraband, as it was known, when they went through the gates into the ammunition compound but only a complete body search could have ensured that they were not concealing cigarettes and their means of ignition, which was not a feasible proposition. Repeated warnings about the dangers were ignored, this being a classic case of familiarity breeding contempt.

When I arrived in 1954 the depot was packed full of assorted rubbish, some of it highly dangerous. Safety standards had been lowered during wartime mass-production;

metals and chemicals had not been refined enough; quality control had been sacrificed for volume production. And anyway nobody thought this stuff would still be lying around ten years after it was made. The result was that truly horrifying sights were liable to meet the eye when a box of ammunition, outwardly in perfect condition, was opened. Bofors rounds were among the worst offenders. It seemed I was to be dogged by those beastly things.

The small fuze for the 40mm projectile was made of a zinc-based alloy which contained impurities. The alloy broke down after a time and turned into a grey powder. When opened, the large steel boxes were found to contain rotting, mildewed cardboard packaging in which lay loose cogs, springs and pins — the remains of the fuze. The bare detonator would usually be sticking brazenly out of the end of the explosive just waiting for someone to touch it.

Another offender was the much bigger 3.7" anti-aircraft shell, wherein another mechanism called the gaine had gone badly wrong. (It boosted the detonating wave between the detonator in the fuze and the explosive in the projectile.) Yet another was Fuze 119 in the 25-pounder high explosive shell. In both, fulminate of mercury had been put into a copper sheath to form the detonator; the two interacted and formed cuprous azide, a highly sensitive chemical liable to detonate if aggravated — rather like Robin Scott-Moncrief. We found out about the 25-pounders because the French, who were using them against the Viet Minh in IndoChina, reported an abnormally high incidence of bore-prematures: that is, the projectile, very antisocially, went off in the barrel of the gun instead of at the receiving end.

A National Service corporal, whose name I regret I cannot remember, a nice-looking, red-haired, intelligent fellow who is now probably an affluent, sane and respected family man, spent months of his young life unpacking crumbling Bofors ammunition and preparing it for demolition, a task of debilitating boredom and mind-bending repetition even had it not been attended by the possibility of serious amputation or even extinction. Other Ammunition Examiners, as they were called, spent weeks on end defuzing shells in one-man-risk bays, small cubicles constructed of sandfilled ammunition boxes bound together with steel tape. If the fuze or gaine went off by itself the damage was relatively small: a few metal splinters were thrown around. It was another matter if the whole shell detonated, hence the need for the man to be isolated. The dicey object was fed in to him on a felt-lined tray, he clamped it in a vice, unscrewed the gaine or fuze with a key, put it in a box, breathed a sigh of relief and pushed the shell, its teeth drawn, out of the other side of the claustrophobic bay. When soldiers began this task their attitude was of excessive caution; then they worked for a time with the right balance between caution and productivity; then they became fatalistic and incautious: if the gaine or fuze stuck fast in the shell they were not supposed to hit it with a hammer, but human nature being what it is they sometimes did, as I found when I poked my head around the entrance to see what they were up to. When the man reached that point I would switch him to another task and feed another Technician into the bay. (Interestingly, none of them ever cracked up, despite the stress of the job.)

Scientists had established that, at random, one in every three hundred or so of these shells was liable to go off at the slightest provocation. This information was duly passed to the Pioneers who handled the stuff and when they could be bothered to do so they solemnly counted the boxes, taking particular care over the one containing the three-hundredth but bashing the rest about if nobody was looking.

At a time when most of the British Army was leading a quiet life, millions of dangerous projectiles were dealt with in this way at RAOC depots at home and overseas. For years, obsolete or useless stuff was shipped from Cairnryan in Scotland to a watery grave as stocks of wartime ammunition were sorted out. For my part I had the task of overseeing these activities and destroying the dangerous stuff from which the fuze or gaine had refused to be parted.

None of the dangerous ammunition could be moved out of the depot, so it had to be destroyed inside it. There was no demolition ground in the depot when I arrived except a small area with a one-pound explosive limit, so I set about making one in a place as far away from storage locations and human habitation as possible. My aide was a big man by the name of Wallace, a Staff Sergeant technician of great experience. We marked out twelve pits, had a very strong splinter-proof bunker built on the far side of a railway embankment nearby, positioned some large concrete drainage tubes — upended — at strategic points around the area where they could shelter lookouts, erected some poles from which to fly red flags and then, more in hope than anger, began to blow up all this foul stuff. Soon, the Warwickshire countryside was rocking to the sound of loud bangs as piles of shells disintegrated. And soon the headquarters was being besieged with complaints from local residents who strongly resented the fact that the odd tile was being dislodged from their roof. We could not, unfortunately, explain to them that unless we cleansed the stables with these explosions the whole roof was liable to vanish.

This shattering of the peace of the countryside went on for months as winter approached and then descended on us. I remember well a clammy, foggy November afternoon when I had finished a series of demolitions and was doing the routine check to make sure that everything had been fully destroyed. I had to jump into the pits to do this but by this time they were eight or ten feet deep and the landscape resembled Passchendaele in 1918. I leapt down into one and went straight up to my knees in slimy clay. It closed like cement around my Wellington boots and I found myself quite unable to move. Darkness was descending as I lunged about like a marionette and I had visions of being there all night, since I had dismissed the attendant crew of lookout men. I called weakly, struggling to extricate myself then, in desperation, more loudly. Suddenly, the grinning, bespectacled face of the man Wallace appeared over the edge of the crater. He had heard me calling as he locked up the bunker. Mouthing obscenities, I asked for his assistance, and off he went to get a rope. In the gloom I looked around for destroyed chunks of lethal metalware and there, where I could reach out and gently prise it out of a slab of clay, was part of an enormous ammonite, hundreds of millions of years old — the fossil of a sea creature several feet under the Warwickshire clay. Mick Wallace returned, got the rope under my armpits and dragged me out of my boots, which I wrote off to experience. Clutching my prize I squelched in my stockinged feet towards the warmth of a large whisky.

The officers' mess was a couple of Nissen huts joined together. Nissens were made of rounded corrugated iron with a soft-board lining. In ours, rats ran up and down the space between the two and the wind whistled through the gaps where windows were ill-fitted into the walls, gently billowing the curtains. The few single or separated officers, most of whom were either mad or poor company, or both, would sit morbidly around the belching apology for a fire getting quietly sozzled until they eventually got up and staggered off through the blinding blizzards to their rooms. These consisted of half of another, smaller but equally decrepit Nissen hut, a group of which surrounded the mess like bedraggled chicks around a half-plucked hen. Not surprisingly, the married men disappeared in a cloud of small stones and dust to their wives and civilisation just as soon as they possibly could.

One of my few recreations was small-bore shooting and then later, due to the encouragement of a dour Scots major, full-bore. I joined the London and Middlesex Rifle Club at Bisley and would go off there for the weekend, sleeping in the Army Rifle Association hut, a very pleasant clapboard building stuffed full of photographs of past champions and teams and trophies and memorabilia — and taking my army issue .303 rifle and ammunition with me in my car, a practice that would be frowned upon these days. After a day's shooting I would join old gentlemen at the benches where, talking about old times, they lovingly stripped and cleaned their weapons. Some came from many miles away, one old Group Captain in a Bentley all the way from Cirencester. (One day I told him he had left the engine of his car running: he glared at me and said, 'What's wrong with that? We always ran the engines of the Sopwiths for fifteen minutes before we took off.') Some of these men may have come to Bisley to get away from their wives for a while (or may have been encouraged by their wives to do so) but most of them were hooked by it all: the snap, snap of distant rifle fire; the targets smoothly rising and falling in the butts, the sight of the markers waving back and forth indicating an inner or a bull, the sound of pistols cracking on the thirty-yards range, the smell of cleaning oil and polished wood. And the strange, solitary challenge of sending a small slug of lead a thousand yards to hit — against all the odds generated by distance, wind, heat, humidity and one's all-too fallible eye and body — a target just a few feet in size.

In Kineton the soldiers had a pretty deadly time of it, except that there was a detachment of WRAC there with whom they could while away the odd half hour, tucked into the corner of a damp, evil-smelling concrete corridor groping around warm and pungent flesh with numb fingers. Judging from the number of girls who became pregnant under the most difficult of conditions the human race has nothing to fear about its ability to continue fertilising the species. (They knew that if they became pregnant they would have to leave the service, that was part of the deal;

and so did the women who, years later, got thousands of pounds of compensation for letting themselves be made pregnant.)

The only time I came near to physical injury from my fumbling dealings with explosives was when I had to destroy tons of past-its-shell-by-date gunpowder. This had been extracted from blank cartridge cases used for saluting purposes on ceremonial occasions; some had failed to go bang at a crucial moment and the whole lot had to be got rid of. Gunpowder burns very fast but, fortunately for me, does not generate much heat — unlike cordite propellant, which can fry a kipper at a hundred feet. Wallace and I laid out hundreds of these charges, I told him to push off to a safe distance and then lit a long length of safety fuze. I had walked three paces when the pile of gunpowder behind me went up with a mighty, thundering whoosh, sending a nuclear-type mushroom-shaped cloud of grey smoke high into the sky: the wind had blown a spark from the safety fuze into the gunpowder. I froze and waited for the pain but all that had happened was that my battledress and the hairs on the back of my neck were slightly singed. I followed Wallace's advice and went and had a large gin. (And vowed never to use safety fuze again, and I never did.)

He was a tower of strength to me, that man Wallace. While I was nervously learning the business and wondering not if but when I was going to blow myself up he kept me going with his good nature, good humour and contempt for all the hazards of our job. He had a fatalistic attitude about it all — if my number's on it, I've had it; if not, why worry: the sort of harbour in which most people will take shelter if they are caught in such inclement weather — but he was never cavalier when handling the stuff, never took unnecessary risks. He thought too much of his wife and family for that.

Cavaliers and the others are supposed to haunt the battlefield at Kineton and on the anniversary in October people kept an eye open at the base of Edgehill, especially the psychical-research nutters who appear out of small crevices in the rock on such occasions. Large men with straggly beards and wild-eyed women with long black skirts have been known to sit crouched in the rain holding flash bulbs at the ready in the hope of seeing a spectre wandering around looking for his severed round head. As far as I know, there has never been a manifestation, though the guard-dog handlers used to swear that their animal's hackles would rise on a dark and windy night. (I think this was just an excuse to get back into the warm.) These men and their canines did not always do a good job of guarding: some enterprising scrap-metal merchants from Birmingham removed tons of lead and copper in Drill ammunition by the lorry load from a remote part of the depot over a period of weeks and it was months before anyone noticed. (Drill ammunition is inert stuff shaped like the real thing and used for training.)

As you would expect, things looked better in the Spring. The dem ground dried out a bit and the birds sang in the trees — until they were blown out of them by the blast from my pits. Having just let off a blast about psychic people, I must now record a strange event.

The system was that Wallace and I filled the pits with the nasty stuff, applied plastic explosive or gun cotton to vulnerable parts, connected it all together with cordtex (a cable that looks like white electric wire but contains high explosive, and detonates along its length virtually instantaneously) taped electric detonators on to the cordtex, connected the detonators to our electric wiring, tamped the whole thing down with earth to muffle the explosion — hard work, blast those tiles — then retired to the safety of the bunker. There, I had a board with twelve sockets in it.

I would fit a two-pin plug, connected to an exploder dynamo, into each of these sockets in turn and then set off the charge by winding up the exploder to generate a charge. When I pressed a button it released an electric charge all the way down the separate cables to the detonator in the pit.

On this particular occasion we had prepared everything, I put the plug into Number One Pit socket and wound up the exploder. Then, as my finger went towards the button, something made me stop. I took the plug out of the socket, climbed out of the bunker, looked over the railway embankment and there, walking right across the middle of the demolition ground was a real, live, Royal Pioneer Corps Lance-Corporal. I politely asked him what he thought he was doing and he calmly informed me that he had gone to the wrong lookout post and was now making his way to the right one. I wished him God speed, gave him two minutes to get there and then pressed the button.

But what was it that made me not press it the first time?

★ ★ ★

For me, 1955 was the Year of the Rabbit, even if it wasn't for the Chinese. Myxamatosis struck, and as I walked to and from the demolition ground I would come across dozens of these poor creatures sitting lost in a haze of blind pain. I have been told by a doctor that there is no reason why a similar sort of disease should not strike the human race; that is, that a newly-evolving microbe might one day mutate and sweep through the population just as the Black Death did in the 14th and 17th Centuries. If this happens I trust I will not have to rely on the tender mercies of the medic we had in Kineton in 1955.

One evening there was a car accident. I had retired to bed and was awakened by Major Mike Pritchard-Davies, who stumbled into my room with his face covered in blood: he had omitted to turn sharp left at a ninety-degree bend as he and his wife left the depot on his way home after visiting his friends in the mess. When I hurried in there glamorous blonde Jackie, who was six months pregnant, was sitting in the ante room looking deathly pale. I quickly telephoned our medical officer, who lived nearby, and explained what had happened, but he told me he was not on duty and that I must get the doctor from the Engineer Stores depot at Long Marston, fifteen miles away. He rang off. I called him again and explained the urgency of the need to administer something to the wife, who was shuddering and looked as if she might miscarry at any moment. He firmly told me to call the other doctor and hung up again. I rang our man for a third time and asked him if I was correct in assuming that he was a medical practitioner who had taken the Hypocratic oath.

Several weeks later I was summoned to the Commandant's office and given a formal but unrecorded (I think) reprimand by a Medical Major-General, the senior doctor at Headquarters Western Command in Chester, for having called our man a bloody quack. I was, and remain, unrepentant, but to redress the balance I have to record that the same doctor struggled desperately but in vain for many hours to resuscitate a soldier who had accidentally electrocuted himself; he had touched a pipe outside a barrack block which one of his pals had inadvertently wired to the mains while making a faulty aerial connection on his radio.

In the end, on the night, I took my injured friends up the road to the RAF station at Gaydon where, in the medical centre, a doctor applied some sedatives and inserted a few stitches, and all was well.

One of the things that offset the unpleasantness of those noisy days was the Memorial

Theatre at Stratford-upon-Avon. For month after month I went (alone, I had no girl friend at the time) to see the plays there. Richard Burton and Anthony Quayle in Henry IV Part II. Laurence Harvey and Margaret Leighton in As You Like It. Michael Redgrave and Peggy Ashcroft in The Merchant of Venice. (When she came on stage, then being a tyro in such matters, I raised my programme to find out who she was. Sitting in the second row of the stalls she saw me, and gave me a very sharp look: well, he might at least know who's playing Portia, mightn't he!) Marius Goring and Rachel Kempson in Richard III. Laurence Harvey and Zena Walker in Hamlet. Barbara Jefford and Keith Michell in The Taming of the Shrew. Vivian Leigh and Michael Dennison in Twelfth Night. Laurence Olivier and Vivien Leigh in Macbeth. They were vintage years. And, to make a change, Moira Shearer in I am a Camera, and the Saddler's Wells Theatre Ballet performing Les Sylphides, danced by Annette Page.

★   ★   ★

I was minding my own business in October 1955 when I was again summoned to the Commandant's office, this time to be told that a bomb disposal expert was urgently needed in Cyprus and would I kindly transfer myself there as soon as possible.

I was not sorry to leave Kineton but amongst my possessions treasure a very ancient fossil of a sea creature that lived about six million years ago which I unearthed in the middle of England on a gloomy winter's evening.

6

Tulips, thyme and tension

I arrived in Cyprus carrying £45,000 Cypriot notes, mint, heavily wrapped, the equivalent today of about half a million pounds. I had once again been minding my own business in the lounge (lounge? Who can lounge in an airport?) at Stansted when I was summoned by a peremptory voice over the loudspeaker to report to the Military Traffic Office immediately. There, I was handed three large bulky parcels and told to take them with me on the plane; and on no account to break the wax seals. I tucked one under each arm, picked the other one up by the string and, of course, splintered its seals into a thousand pieces. Yet another farcical beginning. Under the contemptuous eyes of the staff I staggered out and eventually clambered on to an Avro York.

I had a difficult but interesting journey, the former on account of the parcels, the latter on account of the company. One of my fellow passengers was Group Captain Tate (he became an Air Vice-Marshal), who sported the biggest array of DSOs and DFCs I had ever seen. He had, so I was later told, commanded the Pathfinder Squadron after Guy Gibson's death and reached his rank and been awarded all those medals by the time he was twenty-four. Follow that, as they say. He it was who helped me to carry the parcels over to the restaurant when we stopped-over to refuel at Rome, and guarded them while I collected my dinner tray from the self-service. (And who better?) Tate was very conscious of the fact that eyes were drawn to the splendid array on his chest and when possible hid them by nonchalantly letting his right fore-arm lie over them as he ate, using a fork with his left hand. The passenger I sat next to on the plane was a Major Iain Macdonald of the Border Regiment who was returning to Arabia for a third tour of duty with the Trucial Oman Scouts. He was a big, silent man, not given to saying anything except when questioned, but the answers were enlightening. He was travelling very light, with only one holdall, and when I commented on it said he needed nothing much as most of his time was spent in the desert trudging the sand-hills, and his wants were few. He was a loner, obviously, and one of that small band of British Arabists, like Burton and Thesiger who, once exposed to that spartan existence become addicted to it. Yet another companion was Major Brian Coombes of the Royal Engineers, who within weeks was to win a George Medal for fighting off four terrorists who ambushed his Landrover and shot his driver dead; he killed one of them with a bullet from a Sten gun and the rest decided they had had enough and ran away over the hill. Having refuelled the York and ourselves we carried on to Nicosia, arriving with the dawn.

After Europe, to me the change of scene was startling. The central plain was barren and yellow and as the plane banked steeply a long jagged dorsal fin of mountains — the Kyrenia Range — floated up into the sky and then back down again. The earth came towards us quickly, pale and parched. A cluster of olive trees in a grove, yellow-earth houses. Then, in a flash, almost under the plane, a great flock of sheep that scattered like grains of wheat blown out of the palm of your hand, their shepherd holding a long stick and looking up at this clattering mass of metal that was gliding down with its lights flashing and its wheels appearing from under its belly. On the ground I was met by a major in the Pay Corps who grumpily relieved me of my load.

I was to become fascinated by Cyprus. The

air was as clear as a bell, the colours startling, the weather fine and the smells interesting. Most of these were pleasant — carobs piled up on the dockside at Limassol, groves of eucalyptus on the road to Famagusta, jasmine draped over low walls in Nicosia, kebabs roasting over charcoal in Kyrenia, Turkish tobacco smoke wafting from hubbly-bubblies smoked by old men who sat at tables on the pavements in Lefka. Even the earth itself was scented by thyme and basil and in the Spring was suddenly host to millions of tiny wild crocuses, tulips, narcissi and other flowers I could not name. They died almost overnight but while they lived their display was astonishing.

* * *

My job, it turned out, was to be in charge of the bomb disposal operations on the island. (Since people are generally unaware of who does what on the bomb disposal scene a word or two here would not be amiss. Each service has its experts to deal with explosive ordnance. At sea and in their shore-based depots, and on land below the high-water mark, it is the Royal Navy's responsibility. On land, the Royal Engineers deal with unex- ploded enemy aircraft bombs, because mining and tunnelling skills are often needed to get at them. The Royal Army Ordnance Corps — now extinct, after hundreds of years, and part of the Royal Logistic Corps — dealt with army ordnance and with terrorist bombs. The Royal Air Force with their own ordnance and with enemy aerial bombs inside the perimeter of their own airfields.)

At the beginning of the insurgency in Cyprus the work had been done on an ad hoc basis by Ordnance technicians in between normal tasks — like defusing 25-pounder shells — but as time went on the volume of work grew to the point where they could not cope with it. EOKA, the Greek Cypriot terrorist organisation, had raised the curtain on the 1st April 1955 by burning down the office of the British Association in Nicosia, accompanied by a display of pyrotechnics, but by October incendiaries and petrol bombs had given way to more lethal things.

I found myself on the posted strength of Headquarters Cyprus District, commanded by Major-General Douglas Kendrew. (Another man with four DSOs; a moustached, rather intimidating figure who didn't, as far as I could ascertain, have a lot upstairs.) I had one Ammunition Examiner NCO stationed in Famagusta and another in Limassol. With me in Nicosia I had a little lad by the name of Corporal Davies. Later on, I also had an NCO in Paphos. Between us we covered the whole island, responding to calls from the police and from military units.

My base was in Kykko Camp East, near Nicosia airport. (There was also a Kykko West, occupied by Paras.) The camp consisted of the ubiquitous Nissen huts, large ones, painted silver so as to reflect the heat of the sun, and rows of tents. The huts were the offices and messes; the India Pattern tents, about fifteen feet square, were the sleeping quarters. They had two roofs, the idea being that the space between them acted as insulation in summer and winter. I was allocated to one occupied by another Ordnance captain by the name of Ossie Logan. It was furnished with a wardrobe, chest of drawers and a proper bed each and not, as I had expected, with camp kit. It had electric light and even tatty condemned carpets on the floor. The point was, that the headquarters was permanent (Cyprus would remain a British possession for all time, a singularly foolish politician had announced to the House of Commons not long before, in part triggering the insurrection: he was to be proved quite wrong, quite quickly) whereas infantry and other units had a very spartan existence in temporary camps. Before we finished, there would be more than thirty thousand British soldiers scattered around the island living like that. (50 Regiment RA had re-appeared on my scene, this time as a Medium Regiment converted to the infantry role and stationed at Paphos.) Anyway, physically I was quite comfortable; mentally I was a shade ill at ease, so I became, suddenly, very interested in Christianity.

By the time I was in my mid-Twenties I had reached a benign condition whereby I went to church now and then, if something special prompted it, and prayed likewise. However, when I arrived in Cyprus after spending many months doing an unpleasant job and found myself exposed to even more potentially damaging situations I must have decided that my efforts alone were not enough to safeguard me. Accordingly, I 'got religion' again, and at night prayed on my knees beside my bed, and after that read a chapter of the Bible before turning out the light. I conscientiously read the New Testament right through from beginning to end (twelve years later I was to do the same with the Koran, but for a different reason: as background research for a book I was writing) and when I told the padre in the mess, he showed some enthusiasm. But when he asked me why and I pompously replied that I had read a lot of what were said to be the best books in the world so thought I had better read this one, too, perhaps not surprisingly he lost all interest. In a way, and quite contrary to the original intention, as the weeks went by, so did I.

Ossie was good enough to ignore my religious observances. At least I thought he was turning a blind eye but I could have been wrong because after a few weeks he announced that he had had enough of this — I thought he meant living in a tent — and was going home to get married, a statement that surprised me since he had never mentioned the existence of a woman in his life. Anyway, he did, and soon came back with Betty. Meanwhile, he had tried to distract me by introducing me to the Nicosia Club, bridge and squash.

My working day began with stepping around Ossie's discarded clothes. After abluting in a basin (we had a Cypriot 'batman' who carried water and emptied slops) I put on my tropical uniform, rolled my puttees around the tops of my boots, put on my cap and went over to the mess for a civilised breakfast, calling en route at an evil-smelling, deep-trench latrine. (One evening a Gunner Air Observation Post pilot fell into a half-built one on the way to the showers, wearing only a towel. His faint cries for help brought relief in the shape of someone who went off and got a rope. He was a better pilot than he was a navigator.) Then I would go down the path to my cubby-hole of an office to see Corporal Davies and read the incident reports that had come in from my out-stations. After that, I would drive down the road to the police Criminal Investigation Department, sitting in the front of my sand-coloured Landrover with my Luger (swopped when I was a Lieutenant for a Smith & Wesson .38 plus £3) stuck in my belt and Corporal Davies looking out over the tailboard clasping a loaded Sten gun. Just past a cafe at a crossroads we would turn right again and drive along the outside of the old Phoenician walls of the city.

Paphos Gate police station was entered through an arched gateway. Sand-coloured buildings surrounded a cobbled courtyard, and for all the world it was like the fort in Beau Geste: I expected to see kepi'd heads looking down at me from the ramparts, their white neck-pieces flapping in the breeze, and encounter a martinet sergeant as I stepped out of my vehicle. But the man I usually spoke to first was a giant, negroid-looking

Turkish Inspector by the name of Salih, who had perfect manners and great natural courtesy. The Superintendent, Tom Lockley, would often be the next person I saw; like many British policemen in Cyprus he was seconded for the duration of the emergency, in his case from the Staffordshire Constabulary. With him I discussed the latest bomb attacks. Then I read some more situation reports and looked at photographs — often of mutilated corpses. Then I would visit Dickie Bird in the forensic department, who since 1946 had followed trouble around the world with the Colonial Police, serving in such places as Malaya, Hong Kong and Kenya before arriving in Cyprus.

I came to have a lot of respect for these policemen, especially for the Greek Cypriots, who were prime targets. Many of them had served the British Crown with great pride for years, only to find that suddenly they were obliged to have sharply divided loyalties. If it became evident that they were trying too hard to do their job there was every likelihood that they would get a bullet in the brain. It is to their great credit that so many of them remained loyal.

★ ★ ★

Not long after arriving in Cyprus I was sent to Malta to investigate the crash of an AVRO York of Scottish Airlines. The plane had taken off from Luqa airfield, flown out over the sea, turned back, turned turtle and nose-dived into the ground in a ball of flame, killing all fifty RAF passengers — boys returning to the UK to be demobilised — and the crew. Because a Dakota and a Hermes had been sabotaged at Nicosia airport a few weeks before by EOKA someone, rather belatedly, decided the York might have been sabotaged too, and that the matter should be looked into.

I spent five days investigating the crash — examining the wreckage and talking to eye-witnesses, airport employees and Maltese officials. Because the plane had just refuelled, the biggest piece left by the fireball that erupted when it hit the ground was the size of a door; the rest was a tangle of fused metal and scorched material, as big as a house, stacked up in a corner of the airfield, where it had been brought from the olive grove in which it had exploded. There were other things there too, of course: dried blood, and objects that did not bear too much scrutiny; and a pervading smell of burnt flesh. (I believe the whole lot was bulldozed into a huge hole in the ground after the investigation had ended.)

Normally, when trying to establish whether something had been deliberately blown up the procedure is to find the root of the explosion, then try to find what is left of the initiating mechanism, then try to assess the amount of explosive used by studying how much damage has been done. In this case the whole plane had gone off like a gigantic napalm bomb, so it was impossible to find the point of detonation, let alone estimate how much explosive had been used. Talking to people, I was given a lot of conflicting information — someone had seen a door open on the side of the plane where there was no door; someone else had seen flames coming out of an engine but other people had not; the plane had been upright when it crashed, not inverted, and so on. But the clincher, to me, was that the time-lapse between leaving Cyprus and arriving in Malta (and calling at El Adem in Libya en route) did not match the time delays available to the bomb makers: the triggering mechanisms they had could not be set for such a long interval. I concluded that though I could not prove the plane had not been sabotaged it was unlikely that it had.

Some weeks later I was summoned back to

Malta to give evidence at the Tribunal of Inquiry, which was held in the Palace, Valetta. A legality of lawyers sat among the suits of armour in the throne room representing the interests of the airline, the manufacturers (of the airframe and the engines) the Airline Pilot's Association, the airport authorities, and all of them had a go at me, for a verdict of sabotage would have got them all off the hook. I could only reiterate my conclusion that it was highly unlikely. (The son of one of the ministers in the post-war labour administration, Edith Summerskill, was one of the barristers.)

On the third day a Mr Nelson of the Ministry of Aviation crash investigation department gave evidence. He said that the engines had survived intact, splaying out from their housings as the plane hit the ground, and had been sent home to Rolls Royce for examination. There, it was found that a boost capsule in one of them had failed due to stress, allowing neat petrol instead of a mixture of air and petrol to enter the carburettor, where it had burnt out the flame traps on the inlet manifold and then the valves behind them, causing the engine to seize up. (A boost capsule was a small copper bellows fixed to the carburettor that expanded and contracted relative to the air

176

pressure around it, compensating for the drop or rise in pressure as the plane ascended or descended and thus maintaining the right mixture of fuel and air. It had cracked, breaking the vacuum inside, making it inoperative and allowing pure petrol to flood in.)

As the plane roared down the runway the pilot must have realised that something was wrong but could not tell which of the plane's four engines had failed, since the propeller rev-counters on his instrument panel were all indicating that they were turning. Consequently, he did not feather the propeller on the faulty port inboard engine — turn its blades head-on to the airflow instead of biting at it. Feathered, the propeller would have allowed air past it over the wing section behind and created lift; not feathered, it was pushing against the air flow and cutting off the lift. The pilot turned back to the safety of the runway but the combination of lack of power on that engine plus the drag of the labouring propeller plus the lack of lift on the air-foil section behind it, and the fact that he turned into the drag instead of away from it, caused the plane to turn over and fall out of the sky. The whole sequence of events from take-off to crash lasted about two-and-a-half minutes.

The Tribunal returned a verdict of pilot's error, but added a rider that all aircraft of that type should in future be fitted with extra instrumentation to enable the pilot to see instantly the power output of an engine as well as the revolutions of its propeller.

Flying back over the Libyan desert, very low and bumping a lot in the gusts of hot air that rose up off the sand, on what was known as the Medair Route — Malta, Tripoli, Benghazi, El Adem, Nicosia — I could see vehicle tracks made by Monty's and Rommel's armies fifteen years before etched into the top crust of sand. As well as making a complex pattern of criss-crossing loops and tracks, here and there they came together where units had rested for the night (laagered, a word that had its military roots in the Boer War) before resuming the battle the next morning. One of the tracks could, perhaps, have been made by the wheels of the vehicle that towed my brother's 4.5' howitzer towards Tobruk. (More than fifty years on, Arabs are still scratching a living by selling the metal they pick up in the desert. If they don't blow themselves up first, that is.)

The crash enquiry was a sad but interesting interlude as far as I was concerned, and the nights spent in the luxurious Phoenicia Hotel — paid for by the Maltese government — a

welcome change from sharing a tent with
Ossie and assorted winged and crawling
creatures. But I had to get back to work.

★ ★ ★

My life was a strange mixture of socialising
interspersed with terrorist warfare and,
occasionally, danger. I was on call at all times
and had to leave a contact telephone number
if I was away from the mess or my office, so
danger could arrive out of the blue without
warning in the middle of quite normal
pursuits: during a game of squash at the
Club, perhaps, or when out to dinner at the
Dolphin on the Kyrenia road. Outside the
city walls restaurants were doing a good trade
but as is so often the case during insurgency
situations there was a deadly undercurrent of
activity that the population at large was
totally unaware of. For all the normality of
my daily life I was at some risk. (So? That's
what I was paid for, wasn't it? Oh, all right, I
know.) But just how much risk was there?

The chances of being killed were much
greater than they were for the infantry on
patrol in the towns or searching for General
Grivas, the EOKA leader, up in the Troodos
Mountains but they were far far less than
they had been for infantry in the First World

War, and a good deal less than for bomber crews in the Second. So it was all relative. And all was not gloom. The British soldier as usual supplied droll humour, as on the occasion when a Jock in the Highland Light Infantry in a camp near Lefkoniko in the 'Panhandle', the Karapas peninsula, threw a 36 grenade into the officers' mess. When arraigned before his colonel the next morning and asked why he had done this evil deed he replied: 'Och, surr, it was just a wee bi' of a joke.' He had time to reflect on its humour at leisure. Fortunately, nobody was hurt by the explosion.

After the end of World War Two the British had got rid of unwanted ammunition by dumping it into the sea off Famagusta harbour. However, the water was very shallow and it was possible to dive down and retrieve some of it. In particular, EOKA had got hold of hundreds of old tin-plated Italian anti-tank mines that contained around three pounds of TNT. Solid crystalline TNT can be chiselled or sawn without risk, and this is what was principally used in their bombs. In small workshops around the island piping was cut up, sealed at one end, filled with granular TNT and fitted with a detonator. (Sounds familiar?) The pipes could be three inches long and two wide, or as big as sixteen inches

180

long and four wide. Either way they made a good anti-personnel grenade, and if big enough could do quite a lot of damage to a building.

Another popular device consisted of parcels containing TNT, or gelignite that had been stolen from the mines, principally those at Lefka, where copper was blasted out of the ground. (Cyprus was celebrated in antiquity for its copper mines; our word 'copper' derives from the Greek 'Kypros'.) Stockpiling had been going on for some time before the insurgency began, pilfered by Greek Cypriot employees, so there was a significant amount of it available. As well as stealing explosives, EOKA had acquired timing 'pencils', some from Russia but most of them of British origin. Also, from Greece, they had managed to get American hand grenades, sent there under NATO 'Hands Across the Seas' auspices.

Time pencils are so called for the simple reason that they look a bit like a pencil. One type consists of a plunger under tension that is held back by a wire that is eaten into by a corrosive acid once an ampoule containing the acid is squeezed and broken: the delay depends on the thickness of the wire, and therefore how long it takes for the acid to eat through it. The other works on the same principle, but in this case the wire is made of a special alloy; after a pin is withdrawn the wire comes under tension from a spring and its molecules slide over each other at a pre-determinable rate until the wire snaps. At the end of both types a detonator is crimped which initiates the charge of TNT or gelignite, or whatever.

EOKA's principle weapon was the pipe bomb, used against soft targets such as vehicles and people and initiated with safety fuze or an electric detonator. Prestigious 'hard' targets, such as the GPO in Nicosia, were attacked with parcel bombs initiated by a time pencil. In the former case there was no time element involved in defusing the bomb: the fuze had fizzled out or the spark had not reached the detonator and it was removed by twisting it out carefully. The pipe could then be emptied of explosive or blown up. In the case of the parcel bomb (and some pipe bombs), there was a 'ticking' element to it: the time pencil had been activated and was liable to go off if interfered with — like a touchy young female, I suppose. But after the pencil had been removed, again with great care, the remnants could be handled without danger.

During the whole EOKA campaign some seven thousand bomb incidents were reported. In my time I suppose I was concerned with over a thousand of them. That is not to say that I dealt personally with them all or that they were all fraught with danger — I would guess that about a twentieth of them were — but in those days there was no sophisticated equipment with which to tackle them: no remote-controlled robots, no closed-circuit television, no disrupting devices. It was a matter of cornering the bomb, grabbing it by the throat and then cutting its heart out — with a Stanley knife. Much of the time, neutralising the bombs was routine work — removing detonators from pipe bombs, emptying the explosive out of bombs, occasionally extracting time pencils from parcel bombs — but sometimes there were unusual incidents. One that remains very clearly in my memory is of being asked to go to Famagusta to sort out a bomb that had been placed in a water tower.

When I arrived on the scene my sergeant was waiting for me and reported that a bomb was inside the tower, the lid of which was about forty feet above the ground. (The police had been alerted by a local man who had noticed electric wires trailing from the tower down to the ground.) The sergeant had gone up to have a look and had seen some sort of device, suspended from the other ends of the wire, in the water. Feeling that he was a bit out of his depth, he had sent for me. (There was nothing wrong with that; the rules were, and are, that if an operator is stymied he should call on the next man up the chain of responsibility: in this case, me.)

I climbed up on to the roof of the tower, which was convex in shape, edged my way to the centre and looked in. Sure enough there was a large object dangling in the water. I called for a another ladder — which took some time to arrive, of course — hauled it up and then lowered it into the water, which was about four feet deep. Descending the ladder I gingerly entered the water (like a bather, slowing down as sensitive parts made contact with it) and then groped around until I got a firm grip of the thing. It turned out to be a large pipe bomb. I ascended the ladder (this sounds like one of Gerard Hoffnung's monologues, doesn't it?) clumped over the booming top of the tower and descended to the ground after lowering the bomb on the rope with which the ladder had been pulled up. The detonator had been pushed through a hole in the screw-in plug at the top of the pipe: when I tried to unscrew it, its leads twisted, so I took the pipe away and blew it up. For me, the worst part was going up and down the ladder and hanging about on the top of the tower; I don't have a very good head for heights.

Another memorable incident was the bomb in the Governor's bed. Field Marshal Sir John Harding had had a good night's sleep, woke refreshed and went about his business. A couple of hours later his batman discovered a suspicious object under the mattress. The commander of the Government House guard was sent for and removed the bomb — which had been put there by a Greek Cypriot employee — carrying it out of the house on the end of a spade and then throwing it into a slit trench. I too had been sent for and arrived a few minutes after it went off: I heard the explosion as I drove through the gate. All I had to do was take away the shreds of evidence, of which there were not many. The subaltern in charge of the guard, a Second-Lieutenant in the Middlesex Regiment, was awarded an MBE for gallantry. (As a matter of technique, it would have been safer for him to grasp the bomb firmly rather than risk it rolling off the shovel and going off at his feet. And it wasn't a good idea to throw it into the trench either, which is probably why it went off a minute or two after he turned away. But then if he hadn't done so, perhaps it would have gone off when I tried to defuse it.)

Another incident that I have not forgotten was being called to that cafe beside the cross-roads one evening. A hand grenade had been tossed through the door, had bounced across the floor and exploded between the feet of a young, newly-married American girl. Several other people had been injured.

The girl was pregnant. She lost the baby and would never be able to have another — or anything else, much; her life as a wife was over. Nobody could stop the blood from pumping out of her thighs and groin as she lay there groaning, with her husband ashen-faced beside her, slumped over the table.

★　★　★

Another late-evening call was to the Ledra Palace Hotel, scene of the Caledonian Ball. Two hand grenades had been tossed on to the dance floor after the lights were turned out by one of the throwers. One grenade had gone off, its fragments slicing into ball gowns and dinner jackets. There was a lot of blood there, too — and so was the other grenade. I picked it up and put it in my pocket under the admiring gaze of a distant policeman, who was unaware that it was perfectly safe since the thrower had omitted to pull the pin out.

186

It, too, was an American fragmentation grenade. It was political dynamite, but that pin wasn't pulled either . . .

The Ledra Palace was a luxurious, modern hotel used as a base by the gentlemen of the Press, who occasionally dragged themselves away from the bar to send a report to Fleet Street. I have several friends who used to work in EC4 for whom I have the greatest affection but I must report that sometimes the behaviour of some of their colleagues was lacking in finesse. One morning an Ordnance captain, Peter Lane, was shot dead as he waited on a street corner for a lift to work. I accompanied my colonel down to the town, where he had the unenviable task of telling the new widow what had happened to her husband, and as he went in I had to physically restrain a reporter from entering with him, his camera at the ready. This did not deter him, I heard later, from barging in on the unfortunate woman a few minutes after we had left.

The officer commanding the little ammunition depot in Cyprus was a major — WC Harrison by name, known as Flush — though the appointment was a captain's. After a time someone cottoned on to this and decided the situation must be regularised, so we were swopped around. Flush talked nineteen to the dozen and flashed around all over the place, his sunken eyes deep in his skull-like face, his long-fingered hands flapping about. He would grab you by the elbow and impart the latest gossip and information sotto voce, drawing you further and further towards the ground the more sotto the voce became. I was not sorry to hand over to him, being in the process of taking on new personal responsibilities.

One of my first acts in my new job was to fire a salute of farewell to bomb disposal — for the time being.

On my first tour of inspection around the little pre-emergency depot at Waynes Keep I asked Warrant Officer Ken Nash (now a retired major) what was in a couple of small sheds. He replied that they contained explosives that the police had said we must keep as evidence in forthcoming trials. I could smell almonds at fifty paces, an indication that amongst other things the sheds contained gelignite that was exuding; in other words, it had gone off a bit — broken down in the heat from its relatively benign state into one where the scrape of one box against another was enough to detonate it. Apart from anything else, the smell of exuding gelignite gives you a fearful headache.

Opening the sheds and examining the contents my fears were confirmed: there were dozens of boxes of this stuff plus hundreds of pipe bombs and assorted parcel bombs (minus detonators). Having enough headaches to go on with I decided something had to be done.

I rang Dickie Bird and told him that I was not happy to have all this rubbish in the middle of the army's stocks of ammunition. He said there was nothing I could do about it; it must be retained or I would be in contempt of court. I told him he had twenty-four hours to persuade someone to let me get rid of the exuding gelignite, if nothing else. When I heard nothing from him I rang again the next morning and told him that the next day would be too late. It was. While peering intently through a microscope at some piece of forensic evidence he heard the bang that travelled many miles across the Mesaoria Plain to rattle his windows at Paphos Gate.

Nash and I and a few luckless lads had dragged all the rubbish out of the sheds, piled it in the back of a three-tonner and set off westwards. There was a Landrover front and back — with armed soldiers in them — and an armed soldier in the back of the three-tonner — who looked a bit green when we finally arrived at our destination. We drove to a place that I had recced the previous afternoon. Getting off the metaled road I led my little convoy bumping along a rutted track, climbing higher and higher into the lesser foothills of the Troodos Mountains until we reached an escarpment where I had found a cave, and into it we put all the dynamite — plus a lot of other rubbish: I thought that while I was at it I might as well do the job properly. When all was ready I told my companions to make themselves scarce, placed the detonator carefully in the middle of the pile, took a last look around to see if anyone was skulking in the black depths of the cave (with a bit of luck it could have been a terrorist hide-out), decided that as far as I could tell nobody was, went out of the cave and around the corner, wound up the exploder dynamo and pressed the tit. The explosion lifted the roof off the top of the cave and opened it up to the sky.

I suppose, looking back, that it was a cavalier thing to do, wasn't it? to use someone's land as a demolition ground without so much as by-your-leave, but at the time it seemed eminently sensible. Getting formal authority would have taken months of explanation and haggling, meanwhile the gelignite would have deteriorated further and maybe gone off spontaneously. I heard nothing about contempt of court but I understand there was a bit of tut-tutting in police and military circles.

★ ★ ★

It was in the Ledra Palace that I spent my curtailed honeymoon. One day when I was in the CID offices someone mentioned that Fred Carter, then the big boss of the CID, was getting a new personal assistant, who was being flown out from England by the Colonial Office. For some inexplicable reason the thought flashed through my mind that I would marry her. Whether the thought was father to the deed I do not know, but after a short but enthusiastic courtship I did, the Commissioner for Nicosia, Martin Clemens, officiating.

Sybil was a pretty girl with a lovely figure and long dark hair with auburn tints. She was vivacious, friendly and kindly. Her widowed mother lived in Liverpool, in Bold Street, where she was a milliner: another closed loop, in a way.

On the first night of our honeymoon I went to bed and turned for a few moments, as was my habit, to the on-going book. (By this time I had finished the New Testament and, let's face it, with my release from imminent death, with manic religion, too.) Sybil sometimes referred to this act as an unpardonable breach of marital etiquette; I used to remind her that the book's title was Defeat into Victory, by a man by the name of Slim.

I was recalled from leave (wishing we had gone to Beirut instead of staying on the island, which had been mooted) because the British and French — and the Israelis too, it later transpired — were about to 'intervene', as it was called, at Suez. Without warning Nasser, the president of Egypt, had nationalised the Canal, which was mostly owned by the British and French governments. I have read all the reasons why we should not have intervened but am not convinced. At the time, the Soviet Union was in the process of raping Hungary (4th November); its leaders made the most of diverting world attention from what they were doing by threatening Britain and France with the use of nuclear weapons. The USA was on the brink of a presidential election (6th November); its usual nervous twitchings at such a time, plus Dulles' distrust of the British and dislike of Eden, made Eisenhower, who, like Eden, was a sick man, behave petulantly, threatening to destabilise the pound and the franc. We and the French chickened out and aborted the operation. (Dulles, the Secretary of State, was a not very likeable man who came from Cape Cod, Massachusetts and was known to some people as The Piece of Cod Which Passeth All Understanding.) What I am convinced about is that we should have had the guts to establish a presence on the canal, open it to international shipping and then talk about its future in the UN. It is inconceivable that the Russians would have nucleared London and Paris, an act that would have brought retribution from America's Strategic Air Command and triggered World War Three; or that Eisenhower would have brought the economies of France and Britain crashing to the ground, thus weakening the Western Alliance. Instead of calling the bluffs, Eden and Mollet, the French premier, funked it. Winston Churchill said of this debacle: 'I don't think I would have dared to begin this enterprise, but having begun it I would not have dared to stop.'

★　★　★

For me as a twenty-eight year old captain such things were in the stratosphere. My concern was to expand the contents of the ammunition depot, now at a different site, from fifteen hundred tons to fifteen thousand. The perimeter fence grew yard by yard, hour by hour, day and night as the acreage of real estate and munitions at Lakatamia, a few miles west of Nicosia, increased. I have never understood why EOKA did not slip a time pencil into a box of plastic explosive when it was being handled by Cypriot labourers at Limassol docks. The result would have been a very loud bang indeed, the sound of which would have been heard in the United Nations building in New York — even louder than my parting gesture to bomb disposal had been.

Not only did the size of the depot increase, so did its numbers. Army Emergency Reserve officers and soldiers arrived from the UK and I, a captain, ended up commanding a major, Arnold Groves, and his unit as well as my own, a somewhat unorthodox situation. Before the assault on Egypt, French forces too arrived in droves, landing in Nord Atlas transport planes on the disused wartime airfield at Tymbou and transforming it in short order into a major base. Then their ammunition began to arrive and was put into the same perimeter as ours.

I thought the French army was very impressive. They had been fighting in

Indochina for eight years and then in Algeria, and were highly experienced and professional, especially Les Paras and the Foreign Legion. The French had made a nonsense of their financial arrangements and were able to pay their men only a few francs a week. The two elite corps quickly found the red light district in Nicosia and now and then flogged their weapons in order to fund their visits to it. Furthermore, a lot of the legionnaires were German ex-soldiers, who had few qualms about disposing of carbines that could be used against the British.

We took some French officers into our little mess — one was called Edward Lawton — where for several nights we much enjoyed each other's company — as you would expect, they provided the wine. Then with no word of warning one evening they did not arrive for dinner. When, the next morning, I asked Edward why, he shamefacedly admitted that they had no money with which to pay their mess bills. He and the others went back to sharing food and company with their Warrant Officers in a tent at the far end of the ammunition lines. Then, just as quickly as they had arrived, they all went away. No doubt there are a few Gallic Cypriots with a special taste for wine enjoying life on the island today.

On that subject, we had, working in the ammunition laboratories, as they were called, where ammunition was inspected and repaired, a Turkish Cypriot named Ginger, for obvious reasons. One day when I commented on his colouring to Mehmet, a grey-haired, rubicund, mild-mannered man, the senior Turk in the depot, he smiled and said it was due to the presence on the island before the war of a Company of the Black Watch. Which prompts another reflection. In those peaceful days the garrison of Cyprus consisted of a company of infantry, detached from its parent battalion in the Canal Zone in Egypt. In the early 1930s another Enosis campaign had been initiated by the then archbishop. A mob marched up the hill to Government House, laid siege to it then tried to burn it down. The company of infantry was at the time at its hot-weather station in the Troodos Mountains. It was marched down the hill to Lefka, where it boarded a train that took it to Nicosia. (A railway used to run across the Mesaoria Plain, using wood-burning engines.) There, they marched up the hill and took station line abreast. A banner was unfurled enjoining the mob to disperse, a magistrate read the Riot Act and repeated the instruction, saying that if they did not go home the soldiers would fire; they did not, so the soldiers did, killing a few people. The rest then dispersed. The next day the archbishop was shipped out of the island. Nothing further was heard about Enosis for more than twenty years.

I am not advocating such a course of action as a remedy in all circumstances, merely commenting that there must have been many occasions in history when timely positive action would in the long run have averted a lot of trouble and saved a lot of lives, anguish and money.

★   ★   ★

Sybil and I lived in a modern bungalow at Kermia, just north of Nicosia, one of five prefabs imported from Norway and erected rather incongruously in a grove of eucalyptus trees. We decided it would be nice to invite Mehmet and his wife there for a drink and on the day put some small eats and cheesy biscuits on a table and awaited their arrival. After forty minutes had passed we came to the conclusion that they had thought better of it and were not coming, but then the black and green bus which the villagers used to transport almost their entire male working population to and from the depot drew up outside. Mehmet descended, followed by his wife, their many children, some unidentified females, Ginger and the driver. They all trooped in and stood or sat smiling silently at us. Unlike Mehmet, who was used to British ways and was prepared to incur Allah's displeasure once in a while if he was assured that gin was non-alcoholic, none of the others would touch a drop, so ersatz orange juice was pressed into their hands (they could pick the real thing straight off the trees outside their windows). Politely, they unenthusiastically nibbled at Peak Freans cheesies. Silence reigned but smiles never waned. On being given the nod by Mehmet, after an hour or so they solemnly filed out and departed on the bus with much waving.

The man who owned the estate on which we lived was a German by the name of von Bissing, whose father was the general who had ordered the execution of nurse Edith Cavell during the Great War. In order to escape the post-war opprobrium that this act brought down upon him he emigrated to Cyprus and bought, for a small sum of money, a large tract of land that stretched in an arc from the Nicosia race course round to the Kyrenia road. The son had plans, which he showed me, for a modern housing estate — spacious villas surrounding a shopping centre, sports complex, swimming pool and a church. When Archbishop Makarios and General Grivas began their campaign against the British, five bungalows and a network of roads had been built. Then several tented camps were erected on the estate and within weeks von Bissing found himself beleaguered by bugle calls and tramping feet. (The XXth Foot, the Lancashire Fusiliers, lived just behind our back fence and drilled up and down the road.) He decided enough was enough, sold out to the Bank of Cyprus — allegedly for a lot of money — and took himself and his English wife and their children off to Africa. I hope, for his sake, not to Uganda. (The area is now in the Turkish zone. So much for von Bissing's dreams.)

⋆   ⋆   ⋆

Unlike the Greek Cypriot population which venerated their Greek Orthodox priests, I had a rather different view of them.

One night I was tasked to accompany an infantry group commanded by the CO of the 1st Battalion of the South Staffordshire Regiment, (Cummings) which was going to search Kykko monastery on the outskirts of Nicosia. If any explosives were found, and there was good cause to think that they would, Kykko having been Makarios' alma mater, it would be my job to deal with them.

The colonel spoke to the commissioner, nodded and then walked over to the great door set in the walls of the monastery. This is a strange business, thought Ben. I never thought I would be standing outside a place like this in the middle of the night waiting to burst in and tramp through the cloisters searching for bombs and weapons. The whole thing was inconceivable somehow and he felt decidedly uneasy as he stood there. The heavy thump on the gate brought no response: no light glimmered, no voices or footsteps were to be heard. The CO banged again with the ancient iron knocker, harder this time, and the sound echoed away into the distance through the olive groves that surrounded the buildings. These stood out black against the sky and the stars: great slabs of stone rounded over with arched pediments, and in the middle of them all a thick tower, like a truncated barrel, capped with a flat dome, on the top of which was a squat stone cross: Byzantine Gothic. Cypress trees, like accusing fingers, pointed up through the night at God in His heaven. Ben shuffled his feet and smiled in the darkness at the Lance Corporal and the policeman who had been allocated to his team. 'Nothin' happenin', sir,' said Lance Corporal Jenkins: 'Mebbe we'll have to break the bleedin' door dahn!' The idea seemed to appeal to him. Ben didn't know what to say, so he just grunted. Then, as the colonel was about to turn away from the gate there was a grinding of bolts and the postern opened a crack. He could not hear what was said but after an altercation between the monk who had opened it and a policeman who had been beckoned forward to interpret the main gates swung open and they all moved forward through a cobbled yard and into the main building.

It looks like a cross between a school and a church, thought Ben — but then that's exactly what it is! He stood with his team in the high vaulted entrance hall, waiting to be assigned to a task. The CO had gone upstairs with the Commissioner and the monk who had let them in, and reappeared again in a few minutes. 'The abott's extremely old, and bedridden,' he said peremptorily. 'The senior man's been told to get up and dress. We'll get on with it.' Great Scot, thought Ben, the old monk must have thought he was dreaming, to wake up and find an armed soldier standing in his bedroom.

After a few minutes Ben's company commander came over and told him to search the priests' bedrooms on the first floor. He tramped noisily up the stairs and came to the head of a long stone corridor. At the far end was a window, but otherwise it was a bare brown tunnel, dimly lit by low-wattage bulbs, with ten or a dozen doors opening off to left and right. He swallowed hard and knocked on the first door on his left. There was a pause and then it opened and he stood facing the occupant, who stared at him blankly. The man was about thirty-five, bearded of course, and wore a rather dirty-looking white shift. His long hair hung down over his shoulders and his bare feet stuck out from under his nightshirt. In some uncanny way he looked the archetypal Messiah — even the calm long-suffering look matched the picture Ben had seen so many times. He flushed for shame, stammered something and then realised the monk would not understand him. 'Tell him to get dressed,' he told the policeman. 'We'll need a couple of chaps up here to see that no-one skips out while we're in the rooms.

Double off, Corporal Jenkins, and tell the Sergeant-Major, all right?'

Bloody hell, Ben thought, I don't like this a bit. What a thoroughly nasty business. Nothing could justify the tramping of iron-studded boots up and down this corridor. He waited, ill at ease, outside the door, avoiding the eyes of the Cypriot policeman, who seemed quite unperturbed and leant against the wall smoking a cigarette and flicking the ash on the floor. That can't be right either, Ben thought, but hesitated to say anything. Presently, Jenkins came back with two soldiers, whom he posted at either end of the corridor. 'Ready then?' he asked, and the three of them went into the bedroom.

It was not at all what he had expected. It was basic, yes, but no more so than a barrack room. In fact it was much more comfortable than any barrack room he had ever seen. There was an oak bed, a heavy dark chest of drawers against one wall and a large wooden cupboard against another, a big leather-covered trunk in a corner and a rug on the floor. He had expected an iron cot, a crucifix above it and not much else, but this place could have been a rather tatty hotel room.

Except that a picture of Makarios dominated it. On the chest of drawers there was a framed photograph of a priest at the head of a horde of schoolchildren who were waving their arms and streaming down a road behind a black-robed man; a modern Pied Piper leading his children to what manner of follies? Ben looked closely at the priest in the photograph and then at the occupant of the room but he couldn't tell if he was the same man: they all looked alike, with their beards and stove-pipe hats. The priest had donned his robe and drawn his hair back and knotted it above the nape of his neck. He looked surly. Not surprising, thought Ben, it was enough to anger a saint! 'Tell him we have to look everywhere,' he told the policeman. 'You look under the mattress. And you see what's in that trunk,' he told Jenkins.

Silently they went about their tasks, the priest standing there watching them with his arms folded. Reluctantly Ben made himself open the top drawer of the chest. He rummaged carefully. The usual things you would expect to find were there: an old broken watch, odds and ends of small change, pens, pencils, some snapshots of the family, some spare shoe laces — yes, they wore ordinary brown shoes, which seemed incongruous, you expected sandals — and a tin half-full of biscuits. He opened the next drawer and looked down in disbelief. Jenkins straightened up from his task. 'Nothin' special in the trunk, sir,' he said: 'Just clothes.' He came and stood beside Ben and looked down, then gave a snort of laughter. 'Christ,' he blurted out 'Fuckin' condoms!'

As a matter of fact, several sticks of gelignite were found in a safe behind the alter in the church, and other assorted bits of warlike material here and there elsewhere in the monastery.

I had early on been struck by the stupidity of what two men — the would-be Messianic, egocentric archbishop and the megalomaniac colonel — were doing to the island. Enosis, union with Greece, had long been the rallying cry for Greek Cypriots, a lever with which to court popularity and votes, but in truth the links with Greece were tenuous. Cyprus had belonged to the Phoenicians and Romans, to Persians and to Cleopatra. Frenchmen of the Lusignan dynasty had ruled it for three hundred years, then it belonged to Turkey, until Disraeli 'bought' it in 1878. You had to go a long way back to find the Greek connection.

Until Makarios intrigued his way to the top of the Greek Orthodox church on the island Greek and Moslem Turk had lived amicably together for centuries. They never intermarried, the religious and cultural differences being too great, but they shared villages and towns and drank coffee together in the pavement cafes. Now look at it, with Turks in the north and Greeks in the south and the border between them patrolled by armed soldiers of the United Nations to keep them from each other's throats. (Recently, examination of the DNA of Turkish and Greek Cypriots has established that, irony of ironies, they all stem from the same ancient genetic root!)

Those two men have a lot to answer for, but such is the way of human nature that both are regarded by their countrymen as heroes. But not in my book.

One of my jobs during my bomb-disposal duties was to attend the Special Court in Nicosia, in Ataturk Square, to give evidence as an expert witness during the trials of men accused of in some way being involved with terrorism. (Not all of them were Greeks: there were Turks, too, who were drawn into the inter-communal nastiness.) Some of these people were hanged for their trouble, but before being subjected to the drop were defended by lawyers of their own persuasion. Strangely, two of these, with whom I had peripheral dealings, were Rauf Denktash and Glafcos Clerides, who were, in the fulness of time, to become the Presidents of the divided Cyprus.

★   ★   ★

My son Simon was born in the British Military Hospital in Nicosia. He was brought home to the bungalow in Kermia a week later and from the word go showed himself to be an independent spirit. He seemed very angry to find himself having to put up with the minor irritations of life; with mosquitos, wet nappies, safety pins (which now and then pricked him as he twisted, bawling, under Sybil's struggling fingers) milk that came out of the bottle too hot or too cold, skin rashes that erupted in tender places. It was as if someone somewhere had said to him Life's great down there, you'll find it a marvellous experience, full of fun and laughter, only to find when he opened his eyes that it wasn't like that at all, and so he felt resentful. But he was a beautiful baby; blonde, blue-eyed, with a skin that smelt of honeysuckle and an enchanting smile.

It wasn't long before I made one of my periodic stupid decisions and accepted from another smiling Turk a bundle of leaking fur that turned out to be a pi dog.

Bonny was totally untrainable — how could she be, coming from an unbroken line of wild, half-starved, mangy, sneak-thieves who had skulked around the fringes of human habitation for thousands of years? Perhaps one of her forebears had been kicked in the guts by Richard Coeur de Lion as he strode towards Berengaria's tent in Limassol (or, more likely, staggered out of his boy-friend's) but she had an inborn distrust of all things human and we made little impression on her lack of manners, tying her up on a running lead most of the time when it would have been far more to the point to let her high-tail it back into the hills.

When the time came to leave Cyprus it was clear that we could not take Bonny home with us. Through no fault of her own she had never become domesticated; she was, after all, essentially a wild canine. So I decided I must find a home for her. At the time the situation had been made more complicated because we had been adopted by a stray mongrel bitch who had the nicest nature a dog could possibly have; she was obedient, eager to please, eager to welcome. She arrived one day, looked up at us with a smile on her face the way dogs do, wagged her tail, won us over and stayed a night or two. Then, realising that we could not cope with two dogs, I put her in the back of the car and dropped her off on the other side of Nicosia: if she had found us, surely she could find someone else who would be willing to look after her. Two days later she reappeared at our door. A week after that, she produced a litter out in the garage. As the weeks passed we found homes for the pups but as the day of our departure loomed we had two dogs, not one, who needed a home. I asked people, I advertised, I pleaded, but no-one wanted them. Eventually, rather than leave them to die slowly, scavenging garbage as I had seen so many dogs do in Cyprus, I took them to the Veterinary Corps camp at Lakatamia to have them put down. Wagging their tails as they went . . .

A few weeks before, I had nearly used my Luger to put an end to the misery of a dog, mangy and skeletal, that I saw padding about day after day while I was going to and from work. But then I thought: he's no worse off than hundreds of others on this island, why should I be the judge and executioner? In the end I was obliged to be both to those two dogs who had put their trust in me, and was not at all happy about it.

★ ★ ★

I now had a wife, a son, two dogs and somewhere for us all to live — and had brought all these things upon myself out of a cloudless sky. However, I welcomed them all with open arms.

I had also been Mentioned in Despatches, though the gilt had been slightly scratched off the letter of congratulation from the director of my Corps because it was addressed to Staff-Sergeant MacDonald . . .

My parents had not met my wife and it must have been strange for them to receive letters and photographs charting the development of a new branch of the family and yet be so distant from it all. In a way history was repeating itself, for their parents too must have felt even more remote when they received letters from Chile and Peru.

Bet and Mac were still in Orchard Croft. He had now retired and in order to bring in a few pennies had rented off parts of it. The wing, self-contained above Roger's claw-scratched door, was occupied by a dark recluse who cycled each morning to the station, worked at unspecified tasks at an oil refinery in the marshes, returned in the evening and bolted himself in. He stayed for years, paid his rent regularly, said little and was never known to entertain a friend. He drank not, neither did he smoke, but seemed, for all that, contented enough, in a puzzled sort of way. I can't remember his name . . .

In Orchard Croft itself other people lived in closer proximity to my parents, more's the pity for all concerned. They came and went and I knew little about them except that a young couple who lived upstairs were masochists. On Tuesdays, Thursdays and Saturdays the upper floor would shake to the sound of the lash, blows and shrieks of joy as they belaboured each other into some sort of weird sexual enhancement. Sunday was a day of rest, not least for the elderly couple who lived downstairs.

Another branch of the family was nearer to them and also growing. Brian, after leaving the navy, had joined a firm that sold animal foodstuffs. In 1950 he married Margaret, a tall, leggy, bonny girl who bubbled with laughter — and against all the odds has contrived to do so ever since. They had two nice children, first another Andrew, who took after his mother in looks, and then Caroline, who took after mine: as a little child she was a miniature version of Bet, with deep blue eyes and soft brown hair. They all lived at Lytham St Annes, within easy commuting distance of Orchard Croft on a Sunday. Not so we, who were guarding the outposts of a crumbling empire far away.

I stayed in Cyprus for three years, during which I did three jobs. The first was bomb disposal, taken over by Flush Harrison, who did a good job, even though he was a bit of a menace. Ironically, on account of its greater size the ammunition depot was upgraded to a major's command and given to a fat man who liked his liquor and was surplus to establishment in Headquarters Middle East Command at Episkopi — and everywhere else too, I imagine. During the handover I had occasion to waken him by kicking his feet as he lay in a stupor on his charpoy at eleven o'clock in the morning.

The sergeant who was with me at the time (I know he should not have been present when I assaulted a senior officer, but I was incensed to find the man sleeping off his hangover at such a time) was later accused by his wife of molesting their daughter. I did not want to believe it, the man was a smart, soldierly NCO, and when she told me I stared at her and stupidly asked 'Are you quite sure?' She was sure all right, and left the island, and him, very quickly.

My third job was as a lowly staff officer in Headquarters Cyprus District, by now accommodated in Wolsely Barracks, just outside the city walls, where I worked for a lieutenant-colonel in the Middlesex Regiment by the name of Tom Chattey.

★ ★ ★

Looking back over those years my predominant memories are of blue skies, sunshine, sand-coloured houses and smiling, courteous people, Greek and Turk. We even had a Greek Cypriot girl, Neophyta Christou, working for us as a maid/nanny who spoke not a word of English but somehow contrived to communicate — at least, Sybil did.

I remember red wine and goat's milk cheese. And swimming alone in the warm tideless Mediterranean while my wife played with our baby on the beach and kept an eye on the Luger hidden under a towel. I remember returning from the beach and being nearly forced off a hairpin bend by a young Greek who was trying to do his bit for the cause of Enosis; Sybil pointed a shaking Luger at him out of the window and he blanched and sped off.

I remember, too, soaring away in Auster

light aircraft from one dirt strip to another to visit the bomb disposal men around the island who got on with their job cheerfully and with no need of encouragement from me. (It was that same pilot of DTL fame who took off one day with a very fat brigadier sitting in the back when the propeller fell off. He must have been accident prone. When they landed, the brigadier lost a pound or two in weight.)

I would rather not have to remember the funeral with full military honours of Staff-Sergeant John Culkin, who went to look at a cache of explosives found in a cave near Limassol, told the policemen who were with him to go out while he dealt with it, and was buried in very small pieces. He was stocky, quiet and stoic, and had a lived-in face. Like all of us he didn't know exactly what he was dealing with — since the opposition didn't know, either. Most of it was in a foul condition and no two bombs were alike.

I also remember the guard dogs. They were Alsatians, and were demonic or daft. Some would eat you alive, given the chance, and occasionally tried it on with their handlers, but some were so soft that when they were unleashed and ordered to attack a padded victim, like Ferdinand the Bull they stopped and sniffed the daisies. One night, after a long search, I found a handler sound asleep inside his dog's kennel. They both emerged, with whisps of straw clinging to them, blinking, into the beam of a torch held by Conductor Nash, as Class I Warrant Officers were known in the Royal Army Ordnance Corps. The army psychiatrist at the British Military Hospital told me when I consulted him about this strange phenomenon that behavioural problems were an occupational hazard for dog handlers: they slept all day and spent most nights with nobody to talk to except their dog.

I remember a Spring day when, not long before we left the island, I looked out of a window at Kermia and saw a goat giving birth in a bed of wild flowers while a bearded herdsman with a lined face watched over her. The Kyrenia Range rose, blue and misty, beyond the shivering silver leaves of the eucalyptus trees; the bells on the necks of the goats chimed as they grazed beside the newcomer.

Sybil remembers most vividly the day when she picked up the phone in her office and was told that a man had been shot dead in Ledra Street. When she asked his name she was told it was Macdonald. When eventually someone took the phone from her shaking hands and asked for more information he was able to tell her it was not me but an unfortunate civilian who had died.

I remember the nameless married corporal who shot himself dead playing Russian Roulette in the Guard Room at Kykko Camp, and wonder why. And I ask myself, now and then, if I could not have done more when a sergeant was killed by a bomb hidden in the carrier bag of a bike propped up against the wall of the tin Sergeant's Mess. I was in my tent thirty yards away when a mighty explosion blasted the canvas walls inwards. I ran out and saw a smoking pile of twisted, silver-painted corrugated iron and, when I looked more closely, a booted foot and a putteed leg under it. I ran shouting for help towards the medical centre then thought twice about it and went back and pulled at the sheets with other people who had come running, but by the time he was extricated the man had bled to death. It was small comfort to be told by Simon years later, a propos something quite different, that a human being will bleed to death in three minutes if the femoral artery is severed. All the same, I wonder if I could have done more.

7

Matters of Life and Death

As we approached Southampton the tannoy on the troopship was playing 'Around, the World, I'll search, for you.' Sybil's mother, a grey-haired, black-coated, well-dressed, bird-like little figure, was standing on the dockside waiting to meet her grandchild and her new son-in-law.

We all took the train northwards, then went our separate ways, she back to Liverpool, we to Orchard Croft where, quite soon, our second son, Alexander, was conceived. Sybil assures me that while we were about it she got a fit of the giggles and I told her to stop laughing because this was a serious business. What an extraordinary thing to say. But then, yes, I suppose it was. She had to go to see a doctor soon after, at Greythwaite in the Lake District, because Alex wasn't too sure whether he wanted to go through with it. Perhaps he had been tipped off by Simon. However, she was all right, and we set about enjoying a holiday in a haunted cottage.

This grey stone building, nestling in a fold

of very green hills, was near The Tarns, was very old indeed, belonged to the Sandys family, on whose estate it stood, and abutted on to a larger building that was said to have been used as a barracks by Royalist soldiers during the Civil War. We drove about the beautiful countryside by day and in the evenings sat beside a log fire and talked, with little Simon asleep upstairs. TV had not yet placed its intrusive eye in the corner of the room.

The house had two sitting rooms, one downstairs and another, with a fine view, upstairs. In that room there were two high, old-fashioned wing chairs and I would sometimes sit in one and read quietly while Sybil wrestled with Simon. I found that, now and then, I would have an uncomfortable sensation, feeling that if I were to lean over the arm of the chair and look behind me a man with long grey hair would be standing watching me. Once in a while this sensation would become so compelling that I would actually do so, but of course there was no-one there.

I did not tell Sybil about this, thinking it was too stupid for words, but as we were driving away in the little black Ford I had brought back from Cyprus I remarked that it had been a good holiday, and how nice the cottage was. 'Yes,' Sybil replied, 'but there was something about the upstairs room I didn't like. Whenever I had to go in there to get fresh nappies out of the airing cupboard I always felt that if I looked over my shoulder at one of the wing chairs an old man with long grey hair and dressed in ancient costume would be leaning forward and looking at me. It gave me the creeps.'

I make no comment, just record these facts for what they are worth.

After my disembarkation leave I spent three months with the Ordnance Training Battalion at Deepcut, filling in time before going to the Army Staff College nearby. While with the battalion I learned to drive a Centurion tank, which was not difficult. Indeed there are times when I wish I had one now, to make life simpler on the choked highways of the late-1990s.

The Staff College was commanded by Major-General Reggie Hewitson, who went on to become the Adjutant General, one of the five military members of the Army Board. This group of distinguished officers runs the army with the assistance of a Government Minister (though what he knows about it can usually be written on the head of a pin) and a top Civil Servant — who knows quite a lot, having made his way up through the civilian ranks of the Ministry of Defence over a period of years, calling en route in other places, such as the Treasury, to gain wider experience.

There were one hundred and eighty students at the Staff College, sixty in each of three divisions; a hundred and twenty British officers in all, including a few sailors and airmen, and sixty foreigners from the Commonwealth, NATO, the USA and pro-British countries in Africa, the Middle and the Far East. The British tended to be about thirty years of age and the others a bit older, though there were one or two young rising black stars among us.

I was sent to the splendid, red-bricked, turreted, chateau-like, Minley Manor built, I believe, by the man who made a fortune out of sewing machines, two or three miles south of Camberley, to Division Three, which was under the control of a colonel of the Sappers who had the unfortunate name of John Thomas. He, too, went far, becoming Master General of the Ordnance (another member of the Army Board) which, given his smooth and purposeful character, was quite predictable.

The year's instruction at Camberley was split into six terms, in which we learned army organisation, the defence, attack and withdrawal phases of war, Internal Security (riot control, aid to the civil power) and, lastly, nuclear warfare. We went to fire-power demonstrations at Warminster and Larkhill, where earnest officers described perfectly obvious events to us, and to a Royal Marines demonstration at Portsmouth of how to jump out of a landing craft and get wet. Looking beyond the bedraggled marines struggling up the beach it was possible to see the first-ever Hovercraft bouncing around on the waves doing its first-ever test flight. (It wasn't supposed to fly, of course, but from time to time it did.)

Ours was a vintage year: several of the students and most of the Directing Staff went on to achieve high rank. One student, Richard Lawson, a dapper little blonde gamecock in the Royal Tank Regiment, had the distinction of arriving at Camberley as a captain, temporary major, local lieutenant-colonel, having achieved that eminence in Iraq as Assistant Military Attaché, elevated beyond his station when his boss became hors-de-combat during the coup in which King Feisal was assassinated. Dickie — he of the barathea battledress, when everyone else wore serge — went on to become GOC Northern Ireland, and then took over Allied Forces North in Oslo before retiring. (His wife was Norwegian, which no doubt had something to do with it.) Dwin Bramall of the Green Jackets, one of the Directing Staff and yet another old-Etonian, was to become Chief of the Defence Staff and a Field Marshal — and after that, the Lord Lieutenant of London. A student, John Acland of the Scots Guards, was to find fame as the major-general commander of the military element sent to oversee the change of administration in Rhodesia/Zimbabwe — despite having incurred the displeasure of the Army Board by writing to the editor of the Times deploring the activities of the Army Board. Another student, Sandy Boswell of the Argylls, became GOC Scotland; Martin Farndale of the Gunners became C-in-C BAOR and then Master Gunner, and so on. Interestingly, some of those obviously favoured and marked out for high command by the instructors fell by the wayside, while some thought to be in the second eleven did well. The system favoured the extrovert, the great talker, but in practice some of them turned out to be booming, empty vessels. To me, it proved that a person's true worth cannot be judged in the false atmosphere of a course; or at the age of around thirty, when vestiges of callow youth still linger with a man.

My family lived in a very pleasant army

hiring at Hawley Park, near to Minley Manor. Hot summer days followed upon each other for months on end and in between doing many other things I grew an enormous crop of tomatoes, a great achievement never since repeated. Alexander was born in the Louise Margaret Military Hospital at Aldershot in March 1959, so my attempts at studying were not exactly helped by midnight feeds. I have sometimes reminded him that he first saw the light of day in the Home of the British Army, but the knowledge leaves him cold. As an artist, military life held only a fleeting attraction for the few weeks he lasted as a Combined Cadet at school. He was christened in the little chapel at Minley Manor. As a baby he was cuddly, red-cheeked and placid and, unlike his brother, had little to say for himself. He has made up for it since.

During the three warfare terms we students did Tactical Exercises Without Troops, tramping the hills east of Basingstoke, now cleft by the M3 Motorway, putting in a battalion-group attack and laying out battalion defensive positions; and then, later on, conducting a withdrawal, followed by a counter-attack, near the Thames at Goring. In June, we went to France, to Cabourg, from whence we visited the Normandy battlefields: Pegasus Bridge, the Mulberry Harbour, the bocage near Caen where that other fine artist Rex Whistler was killed by a German mortar bomb. (I stress the fact that it was German because at about that time the start-line for a major British attack was heavily bombed by the United States Air Force. Such things happen in war.) And on the tour I saw, fifteen years on, the beach where Brian's landing craft had ground ashore on D-Day.

* * *

Instruction at Camberley was generally based on the lessons learned from campaigns of the Second World War, on to which nuclear weapons were grafted as a sort of bonus. Using conventional tactics the enemy was to be lured into killing grounds, and then zapped with nuclears. We would sit with a template laid on a map working out the radius of damage of a burst and where the plume of fall-out would go, and try to estimate how many casualties the enemy would suffer, but not enough thought was given, in my view, to the cumulative effect of all those bright bangs on the battlefield. Buckets of instant sunshine, the RAF called them. Could human beings, even specially disciplined ones like soldiers, really take in their stride hundreds of nuclear explosions in a day? The putative yields were far far greater than the 10-kiloton bomb on Hiroshima, yet consider the effect that had on the recipients — and the world. Would whole populations not panic beyond control if the northern hemisphere was being covered with a pall of radio-active dust? (What price the appalled and on-going reaction to the, in comparison, piddling reactor failure at Chernobyl?) I was, and remain, unconvinced that such things could be used like glorified artillery shells; after the first few have been detonated the carnage and confusion caused would wither all military plans on the vine. A few big bangs and organised warfare would quickly grind to a halt, not least because radio communications would virtually cease and there would then be no control over the battlefield.

So far, the matter has not been put to the test — but one day, I fear, it will, probably in the Far East.

★ ★ ★

All that plodding around the countryside was only part of the educative process that went on at Camberley. We also heard many visiting lecturers, top people in civil and military life, and an interesting lot they were, too. Lauris Norstadt, Supreme Allied Commander in

Europe, a clean-cut, all-American boy, came to talk to us, and so did Frankie Festing, the less clean-cut Chief of our General Staff, the front of whose uniform was usually dusted with snuff as well as medals. Smoothie Duncan Sandys the Defence Secretary, jovial Solly Zuckerman the Chief Scientific Adviser, comical Vic Feather, General Secretary of the Trade Union Congress — they all had their say. Mind, some said more than others; for some, it was a case of reading out a speech written by an aide and glanced through in the car on the way to Camberley. Others, though, told us a lot: one of them was a man called Douglas Hyde, who had been editor of the Daily Worker and a rabid communist but who, on the principle of knowing your enemy, had studied Roman Catholicism prior to defending a libel case brought against his paper by the Catholic Herald, and had become converted. (I'm not sure that there is a lot of difference between a rabid communist and a rabid Christian: it's just that the focus is different.) He made some memorable points: that communism contained the seeds of its own destruction, in that as the lot of the proletariat improved, so would the need for a communist system decline; that capitalism, too, was doomed — as firms and nations grew closer together financially, eventually all would founder when they were hit by massive international depression caused by forces out of their control. (The Millenium computer bug . . . ?)

Of the personalities I saw and heard the most impressive of all was Admiral of the Fleet Lord Louis Mountbatten. His tall, handsome figure, his chestful of medals (only out-done by Monty's and some low-ranking American officers I have met), his self-confidence, his mode of address, made him a charismatic figure. The fact that I have since heard on good authority that he was an absolute shit, disliked by most of the people who worked with him, does not alter my assessment of his overt personality.

I have been told by someone who was present that when Mountbatten came to leave the MoD on retirement his successor smartly saluted the back of the departing staff car then turned to the assembled brass standing on the steps and said 'Thank Christ.' Mountbatten's subordinates seem to have weighed him up, too. A retired Captain, Butler-Bowden, whom I met at Osborne House on the Isle of Wight when I was recuperating from an operation, recounted an incident in 1941 on HMS *Kelly*, Mountbatten's ship, on which B-B was the navigator. As the *Kelly* approached Crete they were all on the lookout for Stukas and, sure enough, with the dawn came the Stukas. One put a bomb right through the forward turret of the *Kelly*; it went down into the depths, exploded and opened part of the hull like a giant scoop. As the ship began to corkscrew down into the water Mountbatten yelled to B-B, 'Swim for your life, pilot.' They both took a header into the ocean and when they surfaced bobbed around, watching with horror as their ship's stern rose high into the air. Suddenly a great bubble of air billowed up beside them, in its centre a grimy Petty Officer stoker. He shook his hair out of his eyes, looked around, saw Mountbatten, grinned and said: 'Funny how the scum always comes to the surface, sir, isn't it?'

I'm not sure Mountbatten got it right in India either, when he was Viceroy. The unseemly speed with which we scuttled out of that jewel in the crown let loose totally uncontrolled mayhem, and resulted in millions of deaths. But then he was under enormous pressure from the politicians back home to pull out, and so save money that could be diverted to the Welfare State. Plus ça change . . .

No, not all the great ones were admirable. Some fluffed their lines and others muddled their answers — and the students — but one and all it was an education to see and hear these people. We also had the pleasure of listening to eminent men discoursing informally over a glass of port after dinner. After we had eaten, dressed in a dinner jacket and not Mess Kit, as was usual when entertaining guests, we would adjourn to the ante room where the man of the evening would be asked to reminisce. Lord Goddard, one-time Lord Chief Justice and then 83 years old, told us about his young days as a barrister — and switched off his hearing aid when an intemperate New Zealand gunner major voiced his poor opinion of our legal system: he was most upset to have read that a man had been given *three* years for manslaughter and another man *seven* years for rape. 'Call that British justice?' Monty, in a euphoria of self-esteem, made some more waspish comments about military and civilian personalities. Lord Boothby and Richard Crossman did a political comedy-cross-talk act.

At Camberley I learned a lot. About things, about people in high places, about the army. It transformed me mentally. Some years later I was at the receiving end of an acid remark from an officer who had failed to get a place on the course even though he had passed the entrance examination. 'Camberley counts for far too much in the army,' he told me: 'You'd think people who went there had two heads, or something.' The fact is that if you have benefited from hearing all that information, had your horizons broadened and been made to think, as I was, you must be better off than if you had not. And that, I suppose, applies to the whole learning process, whatever it may encompass.

* * *

Toward the end of the year Neophita Christou persuaded somebody to write to ask if she could join us in England. On a captain's salary, with a wife and two children to support, I could hardly afford to pay her a bean a week, but she pleaded and I duly met her at Victoria Station. She was small and not one of Aphrodite's most beautiful daughters but she dearly loved the little boys, especially baby Alex.

I was posted from the Staff College to Headquarters Southern Command at Wilton and was allocated another army hiring, this time in the village of Swallowcliff, just off the A30 near where the regimental badges were carved out of the chalk hillsides by the doomed young men who were about to go off to fight the battle of the Somme. (A few years ago someone began to carve the CND symbol there but I think their fervour waned before they finished the job, unlike the enduring patriotism of their forebears.)

We arrived at Swallowcliff a few days before Christmas and took Neophyta with us to the midnight service at the Anglican church. What she, a staunch Greek Orthodox Christian made of it I do not know, especially as the vicar, Roome by name, would periodically lose his place in the scheme of things and burble on unintelligibly until his memory returned and took him back on track again. He was a small bespectacled man with a very large, galleon-in-full-sail type of wife and nine daughters, one of whom married a Moslem; I have never been able to decide if there was any special significance in that. One evening he took me into his sitting room for a chat. During a long pause in the conversation I commented that I could hear pigeons cooing. 'That's not pigeons,' he snapped, 'that's my asthma.'

Neophyta stayed with us for a few months and then announced out of the blue — by way of a letter written to us by her relatives in London — that she was leaving to marry, sight unseen, a cousin. Some years later I trudged up and down many dusty stairs in the rag trade area of Soho trying to find her, but without success. I expect she is now a grandmother, sitting on a rickety chair somewhere in the sunshine sewing fine lace.

On 1st July 1960 I went to the Royal Armoured Corps School at Lulworth to watch a demonstration, the aim of which was to fire 105mm tank guns at assorted targets with the object of impressing lots of foreign visitors and persuading them to buy the guns and ammunition. (Some did, and they were subsequently used in earnest during the Arab/Israeli and Indo/Pakistan wars.) It was a beautiful summer's day and I was very glad to be able to escape for a while from the big, fat, bossy WRAC officer I had the misfortune to work for. She was not the last person I was to come across who piled the desk high with paper because it was thought to impress people; and for the same reason stayed late in the office even when there was nothing to do. (Since then I have never been a strong supporter of the view that women should have an equal share of authority just because they are women.)

At Lulworth we all wined and dined well, by courtesy of the tax payer, since much was at stake by way of millions of pound's worth of orders, and in due course, replete, meandered off down to the firing range. The tanks began to bang away, accurately picking off one target after another while the commentator nonchalantly described what was going on; the target next to be engaged, the thickness of its armour, the slope of the plating to be defeated. Then, at precisely one minute to three, he said: 'We will take a break now, gentlemen, and listen to the Derby commentary.' 'Tarby?' a German colonel sitting next to me asked: 'Vat is zis Tarby?' I explained that it was a very important horse race. Total disbelief registered on his face.

Whether the Derby assisted sales I do not know, but judging from the groans at the end of the race most of the British officers had not backed the winner.

★ ★ ★

In 1961 I was made a major and sent to the North East of England, to a headquarters that administered the Regular and Territorial Army in Cumberland, Northumberland, Durham and North Yorkshire; it was commanded by Major-General the Right Honourable the Lord Thurlow, a much-decorated officer who had served in the Seaforth Highlanders, commanded a brigade during the Rhine crossing and looked remarkably like Mr Pastry, a weedy character played by Richard Hearn who used to appear on children's television: appearances can be very deceptive.

Harry Thurlow was a bachelor who lived in a mansion near Northallerton, miles away from the headquarters. We did not see much of him, for he was always around and about his parish, but when we did he was pleasant, if somewhat preoccupied. His successor was Tony Read, about whom more later.

Though I do not regret that tour of duty, which took us to a remote and lovely part of England, I do regret having taken to heart an old army saying: 'Never volunteer for anything', said gleefully by sergeants to new recruits and often accompanied by the tale of the NCO who asked if anyone was interested in music and when someone put his hand up told him to move the piano out of the NAAFI. The moral was that if you didn't volunteer you could never reproach yourself if things turned out badly. Because I accepted this as being a wise injunction, and because one was not encouraged to question the decisions of the amorphous 'they' who ruled one's destiny, I did not try to influence events but took things as they came. This might have been the right, soldierly thing to do, and for all I know may have worked out for the best, but I do regret not having spent more of my army life on active service and abroad, in particular East of Suez; it was to be ten years after I left the army that I finally made it to the Far East, to Vietnam (and it nearly was finally, too). Instead of the torrid bazaars of the Gulf or the humid markets of Singapore I had to make do with the tatty emporiums of Stockton-on-Tees.

We lived on the main trunk road from Newcastle upon Tyne to York, just north of Yarm. The traffic never ceased, except for an hour or two late on Christmas Eve. Power lines hummed over the field at the back of the house, which was a semi-detached army quarter, on the other side of which lived an RAF family. They had a cuckoo clock nailed to the partitioning wall and its demented little bird sounded off at half-hourly intervals day and night. It was not a quiet life. However, workwise I enjoyed it.

My office was huge and panelled and had once been the dining room of Kirkleavington Hall, a grey stone mansion erected by a nouveau riche Victorian industrialist. The company was congenial and I travelled a lot; to Berwick-on-Tweed, York, Newcastle, Carlisle, Millom, Durham and all points in the neck of England, once getting stranded on Bowes Moor in a blizzard. The Winscale (Sellafield) towers near Millom, standing silhouetted against the sun setting beyond the sea, looked weird, like something out of a science-fiction film. Their malign influence on events continues to this day: litigation about leukaemia, anxiety about the disposal of nuclear waste. Much pleasanter was the beautiful house in Yorkshire belonging to Colonel Phillip van Straubenzee. Strolling around his garden on a summer's day, sipping from a pre-lunch glass of sherry and listening to the bees bumbling around the hollyhocks I asked him if he had lived there long. 'Oh, about three hundred years,' he replied.

* * *

It was to York that I went, in June 1961, to act as an usher at the wedding of the Duke of Kent to Miss Catherine Worsley. I had volunteered, for once, and was amazed when my name came out of the hat. Imposing-looking envelopes began to arrive from the Lord Chamberlain's Office containing instructions that regulated everything except how often one was allowed to breath: timings to the minute; placings, precedence and protocol with precision. When the great day dawned I donned one of Mr Moss' morning suits and set out. (Regrettably, the ushers' wives were not invited.)

I was in charge of Block 'A' in the North

Transept of York Minster. We were all of us — twenty officers, as I recall, from the Royal Scots Greys, the Duke's regiment, and twenty All-Sorts from Northern Command — presented with a red carnation on arrival and then, having figured out where to stow our top hats, told to take post. The great ones of the nation began to assemble and I did my duty, showing such people as Sir Malcolm Sergeant and Cecil Beaton to their seats. While the television cameras recorded for millions the magnificence and dignity of the ceremony I tried to get a glimpse of what was going on around the back of a massive pillar of stone — whose name I never discovered.

When it was all over and the lovely bride — she still is lovely — had walked back down the aisle with her duke I drove in convoy in my car the twenty miles or so to Hovingham Hall, the home of her parents, a fine mansion that nestles in soft Yorkshire hills and boasts its own cricket pitch, Sir William being a keen cricketer, as so many Yorkshiremen are. On this occasion a huge marquee had been erected on the pitch (but not on the wicket, needless to say), decorated internally with stripes of pastel colours and filled with fine food and drink charged to Sir William's account by Terry's of York. I stood watching the royal family — of whom I thought

Alexandra the most attractive — eating energetically (they and I), drinking copiously (I more than they, pre-breath test days) and counting Field Marshals. Templar was there, and Slim and Hull and Festing. And, of course, Montgomery. But it was Mr John Profumo, the Minister for War, who stole the show and up-staged everyone — probably for the last time — by departing with his wife in a brightly-coloured helicopter. (A few years before, I had seen his wife, Valerie Hobson, with Herbert Lom, in the King and I at the Theatre Royal, Drury Lane.)

For my part, I got into my green-and-white Ford Consul and drove North straight up the road, full of vintage champagne and singing all the way. Now and then, like Toad of Toad Hall, I toot-tooted and waved graciously to the peasants I passed on the streets, as I had done to the crowds that lined the roads all the way from York to Hovingham. Then, they had cheered me enthusiastically, and I could see them asking each other: ' 'Oo's 'ee?' This time, one or two of them made rude gestures back. I arrived home in a state of high euphoria and was greeted by my wife with the news that she had supper waiting for me.

Kippers.

Ah, well, such is life.

★ ★ ★

Years later I met the duke when I was working in the Ministry of Defence. He came into the office I shared with four others and I mentioned that I had ushered at his wedding. He gave me a sharp look. 'Oh, did you?' he replied: 'I don't remember a thing about it.' It was thirty-seven years since my father had met his father in Peru (another closed loop) but I didn't mention it: I wasn't sure he would be interested.

I was sorry that the only memento we ushers received was a red carnation. I still have mine, pressed between the leaves of the order of service, but a pair of cufflinks, say, would have been a nice gesture.

★ ★ ★

One day when I was in the little officers' mess in Kirkleavington Hall I picked up a copy of the British Army Review and read an article — very short, only two or three pages — about the Order of St John, the Hospitallers. The idea of soldier monks, disciplined in faith and fortitude, struck a chord that lingered in my mind and was, five years later, to have a profound effect on my life.

Simon de Morlancourt stood on top of the middle, highest, tower. Everything was very still and quiet. Uncomfortably so. He felt the watching eyes as he looked down, from this reeling height, on the great empty valleys, brown and gold, cleft here and there by dark shadows and smudged by dusty greens. Heat shimmered in the afternoon sun. There was no sound at all except a muted flapping of cloth from the Hospitaller banner above his head. Birds soared distantly, rising on outstretched wings in the hot air.

Range upon range of hills in front of him. Dusty soil and baking heat. He was hundreds of feet high, and now and then great volumes of air seemed to move in the valleys. He felt them and heard them: a thump and a great sigh, the earth breathing heavily under the summer sun.

He leaned forward on the parapet, feeling its heat soak deep into his chest and hands, but it was too much for comfort. The rough cloth of his robe was heavy and clung to his body. He stepped back and walked over to the other side and looked down.

Men lay or sat in the shade, resting until the worst of the heat had passed. The courtyard was untidy: bleached wooden scaffolding clutching the almost completed chapel; heaps of stone; piles of shells and broken pottery to be pounded and mixed into mortar; a great jumble of wicker baskets in a corner; piles of kindling wood outside the bakery door; carts with their shafts thrown back over the driving seat; animals in their pens around the walls.

Three donkeys stood beneath him, heads low, tails flicking, the dark cross of fur enfolding their bodies.

There was no noise, still.

Then a donkey stirred and its small hooves tapped lightly on the flagstones as it swung its weight from one side to the other. A dog lying beside his man twitched and woke up, scratched an itch behind an ear, half stood, followed his heels around twice then lay down again.

Far, far away the horizon merged into heat haze. Beyond the horizon, where the sun set, was the sea which, on a clear day, glinted like a silver thread between earth and sky. It was months ago that he had left it at Tripolis and ridden for two whole days over the hills to Le Crac des Chevaliers.

He pivoted around on his heels, following with his eyes the line of the road until it disappeared from view in the direction of Homs. Homs. An old place. Home of many people. Moslems. Where the road from Damascus met the road from Baghdad and walked with it to the Middle Sea. But there were not many people elsewhere in the county of Tripolis; here and there a few mud houses near a pool or well, but mostly emptiness and dust, hill after hill. Fir trees and olives and eucalyptus; and thyme and sage, crunched under the horses' hooves and sending up a fragrance as they rode. And lizards scuttling away through clumps of dried grass.

To his right the hills stepped upwards into the fortress valleys of the Assassins. He frowned, perplexed. He had never seen an Assassin. Or perhaps he had — they looked the same as any other Saracen, so he had been told.

The whole thing was very strange: the Old Man of the Mountains in his castle. Men waking from drugged sleep in a beautiful place, looking into soft eyes, feeling deft fingers fondling them . . . Then sent on desperate missions with the promise of a re-awakening in that paradise provided they carried out the appointed task.

He turned rather guiltily at the sound of approaching footsteps.

We left the north-east of England, with its magnificent unpopulated beaches — when you have sat on one for twenty minutes in the teeth of a howling East wind you understand why — and made our way to Germany, to a little village called Wulfen, just north of the Ruhr. Today, it is a town, built around a new coal mine, but then it was a sleepy hollow — except for the two hundred tree-covered bunkers that held ammunition, missiles and explosives.

The Forward Ammunition Depot was a splendid command for a young major — I was then 34 — because it was a completely self-contained community. It had a housing estate for the army families, a barracks for the soldiers, a school for young service children, a church, a fire station, a railway and engines, a motor transport pool, workshops, a sports field, an indoor small-bore rifle range and even a broken-down nine-hole golf course. In all, I was responsible for the welfare of more than seven hundred souls, including many German civilians who had worked there for years, some of them when the place was a German depot during the war. And responsible, too, for millions of pounds worth of military hardware.

It was only a week before we left Yarm that Sybil's mother had died in Liverpool. We mourned her, of course, and like many modern young ones who consign their old folks to a home wished we had done more for her. She had lived alone for many years, a tiny, independent little creature who tottered about on spindly legs. Hannah had few friends but was much loved by those she had. She died suddenly of a cerebral haemorrhage in a nursing home, which fortunately she had not been in for long. They found a half-eaten bar of Aero chocolate under her pillow — which they sent to us with the rest of her belongings.

And it was only four days after we arrived in Germany that my father died. By then Andrew had sold Orchard Croft for a ridiculously small sum of money and he and my mother had moved to rooms in Lytham St Annes. We would visit them there from Yarm to find my mother still very active but my father totally bedridden, sitting propped up, gaunt and big-eyed, watching television incessantly but uncomprehendingly — except the football, which he understood very well. His eyes would fill with tears when he looked at my small sons. He was feeble and pitiful but just now and then would grow angry and accuse my mother, then over 70, of having an affair with an unspecified person who, it seemed, lived in the bathroom. He must have loved her very much to still be jealous of her when he was over eighty. Maybe she didn't realise the significance of it, for she was irritated by his outbursts. Then, quite suddenly, he left us, all passion finally spent.

I did not go home for the funeral. I was very involved with other things and there seemed so little point to it. I was probably wrong not to have gone, and have since regretted it, but to me he had died at least a year before when the vigorous man I had always known became unrecognisable inside the trembling, pathetically child-like, wizened shell of a body that no longer resembled his.

★　★　★

Germany entranced me. As a boy I had a large map of the country pinned to a piece of soft-board — a black-out window screen — in my bedroom and would move coloured pins on it to indicate the progress of Patton's Third Army and Dempsey's Second as they drove eastwards. I knew the names, from radio reports of the bombing, of Gelsenkirchen, Essen, Duisburg, Ruhrmond. Now, I found myself living only a few miles from these places, completely rebuilt and inhabited by prosperous, hardworking, polite people.

In many places the planners had taken advantage of the opportunity given them by the destruction of the centre of their towns to lay out wide streets and spacious squares surrounded by well-built offices and shops. In the theatre in Gelsenkirchen-Buhr, for example, during the interval one can stroll around sipping gin-and-tonic while looking down a long tree-lined avenue with rows of twinkling street lights that disappear into the distance. Bristol and Plymouth had the double misfortune of being bombed by the Germans and rebuilt by the British. What a pity the burghers of those cities did not have the same vision, instead of creating tall rat-runs of ugly, soulless concrete.

On arrival we stayed for a few days in an hotel beside a lake, waiting for our quarter to be vacated by the outgoing major. On our first Saturday there the dining room was filled to capacity with people eating, drinking and dancing who departed in the early hours in a fleet of shiny little cars. When the next morning I asked the proprietor who these affluent, well-dressed, well-behaved people had been he said they were miners from the Ruhr. It was my introduction to an aspect of life in Germany that I have since confirmed many times: that it is difficult to tell by looking at a German which strata of society he inhabits. Here, the working man is jeered at by his fellows if he tries to take off his cloth cap or change his accent; there, they have a less class-conscious way of life and people can move more freely up or sideways.

Though the Germans work hard, they play hard too. To go to a schutzenfest — a relic of medieval times when a village elected the best archer to be the Schutzen Konig for the next year — is an eye opener. Now, the men shoot at a wooden cockerel; the one who gets the best results is cheered, chaired and takes pride of place, with his Queen, for the two or three days the festival lasts, and keeps the title the year long. A vast marquee is filled with long tables and benches and a band plays on a dais at one end. Hundreds, sometimes thousands, of people link arms and sway, sitting on the long benches singing their hearts out; couples gyrate on a dance floor, girls carry six or eight flagons of foaming beer at a time from the bars to the tables; chiding women drag their drunken, grinning husbands home. (Generally speaking, Germans become affable when they get drunk whereas a Scotsman's first instinct is to belt someone. Strange, isn't it? And quite the opposite what one would expect.)

The other big festival of the German year, like the schutzenfest a hangover from medieval times, is Fasching, the merrymaking that precedes Lent, when all personal inhibitions and moral constraints seem to be swept away in another two or three days of frantic revelry. On Ladies Day it is the turn of the women to choose a partner — by cutting off the bottom of his tie with a pair of scissors as a memento. Nine months or so later Rosen Montag (Rose Monday) babies are born who, if the mother so wishes, will be brought up in a children's home. There seems to be no condemnation of these births: they are regarded as just an inevitable part of life, the result of men and women coming passionately together after a long winter and before they begin to observe the restrictions of Lent. At least, that was the excuse in the old days.

Not all aspects of German life struck me as admirable of course, how could they? The docility of the people as regards rules and regulations makes for a well-ordered existence but explains how they came to be so easily led astray by the strutting little madman with the Charlie Chaplin moustache. It is difficult to think of any other race that would have solemnly greeted each other for years on end with a childish salutation like Heil Hitler while thrusting an arm up into the air on every possible occasion. (On the matter of discipline, if you are driving there don't ever argue with a German coming towards you if he appears to think you are in the wrong: get out of the way, or he will kill himself to prove his point, as I have seen happen.)

In 1963 most German women walked around wearing a pork-pie hat, square-cut dark clothes, thick stockings and flat-heeled shoes: the archetypal frau with a gimlet eye. They and their husbands were the people who had grown up between the wars, the whelps of the Weimar Republic who were to be hypnotised by Hitler, dragooned by the Gestapo and finally crushed by the spitting jaws of the pincers that slowly closed in on them from east and west in 1945. The Fraus frowned at the Frauleins who wore modern clothes, short skirts and went bareheaded. (And they jived, too, Mein Gott!) But thirty years on the Fraus have gone and the frauleins are the new mothers; different, gayer people. The words Kirche, Kuche, Kinder do not imprison the womenfolk any more. (Discipline, too, has eased a bit — more's the pity, in some ways, since crime spreads in lax conditions. And people don't work as hard as they used to.

That is the other side of the coin.)

As to the jaws of the armoured pincers, they stopped closing while there was still a strip of a hundred kilometres or so of central Germany that remained unbombed. In that strip you will find beautiful little towns like Celle and Rothenburg-on-the-Tauber which still have hundreds of intact medieval buildings, their façades preserved punctiliously even when the insides have been gutted and modernised.

A few miles east of Wulfen there is a town called Dulmen. On one occasion I went there to tell the burgermeister that he would soon be having British soldiers living in his community: a new British depot was being built and some of my soldiers and their families would be occupying quarters there. He showed me photographs of Dulmen before and after: before 13th March 1945 the old town stood, walled, half-timbered; on the 14th there was virtually nothing left. Twenty-four hours before the infantry arrived British and American air forces destroyed every town and village in their path.

★　★　★

In the Spring of 1963 the roads had erupted because of the extremely severe winter we had had and I would hang on to the seat of my khaki-coloured Volkswagen Beetle as my driver, Bernhard, belted down the dead-straight road which, I was told, Napoleon had built from Wesel, on the Rhine, to Munster in order to ease his supply problems on his way to Moscow. (At that point he had hardly begun, so he should have had second thoughts, perhaps ...) The half-timbered farms smelt richly as we passed them, and butcher's shops, too, when Sybil and I entered them: of smoked hams and the sausages hanging from the eaves. The gastattes smelt of beer and cigar smoke, the shops of floor polish, and the smiling shop girls of soap and scent. It was a nice change from the surly looks we were used to in England, and the attitude that the customer is a stupid nuisance who interferes with important things like gossiping about the previous night's escapades with the boy-friend.

It turned out that I was to live in Germany for many years, twelve in all, something that would have seemed inconceivable when I was a boy. The inhabitants were historically our enemies; grim, faceless Huns. They had brought about the Great war, then raped Europe again in the 1940s — and put six million Jews through Hitler's abattoirs. They had, when all was said and done, been responsible for the death of my brother. Yet I liked them in 1963 and I like them now. And never have the feeling that they regard us as their enemies. More than one of them has said to me 'Peter, it should have been Chermany and England against the rest.' A very revealing remark, echoes of the Lorelei Song, of 'Today Germany is ours, tomorrow, the world.'

* * *

My work was varied and interesting and I loved dealing with people, making decisions and seeing things happen as a result. Once, someone said to me 'I hate Monday mornings,' to which I replied, 'I love them.'

We lived self-contained as a community, forty miles from the nearest possible interference from higher authority, and because we employed so many locals were a part of their lives, albeit a small one. (In some ways the British Army of the Rhine was too self-contained: a public opinion poll in Bielefeld in 1977 revealed that only 30% of its population were aware that British troops lived in their town — indeed had done so for thirty years. For our part, the British soldier has no interest in being a tourist; he would prefer to lie on his bed and read a girlie magazine than, like his American counterpart, be up and about with a camera at the high port. He saved every penny he could to go on leave to Cardiff, London, Belfast, Glasgow or wherever and have a big spending spree with his girl and his mates. There was not a lot of communication between us and the Germans at that level — except in the night clubs, where the whores did a good trade. My job, though, brought me into contact with the local people and we began to make friends. In sickness the little garrison was ministered to by Doctor Rolf Eicke, and through him we made many local contacts. His hospitality and generosity to me over the years was to be astonishing. I spent many evenings sitting in comfort and amity in his warm house.

★   ★   ★

But not all my memories of that first tour of duty in Germany are of good food, fine wine and interesting talk. Once, I attended the funeral of an elderly German who had died when an army truck bringing him to work skidded and overturned.

North Rhine Westphalia is predominantly Catholic but this man was a Lutheran. The big sombre church was full of candles and black-clothed people, its high ceiling almost out of sight in the gloom. I stood in the silence, amongst all those people the only foreigner, and in full uniform at that, mourning the death of a man who had fought against us in two wars. But what was wrong with that? His relatives had asked me to go and thanked me solemnly afterwards, our breath hanging in the cold, foggy air. Strangely, they valued the fact that a British officer had come to see an old man laid to rest in his home ground.

On another occasion I went to the funeral of a man who had died far from home.

We had, to guard the depot, a platoon of war dogs, my old friends the slavering Alsatians, tearing their claws out as they tried to get at me through the wire mesh on the front of their cages. These animals were looked after by men known as MSO, the Mixed Services Organisation, displaced persons employed by the British after the war and formed into labour and transport groups and guard units. The Wulfen company was commanded by Hubert Parasanovic, a tall, distinguished-looking, white-haired man who had been an officer in the right-wing resistance forces commanded by Mihailovic. He had a wife and son in Yugoslavia but had backed the wrong horse and could not now return to Tito's communist country. His group of assorted Poles, Latvians, Lithuanians, Serbs and Croats, who had all been bad punters, were responsible for patrolling the perimeter of the camp, hanging on to their straining canines.

These people lived a strange and solitary life and had real cause to be bitter. Life had taken them in their youth from hearth and home and left them stranded on an alien shore with no hope of returning and hardly any hope of betterment in their condition; only a few managed to find a wife and create a new life and family. That the others could still smile was surprising, yet they did. During the 1970s many of them began to die off, and now there are none of them left. One of them died young, in 1964.

As I stood beside his grave I felt very keenly not only the futility of war but even of life itself. He could never have dreamt, could he, when he was a little laughing boy in Bosnia, that he would die alone hundreds of miles from home after a pointless, useless existence?

And yet perhaps he did not see it that way at all. I hope not.

★ ★ ★

One of the contacts I made in Wulfen was a former Luftwaffe pilot who had rejoined the German Air Force in 1955 and was now a Colonel. (The German armed forces ceased to exist between 1945 and 1955, when they were allowed to re-form and contribute to the NATO deterrent.) When I asked if he knew England he replied, with a twinkle in his eye: 'Some places. London, Portsmouth, Coventry, Liverpool. But not very well. Only from a distance, you might say.' Maybe, who knows, he was the man who gave me those warm, bird-song-filled days in North Wales. He was one of the few Germans I met who owned up to having fought us: most admitted only to having been on the Russian front. But then, most of them had, at one time or another. (Some years later I asked a German Brigadier-General where he had won his Knight's Grand Cross of the Iron Cross and he replied, straight-faced: 'In North Africa, shooting down British planes.')

While we were in Wulfen Rolf Eicke, the doctor, arranged for me to go down the new mine that was being developed.

A great tilted seam of coal runs from the Ruhr northeast towards Denmark, very near to the surface beside the Rhine but getting progressively deeper the further it goes. During the war when fuel was in short supply some people living in the Ruhr could dig coal out of their cellars, but by the time the seam reaches Wulfen it is a thousand metres deep — which is a lot of deep: almost as far down as Snowdon is up.

On a dull March morning Rolf and I and his brother-in-law, a mining geologist by the name of Heinz, donned heavy white serge clothes (yes, white, so that you can be more easily found if there is a cave-in) and a helmet with a light at the front, climbed into a great steel bucket hanging from a cable and were lowered, by stages, down into the depths, the bare rock of the walls flashing past in the light from our torches, the bucket bouncing up and down on the elasticity of the cable. At one point we went through a patch of mist, where the cold air on the surface was mixing with the hot air down below, and then we plunged on, interminably, it seemed. At last we grounded and clambered out.

Some years before, on an Officers' Day while at Parkhall Camp in Oswestry, I had gone down a Welsh pit. Its seams were low and the conditions awful: men picking away at a two- or three-feet-high coal face while lying on their sides after walking miles from the pit head. These days they have it easy by comparison, with great steel jaws biting the coal out of the seam on their behalf and conveyor belts to ride on to and from work. Bad enough, mind, I'm not saying it isn't, but in earlier times it must have been sheer hell. I came up out of that pit a confirmed socialist. But not for long.

At the bottom of the Wulfen shaft a long drift had been hacked out (shades of Corsham). We walked along it, in an 80degree F heat, sweating copiously, breathing in coal dust and getting slowly dusted with it, our clothes turning from white to grey, until we staggered into another little cavern where we took breath and stretched our necks: we had had to walk all the way with our heads down because if we lifted them up our helmets tried to crack open the roof. I thankfully clambered into another big bucket and was pleased to see the blanket of fog as we passed through it on our way up a second shaft to a raw wintry day. Later, I was presented with a replica miner's lamp to commemorate the occasion.

★ ★ ★

While we were in Wulfen I made my first personal battlefield tour. I went off alone in the middle of winter and in bright, iron-hard weather walked about on Hill 60 near Ypres, on the slopes of Passchendaele and in the subterranean vaults under Vimy Ridge, where tens of thousands of Canadians had made a strange temporary home. I passed dozens of cemeteries, stopped at some and looked at thousands of grave stones. 'Sacred to the memory of a soldier of the Great War' was what many of them had carved on their white faces. (What a ghastly job that must have been, exhuming decomposed bodies and trying to find the name tag then re-burying the stinking pieces in straight lines.) Some of the cemeteries were right in the middle of what had been scenes of carnage. In the very first I stopped at the gum-booted, leather-jacketed attendant turned out to be a British soldier of the Second World War who had married a Belgian girl and stayed on. He told me that only the week before he had been re-aligning a path and had dug up two Germans. 'How did you know they were Germans?' I asked him. 'Because their leather jack-boots had not completely rotted,' he replied. In the evenings I returned to a lovely old hotel in the Place de la Croix Rouge in Arras, ate and wined well and appreciated it. Especially after seeing Tyne Cot, where thirty thousand British and Imperial soldiers lie, including Chinese brought from Hong Kong to Flanders to do labouring tasks.

While in Wulfen Alex nearly died, too. One day he began to run a very high temperature and developed spots. Rolf thought it was measles, but then Alex became really ill and he decided that hospital was the right place for him. In the British Military Hospital at Munster Colonel Webb, a physician, recognised the symptoms as being those of Stephen Johnson's syndrome, which in the past had always been a killer. Alex was pumped full of penicillin and while Sybil stayed at his bedside day and night, slowly recovered. We thought perhaps he had picked up the bug at the Zuider Zee, which we had visited a couple of weeks before. Since they put a road across its mouth, it tends to be a lake full of sewage.

It is said that everyone remembers where they were when they heard that John F Kennedy had been assassinated. I certainly do. The officers of Wulfen Station, wearing Mess Kit, were all sitting at the dining table in the Officers' Mess attending a formal dinner night when the German manageress, Raisie Gauler, came to my shoulder and whispered to me. I tapped my glass and announced the news to the officers. There was a long silence. It put a damper on the whole evening, which tailed off as people drifted home.

Kennedy's death certainly had a pronounced effect all over the world, far more so than it would have done if he had lived longer and his true character had become apparent. Then, he and his pretty Jackie were symbols of a new age. But it was one that would never have dawned.

★　★　★

And it was from Wulfen that my little family made our first visit to Berlin, not long after the Wall had been erected. (It looked as if it would be there for all time.) It was brutal, slicing through the living heart of the city; apartment blocks *were* the wall in some places — until they were later razed to the ground and an open space torn out so that mines could be laid — and so too was the front of a church, which carried in big letters the words 'In Tyranus'. Along its length there were crosses and bunches of flowers, marking the places where people had hurled themselves out of buildings to their death rather than live ten yards behind the barbed wire.

The city was absolutely fascinating, the contrast between East and West astounding. On our side there was a vibrant, pulsing life, with well-dressed people thronging the pavements and the cafes of the Kurfursten-damm. There were shops full of glittering goods, and hundreds of cars racing up and down the road beside the Tiergarten. On the other side of the Brandenburg Gate the same road continued, the Unter den Linden, the two halves slicing for miles like an arrow right through the middle of the city. But the other side of the gate was a different world. Looking out at night from the restaurant half way up the Western TV tower was like being at the seaside: on either side and behind were ribbons of light and sparkling neon signs; in front, in the East, profound darkness. Only their new TV tower was lit up, and that had been secretly designed, so the West Berliners said, so that the lights in its bulb, standing on its long stalk, formed the shape of a cross ... Sybil and I went to the Berlin Philharmonic to hear Brahms and Sibelius, to the opera to Puccini's Tosca, to the Dahlem Museum to see all the Rembrandts — all thirty-four of them. And we went through Checkpoint Charlie into the Eastern Zone.

In the Russian military cemetery there is a gigantic statue of a soldier holding a child in his arms. They are looking down over green plots of grass under each of which are buried five thousand Russian soldiers, standing up shoulder to shoulder in order to save space.

We also went to the Pergammon Museum where dowdy female attendants watched over the empty corridors and asked us eagerly, with tears in their eyes, about life in the West. We saw the site where Hitler's corpse had been burnt in a Wagnerian pyre; still, twenty years after the event, an empty tract of rubble watched over by soldiers holding binoculars to their eyes in the guard towers. And we saw, in the West, the big derelict houses whose legal ownership had not yet been established because their one-time occupants had died in Dachau, Ravensbruck or Auschwitz.

8

More hope than glory

We came home in June 1965 and took up residence in a house in Bovingdon Green, Hertfordshire.

Little Bushey, then owned and rented out by a Group Captain, was charming; not very old but built in an old-fashioned way, with a large inglenook fireplace in the sitting room, plank doors which fastened with wooden snibs, and unplastered walls. We were told that the reason for the bare bricks was that the original spinster owners had run out of money when the place was being built.

At about ten o'clock on most nights the door in the sitting room opened though nobody was there. I expect the snib slowly lifted due to draughts coming down the stairs and after we had been sitting for a while, usually watching television, it would rise above the retaining catch and allow the door to swing open with a soft click. This is yet another example I have recounted of what some people would call the paranormal. I have mentioned these not because I believe in such things as the paranormal but because these things happened and I don't really understand why.

★　★　★

Television has played a very time-consuming part in my life. I first watched it in 1953, in Robert's Hall, one of the big officers' messes at the Royal Military College of Science. The steam-age set projected a fuzzy image on to a 5- by 3-foot screen on which Isabel Barnett and Gilbert Harding seemed to appear a lot — poor Isabel, the magistrate who couldn't help shop-lifting — Gilbert pompously declaiming about all sorts of things he knew nothing at all about, Eamon Andrews oiling along in his smooth Irish way.

When we returned from Cyprus in 1958 and were living briefly in Frimley Green, in the house of a retired colonel of the Indian army who grew mushrooms and small children, we rented our first set. One evening I sat impatiently waiting for a tenuous link-up with La Scala Milan to be made, where Maria Callas was to sing Tosca. Something went wrong and the BBC filled in for about an hour until we were able, at last, to see the great diva. She was just reaching High C and

I was drifting away on wings of song when Sybil, who is a matter-of-fact sort of person, said 'She looks as if she's in terrible pain.' For me, Maria Callas was never the same again, on or off Onassis' yacht.

My television years are a haze of flickering gibberish wherein it is difficult to remember many really worthwhile moments. The trouble is, as we all know, that it mesmerises. I sit ever-hopefully waiting for something better to appear, or for some unforeseen catastrophe to occur; in the 1980s for Jan Leeming to blow her lovely little top and bellow at the cameraman, perhaps; in the 1990s for a politician to tell one of those rudely intrusive interviewers to push off, or — even less likely — to tell the truth! It is rather like watching a bull fight or a Grand Prix motor race: I don't want to see the pass or the pit stop, I want blood. Of that there is plenty. Older people must all have watched fifty thousand people mown down in stereotyped carnage, and even more punishingly socked on the jaw. I believe one blow on the face with bare knuckles is enough to finish most men, yet in films and on TV men take a terrible thrashing that in real life would kill them then walk away with a grin, not a grimace. All over the world, in mud huts in Africa and corrugated iron igloos in Alaska (eskimos — inuits, as we are now obliged to call them — don't make snow ones any more) people watch the same programmes. They revisit Brideshead; ride with The Lone Ranger; go Upstairs and Downstairs (I have heard 'Achtung, Silber, fahrt' in Deutschland, and 'Hudson, donnez moi le bifsteak,' in France); watch Dallas, alas, and get the Hill Street Blues. Much is great entertainment, but much is pernicious. The effects of malignant, amoral nonsense on peoples' attitudes and thought processes should be scientifically assessed, but regrettably it seems there is no way to do it. Death without pain or grief, blood-letting without shock, sex without tenderness, let alone love. Perhaps it is not one of the many world-threatening catastrophes that loom on the horizon — over-population, global warming, rain-forest denudation — that is the greatest menace to civilisation but decay from within.

And yet, and yet . . . How much better informed we all are, how our horizons have been widened, how much more we know and understand about people, animals and events the world over. And how amazingly people's vocabularies have increased over the years: in pubs and in bus queues and in the shops men, women and children are articulate in a way they never used to be. And how much pleasure there is, too, in watching the sheer artistry that human beings can create; in paintings, drama, music, ballet, opera. There is a sizeable and laudable weight on the other side of the balance. At least, that's the excuse I shall make to myself for watching more moving wallpaper tonight.

There is no doubt at all about the power of TV to influence. I am quite certain that the 'knocking' cult originated by that objectionable man David Frost was responsible for the great wave of contempt for established institutions that swept through the nation in the 1960s and has never receded. He discovered a rich seam in which to dig in order to unearth his snide jibes; a profitable source of cheap laughs. While he and his cronies subtly undermined our way of life, created over centuries, making the British giggle at his 'awfulness', he sniggered all the way to the bank. (And now, blow me, he has been given a knighthood and attained the status of a guru!) Other TV personalities quickly cottoned on to his ideas, but these days to achieve anything comparable in shock value they must plumb ever greater depths of dirt and depravity; go Right Over the Top, in fact — ROT! There is a ratchet effect whereby once shown, any act is permissible again, even if it has gone beyond the previous pale. And so on ad infinitum. But to what ultimate end?

* * *

The reason for our unexpected and hasty return from Germany was that someone had broken his neck and thus created a vacancy on a course at the Joint Services Staff College at Latimer, and I got it. And so began seven of the most pleasurable months I have ever spent.

Latimer was commanded by an Air Vice-Marshal, Paddy Menaul, had a tri-Service Directing Staff and took eighty students at a time on its courses — sixty Brits and twenty foreigners. Only this time they were mature men, aged around 37, who had been in charge of various fairly responsible enterprises — like John Slessor, son of the great airman, who had commanded a squadron of Vulcan bombers armed with stand-off nuclear missiles.

The students did in-depth studies of the Soviet Union, of the world balance of power and Britain's part in it, of combined operations, and of the problems arising from trying to divide the defence cake reasonably and effectively between the three Services. We went to sea with the Navy, in my case on

HMS *Tiger*, the cruiser that was soon to be the rendezvous for Premiers Smith and Wilson during their abortive talks about Rhodesian UDI; there was a moment I did not fancy much when I had to make a dash from a door below the bridge to a hole in the deck up near the bow as waves came crashing over it. I decided I would not really have liked to have been a sailor. We went up in the air with the RAF, I to the V-bomber base at Scampton, from whence 617 Squadron had flown its many wartime missions — a closed loop with Group Captain Tate and loadsa money in Rome. (One of 617's tasks was to breach the Mohne Dam, which I had first gazed at in 1964, Alex standing beside me with his head in a red balaclava because he had mumps. Incidentally, the majority of the people who died as a result of the outrush of water from the dam were displaced persons living in forced labour camps downstream of it.) And with the army we went in sub-zero weather into snow-filled slit trenches near Osnabruck, where men from the other services decided they would not really have liked to be in the army. I have a home movie which shows a very cold but broadly smiling black major by the name of Jack Gowon blowing on his hands as Centurion tanks and Armoured Personnel Carriers scrunch up the hill towards us. Jack, much to his surprise, was to become president of Nigeria not long after.

In 1966 Nigeria was divided into three military districts, each commanded by a brigadier. When they deposed the major-general who was acting as president they could not agree among themselves which of them should take over, so they appointed Jack (then a lieutenant-colonel commanding the Presidential Guard) because he was a Hausa from the north but a Christian, not a Moslem, which nearly all Hausas are. He was, therefore, not fully tribally aligned, as the three brigadiers were. They thought that he would be their puppet but he was not, and ruled well until he himself was deposed in a bloodless coup in 1975. He then went to Warwick University to get a degree, and has since dropped out of sight. A nice man.

Not all the overseas students fared so well. One, John Bangura, from Sierra Leone, was on the wrong side of a coup and thrown into prison, was released after a counter-coup and sent to be military attaché in Washington, was ordered home after a counter-counter coup and shot. Happily, no such fate awaited those members of the course who became exalted British personages: Deputy C-in-C of the Central Region of Allied Command Europe then Black Rod in Parliament (John Gingell), C-in-C Fleet (Jim Eberle). The army produced one full general, Jim Glover.

One of the most pleasing things about Latimer was the speed with which we achieved a high degree of accord amongst ourselves. We felt that given the same amount of understanding and good will the world's leaders would soon be able to sort out the mess. However, all that was rudely shattered one morning when Enoch Powell, Shadow Defence Secretary, came to talk to us. In forty-five minutes, as one incensed artillery major told him, he undermined everything many of us had believed in for the last twenty years: he sneered at the special relationship with the United States, denied that there was anything of value in the Commonwealth, pooh-poohed the advance of communism in the world (he was right about that, but for the wrong reasons).

Now it happens that Service officers are usually very polite and respectful to people who are invited as guest speakers. It takes a lot to provoke them into aggressive questioning and yet about fifteen of us stood up, one after the other, and had at Powell. Not that it did any good. From his cold-eyed pinnacle of spurious logic he told us, in scarcely disguised terms, that we were a pack of nincompoops. One of the questions he was asked was: 'Will the Russians not move in to fill the vacuums we create when we move out of such places as Aden?' to which he replied: 'Of course not. The people there don't want them any more than they want us. Such people, like water, will find their own level.' Well, we know whose navy tied up at Steamer Point within months of our departure, don't we, and whose planes took off from Khormaksar? This was not the first or last time I heard him propound what seemed to be a closely argued case based on unanswerable logic only for him to arrive at the wrong conclusion — but presented with such clarity and self-confidence that it appeared sound even when, with hindsight, it was nonsense: like castigating socialism for thirty years and then advocating that Tories should vote Labour in the next election.

I heard Mountbatten again, this time a week before he finally retired. An hour before he was due to arrive all the lights fused in the lecture hall. Consternation! He stood at the lectern flanked by two guttering candles and in the gloom made some very unfortunately phrased references to Africans which, today, would bring prosecution for racism, e.g. 'The problem is to decide whether you are going to fight a nuclear war in Germany or go nigger-bashing in Africa.' Only when the lights went up, presumably, did he see the black faces sitting facing him on the front row.

Denis Healey, Defence Secretary and embarking on the first of the many defence reviews that have followed since 1966, also came and talked down to us. Like an avuncular, red-faced teacher explaining the facts of life to primary-school children the presentation was nice enough but the information was difficult to believe.

And the heads of the three Services came too. James Cassels, the CGS, looking as if he would have much preferred to be back in command of a battalion of Jocks or the Commonwealth Brigade in Korea; the airman and the sailor trying to hide the fact that their horns were locked on the question of whether aircraft carriers should be scrapped or not.

Sometimes, we visited major British institutions: the BBC Television Centre, Heathrow Airport, the Daily Telegraph. We saw a Dalek gathering dust in a cupboard, the dirty ashtrays out of camera shot in the news studio; saw air-traffic controllers doing their vital but boring old thing in front of a radar VDU in the control tower; heard an editor discussing how to reshape the front page because even newer news had just arrived: and the highly overpaid compositors down in the cellar grouped in a corner debating whether to actually print the paper that gave them a living.

We had a ball to end it all and then departed regretfully to sterner business, I to the Ministry of Defence.

★   ★   ★

In August 1965 Aunt (Tia) Jean had died. Her heart had gone and it slowly wound down and finally stopped — before we had had time to realise that this was the end we were hearing about, not just a short remedial stay in hospital. Despite the depredations of the tax man I found myself a few thousand pounds better off. It seemed a good time to buy a house so I looked at a map and at railway timetables and opted for somewhere from whence I could reach Charing Cross station, a five minute walk from Whitehall, within half an hour or so. It turned out to be Sevenoaks, and we moved in just in time for Christmas.

The house was at the top of a cul-de-sac, Croft Way, on the edge of the Green Belt. In one minute we could be in the country, in three in a lush green, sloping field that still bore traces of the Army's presence there in the early 1940s: old telegraph poles with drooping, broken wires strung along the edge of a wood — which may well have been where Basil camped before he went off to sandy North Africa. He certainly must have walked the streets of the little town, and probably had a pint of beer in one of the pubs I went to now and then.

★ ★ ★

Because Poland was behind a heavy iron curtain it was not until I left the Army that I was able to visit his grave in Cracow.

In the process of obtaining my visa I went to see the Military Attaché in the Polish Embassy, which occupies the house once lived in by Field Marshal Lord Roberts of Kandahar. The Polish colonel led me through three layers of security screening into an inner sanctum: into the Chinese Room, in fact, where without a word he opened a cupboard, took out a bottle of vodka, poured two generous measures, handed me one, lifted his glass and said: 'We are soldiers together, we should drink together. Good health!' and downed it in one. At two-thirty in the afternoon. He told me that the Polish authorities would arrange my visit and welcome me in Warsaw but as time passed it became clear that they wanted nothing to do with it; no doubt they thought I would be spying. In the end I went as a private citizen.

Their Sun Went Down Before The Day Had Ended is the title of an article I wrote for The Contemporary Review after I returned from Poland. Here is part of it.

'In my experience Commonwealth War Graves cemeteries are separate, walled-off parts of a foreign field that is forever England, but that is not the case in Cracow. The soldiers, sailors, airmen and civilians who lie there are in a distant part of the biggest civilian cemetery in the city, sharing it with the remains of more than a million Poles — and with several hundred Russian soldiers. However, within that great burial ground our plot looks the same as do our war cemeteries the world over: row upon row of white stone slabs, the whole place dominated by a tall stone cross on which is an inverted steel sword.

The graves register had been removed, so I was unable to tell how many people are buried in that cemetery, but I counted more than five hundred, who died between 1940 and 1945. Men of many religions share the place — mostly

Christians, but also Jews, Moslems, a Hindu and a Buddhist. A gardener of the Imperial War Graves Commission, who died in 1942, lies among the graves he tended, and there are some other civilians there too, caught in the confusion of war. There are a few sailors buried there — captured who knows where? Fished out of the Atlantic, perhaps, only to perish years later — dozens of airmen (many of them Polish) and hundreds of soldiers. They came from the British Isles, South Africa and Australia; from Canada, India and China. And even from Nepal — a Jemadar of the 8th Gurkha Rifles lies there, a long, long way from home. As is Gunner RA Ansell of the Royal New Zealand Artillery, who lies on one side of my brother; on the other, is the body of Private GA Murray of the Gordon Highlanders, who probably came from Aberdeenshire, where our own father was born.

The prisoners must have had a bad time during the summer of 1944 for many young men died — most of them in their early twenties. Some had been taken prisoner at Dunkirk, some in the desert, some in Italy. All had survived for years on poor food and become slowly debilitated, to the point where they had no bodily resistance with which to combat illnesses which young men would normally have shrugged off. One of the few older men who lies there is a colonel of the Royal Army Medical Corps, a veteran of the Great War. He and the few other doctors in the camp would have done their best, but they had few drugs to help them. In general, the Germans treated their British and Commonwealth prisoners reasonably well (it was not through calculated acts of ill-treatment or neglect that most of the British deaths occurred) but other nationalities did not fare so well — more than one hundred thousand of Lamsdorf's prisoners died, most of them Slavs. But as well as malnutrition and lack of medical resources there was another factor that was partly to blame: some of our young men, after years of privation and with no end to the war in sight, gave up hope, and when sickness struck them down turned their faces to the wall and died.

The memory of my visit to the cemetery that lingers most strongly with me is the heartbreak and anguish felt by the bereaved for those who never came back. On one grave a young wife had asked for these words to be inscribed: 'There's never a day goes by when I don't long for you.'

It struck me, too, at the time — as I walked around and looked at every grave there as a sort of tribute, feeling that perhaps some of them had never had a visitor — that these men had given their lives to no purpose. On the grave of an 18-year-old Warrant Officer of the South African Air Force are carved those famous words 'One crowded hour of glorious life, is worth an age without a name.' I wondered, as I stood looking down at it, if he would have agreed. But then two days later I visited Auschwitz, and after seeing that place, which must have been the greatest hell ever contrived by man on earth, I had not the slightest doubt that their lives, wasted though they were in a sense, had not been sacrificed worthlessly.'

I began work at the beginning of January 1966 in the branch of the General Staff that was reorganising the Reserve Army.

The Territorial Army had an establishment of well over a hundred thousand men and women but the numbers recruited were nothing like that. The officers' and sergeants' messes tended to be up to strength because ex-army people like to maintain the connection but there was a dearth of young men in the junior ranks: too many Chiefs and not enough Indians. Also, the structure of the TA was based on a hangover from the war; formed around divisions, but ones which in 1966 had no planned role in the event of war. (While in Yarm I had been with the headquarters of the renowned 50th Northumbrian Division, which was one of them.) There were dozens of under-strength infantry battalions, and scores of Gunner regiments that would never fire a shot in anger. Clearly a sort-out was long overdue.

By the time I arrived in the Staff Duties Directorate it had been decided to cut the strength of the TA to around sixty thousand, to tailor its organisation to meet planned contingencies, and to recruit in those places where there were likely to be volunteers. Also, the Army Emergency Reserve was to be restructured. All this meant a massive reorganisation, which, as you may imagine, brought on apoplexy in many an ancient military body. But the new force would have modern equipment, be better trained and better paid, and have more regular-army soldiers in its units to administer them.

I had hardly begun to get in to my new job when on 7th February, her birthday, my mother died. She had by then moved to a hotel on the East Cliff in Bournemouth with her brother Sam, the twin of Jean. Bet and Sam had never really liked each other much and seldom went out of their way to do more than pass the time of day, but it comforted them to know that their own flesh and blood was close at hand. They both ate like lords and constantly complained about the food; strolled up and down the cliff in the sunshine with their friends and moaned about the weather; wandered down to the Square and said what a dreadful place Bournemouth was ('They don't bury their dead here, they let them walk around.' 'It's Dover for the Continent, Bournemouth for the incontinent!') watched TV avidly and said what a lot of tripe it was. In other words, behaved like normal British human beings.

For most of her life my mother had been convinced that she would die in agony, lingering in pain. In fact, on her seventy-fifth birthday she had a good day, shared a bottle of wine at dinner, played two rubbers of bridge and then went upstairs to bed. In the morning the maid decided to let her have a lie-in, she was sleeping so peacefully . . . If only Bet could have known it would all end peacefully.

I went to see her in the mortuary, kissed her cold forehead, touched her cold hands, wondered where she had gone.

I felt her death very keenly indeed. For all her many faults, the point was that she really cared. She could be cantankerous and on occasion vitriolic, was often irrational and infuriatingly illogical — in other words, typically feminine. But she was very wise and had a lot of character. When she came to visit us at Little Bushey we had a party at which she was the centre of attraction; flirting with Major Narindar Singh of Hodson's Horse, joshing Jack Gowon and holding his hand.

I went to the crematorium for the second time in six months and wondered if they really burnt that expensive, silk-lined, highly-polished coffin or if they whipped the body out as soon as the curtains had closed and used the box again the next day. Then I went back to work.

★   ★   ★

My immediate boss, Giles Mills, yet another old-Etonian, was a Green Jacket, and was married to an American lady, Emily — who was a descendant of General Robert E Lee. He had considerable calm ability and was a pleasure to work for. His boss, the Director of Army Staff Duties, Major-General Michael Carver, was not such a pleasure to work for. He was a Wickhamist who had been commissioned into the Royal Tank Regiment, had been one of Monty's aides during the middle part of the war and had commanded an Armoured Brigade during the crossing of the Rhine — when he was thirty-two. The long journey to his desk in the corner of his office overlooking the Thames seemed to take an age, the return trip was accomplished in a flash. Though he was not a very friendly person I have never met a more able one. The amount of work he got through in a day was astounding.

Broadly speaking, the Director of Staff Duties implements the army's policy as set out by the Director of Military Operations, who follows the guidance issued by the Army Board. In 1966 de Gaulle had called for the withdrawal of NATO forces from France, the army was deeply involved with the insurgency in Aden, with the Defence Review and the TA reorganisation, so there was a lot going on. Carver coped with all this with icy efficiency, issuing a constant stream of direction and guidance, usually on a slip of bumf on which he had summarised a lengthy position paper in three cryptic sentences and added a fourth telling us what to do. The secret was that hardly anything came over his desk twice. Where others would have asked people to comment — say, the Director of Infantry — or set up a working party, he made an immediate decision. This upset some officers who felt insulted if not consulted, but that was too bad: time was, as they say, of the essence.

'The street was similar to those Ben had seen in Crater: a clutter of signs in Arabic and English; tatty shop fronts, some of them boarded up; ramshackle buildings cheek by jowl with more prosperous premises. Home-made Egyptian flags fluttered lazily. There was a hint of wind in the air, and a swirl of dust came round the corner by the mosque. The reserve platoon came into sight at the double and spread out across the street. Orders were given and the men in the front rank began to lean forward. Ben could see the pick helves rising and falling and very slowly the line began to move. The rain of missiles increased and so did the noise level. Suddenly, from somewhere down the street behind him, a shot rang out. A soldier, hit in the back, dropped to the ground with a thud and a clatter of falling equipment. A moment later a grenade was lobbed over a low wall. Ben judiciously took cover behind his Landrover.

The grenade went off with a loud bang and fragments of metal whistled through the air. Two men of the platoon clutched at themselves and doubled up. 'There he is!' Ben's driver shouted as he stood up, pointing over the bonnet: 'Look!'

Quickly scanning the opposite side of the road Ben saw a figure lurking behind an upstairs window. Behind him on the pavement a paratrooper kicked open a door with a crash and dived inside, his boots thumping. The next moment he had smashed an upstairs window with his rifle butt and the next he had fired across the road at the sniper.

There was a pause. Ben's heart was thumping like crazy and his mouth was dry. His 9mm Browning, dragged without thinking from its holster, had found its way into his hand. He eased the safety-catch off.

Suddenly a door in a low wall burst open and three Arabs ran down the street. Before he had time to react the soldier above him in the window fired once, twice, and two of the terrorists dropped to the ground. The third, screaming, dived into a shop. After a few moments its plate-glass window starred then broke; behind the shattering glass Ben saw a man, his arms flung out, fall to the ground.

For an instant everything seemed to be in slow motion and he stopped breathing. When he looked to his left again the troops were on the move and the crowd was falling back. The soldiers were wearing gas masks now, and a grey smoke-haze hung above the crowd. The soldiers broke into a run. The pungent smell of CS gas began to bite at his mouth and nose. The soldier who had killed the two Arabs and wounded the third came slowly out into the street looking white-faced and taut. He walked over to where the bodies lay and stood staring down at one of the sprawled, bloody figures with total disbelief on his face. 'That was pretty good shooting,' Ben said quietly, coming up behind him: 'Copy-book stuff.'

'Aye, it was that, sir,' the man said: 'Just like pickin' off them snap targets on Ash Ranges. Only more excitin'.'

He looked about nineteen.'

At my lowly level I beavered away at organisation and manpower, taking decisions of greater financial magnitude than I was ever to take again at much higher rank. Douglas Miers of the Queen's Own Highlanders was the policy man, a nice Wykhamist with deplorable sartorial taste given to wearing his grandfather's green-with-age bowler and carrying a Mrs Gamp brolly. I was the implementation man, desk-, phone- and committee- bound from morn until night, leaving home at seven thirty and getting back at seven twenty-five. Five days a week I fell exhausted into bed, Saturdays I went shopping, Sundays I worked in the garden. On Mondays the treadmill began all over again. How people do it for thirty or forty years I just do not know. Some don't, of course: they die in the attempt.

Standing on the station platform on my first day I got into conversation with a middle-aged man who told me he had been doing the journey for decades. We crammed ourselves into a train when it arrived, said a few pally words on the journey and then went our different ways. Three days later as I hurried into the booking hall he was lying dead on the floor, his umpteenth sprint for the train having been his undoing. (Wife pottering about in the kitchen washing up the breakfast dishes. Going upstairs to dress. Making the bed. Going downstairs to answer the door-bell. 'Mrs . . . .? I'm very sorry to have to tell that I have bad news. Your husband . . . ')

I came to have great admiration for the much maligned Civil Service. I think few people realise just how hard the senior levels work, how much information they have to absorb in a day, how weighty are the decisions they make. And without company perks or expense-account lunches, either. There were some enormously capable and dedicated men at the top, and the lower levels, too, were conscientious and loyal citizens.

I usually snatched lunch in the Greasy Spoon in the basement of the MoD, sometimes with Dickie Lawson, who was working a few doors further down the corridor. He told me once that his postings branch had assured him it was very unlikely that he would ever get command of a tank regiment — which doesn't say much for their ability to pick a winner.

Another major who worked down the corridor was Peter Inge of the Green Howards, who was to become Chief of the Defence Staff when the airman incumbent became too intimately involved with a titled tart. Twenty-five years after we worked together in the MoD, by then commanding the British Army of the Rhine, he walked into an officers' mess, shook me by the hand and said 'Hello, Peter, how are you?' We had never met in the interim. Meeting him again not long after I asked him if he knew the Army was smaller than at any time since the Peninsular War. He gave me a funny old look and said: 'Yes, but it's got a lot more firepower.' True. But history shows that at the end of the day it's bums on seats that matter. (Inge is now a well-earned Field Marshal and Lord.)

Sometimes, too, rather than risk the MoD food, I would take half an hour off to look at the faces in the National Portrait Gallery. I admired Nelson's admirals greatly, but they came a poor second to Romney's portrait of Emma Hamilton, and the tranquil loveliness of Sarah Siddons. I have always been a sucker for a pretty face.

They were sitting in the cafe in the basement of the Tate Gallery, surrounded by the Rex Whistler mural: in a dream world.

'It's a pity he had to die,' he said.

She looked startled. 'Who?'

'Rex Whistler.' He nodded towards the mural. 'He had a quite extraordinary facility for creative art — for being able to transpose a thought on to paper or canvas. I mean, a lot of artists can paint what they see in front of them but they can't paint a vision.'

'He couldn't,' he said later as they stood in front of an Atkinson Grimshaw of a waterfront at night: wet, cold and foggy, the street lamps sparkling, reflecting in the puddles. You could almost feel the damp air. 'He could only paint what he saw. Sometimes painted over a photograph.'

'Maybe, but what a marvellous talent,' she said. 'He could capture a scene like that wonderfully. It's really beautiful. Fantastic.'

'Just think,' he said, 'tomorrow we will actually have six or seven hours alone together. Isn't that incredible? For the very first time, a few hours alone together.'

* * *

'The bed looks like a battlefield,' she said, sitting up and surveying the scene; half disdainfully, because of the evidence of their love-making, half approvingly, because it proved a lot. She stood up and went over to the bathroom. When she returned he sat up in bed and watched her dressing.

She clipped her earrings on first. 'You do everything backwards,' he said mockingly. She turned and looked disapprovingly at him, an eyebrow raised. 'I mean, earrings should come last. Shouldn't they?'

When she was dressed — made-up, cool, clean and chic again, she came over to him. 'As long as I have my earrings on, I feel fully dressed,' she said, laughing. 'And a dab of perfume, of course.'

★ ★ ★

'What are we going to do?' she asked. They were standing on the bridge over the lake in St James' Park, leaning on the parapet watching ducks dabbling. Beyond the green stipple of leaves painted on a blue sky the outlines of the Foreign Office building and the Horse Guards stood out palely. It was lunchtime, and people were strolling in the sunshine or sitting on deckchairs or on the grass, enjoying the warmth of an English summer's day. The band of the Coldstream Guards was playing selections from Fiddler on the Roof in the stand beside the weirdly-shaped cafe. 'What are we going to do?' Sarah repeated, pressing his hand. She was wearing a little grey tailored coat despite the summer weather because she never felt really warm.

'I don't know,' he answered. 'I just don't know. But there's got to be an answer.'

There wasn't, of course.

As part of my job I became involved with the planning of a major Anglo-American exercise to test the feasibility of monitoring disarmament agreements. It was code-named Cloud Gap and the object of it was to assess whether it would be possible to monitor any arms limitations agreed with the Soviet Union. The British brigadier in charge was Paul Ward, late of the 5th (Northumberland) Fusiliers, who looked extraordinarily like Cruikshank's cartoon of Mr Pickwick — except that never, in my presence at least, did he wear those folded-down riding boots. The conclusion drawn after the exercise had ended was that yes, it would be possible to monitor arms agreements but it would require the very costly deployment of a very large contingent of men all over the Soviet Union. What a prospect! However, like many things this problem was to be solved by the passage of time, for technology soon gave us the ability to photograph what was going on all around the world, even through cloud when there was no gap in it; to such an extent that the words on the page of a newspaper held by an old gentleman sitting in Gorki Park can be discerned from a satellite orbiting high above the earth; there was no need to have people swanning around counting rockets.

There are two more memories that stand

out from those times. One is of attending a conference in the MoD at which the Joint Working Party was to be wound up. This body had been given the task of overseeing the reorganisation of the Reserves and consisted of the Chairman of the TA Council — the Duke of Norfolk — the Vice Chief of the General Staff — General Sir Charles Harrington, lately in command in Aden — and various other people who sat on both sides of the fence. I was there as general dogsbody and secretary.

After the business of the day had been completed one of the members of the Working Party stood up and announced that in order to commemorate the occasion a special tie had been designed. It was blood red in colour and on it there was a motif of carving knives crossed over meat cleavers. The name of one of the hatchet-men (as the TA thought) was Hacket — the Deputy CGS — and the other was Carver. The ties were solemnly distributed, amidst embarrassed smiles and half-hearted clapping, to those on the top table but when Carver came out of the door he thrust his into my hand and snarled 'I don't want to see that again!' I had it framed, and hung it beside my desk.

The other recollection is of being in the Box Party in the House of Lords.

Whenever a Bill is being passed in Parliament the Ministry concerned provides so-called experts to be on call in the chamber while the debate is progressing. If the Government sponsor gets stuck for an answer he sends a flunkey along to the box, where one of those present, he hopes, scribbles the relevant facts on a piece of paper, which is then passed back to him so that he can quote them and get himself off the hook. On this occasion the Minister was Lord Shackleton, actually politically in charge of the RAF but because he was in the Lords, having to speak on all Service bills. I went upstairs to brief him on the subject before the debate and was amazed, not for the first time, at the extent of the knowledge that such people have to absorb in the course of their working day. Looking at him I thought about his father's incredible fortitude during his expedition to the South Pole. His ship *Endurance* had been crushed by pack-ice and twenty-eight men had taken refuge on drifting ice-floes. Shackleton and five others set off in a small boat for South Georgia, 800 miles away. They survived awful hardships, landed on the coast and then walked thirty miles across glaciers to raise the alarm, as a result of which the men waiting on Elephant Island were rescued. Which led my train of thought on to

Amundsen and Scott. And Captain Oates: 'I am just going outside, and may be some time.' I came back to earth, said my piece, then got up and went back to my piles of paper. (Years later I was to hear Beryl Bainbridge speak at the Cheltenham Literary Festival about her novel The Birthday Boys, based on Scott's exploits. She looked a bit dotty and her appearance was not kempt but the talk was utterly enthralling, one of the best deliveries I have ever heard.) On my day in Parliament one of the speakers was Harry Thurlow, Major-General the Right Honourable the Lord, retired; dry, incisive, pertinent.

For me, being present during the passage of the Reserve Forces Act of 1967 was an intriguing experience; for many of those sprawled on the red leather benches it seemed to be an opportunity to catch up on lost sleep while drawing their Attendance Allowance. Nowadays, I imagine the presence of TV cameras ensures that most of the sleeping is done in the library, out of sight of the prying lens.

★　★　★

The TA was not the only part of the army that was going through a period of intense disgruntlement — and it was not the army alone that was discontented; on three occasions in a few months civilians had come up to me and asked, in all seriousness, when the army was going to take over the country and sort out the mess. Within weeks I was to hear an infantry CO say: 'If someone wanted my battalion outside 10, Downing Street tonight, I'd take it there.' We were in the depths of Harold Wilson's dismal premiership, a time when some people felt impelled to try to halt our slide towards mediocrity as a nation.

One day I suddenly thought: for God's sake stop moaning about it and do something; get into politics. So for the second time I went to Smith's Square, from whence I was directed to the Research Department offices, which backs on to Birdcage Walk.

I turned up at the appointed hour and followed the direction indicated by a cardboard pointing finger stuck to a wall. In a brown back room lined from floor to ceiling with dusty copies of Hansard an ancient crone breathed gin fumes over me and told me to sit on a bench and wait. In due course she escorted me to one of those Dracula-coffin lifts which shuddered its way upwards. (I noticed that on the ground floor of the house there was carpeting, on the first floor linoleum, on the second floor bare boards.)

In another small back room I was interviewed by a bright young spark by the name of Bertram Sewell. We got along swimmingly until we arrived at the dire question of the scale of remuneration I would receive were I to join the Research Department, which I knew could be a stepping stone for some — like Enoch Powell! — into Parliament. When he asked me how nineteen hundred a year sounded my shaking hand reached for my bowler hat and I made a hasty departure. Smiling. The cost of educating my small sons was one of the considerations uppermost in my mind. Shades of Arequipa and my father's dilemma.

Mentally, I went back to the army, and a few weeks later to the School of Artillery at Larkhill, to attend a course for future commanding officers.

A lot of gin had been drunk in the mess since I was last in the area gulping lukewarm tea in roadside cafes. I had changed a lot, but so had the army. In twenty years it had been whittled down to a quarter of its postwar size and there were far fewer places to which its soldiers could be sent. On the credit side, it was far more professional, was better equipped, and was manned by people who actually wanted to be in it. In my early days it had been considered rather pushy and bad form for officers to appear too keen; the image presented was all-important, the results achieved less so. But by the late-1960s an intensive training system, geared to promotion — officers had to pass examinations and, if they were to do well, had to be selected for the right courses — plus the onward march of technological progress had changed all that. Computers, electronics, missiles, left a lot of people short-circuited but shocked the rest into mental activity.

Sergeants' Messes and Corporals' Clubs had changed a lot too. In my young days the Sergeant's Mess was often an uncouth working men's club, and if you ventured to an All Ranks dance the odds were that it would end in a drunken brawl, with the Regimental Police arriving with truncheons to break up the party. Now, sergeants wore mess kit, and under it concealed a fit body, for physical efficiency tests had been introduced for everyone. Also, the army insisted that soldiers attained basic standards of education before they could be promoted. The old days of finding six or seven per cent of the intake totally illiterate and literally lousy had gone. It was no longer enough to tell a sergeant to Carry On; most of the people at the receiving end of orders were sharp.

The other side of the coin was that many officers had become very promotion conscious and were desperately disappointed if they did not make it. Where it had once been the summit of ambition to command a regiment or battalion at lieutenant-colonel rank, now a lot of people were miffed if they did not become generals. This attitude injected an unwelcome element of the civilian rat-race into the officers' mess: and not only there; the wives, too, became infected, working hard at socialising the right people and scanning the promotion lists with ill-concealed anxiety. (And, indeed, sergeants' wives did, too: in time I was to hear a woman say that she was going to divorce her husband because he had not been selected to be commissioned from the ranks! But that, clearly, was just an excuse.) I suppose the same sort of thing happens everywhere — in the Diplomatic Corps, Lloyds Bank or the Co-op — but because army rank is so obviously delineated such attitudes seem more blatant. Some people can cope with this nonsense better than others. Sybil was a good wife and mother, hard-working and cheerful, but sometimes lacking in self-confidence, and she found it very trying.

★   ★   ★

300

The course I attended at Larkhill was designed to bring us up to date on the military situation in Europe. The Soviet Union had reached broad parity with the USA in nuclear weapons and their delivery means and had long outnumbered NATO in troops, aircraft, tanks and guns. The only way to stop them from reaching the English Channel, if they felt inclined to try, was by using nuclear weapons. I do not believe that they ever intended to try — covert subversion was a safer option — just as the Americans never intended to march on Moscow: it was a case of mutually assumed distrust, just as mad as Mutual Assured Destruction, the term used to encapsulate the situation that would prevail if ever nuclear war came; smoking, radio-active chaos. It was against this dismal background that I went to Headquarters 2nd Division, which was stationed in Lubbecke, between Osnabruck and Minden, to be in charge of Ordnance services.

Our house was in a row of married quarters built on the lower slopes of the Wiehengebirge, a long forested ridge that runs east and west along the North German Plain. At the Minden end there is a strategically important gap through which the River Weser flows, one which has played a vital part in a succession of dynastic wars. (In 1759 British soldiers, fighting alongside Hannoverians, defeated a French army, achieving what was thought to be impossible: 'I saw,' an eye-witness was to write later, 'a single line of infantry break three lines of cavalry, ranked in order of battle, and tumble them in ruin.' Several British regiments still, rightly, celebrate Minden Day.)

If we went out of the back gate of our garden we could walk for miles along silent woodland tracks — and find ant hills five feet high in amongst the pine cones. I did this now and then to forget about future wars and think about one that had happened a long time ago.

★ ★ ★

When I began to commute daily to London I would buy an evening paper and bury my head in it until I reached Sevenoaks. Then I would hear the same news again on the TV and read it again in the Daily Telegraph on the train going back to London the next morning. I came to the conclusion that this was a pointless exercise, so I began to read books.

The short article I had read about the Hospitallers had plucked a string that still

302

reverberated slightly. And I could see in my mind's eye the Palace in Valetta, with its marble corridors lined with suits of armour that had once belonged to the Knights of St John of Jerusalem.

I went to the headquarters of the Order at St John's Gate in Clerkenwell and to the Ministry of Defence Library and began to delve into historical archives. One book led to another and for the best part of the two years I was in the MoD I read on the train. After a short time I began to take notes and by the time I had stopped fighting for a seat in a crowded compartment I had read eighty-three books about the Order and the Crusades, and filled a sizeable notebook with 280 pages of written and typed facts.

At some point in the compilation of my notes I came to the conclusion that there was a great story to be told about the people who lived in the Holy Land between the Second and Third Crusades, and began to write it; as fiction, because I felt that only in that way could the drama of it be brought back to life. By the time I arrived in Lubbecke I had the outline of a book in my head and was thinking as much about Saladin and Baldwin the Leper King as I was about troublesome track pads on self-propelled guns.

I had to travel a lot in my job, not least

because in a puerile attempt by the Treasury to save DM50,000 a year in foreign exchange one of the Second Division's brigades had been transferred to the Catterick area. (Had anyone figured out, I wondered, what it cost to send the whole brigade to Germany each year on exercise, and staff officers shuttling back and forth constantly, and hundreds of phone calls every day?) In the back of my staff car taking me to visit units in Osnabruck, in planes flying to and from Gatwick, and in the trains taking me to and from Darlington, I wrote a few pages.

I wrote everything in longhand, corrected the previous day's work the next morning (creating a page full of convoluted crossings-out, scribblings and looping arrows that indicated where to insert new blocks of words) and then wrote a thousand more words before lunch. After that I rested the brain by doing other things — except that during the process of writing, especially fiction, it never rests: even in sleep the subconscious is working without the author being aware of it; plotting the next steps in the story, the next exchanges of dialogue.

I had read somewhere that Hemingway worked like that: read his previous day's writing — the act of which brought his brain back on track again — then edited it, then wrote new paragraphs, then read them, then edited them, and so on. It worked well for me, too — and still does.

I had also read that a writer is like a man who pushes a great rock up to the top of a hill, straightens up, stretches his tired muscles then goes down to the bottom of the hill, finds a new rock and begins pushing it, too, up to the top. (Or, if a woman, hoes a five-acre potato patch, I suppose, then starts again!) The analogy of repeated hard labour, however one describes it, is true. If only people knew how much research and thought and work was in store for them the first time they write Chapter One at the top of a clean sheet of paper there would be far fewer writers around. But in blissful ignorance they go on, and then, if they have the determination to keep going, get hooked. It is said that for every thousand people who think they would like to write a book only a fraction of them begin. Of those, only a hundred finish it. Of those, only ten find an agent. And of those, only one a publisher. That too, I am sure, is true. Writing books is not for the easily discouraged.

Anthony Burgess said that a writer never leaves the battlefield: he dies fighting — which is yet another veracious statement. But that is a good thing: there is no such thing as retirement, and wondering how one is going to fill tomorrow's hours. And, for me, writing is not a chore. People have asked if I have to force myself to sit down — presumably because it is a big effort for them to write anything, even a short letter — but when I am well into a book I can't wait to get to my desk each morning.

Apart from my work and my writing I picked up the threads of life in Germany. I went back to Wulfen and stayed with Rolf and his wife Agnes; and heard with regret that Hubert Parasonovic had died. And remembered his 'indigestion'.

Simon and Alex were at this time at prep school at Windsor. They flew to and from Germany in what army people called Lollipop Specials: chartered planes full of children aged eight to eighteen. (The army paid for two trips a year and the parents for the third.) Sometimes I would drive home to see them, and it was on one such trip that I diverted to the battlefield of Agincourt.

Henry V was leading a few thousand bedraggled Englishmen, 'very much wearied with hunger, diseases and marching,' towards Calais and home in a wet October in 1415 when their escape route was barred by a much superior French force. The English were camped at the neck of a V formed by the confluence of thick woods. The infantry cut poles, sharpened them at both ends and then stuck them, slanting forward, into the wet earth in front of their bivouac. As the French knights cantered towards them the next morning, the 25th, our longbowmen let fly repeated volleys of arrows which cut down the horses and their riders. (It's not really 'our' is it? The Scots had nothing to do with it, though there was a man called Edward Mackwilliam there, in the retinue of Sir William Bourchier.) As more and more French knights pressed on they rode over those who had already fallen, until in the end there was a great pile of men and horses six or seven deep, the wounded dying under the weight of those crashing down on top of them. The few who got through that awful barrier of shouting human beings and screaming horseflesh were impaled on the wooden stakes. None broke through. When it was all over more than ten thousand Frenchmen lay dead but only around five hundred Englishmen.

If you visit the place today the woods are still there, in almost exactly the same position as they were then. And the neck of the V. You can almost hear the flight of the arrows and the thunder of hooves, and smell the fear. I picked some of the soil off my boots when I got home and put it in a silver snuff box. Another small treasure.

★ ★ ★

It was while I was with the 2nd Division that I was introduced to BAOR-type exercises. The first of these I was involved in took place in the depths of winter.

After negotiating some icy roads, driving in battle conditions, with only sidelights, and no tail light except for the small bulb that glows over the rear axle to guide following vehicles, we eventually pulled into our designated location. I dropped into my sleeping bag at about three a.m. and awoke again about seven when it was still dark. Putting on a parka I walked across the frozen ground of a snow-covered farmyard and into a gigantic, half-timbered byre, in which were about two hundred cattle, their bodies warming the vast building as though it were centrally heated.

Electric lights up on the beams lit the long rows of beasts in their stalls, who turned their heads to look at me as I walked down the long aisles. In a corner of the byre I found their keeper, a shaggy, misshapen youth, crouched on a pile of straw. He too watched me, with terror in his eyes, his idiot face

308

agape. There was a feeling of timelessness in the scene: it could have been 1768, the date carved on a great beam above the entrance that proclaimed the year in which the byre was built, and the names of the man and his wife who owned the farm at the time — as their descendants did then.

Regularly, our divisional and brigade headquarters deployed into the German countryside and for a week or two 'fought' an imaginary battle, usually without troops but during annual major exercises with the whole complement. In each echelon of command there was always 'one foot on the ground'; officers and men at the previous location would maintain radio contact and control the battle until the new location had been reached and was functioning. Then they would catch up the main party, park up, camp up and fall into sleeping bags in the corner of a barn or under a truck.

The battles were always defensive ones of fire-and-movement, for two reasons. First, because we were theoretically withdrawing under relentless pressure from outnumbering enemy forces; secondly because their electronic counter-measures demanded that our units moved frequently in order to avoid being discovered and zapped, either with explosives or with chemical or nuclear weapons.

It never ceased to amaze me how Germans, for year after year, accepted the presence of our soldiers in their farms and villages with only the occasional protest from an angry farmer. Admittedly, we paid them for the privilege, but only a little, and it could not have compensated people for the general confusion we created.

Members of the Mixed Services Organisation who spoke fluent German would go to a farm or village and give warning that in a few hours the soldiers would arrive; they could not give longer warning because the locations and timings depended on the development of the battle. (On one occasion I was billeted by the MSO in a German household. The owners gave me the best bedroom, and I slept in a great feather bed under a huge duvet, to be awakened in the morning by the man of the house bringing me coffee while his wife prepared a splendid breakfast. Downstairs on the mantelpiece was a photograph of their son who had died in Russia. He was wearing Waffen SS uniform. I was grateful for their kindness and arranged for the local florist to send them some flowers after we had gone on our way.)

Always in the dead of night, because, for real, movement by day would be certain to bring retribution by air attack, our vehicles would move in to farmyards, outbuildings, village halls, taverns. People generally did not get much sleep on account of the night moves. After a few hours rest I would get up, wash, shave, dress and then leave my 'caravan', a tin box mounted on a half-ton trailer. Often, I would find myself under the canopy of a big beech wood — once I was escorted by fireflies up a long path through the woods as I walked alone, trudging through the dead of night, to rejoin my group. Or it could be a richly-smelling farmyard, bustling with activity. Trucks were tucked inside barns or parked under the eaves of farm buildings, with camouflage nets draped over them. Radio aerials sprouted here and there. Soldiers in combat uniform and muddy boots were straggling up the road to where the cook's oil burners could be heard roaring an invitation to hot, sweet tea, bacon and eggs and butties. The offgoing watch could be heard through the door of a box-body truck briefing sleepy oncomers. Drivers were emptying jerrycans of fuel into their vehicles, or were crouched asleep in their cabs. Down the road men, stripped to the waist in all weathers, were shaving and washing out of tin basins. Living, the very act of survival, became a very time-consuming business, especially in winter. Keeping warm, keeping dry, eating, defecating, sleeping, keeping clean, were so much more difficult that one became very conscious of how simple such things are in civilised conditions, and just how much effort is needed if conditions are bad. Even so, nobody, it seemed, ever caught a cold or became otherwise ill. Fresh air, forced exercise, good food, kept us fit.

After an exercise men gave their wives a hard time — depending on how you looked at it. When an exercise ended a potential increase in the population was very likely, for absence in those circumstances certainly made the sap rise. Men would step through the back door of their married quarter (it was SOP that the kids would if at all possible be with a neighbour whose husband had not been on exercise), tear off their boots, peel off layers of smelly clothes and drop them on the floor then rush upstairs with the wife. In due course both would languish for a while in a hot bath before coming down to earth again. (Single soldiers had to wait a while before they could go off and find solace in the local town, though that was not always easy; and, of course, not all of them did.)

I spent two years in the Cross-Keys division. After a while I could tell quite accurately, often within minutes of being with a unit, how efficient it was and what sort of spirit it had. Sometimes the so-called 'crack' regiments lived up to their reputations, sometimes they didn't. It all depended, as I had learned very early on, on the man at the top. I fancy, though, that most of ours, even those not in the premier league, were much better than most of the opposition.

One evening Sybil and I attended the annual function held by Soxmis, the Soviet Mission in West Germany, to commemorate the October Revolution. Soxmis occupied a wired enclosure in the middle of a patch of British officers' married quarters at Bunde. Some of the staff were allowed to have their wives with them and they duly turned up at the Cocktail Party, looking strained but trying to be friendly. Sybil hit it off with one of them and asked her if she would like to visit us at Christmas, to which the woman replied 'I am very sorry but I am going to be ill at that time.' Their 'mess' consisted of two semi-detached houses knocked into one. The British officers, in full Mess Kit, and their wives entered the place between two po-faced Red Army soldiers and were then packed, like commissars in the Kremlin, into two tiny rooms. Vodka flowed like the Moskva: no sooner was a sip taken than a Russian soldier refilled the glass. I and a pretty Grenadier major's wife, Anne Tufnell, sure that the room was bugged, stood under one of the many pictures of the leaders of that luckless land and clearly enunciated very rude comments about their unlovely features. When the geriatric Soviet general was introduced to me he pretended he could not speak English; I say pretended because it is inconceivable that he would have been appointed to the British Sector of Germany if he could not do so. When, rather inanely but for want of other small talk, I asked his eager young interpreter if the general liked being in Bunde, and what he thought of the German countryside, after much confabulation in Russian the answer came: 'My general wants to know what you mean by that question.'

Up against a wall in one of the rooms were two tables loaded with good food, but when at last the vodka-priming, tongue-loosening session had ended and it was intimated that we could eat, there was nothing to eat with; no plates, no knives, no forks, nothing. I have to report that it is difficult to eat caviar with one's fingers. But not impossible.

I left that house and closely-guarded compound despising the people in charge for their stupidity, rigidity of mind and the way they imposed such fear and suspicion on the one or two nice Russian people we had met there. And for thinking we were as stupid as they were.

★ ★ ★

One of my most memorable days while with 2 Div was during a visit I made to Larzac in the Massif Central, where battle-groups — mixed formations of armour, infantry and artillery — were sent each summer from Germany to train. I flew in a Beaver (a single-engine light aircraft of Canadian design) from Bad Oynhausen, via Lyons, to a French military camp not far from Rochefort, where they make the cheese. The Beaver had a Pratt & Witney radial engine that was made in 1929, the year after I was born. It and I were in pretty good shape, considering.

The French army owned a piece of the coastline on the Mediterranean near Montpelier and our soldiers were given three days holiday by the sea after they had completed an arduous spell of training; flogging up and down the hot mountains of the Massif in armoured vehicles, sleeping beside their tracks or in slit trenches. One of the great attractions for them was that the adjoining beach was for nudists, who were required to remove all clothing before they passed the notices that were stuck in the sand. Men, women and children would stop, peel off their clothes and walk on, then find a place and sit down, sunbathe and swim.

On my second day in Larzac I was offered a trip down to the coast in a Scout helicopter that was taking medical supplies down to the camp. We flew up, up and away over very rugged, impressive countryside, all brown and green and gold, dotted with ancient walled villages that had been built by the Templars in medieval times. Then along the coast for a mile or two, slowly descending until we flew across the nudist beach to land on the dunes behind the little camp of army tents — stirring up the sand and the ire of the sunbathers. By the time the rotors stopped the chopper was surrounded by hordes of mostly naked French children, pointing and staring and chattering — and wondering who this immensely senior officer was who had his own helicopter. I spent two hours lying in the sunshine and swimming every now and then in a pair of army PT shorts, and then was flown back. For a few hours I had known what it must be like to be one of the jet set.

As an insight to human nature, beside me on the beach were a young French couple in their twenties, both very handsome. He sat with a pair of binoculars glued to his eyes watching the naked girls on the adjoining beach while beside him, almost totally ignored, and almost totally naked, lay his gorgeous girl. For him, the grass was much much greener twenty yards away.

The next year when I went to Larzac I toured the Rochefort cheese 'factory' with a group of officers of the Royal Scots. The place where the cheese is manufactured consists of layer upon layer of caverns in the rock, each of them subtly different in temperature and humidity. The cheeses start off low down and are then brought slowly higher and higher, week after week, until the mould has grown and spread and the cheese is ripe. Nowadays, the mould is cultivated then sprinkled on to the cakes of cheese, entering holes made in them by something that looks like a large version of the spiked objects used to hold flower stems at the bottom of a vase. The original mould had grown naturally in fissures of rock in a cave in which a local farmer stored his home-made goat's milk cheese. It accidentally infected the cheese and he liked the taste — or perhaps it was his thrifty wife who tried it first. Anyway, some of their neighbours did, too, and out of this serendipitous discovery grew the sizeable industry that now exists. So much so, that today they have to import goat's milk from

North Africa and Italy to satisfy the demand. After we had trudged through the caves we were taken to a reception room, given champagne and then sent on our way with smiles and waves — but with no free cheese. The story of Rochefort has a parallel with that of Mateus Rosé wine.

In 1969 Sybil and I went to Madrid to stay with the British Air Attaché, John Slessor, and his wife Ann. While there we met John's cousin Fernando Calavarez, whose uncle runs the Mateus wine business. Like the Rochefort cheese, the original wine began in a small way in a small vineyard but now is blended from grapes that are brought in from many different places, its chemical consistency checked carefully against the first formula.

I loved Madrid and Toledo, and marvelled at the truly fantastic, awe-inspiring cathedral which, on Franco's orders, was carved out of a solid dome of rock some thirty miles west of the capital to commemorate the dead of the Civil War. The cross on top of the mountain in the Valley of the Fallen — which is in effect on top of the dome of the cathedral inside it — is so big that a bus could stand on one of its outstretched arms, and dominates the countryside for miles around. The Prado's Velasquez' and Goyas are astounding, but so was the beauty of the Spanish women, the vitality of the city and the food (weird but tasty seafood — brought nightly all the way from the coast two thousand feet up the hills to Madrid — steaks straight out of the bullring, rich Rioja wine). Apart from the quixotic charm of its old streets Toledo has stayed in my memory because of the story of the commander of its garrison during the civil war who traded the life of his son, held by his opponents, for the security of the fortress, the Alcazar, in which he and his troops were besieged.

★ ★ ★

Another memorable occasion was, late one evening in a gastatte, sitting in warm comfort after a hard day, playing a rubber or two of bridge with my general, Chandos Blair, and two other officers and bidding, and making, a grand slam in No Trumps on the first hand of the evening. After that, every hand played was an anti-climax. Even great moments have their down side.

Major-General Chandos Blair, then commander of the 2nd Division, is one of the men on the list of much admired senior officers I have met. Like Harry Thurlow he had been in the Seaforth Highlanders. Like him he had had a gallant war: captured with the 51st Highland Division at St Valery, winning the Military Cross, escaping, rejoining his regiment, fighting with it in North-West Europe. Unlike him, he was approachable, energetic and looked like Goya's portrait of the Duke of Wellington. His wife Audrey was also full of character and with her, and her daughter Susan, Sybil and I made a second visit to Berlin.

We did the rounds of the usual sights again but this time also went to a svelte night club called the Red Rose, under the revolving Mercedes star at the top of the Kurfursten-dam, where Angie Le Bubbly did a very exotic dance, contorting and jerking her lovely body in very realistic eroticism. (I really don't want to try to imagine what she looks like today.) Chan Blair was thrown while riding one day, hurt his back badly, was taken to the British Military Hospital at Rinteln, walked out after one night, went home, rang me to ask if I had any books he could borrow and suggested that I come to his house to play bridge. He sat at a table with the sweat of agony starting out on his forehead, played two or three rubbers then announced that perhaps that was enough for today. I and the Commander Royal Artillery, Tony Richardson, and his wife left him to it. (Audrey was in England at the time.) It was an extraordinary example of the power of mind over matter.

Chan Blair went from Germany to be the Defence Services Secretary in the Ministry of Defence, responsible for, among other things, briefing the monarch regularly on matters concerning the armed forces. I imagine she looked forward to his company. He it was who was sent to negotiate with Idi Amin at the time when that jumped-up sergeant was making life hell for people in Uganda. Chan had known him when they served together in the King's African Rifles. Idi kept him waiting for hours in the sun in full dress uniform then had him enter his presence through a door so low that he had almost to crawl in order to get through it. Just to show who's boss, now, mastah.

★   ★   ★

We went on holiday to Denmark, to Aarhus, where one day, alone in the magnificent brick cathedral, I heard a man playing the organ with enormous feeling and panache. I sat enthralled as the music rolled up and around the lofty ceiling: Bach at his best. That is one memory of Denmark during that visit — the music thundering out and shaking me and the building. Another is of my small sons standing with their eyes bulging looking at other sorts of organs on multi-coloured display beside sweeties and beach buckets. Pornography had just been legalised and the shops were full of it; at the border on the way back into Germany long queues of men stood with their tongues hanging out waiting to buy magazines from the porno-kiosks. For my part, there is a time and place for everything, and no inherent beauty in the human reproductive organs. The mast of the Good Ship Venus standing upright beside a packet of cornflakes strikes a jarring note.

One weekend Rolf and his wife Agnes came to stay with us in Lubbecke. Towards the end of a long night of food and drink and talk, after the wives had gone to bed, Rolf suddenly asked: 'Peter, do you think we Germans are the worst people in the world?' I stared at him, then told him the truth: 'I think the things you did during the war were the worst acts in the history of the human race. Other dreadful things have been done in the heat of battle, or because people were barbarians, knew no better and it was part of their way of life, but there has never been such evil, calculated brutality.' He nodded and his eyes filled with tears. Then he stood up, shook my hand, said good night and went upstairs.

What I said was true, but soon we would hear of Pol Pot's Killing Fields in Cambodia. Human beings are easily led. Given the lead, some people will happily kill. We should recognise that fact and not pretend that it is an aberration from normal behaviour. In our backgrounds there are a few hundred years of pretty women wearing ball gowns, scent and dangling earrings but a million years of people having their brains beaten out with wooden clubs.

★   ★   ★

Our two year tour was over and it was time to go home again. By then, as a family we had moved ten times in fourteen years. This was by no means exceptional for people in the army but somewhere at the root of my mind there was an itch to settle down. There were other signs too, though I did not recognise them for what they were.

For one thing I had done some sculpting in the cellar of our house in Albert Schweitzer Strasse; a nude, sitting figure of my wife to put beside the heads of my two small sons that I had done when we were at Wulfen. It made a good talking point at cocktail parties. (It was while I was working on the moquette that I looked out of our narrow semi-basement window one evening and saw my neighbour, the Colonel General Staff, Roger Chandler, sitting out on his patio, apparently relaxing after a day at his desk. When I went upstairs twenty minutes later Sybil told me he had just been taken away in an ambulance. Five hours later he was dead. It seems that he had nourished a stomach ulcer for a long time but had never declared it, being concerned that if he did he would be medically downgraded and lessen his chances of promotion. It had perforated almost as I looked at him, and he died in the local krankenhaus.) For another, I had hired a tinny piano, at which I would sit for an hour or two each week. Also, my novel was all but finished. All I needed was a title. Then one Sunday I found it during morning service in our little garrison church: The Hope of Glory, taken from the Book of Common Prayer. I read: 'We thank thee, Lord . . . for all the blessings of this life; for the means of grace and the hope of glory.' It seemed very appropriate for a book about soldier monks fighting a crusade.

9

Bumf...

I went back to the Ministry of Defence, to be in charge of the military element of the Secretariat that served the Quartermaster General, one of the members of the Army Board. The civilian part of it dealt primarily with money matters and was under the control of John Levinson, a Principal. Both parts were headed by an Assistant Secretary, at first John Blelloch (who was to become the Permanent Under Secretary, the top-ranking civil servant in the MOD), later Ian Petrie.

As one would expect, the generals who constitute the Board almost without exception come from the so-called Teeth Arms, the fighting regiments of the army. In those days they would have commanded a regiment/battalion, a brigade, a division — usually one in Germany — and then gone on to higher things, for example, command of BAOR or the United Kingdom Land Force, before achieving Board status. (The whole composition of the Army has changed since those times: there are fewer divisions, no BAOR, and so on.) The generals have usually known each other for years: possibly attended the same courses, worked as staff officers together in the same formations. They form a very exclusive club: a group of highly talented soldiers who generally get on together without rancour. Just once in a while a maverick will get to the top; someone like Michael Carver, who was so capable that no-one could figure out how to stop him but who was sometimes out of step with some of the rest — as he would no doubt agree, that being the title of his autobiography. Equally, some who might be thought capable of reaching such an eminence do not do so because they are incapable of fitting in; one such was a senior general, a scholar and possessor of a very good mind (he wrote a book about the Third World War) who nearly made it but was thought by his contemporaries to be too clever by half.

My boss was an infantryman by the name of Tony Read, who had taken over from Lord Thurlow in Yarm. The Chief of the General Staff, Carver, had been in the Royal Tank Regiment, the Adjutant General, John Mogg, was, like Read, from the Oxfordshire and Buckinghamshire Light Infantry, the 43rd and 52nd of Foot, by 1968 the 1st Battalion of the Royal Green Jackets. The Master

General of the Ordnance, responsible for the procurement of equipment, was John Thomas, the Sapper who had been my colonel at Minley Manor, and the Vice-CGS was 'Monkey' Blacker, a cavalryman who had been Carver's deputy when Carver was Director of Army Staff Duties. (Carver had shot up the promotion ladder since 1965, in the meantime commanding the Far East Land Forces in Singapore.)

It happened that I had worked for four out of the five members of the Army Board, the exception being Sir John Mogg. As far as I know General Read did not ask for me to go to his Secretariat, but on the other hand he did not object when my name was proposed by the Military Secretary's Branch which controls officer postings. (In the 1930s Mogg had been deputed to meet Read at the railway station when he first reported for duty with his battalion after being commissioned. Having served together for years they ended up as generals on opposite sides of the Seventh Floor of the MOD. I would occasionally be standing in Read's office when the door would be flung open and Mogg would enter. 'What nonsense are you perpetrating today, Read?' he would ask. 'Bugger off, Mogg,' would come the reply.)

The army is part of the Tri-Service MoD

organisation, which has two supremos: the Defence Secretary, appointed by the Prime Minister, and the chief Serviceman, who comes in turn from the Navy, Army or Air Force. In my day each service also had a Minister of State. Heading the Civil Service element of the ministry was the Permanent Under Secretary, who was a member of the Chiefs of Staff Committee — then, Sir Ned Dunnett. Each service board had a Deputy Under Secretary (the Army's was a man called Montgomery, who died of a heart attack after an Army Board dinner. Surely the food wasn't that bad?) and each Board member was assisted by an Assistant Under Secretary, who had under him his Chief of Secretariat. Thus the activities of the three services were monitored by both Parliament and the nation's administrators. (Years later Dunnett appeared in court accused of soliciting in a public lavatory. The mental image invoked does not bear thinking about. What dire compulsion is it that makes a married man with a family, loaded with achievement and honours, degrade himself in such a way?)

When I arrived in April 1969 Dennis Healey was still the Secretary of State and Roy Hattersley was the Army Minister. Admiral Hill-Norton, known to some as

Hoggs-Norton, was the Chief of the Defence Staff. The politicians were soon to change. One day I went to brief Roy Hattersley about a major item of army expenditure. A few weeks later he was no longer in office, all the panoply of power — the Private Office with its obsequious staff, the deference accorded him by his peers, the shiny, chauffeur-driven limousine, the high view over the Thames — all gone. And his salary slashed. Geoffrey Johnson-Smith replaced him, much given, so I was told, to studying his reflection in the mirror beside the door of his office.

When a General Election is due the Board members in all three Services produce a detailed brief which sets out the principal ongoing business. Because the opinion polls had all forecast the return of a Labour administration these tended to assume that our theme would remain much the same, even if our ministers moved in time to the music. In the event, Edward Heath was returned and Lord Carrington became the Secretary of State, the latter a very direct gentleman who had earned a Military Cross during the war serving with the Guards and had also acquired a soldier's vocabulary. (One morning a major in my office announced that he had come up in the lift with Lord Carrington. When I asked if they had exchanged pleasantries the answer was 'Well, I suppose you could say that. I said Good Morning and he said 'Get out the fucking way, I'm in a hurry.' ')

The first thing the new administration did was to cut — if memory serves me right — £700m from the defence budget in order to finance pledges they had made in their election manifesto. One cannot help but wonder why they had not costed things a mite more accurately all round. But then, that is not the name of the game. The defence ship of state veered on its course.

That paints the general picture. The detail was much more mundane. I worked in a poky office on the seventh floor on the Whitehall side of the building. (In my previous incarnation there I had been on the fourth floor on the other side, looking out on to a dismal, pigeon-infested courtyard.) The adjoining office on one side contained two majors, my assistants, who seldom stopped scribbling, and on the other, three officers who seldom stopped talking — the QMG's Military Assistant, Bob Pascoe (who, predictably as far as I was concerned, would one day become a not very notable Adjutant General), Read's Aide-de-Camp, a benign youth who accompanied the general on visits, and an officer commissioned from the ranks who washed the teacups and made the occasional phone call to get QMG's car to the door.

My job was to produce written briefs for the QMG on all Army Board business, all QMG business — that is to say, army logistics — and on matters concerning the tri-service Principal Administrative Officers Committee, of which QMG was a member: in fact, on every subject that concerned the army. QMG had six major-generals under him: a Vice-QMG, a Deputy (Bob Britain) and four Directors in charge of Army Quartering (John Cowtan), the Royal Corps of Transport (Peter Blunt), the Royal Army Ordnance Corps (Alex Young) and the Royal Electrical and Mechanical Engineers (Peter Girling). I also briefed the current VQMG on equipment matters (he was a member of an MGO committee), in my time successively two major-generals from the Royal Corps of Signals — the first a gay old dog by the name of Price who looked a bit like Maurice Chevalier, and the second a large dolourous man by the name of Hancock, who was more of a hangdog. (Price told me one day that he had just been out to buy his last suit: he was fifty-five, and in his mind impending retirement cast a dark cloud over his future. I fancy he has bought several more since then.) I also went across the road fairly regularly to keep the DGMG — at first in the Old Admiralty Building, later in the Old War Office Building — aware of what was going on in the main building. In addition, I sat in as secretary at all QMG's oral briefings, and when he had VIP visitors: the CGS of the Iranian army (I wonder what happened to him when the Ayatollah came to power?), top American generals, and so on. (One of them, General John R. Deane Jnr, recounted how he had been a battalion commander in Berlin when the Wall went up. 'Man, nobody knoo what to do! I told my general: 'Tear it down as fast as they put it up, surr,' but he shook his head. 'I can't,' he said: 'I want to, but I can't. It's all too political.' ' 'I have to tell you,' Deane went on, 'my general aged ten years in two days. His hair went white.')

Mine didn't, but it was a busy job. Almost as busy as the QMG's, but the pay was not as good. I worked like a convict on a chain gang but, as always, there were lighter moments. Like the day I went in to a major-general's office and found him and another man crouched over a street map of Belfast holding a small piece of forked wire over it. When I asked what they were doing I was informed that they were dousing for terrorists. Whether his twitching wire ever revealed one, I do not know. Another light-hearted interlude was a very long lunch at the Guards Club with that Coldstream peer I referred to at the beginning of the book — the fellow with a poor opinion of horses; then Lieutenant-Colonel The Lord Alvingham, later to be a major-general. We sank deeper and deeper into leather armchairs as we drank glass after glass of Port until we reluctantly decided there was nothing for it but to take a taxi back to work. As we arrived at the main entrance of the MoD the first of the worker bees were departing in a swarm down the steps. I sat in my office trying to focus on a calendar on the wall and then, finding I couldn't, panicked and made a run for home, eventually reaching it in a deplorable state. 'What's the matter with Dad?' Simon asked. 'Oh, he's not feeling too well,' Sybil replied: 'He's gone upstairs to have a little rest.' It had slowly dawned on my fuddled brain that it would just not do to stand gently swaying and grinning inanely at one of the members of the Army Board should he decide to send for me.

I can only plead in extenuation of this reprehensible behaviour that my companion on that occasion (whom I had been in syndicate with at the Staff College) also worked hard, and that our break-out happened towards the end of a two year stint in the place. The next morning Tony Read asked me, with a twinkle in his eye, if I had had a good lunch. (Actually, the lunch was not as good as the Port, but was enlivened by the presence of a number of rather worn-out looking Guards officers who had spent the morning in a high-class brothel in Mayfair which was staffed, so they said, by some really classy-looking Chinese bints; and by a bucolic-looking retired colonel whose foot was in a sling and who alleged he had been trodden on by a cow. 'A cow?' sniffed Guy Alvingham. 'A cow? You surely mean a horse, Archie? Not a cow.')

After doing his tour of duty in the MoD General Sir Anthony Read, GCB, CBE, DSO, MC became Commandant of the Royal College of Defence Studies and then, in retirement, Governor of the Royal Hospital. Those old soldiers the Chelsea Pensioners, who brighten the streets of London with their scarlet coats, could not have had a better man to look after them. In all the time I worked for him I never saw him ruffled or ill-tempered, never saw him fail to smile and be courteous. I could not say the same for myself. It made my blood boil to see the long-term future of the army so often jeopardised to make paltry short-term gains; to see years of planning go into the waste-paper basket because strikes and low productivity in industry made a nonsense of Treasury estimates and resulted in cuts in the defence budget.

I find it difficult to remember much about what I did in the Ministry during the two years I was there. This is partly because such was the volume of work that passed over my desk that most of it did not have time to register: I edited, re-shaped and honed information into intelligible briefs that were fed in to my general as if on a conveyer belt. It was also partly because the human brain seems to have a shutter that comes down over things one does not wish to remember. For example, I spent six months in a large Ordnance depot working on what was known as provision; the monitoring of stock and the topping-up of holdings. Every day I had to check the mathematical data and trends on hundreds of record cards that emanated from the pens of dozens of German clerks, men and women, who beavered away with bent heads at rows of desks in a long, stuffy, ill-lit, orange-coloured room. These days the task is done much more efficiently by computers, but in the '60s Mr Quill still sat scratching on his high stool. I walked out of that place without a backward glance and the shutter slammed down. Three years later I received a phone call from someone who clearly knew me well; the trouble was, I had not the faintest idea who he was. Then as he prattled on I realised that I had shared an office with him, poor chap, every working day during those six months. No wonder mass-production workers go on strike: they need to have some days in their lives that are memorable, some days when they have a sense of mattering — a sentiment that lies uneasily with the one at the end of the last paragraph, but surely it must be possible to achieve productivity and self-esteem at the same time.

I do remember, though, that the ongoing theme in the Ministry was cut-backs. There was no money. The phrase 'Not in this financial climate,' which I first heard as a young captain in the 1950s, epitomises for me, as much as any other, the post-war decline of our nation and its army. During the Suez crisis Harold Macmillan made the remark that 'if we are not careful we will end up like the Dutch,' meaning that we would become a small nation with little influence in the world. Well?

But back to the Ministry . . . The system was that Army Board papers were sponsored by the Director of the branch concerned and presented by the appropriate Board member. For example, VCGS might present a paper sponsored by the Director of Training on the need to develop Suffield in Canada as a battle-group training area to replace Larzac, which the French would no longer allow us to use. (When in 1968 I had asked a French colonel how it was that General de Gaulle permitted the British to drive tanks, guns and trucks hundreds of miles through France to the Massif Central he said, with a lift of his shoulders and a big grin: 'We do not tell 'im.' I suppose he found out.) Or QMG might present a paper sponsored by the Director of Ordnance Services.

Papers would then be tabled on the agenda for a Board meeting. We in the Secretariat would ask all interested parties to comment, and on a walkabout would ascertain the reaction of other Secretariats. Then we would write a brief setting out the background to the paper, add the comments of Directors and incorporate any 'feel' there might be in the Ministry. Just prior to the meeting QMG would hold a discussion briefing, and would thus attend fully prepared.

The Head of Secretariat, John Blelloch, an Oxford graduate, possessed great powers of analysis. When at the end of an oral briefing QMG would ask him to sum up he would do so with unerring accuracy, and then indicate what he considered to be the proper course of action. It was no surprise to me that he went on to achieve great distinction and a knighthood. Ian Petrie, on the other hand, had risen from the ranks. He had begun life as a lowly Administrative Officer but had been repeatedly promoted in recognition of his ability, and despite the fact that in his time it was almost impossible to make the big leap from the clerical to the administrative grades of the civil service. He could write concise briefs in superlative English but lacked the self-confidence to make his mark to the same degree as Blelloch. He was, however, a warm, humorous and kindly man, devotedly served by a secretary, Liz, who had followed him from post to post for years.

However well presented and justified, a case might be dismissed by the Defence and Overseas Policy Committee for reasons we were not made aware of — conflicting demands for available funds between Ministries, or sudden changes in foreign policies, say. And always in the background there was the Treasury. Like a tired juggler dropping a ball now and then it would cancel this or postpone that: not directly, of course; decisions to make another financial cut-back came through the Cabinet to the Secretary of State, but the effect was the same.

★　★　★

Though such matters took up nearly all my waking hours they were overlaid on normal family life. We were again living in Sevenoaks and my sons, aged thirteen and eleven, had gone to a minor public school in Kent. Their characters had not changed markedly from the time of their infancy. Simon was an especially handsome boy but felt the injustices of life keenly. It was not in his nature to temporise — he had to be convinced or persuaded — but quite often he was harshly made to toe the line by a short-of-time or short-of-patience schoolteacher, or by bigger boys in the school. Alex was, in contrast, very appealing looking, had a warm, loving nature and was liked by everyone. He drifted, smiling, through life. They were both highly intelligent, as has been proved over the years, but where one needed painstaking encouragement, the other needed prodding into greater activity. Neither was handled correctly. It seemed as if the boys who posed no problems to the school sailed along but anyone who demanded extra care or time was a nuisance. It seemed as if the gladiators — the star batsmen or try-scorers, or the one who might make Oxbridge and thus glorify the school — had to be the recipient of all the plaudits, while never a pat on the back went the one who, in the beginning, had stood with an eager expression on his face waiting for a smile and a word of encouragement.

It is evident that I have little time for the teaching profession. At primary school Simon was frequently forced to eat badly-cooked carrots, which he loathed. He would then go to the lavatory and vomit. In the end Sybil made plastic linings for his pockets so that he could spirit the carrots away while the young virago in charge was directing her nasty attentions towards another child. At prep school his housemaster once told me that one of his plump charges was 'A silly young ass, quite useless except for digging my garden.' Did he refer to my sons in a like manner to other parents? At the public school living conditions were appalling — far worse than in any barrack room — the food uneatable, the discipline lax at a time when the flower-power people were infecting the country with their love of drugs and anarchy. Schoolteachers did not know how to react, but generally tried, mistakenly in my view, to be liberal and go along with the sloppy trend. See where that has got them.

One might well ask why, in these circumstances, I took no action to change things? The upheaval of transferring them to another place might have done more harm than good: at least they had a circle of friends. And would another place that they joined late have been any better? As to sending them to a day school, which would in many ways have been preferable, we were sure to move again. It was not a tenable option.

In the event, both my sons overcame the fact of being academically impoverished when they left school. As a boy, Simon went to sea with the navy, flew from Manston with the RAF, shot at Bisley with the army. He hitch-hiked across Canada when he was seventeen, worked with the Rhodesian Police for a while, and for a few months was Second Mate on a tramp steamer plying between the Cayman Islands and Florida, though what he knew about seamanship could have been written on a postage stamp. (All the more credit to him.) Already he has a lot to look back on, including having once been a member of one of the most elite regiments of them all. He is a successful author, with half a dozen fine books to his credit, and now, after taking a late degree, teaches War Studies at a university. Alex is totally dedicated to his art, prepared to spend most of his income on buying materials for his ongoing work; prepared to do without the things other people regard as essential in order to do what he regards as essential. He paints fine portraits and pictures, has won prizes at the National Portrait Gallery and exhibited in several prestigious galleries. While his brushes make strokes with incredible skill his mind goes questing in all directions. He is very knowledgeable, full of fun as well as wisdom, and is a stimulating companion to be with. It is a pity their path was so unnecessarily pitted with potholes along the way.

I think the problem teachers have is their sense of power. They are so used to obedience, to Yes sir, No miss, that they begin to believe in their omnipotence. It takes a good and rare man or woman to deal with each child as a unique individual. I have not encountered many Chipps off that old block called education. Strangely enough, for many people would expect otherwise, I do not think military men have a power complex. They are obeyed, yes, but they are dealing with mature men whose character has been moulded. You cannot today — indeed you never could, since 1918 — expect unquestioning compliance as of right. This tempers the approach in a way that teachers do not have to consider.

★   ★   ★

Because I was so heavily committed The Hope of Glory had to take a back seat for a while but eventually I polished it up and decided it was time to push it gently into the stream and see if it would float.

In Germany I had met an author by the name of Alexander Fullerton, who was a relative of Audrey Blair, Chandos' wife. He gave me the name of a literary agent friend of his and I took this gentleman to an expensive lunch at Simpsons in the Strand. He uttered a few platitudes and in return for his cut off the joint on the trolley agreed to read a chapter or two of my book. After a few days I received his comments.

His first suggestion was that I should rewrite it as non-fiction. Fiction was terribly difficult to sell, he wrote; it would be better to do it all again. Having just completed seventy thousand words of fiction and spent two years doing it, that suggestion put great strains on my good will. He went on to say my manuscript showed promise but he deplored the use of three full stops at the end of a sentence to suggest that the reader should draw his own conclusions . . . I had already drawn mine when I saw the quality of his shirt and suit, which indicated that he was not a successful agent.

I put the book aside again and

concentrated my efforts on the daily word-processing grind. Then I had a thought: the story would make a marvellous film. (So it would.) I sent it off to a film company in Wardour Street in London and waited. And waited. And waited.

My authorship came about as the result of the bloody-mindedness of Mr Ray Buckton's train drivers.

The train service from Sevenoaks to London was deplorable at the best of times — smelly, non-corridor stoppers or slightly less smelly less frequent non-stoppers that began at Hastings and were full by the time they reached Sevenoaks. One morning ASLEF flexed its hide-bound brain and declared one of its many go-slows, with the result that I reached my office late and not in the best of tempers. The morning did not go well, and by lunchtime I was gently simmering. I decided to phone Film Rights and was fobbed off yet again by a patronising young popsie who would have greatly benefited from a smacked bottom. Since I was not in a position to administer the improvement I did the next best thing and gave her a sharp blast down the phone. She hurriedly put me through to her boss and he got an earful, too. Strangely enough he melted like butter, apologised profusely and

344

said that a reply would be in the post in the next day or two. It was, and in it he agreed that the story would make a great film but that unfortunately it would cost about ten million bucks; he thought it wouldn't stand a chance unless it had been published first, and had taken the liberty of sending the manuscript off to a friend who was a literary agent. That gentleman, Michael Thomas of AM Heath, accepted the book and found a publisher within days, which only goes to show that bad temper sometimes brings results, and that even bloody-minded train drivers have their uses.

In 1971 I returned to the scenes of my boyhood for a brief visit. Sybil and I went to stay with my brother and his family, then living in Bramhall, Cheshire. Brian had tried various money-making schemes but had not been very successful with any of them; as had been the case with his father, hope triumphed over experience — and, like him, he trusted people too much. Hard as he tried, the expected good results never materialised. Yet he seemed happy, his disappointments largely offset by the reciprocated warm affection of his family. One day I borrowed a car and drove over to Helsby.

Orchard Croft had vanished, and where it had stood, and in its orchard and garden, five houses had been built. I stared aghast and then called on a one-time neighbour who told us that developers had strung great hawsers around the house then attached them to a bulldozer, which had heaved and heaved until the whole structure collapsed inwards in a great pile of rubble and dust. What a shocking waste. All that carved oak and teak and decorated plaster work. And the big mahogany throne-like loo that sat on a wooden pedestal two steps up from the floor.

In 1971 we took a holiday in Scotland, going there by moto-rail and renting a cottage at Lagan, near Kingussie in Invernesshire. I took Simon and Alexander fishing on the Spey, once on the edge of a quicksand; it was only as we were leaving that we noticed, painted roughly on the rock behind us, a sign warning people of the great danger of venturing near the place. Maybe that impish spirit was in attendance again, keeping an eye on things as she did on the day I did not press that button and blow the soldier to pieces on the demolition ground . . .

We loved the scenery in Scotland and the warm friendliness of the people. I felt as if I had been there before, and Glencoe in particular had an atmosphere for me — but perhaps it was only my imagination. At Lagan Bridge we climbed a mountain called the

Black Crag and found the remains of a Pictish fort where the local water-bailiff, another Macdonald, had told us it would be. They must have been hardy people, those Picts, living up there in the dead of winter with only a scrap of food and fire for sustenance, and a plaid draped over their bones to keep body and soul together. But not, of course, for long; they died in their thirties. Shivering, no doubt.

There are some five million Scots in Scotland, just a fraction of those scattered around the world. In that respect they are like the Irish, of whom there are around five million in the whole of the emerald island and nearly twenty million in the United States alone, mostly Roman Catholics — and therefore pro the IRA, about which more later. The highland clearances did for one what the potato famine did for the others.

The Scots who are left in Scotland strike me as a mite smug. Like the Welsh they have an inferiority complex that impels them strongly to assert their nationalism. To my mind — and I won't get any gifts of haggis at Hogmanay for saying so — they make themselves ridiculous with their insistence on flaunting the Harry Lauder image. The vision of a whisky-sodden ass reeling around whooping like a Red Indian around a totem pole and asserting that Glasgow belongs to him makes me cringe. And would be regarded with scorn by his highland ancestors if they could see it. Clan tartans, for one thing, only reached their present complexity in Victorian times, and with them all the paraphernalia that surrounds them — dirks and sporrans and bonnets and feathers. The hard men of Culloden would be horrified to see their modern image, I'm sure.

* * *

One of the few nice things about my office on the seventh floor of the MoD was that I had a view across Whitehall to the Horse Guards building and the London skyline beyond. On state occasions I could open my window and gingerly step out on to a narrow flat roof and watch the procession passing below: the jingling sparkling escort of the Household Cavalry; the open carriages with their resplendent gold-liveried coachmen and out-riders; the lines of flags fluttering along the route; the troops, scarlet, immaculate and rigid lining the road. It was good, too, to feel at the centre of things and be able, in some small way, to do my best for the soldiers who were doing their best in Belfast, Belize and Berlin, but all the same I was glad to be on the move again when my two years were up.

I was to go as a full colonel back to the ammunition world, still in the Ministry of Defence but in one of its out-stations. Before taking up my appointment I was sent on a bomb disposal refresher course at the Army School of Ammunition. I was brought up to date on developments, shown — and used — the equipment we were using to deal with bombs, and introduced to the people who were doing the training. Then I went to the Inspectorate of Land Service Ammunition.

10

...and bombs

For a number of reasons, some professional, some personal, my stay in Didcot turned out to be one of the worst episodes of my life.

The pressure of work was less than I had experienced in Whitehall but there were two sharp edges to it: one was that some decisions were a matter of life and death; the other was the frustration created by other army departments. Of equal concern was the fact that Simon was entering the traditionally difficult phase of teenage life; and also that my wife was undergoing her own personal crisis, not unconnected with her age. At work and at home I had a lot to think about. Responsibilities crowded in.

I found I was to work for a highly-strung, efficient but humourless brigadier, Peter Dutton — a combination of attributes that is difficult to deal with but not all that rare. My team had to monitor the condition, safety and performance of all munitions in army service world-wide. Under me I had three lieutenant-colonels, one overseeing conventional ammunition (projectiles, mines, grenades, pyrotechnics), one responsible for missiles (Thunderbird, Rapier, Blowpipe, Lance) and one, George Styles, GC, in the bomb disposal business. I also had a very good major, Fred Cantrell, who dealt with safety in storage and transit. A propos that aspect of things I was, ex-officio, a member of one of the Ordnance Board standing committees in London and chairman of its electronic sub-committee.

I was also part of a government committee that met periodically in the Cabinet Offices in Whitehall to discuss security, my input being concerned with bombing trends. Nameless men presented themselves, sat down, said nothing, got up, gathered their papers together and departed in silence. I am not sure who they were or how much they, or we, achieved but judging from the amount of time the rest of us spent discussing the matter it seemed there was a great shortage of money: though every bomb blast in Belfast cost the tax payer about £ 50,000, the man in charge could not persuade the powers-that-be to let him engage a typist at an eighth of that cost.

It was Fred Cantrell whom I met very early one Sunday morning under some railway arches in the East End of London soon after I arrived in the job. We were there to supervise a team of Ammunition Examiners who had to remove hundreds of boxes of potentially very dangerous chemicals from dilapidated storage bays built into the arches.

Several years before, an enterprising scrap merchant had bought a job lot of government-surplus chemicals on the assumption that some day, somewhere, someone would want them and he would be able to sell at a profit. Nobody did, and a few tons of potassium di-phenal/di-nitrazene lay quietly mouldering until an official got to hear about it when the old man died, his clock having stopped. The stuff was highly sensitive because it had interacted with the damp atmosphere to form crystals that would ignite if scraped.

Our men wore special protective clothing from top to toe, and a gas mask. They padded around like astronauts, gently carrying the crystal-sprouting boxes to the back of trucks, into which they were carefully loaded. All through the quiet morning, while worthy citizens, all unknowing, lay mouldering nearby in their beds, the ATs sweated away. By the time the East-Enders were thinking of tottering down to the Queen Vic for a few pints while their wives sweated over a hot stove the convoy was on its way to Essex, where the contents were chemically broken down and disposed of.

Once I got into my job I found that I devoted sixty per cent of my time to bomb disposal matters and the rest to what, in normal times, would have required ninety per cent. It was not surprising. I arrived in March 1972 and departed in October 1974. In Northern Ireland in 1972 4,300 bombing incidents were dealt with, in 1973 3,800, and in 1974 2,650, an average over the period of more than seventy a week, with the top scorer being 170 in one week alone. (Between 1969, when all the nastiness began, and 1976 there were more than 20,000 incidents. In the same period, of that number 5,500 were false alarms and 2,750 were hoaxes.) For me, the matter demanded a lot of attention. Copies of some of the reports came across my desk every working day and one morning I was saddened to read that the Sandys Home in Ballykinlar, in which I had enjoyed my 5p meals in 1946, had been destroyed. A van bomb left outside had gutted it. Another closed loop . . .

I was involved in three main areas of decision making: equipment development, the selection of personnel for duty as bomb disposal operators, and their training. Regarding equipment, there were two things that concerned me a great deal. One was the development of something that would deal with the hard-cased bomb, the other was the continued improvement of remotely-controlled means of tackling a bomb.

Bomb incidents are recorded under five headings: 'live' bombs, bombs that have already exploded (requiring post-explosion reports), false alarms, hoaxes and finds. Live bombs are those that are armed and waiting to go off when the operator arrives on the scene. Post-explosion reports are written in order to record the estimated amount of explosive used, give a positive or assessed identification of the triggering device, list the evidence found on the scene (which may be used during any subsequent trial, requiring the attendance in court of the expert witness who logged the evidence) and provide statistical data which forms part of the intelligence picture about trends, the availability of explosives and detonators and the location of incidents. Since bombs tend to have a 'signature' in their construction it may even be possible to identify who the bomb-maker was — though seldom by name, of course. False alarms originate when members of the public or the security forces genuinely believe they have found a bomb or know its whereabouts. Hoaxes are reports of bombs originated with malice by terrorists or by members of the public — to confuse the security forces, to create disorder, or for personal reasons such as scoring off a business rival. The public or the security forces can come across explosives or bomb-making materials and report their 'find'; operators must then attend to ensure that the objects are safe to move and be disposed of, and to catalogue all items after identification.

All reports must be treated as potential live bombs: only when the full render-safe procedure has been followed can it be known for certain whether a bomb existed. Ironically, some of the bravest deeds done by bomb disposal men over the years have turned out to be during the 'neutralisation' of hoaxes; men have consciously braced themselves to risk their lives when in fact there was no risk.

Eyeball-to-eyeball confrontations between an operator and a ticking bomb took place on average twelve times during a man's four-month tour of duty in the Province — about 10% of the number of incidents he produced a report on. This was because roughly half the bombs had exploded before he got there and also because of the large proportion of false alarms and hoaxes.

Due to the advent of transistors and

micro-electronics, bombs had become much more sophisticated since the days when I was in Cyprus. To give an extreme example of how complicated a scenario can be, in Cairo in 1971 a man had his head blown off by remote control when he lay down on his hotel bed and put his head on the pillow: its weight triggered an electrical impulse that told a man in a nearby building that his target was in position; he then pressed a button which transmitted a radio signal that detonated explosives under the pillow. In the mid-1990s a man using a mobile phone had his head blown off when he pressed one of the dialling buttons.

By early 1972 the Provisional IRA were creating hell in Northern Ireland, especially in Belfast. They had large quantities of explosives and detonators and a mass-production system for making bombs. They had graduated from petrol bombs and six-inch nails taped around sticks of gelignite to complex, radio-controlled devices — and had begun to make deadly use of the car bomb: in March 1972 two senior bomb disposal NCOs were killed when trying to remove a bomb from the back seat of a car; in the same month Major Bernard Calladene was killed when a car bomb exploded as he walked towards it. Big, smiling Bernard, second-row forward, an Army and Corps player, a nice man whom I had first met when I was in charge of Corps rugby in BAOR in the late Sixties. His great size and strength did not save him when he was picked up by the blast and hurled through a plate-glass window.

Step by step the Royal Army Ordnance Corps counter-measures department had met each IRA challenge as it came, even, thanks to the boffins in one of the research establishments, being in possession of a piece of equipment that could deal with a bomb assembled in a package, cardboard box or holdall. But at the beginning of 1972 we had nothing that could deal with the hard-cased bomb, usually in a car but sometimes in other forms of metal casing, such as a beer barrel. The solution to that problem arrived to some extent by chance.

An Ammunition Technical Officer, a captain who had done a tour of duty in Northern Ireland, had been attached as a liaison officer to the Royal Armaments Research and Development Establishment at Fort Halstead, near Sevenoaks. One morning he came into my office to tell me what was going on. There was some progress, he said, in finding the solution to the hard-cased quandary, but nothing conclusive. He went on to describe various lines of experimentation. When he got to one of them I nodded. Then he began to talk about something else. I stopped him. 'But surely that's it,' I said. He frowned. It was a classic case of standing too close to a problem: he and the scientists involved had stumbled on the solution without realising it. He went back, persuaded people to test and re-test the idea, and in due course it was taken into use.

Printed circuits and transistors were also revolutionising our ability to deal with bombs remotely. A very small Japanese television camera mounted on a robot and connected by an umbilical cord to a screen some distance away enabled the operator to see the target and decide how to deal with it in relative safety. What we needed was a really sophisticated robot. The Atomic Research Establishment at Harwell had developed one for use in the event of heavy radiation contamination: it could drag people out who had succumbed, or isolate radio-active sources. I went to see a demonstration of it. Two men carried a plywood box into the room, took the lid off, plugged in an electric cable and stood back. One of them then pressed buttons on a small hand-held control unit and the robot climbed out of its box and trundled around the room waving its arms about. It was a masterpiece of inventive engineering.

Harwell offered it to me there and then, complete with all its blueprints. I proposed its use to the Ministry of Defence equipment sponsor branch, but they, sight unseen, did not enthuse. To make things worse, and put the lid on it, neither did our senior bomb disposal man in Northern Ireland, a lieutenant-colonel. It was a glaring example of that not uncommon human reaction known as the Not Invented Here Syndrome — if I didn't think of it first it can't be any good. The MoD asked two research establishments to design a robot of their own, and quite predictably each went its own way, one towards hydraulics, the other towards electro-servo mechanisms. Eventually a hybrid was made which was so complicated it did not work — and what is more, cost six times as much. In the end the Wheelbarrow, the machine that had been developed in the first place, was refined.

As to personnel selection, there were two aspects to which I gave a lot of thought. The first was psychometric testing, in which I became involved with the Army's psychiatrists and psychologists at Netley, near Southampton.

We were taking casualties at the time, amazingly few, considering, but too many all the same — and far too many for some people. One day when I was addressing a course at the School of Ammunition, of men who were just about to begin a tour of duty in Northern Ireland, I was summoned to the phone to speak to the deputy director of my Corps, a brigadier. He asked me if I had heard that one of our men had been killed that morning. I said yes, I had. He then asked me what I was going to do about it. I replied that I did not understand the question. 'It's got to stop,' he said. I told him that risks were high and casualties were inevitable. He then instructed me to send an order to the effect that our men were to stop risking their lives: they were to tackle bombs only if there was no possibility at all that they would blow themselves up. I declined to do so, and suggested that he should send the order himself. I think the problem, which I had encountered before, was a lack of understanding by non-ammunition people in the Corps of what it was all about.

The existing procedures were anyway quite clear: the only time when a bomb disposal man's life should deliberately be risked, regardless of the consequences to him, was when he was tasked to incidents when other people's lives were at stake; for example, if a bomb was near a hospital from which it was not possible to evacuate the patients, or, say, if people were trapped by the effects of a previous explosion. Then it was mandatory that he should tackle the bomb. I could think of nothing more calculated to undermine morale than the sending of such an order, which would have instantly changed the mental attitude of our men into one of great uncertainty. They knew that risk to life was inherent in their job, that if things became difficult they could call on the next man up the chain of responsibility for help and advice, that in the last resort they could draw back if other people's lives were not at risk. To tell them never to take risks would have made a nonsense of all we were trying to achieve. Needless to say, on reflection the order was not sent.

A number of the men who had died had done so without due cause. In other words, they had acted in ways that were inexplicable, and contrary to all the precautions they had been taught during their training. There had to be another, personal, factor that had made them do what they did. I consulted the head-shrinkers and they suggested that psychometric tests should be taken by all men before they were trained.

Such tests were already in use to exclude unsuitable men for service in submarines: to identify people with latent claustrophobia and debar them from undertaking that speciality. In some armies similar tests were applied to identify men with vertigo and exclude them from parachute training. Why should we not exclude men who were impulsive, irrational; who, perhaps, harboured a hidden death wish? I found the subject fascinating, and directly it brought no frustrations to me. The problems arose when it came to persuading people that it was a good idea. Some said the whole concept was nonsense; who ever heard of such a thing? Soldiers always did their duty, didn't they? It was part of the unwritten contract, wasn't it? To suggest that some were incapable of doing so was to undermine that whole principle. (A good point, but consider how attitudes towards stress have changed over the years; how in the Great War more than three hundred men were shot for what was then called cowardice, but which today, in most cases, would be attributed to extreme stress, which some men are more capable of withstanding than others.) Other people shied away because to them anything to do with psychiatry implied proximity to madness: if a man failed, was he trembling on the brink of insane incarceration? (Good grief, I might fail the test myself! No thanks.) However, at the beginning of 1973 the tests were introduced: some six hundred questions, spread over three test papers.

One paper consisted of Yes/No answers to simple but sometimes apparently pointless questions. Do you pick flowers? (What, me? Pick flowers? What do you think I am? Not likely.) Do you visit relatives? (Not if I can help it.) Do you like rich creamy foods? (Yes, of course.) Medicine bottles? (Hardly. Gin bottles, yes.) The second paper asked for Yes, No, Maybe answers to straight questions: Do you often get angry with people? (Naturally.) Do you like reading about sex? (Only as a last resort.) The third paper contained questions the answers to which could be fudged, but if they were, showed up in contradiction to the answers in the first two papers. If there were too many, the person was asked to answer a fourth set of questions, which resolved or confirmed the contradiction.

The screening of potential bomb disposal men was only part of the selection process I was involved in. The other was deciding which officer was to go where; sometimes, who was to be put into a position of greatest risk. Once I had to choose between two captains who had come out joint top of their bomb disposal course, as near as made no difference. I picked one to go to Belfast — I don't think his pretty young wife ever forgave me — and the other to go to Hereford. He it was who was killed by an IRA bomb in Birmingham; the other is still prospering.

The wives of our men were incredibly stoical. One of them, a pretty woman with two delightful young children, lived opposite us in Didcot during the time her husband was in the thick of it all. Based in Belfast, he had to travel everywhere to visit the EOD (Explosive Ordnance Disposal) teams, as they were known in NATO parlance — to Londonderry, to Omagh, to Bessbrook near the border. As the months went by his wife lost pounds in weight and the strain showed on her face, but she never uttered a word of complaint or misgiving, despite being well aware, generally, of the risks he was taking. I don't suppose he told her, though, that on his first weekend in the Province he had spent two hours picking fragments out of the bodies of two soldiers trying to establish what sort of bomb had killed them.

Sometimes after an explosion nothing of any significance at all is left of a man. On one occasion one of our staff-sergeants was tasked to go to the scene of some explosions out in the countryside. He flew over the field in a helicopter, saw nothing apart from some new patches of earth where the bombs had gone off and, as it was getting dark, decided to return in daylight. The next morning his lieutenant-colonel, John Gaff, said he would go along, too. From the air they could see that there were six craters in a rough circle, with a gap as if there had been a place for a seventh bomb that had not gone off. They landed, cast around and found a command wire running towards the craters. They began to follow it carefully, keeping a look out for booby-traps. The wire disappeared into a pond, and the colonel said he would follow it. He waded in while the staff-sergeant walked around the pond and began to follow the wire again where it came out on the other side. It went through a dry-stone wall and he, with the Welsh Guards sergeant in charge of the infantry cordon not far behind him, walked down the wall to the gate, checked it, then went through and down the grass verge on the other side. He saw that a bit of turf had been cut out and that the wire disappeared into the ground underneath it; called out that he thought it was one of the new remotely-controlled bombs; bent down to take a closer look and it went off. I visited the place the next day in a helicopter. There was nothing to be seen at all, except the scars on the ground. The colonel and the Guards sergeant were unharmed but the man had just vanished.

I went to his funeral in the Midlands a few days after that. His wife had asked to be allowed to see him in his coffin, but somehow the undertakers had persuaded her that it was not a good idea. There was nothing in it, you see, except a few pieces of flesh and some stones to weigh it down.

'The captain and the sergeant were coming back. Good, thought Ben: now they'll get on with it. 'What's next?' he asked. 'The thing's tied to a telegraph pole, sir,' the captain said. 'I'm going to attach some rope to it and pull it away with the Landrover. From a distance. If it's booby-trapped, that will set it off. If it isn't, then I'll open it up and disarm it.' Ben nodded. That seemed straightforward enough.

While they were getting on with it he went behind a hedge and had a pee. By the time he got back the captain had fixed a long rope to the churn and the sergeant was tying his end of it to the vehicle. 'All right, MacKinnon,' the captain called as he walked towards them, 'let the clutch out slowly and give the thing a pull.'

MacKinnon leaned out of his window and, looking back down the road, gently eased his vehicle forward. The rope went taut, the churn suddenly came adrift from the pole, clanked on to the road, then rolled over twice. 'Great!' the captain said with relief: 'It shouldn't take long now . . . I'll do this bit on my own. Give me the tool kit, please, Sergeant Ridley.'

He took his peaked cap off and put it on the bonnet of the Landrover, thought about taking his belt off, with its holster and pistol, decided it would not impede him, picked up the metal tool box (a small, converted ammunition box, painted red) and stepped out down the road. Sooner him than me, thought Ben. Being in the parachute regiment was one thing, doing this sort of thing was quite another. 'What's next?' he asked the sergeant. 'He'll have to get the lid off. We haven't got anything that'll get through metal that thick. Well, we have, but it's very cumbersome and might do more harm than good.'

'Set it off, you mean?'

'Yes, sir. If you use heat it could cook off, and if you use a cutter the vibration could activate it. They put trembler switches in bombs sometimes. The best way is to take the lid off and take it all apart, slowly. Besides, we like to see what's in there — see if they've come up with any new tricks. It shouldn't take long now,' he added.

The helicopter pilot had joined the crew of one of the scout cars and Ben could see him standing talking to an NCO of the 16th/5th Lancers. The chopper sat like a disgruntled grasshopper in the field, dozing in the sun but ready to leap into the air. The wires on the telegraph poles hummed, the cows munched in the field, the sun was warm on Ben's back.

Going off on his own, he sat down on a fallen log, pulled a long-stemmed piece of grass and started to chew it. It was all very peaceful. You couldn't believe it, really, that Ireland could be such a troublesome place.

Ever since Henry the Second annexed it in 1172!

It was ridiculous, when you thought about it. A crazy, convoluted maze of a situation.

The country had actually been joined to Great Britain a few thousand years ago, and that was nothing in the life of the world; the blink of an eye. Geographically, the Scottish Highlands extended down into Donegal and Mayo, the Welsh Hills into Waterford and Wexford. In fact, the whole boiling lot had once been joined to Europe. Indeed, some of the first people to live in Ireland had come from Brittany!

The captain was kneeling by the bomb now; had his head down by the lid and seemed to be examining it.

The whole history of Ireland was a saga of mistakes, miscalculations and misunderstandings. Most of the things done had no doubt seemed right and reasonable at the time, they just went awry as time passed. Like Queen Elizabeth the First founding the University of Dublin at the end of the Sixteenth Century but excluding Catholics from it! Right in principle but wrong in execution; giving the Irish the means but not the opportunity to be educated. Though with the Spanish threat that existed at that time educating Catholics could not have seemed a good idea . . .

The captain had got the lid off. He stood up and waved cheerfully to Sergeant Ridley, put his hands on his hips and straightened the cramped muscles of his back, opened the red box, took something out of it then knelt down on the road again. Why doesn't he stand the churn up on end? Ben wondered. Oh, because he might dislodge something.

As if people and politics were not enough — Cromwell, William of Orange, Gladstone, Lloyd George — the potato famine in 1846 had really screwed the poor devils down. The population had dropped from eight million in 1830 to three million a hundred years later because of the famine and the mass emigration that followed it. Late marriages had been a means to control the birth rate and lessen the number of mouths that had to be fed around the peat fires . . .

It was a strange country visually. There was so much water. He had flown over most of the north, where there were great stretches of nothing: just water glinting everywhere, in little lakes, in ponds, in bogland. Rolling hills, heather, sheep running away from the beat of the rotors. A few scattered cottages. Little lanes. Like a great . . .

The sound of the explosion hit him as if a giant had banged his head between his hands. The blast threw him sideways on to the ground.

Oh God! Christ Almighty. He scrambled to his feet and ran instinctively towards the grey cloud of smoke where the milk churn had been, vaguely aware that Sergeant Ridley was beside him and that MacKinnon was galloping along behind. Oaths kept repeating themselves in his head over and over again. As they got nearer, the smoke began to clear. The telegraph pole was standing at an angle, with wires trailing on the road verge. There was a scorched, blackened patch on the road surface, and a bit of a crater, not all that deep. Smoke curled up. 'Where's the captain?' he shouted to Ridley: 'He must have been blown into the ditch or over the hedge. See if you can find him.'

The smell of explosives was everywhere, an acrid, burnt-chemical smell that he knew of old. 'Where is he, for Christ's sake?' he called out. A large piece of the churn, its edges bent, buckled and discoloured, lay in the ditch twenty yards from the site of the explosion but there was no sign of the officer. Slow down, Ben, stop running around like a wet hen! he told himself. He took a deep breath, stood still and looked back down the road at the smoking hole in the ground. Sergeant Ridley was reappearing through a gate on his right and MacKinnon was clambering through a gap torn in the hedge on his left. The pilot and the cavalry subaltern and one of his NCOs were running up the road to the scene. Ridley and MacKinnon, white-faced and gasping for breath, both looked at Ben and mutely shook their heads.

Ben frowned. He must be somewhere!

He walked down the road towards them, looking to left and right. Then he saw a lump of flesh with grains of soil embedded in the bloody tissue lying on the grass. And further on, almost hidden in a patch of nettles, a shoe. He went closer. The remains of a shoe. With a foot in it. The calcaneum, chopped of, looked like the sawn-through bone on the end of a joint in a butcher's shop.

'He's gone, sir,' Ridley gasped. 'For Christ's sake, there's nothing left of him! He's just vanished.'

Yes, vanished from the face of the earth, Ben thought. Poor devil. Ye Gods. Oh Christ, what a mess.

MacKinnon was over by the hedge being sick. The retching noise made Ben's stomach contract in sympathy. He could feel the bile rise in his throat and the skin stretched taut on his face. The young officer stood there looking ashen and terrified.

'His pistol must be somewhere,' Ben said. 'We've got to find it. Here, MacKinnon, you look for it. You too,' he told the subaltern. Give them something to do. 'Got any plastic bags?' he asked Ridley. 'Yes, sir, we have some for forensic specimens.' Forensic specimens! My God!

⋆   ⋆   ⋆

Later, he walked down to the Landrover holding four plastic bags by their necks, two trailing from each hand. In them were what was left of the captain: a few mangled, grisly, bloody lumps of bone and flesh and skin. He heaved them into the back of the vehicle beside the battered red box, which Ridley had retrieved. The scout cars had gone and the helicopter pilot was walking around his plane checking to see that it had not been damaged. Ben joined Ridley at the side of the vehicle. MacKinnon was sitting in the front, stunned and hanging on to the steering wheel.

'The blast must have nearly all gone upwards,' Ridley said. 'That's why the crater isn't very big. He must have got the full force of it. It's unbelievable. Just bloody incredible. He was a good guy, too,' he added desperately.

Ben looked up and saw that the captain's peaked cap was still on the bonnet of the Rover. He stared at it. At the polished leather chin-strap held by two small brass buttons. At the regimental badge with its three cannons on a shield surmounted by a crown. Half an hour before it had had an owner.

When they had the military funeral it would be put on top of the coffin, on the Union flag. Firing party, bugler. Child-widow in black. Weeping mother. Grey-faced father. Uniformed pall bearers, all captains, same rank as the deceased. The rippling crack of the volley echoing. Dust to dust, ashes to ashes. They would put stones or bricks in the coffin to make up the weight.

Good job the widow couldn't see what was in there. And the mother.

They often asked to see the body. What did you say to them, for Christ's sake?

The Union flag! What a joke.

He put out his hand and grasped Ridley by the shoulder and shook it gently. 'I've got to go,' he said. 'I'm late. You've told them on the radio, haven't you? OK, well I'm off then.' He returned Ridley's salute and went over to the helicopter.

'Right, Staff, let's go,' he told the pilot. 'Bessbrook.'

As they took off he looked down at the scene. There was nothing special to see. The birds and beetles would eat the bits, he thought to himself. Life went on.

They banked and soared over the countryside. Like a green, thick roll of green and purple velvet, it was, brown and yellow and purple but mostly green, lying laid out on top of a big puddle. The Emerald Isle . . .

The Friesians scattered, lumbering around the field. 'Eilleen Oag, my heart is growing grey, ever since . . . ' The words of the song rang in his head, he couldn't stop it, it kept coming back all the time. ' . . . is growing grey, ever since the day you wandered far away . . . '

They never did find the pistol.'

The EOD men did a marvellous job and earned many awards for gallantry, but not enough. On one of my routine visits I spoke to the colonel on the staff of Headquarters Northern Ireland who was responsible for screening the citations. He assured me that brigade commanders were submitting dozens of commendations but then said: 'However, we can't have your Corps hogging the gallantry lists, can we? We have to let other people get a look in.' Such an attitude is ludicrous. How can you justify giving an award to, say, a military police corporal who was the first on the scene of a ticking bomb in preference to giving it to the man who disarmed it? I know of many deserving cases of young officers and NCOs, there during those horrendous days when Belfast looked as if it had been blitzed, Londonderry was paralysed and the country areas were minefields, who were cited but received nothing because someone else had to 'get a look in.'

To most people bomb disposal must be the most dangerous of all occupations. In his autobiography Anthony Eden said of our operator's work in Northern Ireland: 'In cold blood, calmly to place life at a desperate hazard in the hope of saving others can never be surpassed and rarely equalled by any deed of daring in the heat of battle.' It is one thing to fight a battle beside comrades in the heat of war, when the risk is a random one; it is another to be alone with a threat that is targeted specifically at a solitary individual. Bomb disposal places that individual directly in conflict with danger. Danger creates fear. Every man confronted with a ticking bomb is afraid; conquering that fear determines his ability to do his job. It seems against the odds that a man can attain the clinical detachment and enormous self-control that is needed, yet given the right training and equipment he does. Esprit de corps and the opinion of one's peers also plays a big part; a bomb disposal man does not want to be seen to be cowardly, either by civilians, policemen, the rest of the army or, especially, by the men he works with day by day.

I can think of no more gutsy performance than that of those men in Northern Ireland: which, alas, nearly thirty years on they are still doing.

As to the Irish, they should grow up. And practice the compassion and forgiveness their prelates preach, in the name of God.

* * *

In 1973 I became involved in the QE2 incident.

While it was en route from New York to Southampton, Cunard received notification that there were six bombs on board. They rang the Ministry of Defence and asked if something could please be done about it? A major in the MOD then rang me and repeated the question. Did we have any parachutists who could drop in and sort the problem out? We had, but the difficulty was trying to find them.

In the days before computers were invented a little man somewhere would have had a well-thumbed Stationery Office alphabetically-listed notebook in which were written all the personal details about our operators. He would have flicked through it and in a few minutes told me who and where they were. In 1973 when I asked our Records Office they rang back to say that the computer was not programmed to provide such information and it would take several days to get it.

After a few hours, memory and word-of-mouth produced a list but when I checked it no-one was readily available: one man was in Hong Kong, another in Germany; another parachutist was not up-to-date on bomb disposal techniques, and so on. I had come to the conclusion that I would have to go myself, even though I had never parachuted, when I was saved by the bell by a call from one of our instructors at the School of Ammunition, Captain Bob Williams. He had done a few free-fall drops, would he do? He would, indeed. Who better?

Within an hour he was in a helicopter with a box of kit, and within three, after a crash course on how to land on water, in a Hercules heading out over the Atlantic, accompanied by an officer and an NCO of the Special Boat Squadron, Royal Marines (who were there to fish him out) and a Staff Sergeant of the Special Air Service, whose role was not clear to me. They had a very hairy time getting aboard the QE2, having to circle it several times and do some sick-making flight manoeuvres each time before they found the right gap in the clouds, but eventually they were fished out of the water. Meanwhile, George Styles had been speaking to the captain of the QE2 over the normal GPO telephone network, telling him how to go about searching the ship and what to look for. And to close the watertight doors, which he seemed not to have thought of himself!

The service team were given anti-seasickness injections as soon as they got on board and then set about searching the ship for the bombs. In the end it all turned out to be a gigantic hoax, but the men who flew hundreds of miles out into the Atlantic did not know that.

We took steps to have a standby team available for any future incidents of that nature and for a few weeks our operators, from lieutenant-colonel rank down to corporal, were dropping into Poole Harbour like guillemots gone ga-ga.

For my part I regret that I did not fly out to the QE2. It would have been a marvellous memory.

★　★　★

In 1974 I became involved in the production of a BBC TV documentary about the bomb disposal men, one of the Fifty Minutes series.

First, they sent a pleasant young woman researcher down to do the ground work, and then a lady by the name of Jenny Barraclough turned up.

When told the producer was coming to see me I had visions of a long-haired Lefty arriving, since in my mind — and in the minds of a lot of people at that time — that was the BBC's image: a bunch of bearded, anti-establishment, radical men surrounded by slightly cookie women. Either I have changed, and become used to them — proof of the brain-washing process, maybe — or they have grown up. Anyway, I was not prepared for the appearance of a very striking-looking, very feminine, highly intelligent woman with long, soft wavy hair and a great deal of charm, even more, maybe, than my old friend Martin Foy, the gardener. Unlike him, she had a will of iron.

She arranged to visit our team in Belfast but did some location shooting in England before she went there. One episode, at which I was present, took place at Stratford-upon-Avon, within sight of the river and not far from the Swan Hotel. (In which I stayed in December 1993, then taken over by Mr Forte and full of piped music from morn till night. By the time I got to the third day A White Christmas was making me choke over my bacon and egg, and bells were jingling in my head. Silent Night it was not.)

Anyway, back to Jenny. At about nine o'clock on a summer's evening she insisted, with no arguments brooked, on shooting a scene of an imaginary bomb under the wheels of a goods train, even though the cameraman, who got paid twice as much as she did, plaintively kept telling her that the light had failed. And, I fancy, his physical stamina. Her's had not. She got her scene, and after that slight contretemps had been resolved, applied the charm. The man's irritation melted away visibly before my eyes and a warm smile replaced his frown. She is a remarkable woman, who is now joint partner in the independent television production company known as Barraclough-Carey.

The reporter on the programme was Jack

Pizzey, one-time husband of another remarkable, if less appealing, to me, woman, Erin, who founded the first home for battered wives. I found him a thoroughly nice, level-headed man whose subsequent appearances on television, regrettably now less frequent than they used to be, always heralded, for me, a worthwhile half hour or two.

Our documentary was successful, but could have been even more so if Jenny had had better luck; though she and her crew hung around for several days they did not get an exploding bomb, as she had hoped. But they did film a scene of an ATO going in to a building to neutralise a bomb, which made rivetting viewing. While all this was going on Jenny had stayed in the EOD team's grotty working and living accommodation opposite the Divis Flats, surrounded by hairy Jocks from the Queen's Own Highlanders. When I visited the place soon after someone had put up a sign saying 'Jenny B slept here.'

Another contact that came about as a result of media interest in bomb disposal was with the Sunday Telegraph, who did a colour supplement article on the subject. Duff Hart-Davis did the reporting and through him I met George Evans, the Managing Editor, a delightful Northern-Irish Catholic who has remained a staunch friend through the years. He took me to lunch in the Press Club several times, introducing me to Claire Hollingsworth — who looked like a little Chinese woman in the Sino-style tunic and pulled-back hair she had adopted after living for years in the Far East. It was difficult to imagine that in Cairo during the war she had been a great beauty. The march of time had had its impact, as it has on all of us, but it had not dimmed the alertness of her mind. I also lunched with Adrian Berry (son of the proprietor, Lord Hartwell), the man who writes extraordinary articles on a Monday in the Telegraph about interstellar exploration. (Long may he believe in it, but I don't: how can, and why should, people travel for many hundreds of years in a spacecraft, breeding replacement generations on the way, to places where they cannot live and from which they will never return, however much they want to? And why spend billions and billions on that when we haven't sorted out the mess down here?) And I perused the same menu with Peter Eastwood, the managing editor of the Daily Telegraph. Standing beside his desk after lunch and watching him vetting input from his reporters I was astonished at the speed and contempt with which most of their contributions were consigned to the waste-paper basket.

* * *

As is usual in life, all was not gloom. When Michael Ramsay, Archbishop of Canterbury, was confirming Simon his aide somehow muddled the Christian names of the young men who were kneeling in front of the altar. The archbishop got the first one right, missed one out then went right down the line using the wrong name. Simon became Mark as the elderly prelate's hands came down on his head in solemn benediction.

Though in some ways this event was not in the least amusing I could see the funny side of it. After all, no-one is perfect — not even an archbishop. Later, I asked Cantaur if the whole ceremony was null and void and would have to be done again. He looked first vague then astonished, blinking at me in his characteristic way, his eyebrows shooting up and down, then assured me it would not. But, I am told that in canon law Simon may call himself Mark if he so wishes. (In fact, he calls himself Peter, that being his second name.)

* * *

I left Didcot in October 1974 and joined a working group that was to study the logistic system in BAOR. I was forty-six years old but did not feel in the least middle-aged. In my own mind the young officer happened to have embellished his uniform with red tabs and a red-banded hat but was inwardly unchanged. The acute realisation of the onward march of time dawned on me during a visit to the Royal Military College of Science.

I went there to speak to captains who were completing their studies prior to becoming Ammunition Technical Officers. I told them how fortunate they were to have had the benefit of being in such a place, and how much I had enjoyed being there twenty years before. And then I stopped dead in my tracks because it struck me that all of them, sitting there with their young faces registering polite if not enthusiastic interest, had been born after I joined the army.

11

A good European

The Hope of Glory was published in November 1974. It was a great moment for me but the real high point had been receiving the 'pull' print of the jacket a few months before. For the first time, I felt I really was going to be an author. But then I told myself that one book does not make an author any more than one crumb makes you swallow. I went to see my publisher in Clerkenwell Green, a few yards away from the headquarters of the Order of St John at Clerkenwell Gate, where I had gone to research material for the book.

John Hale took over the business founded by his father, Robert, and built it up until it published more titles than any other firm in the country. We talked about possible new projects and when I told him that I had been involved with bomb disposal he showed interest. Thus, Stopping the Clock was conceived. During my three weeks' leave between jobs I began to write it.

Because the subject was so fresh in my

mind I needed to do no research — I just roughed out the shape, wrote letters to some of the protagonists to pick their brains, and began to fill in the details. The big constraint for me, of course, was the Official Secrets Act. Not that I was in any way inclined to give anything away, quite the contrary, but from the publishing point of view it would have helped sales if the book had contained a few really startling snippets of information. Nevertheless, over the years, as shown in the Public Lending Rights returns I receive each January, it has been one of the most widely-read of my books. (Authors get around 2p for each assessed lending, a figure so paltry that it is scarcely worth the administrative costs. Less than £5m is allocated per annum for the entire scheme, of which more than half a million goes in operating costs.) I managed to get a couple of chapters written before I went off, somewhat reluctantly, to my new assignment as Chief of Logistic Plans and Operations at a NATO headquarters, Allied Forces Central Europe.

'Dear Sis,
   Thought I'd write to let you know how I'm getting on.
   It's all a bit of a rum do, as you can imagine. The Micks are a funny lot,

387

friendly one minute then chucking things at you the next. We live in what used to be a mill — declared unsafe in 1911! It's used now by a company of infantry and your's truly, God's gift to women and the people of Ireland. It's a great, gloomy, rambling dump of a place with concrete stairs, brick walls, dark passages, and it smells of damp, cooking and Jocks. They're all right, though, the Jocks, a great bunch. We have six of them and a corporal looking after us. They come with the team every time we go on a task and spread out around the scene looking all warlike and keep the baddies off our backs as we get on with the job. Funnily enough, they like being with the team — so do the drivers and signallers who are part of the set-up. Gives them a kick, I suppose, to be with the heroes who calmly deal with deadly devices daily disdaining death. Seriously, though, it's not like that at all. I don't mind telling you I didn't like the thought of coming here, we've had a few knocked off and the stories that go around are enough to give anyone the abdabs and when you go on the course and learn all about it it really makes you wish you'd done what Dad said and gone into the motor trade, but when you've been here a bit you see that life just goes on.

I'll tell you the set-up. You come up the grotty stairs and on the right is a room where the drivers and signallers sleep and beyond them are the escort Jocks and beyond them the lats. Then on the left is our section. There's the office as you go in, with a radio and a telephone and some bumf and the typewriter — and me too, at the moment, with a fag just about to burn Her Majesty's issue furniture. Beyond the office there's this biggish room with a telly in the corner and a sort of bar — not that there's any drinking when you're on duty mind, that would be daft. There's lots of girlie pictures on the walls and a whole row of number-plates that came off the cars we've sanitized (that's a good one, isn't it?) — sort of trophies. Sometimes there wasn't much left except the number-plates.

The food's not bad and everything that can be done is, but you can't change a derelict mill.

I'm going to stop now. Tomorrow one of our senior officer's coming on a visit so the OC's got a bit of a hate on. See ya!'

I went to AFCENT reluctantly because I did not know what I was letting myself in for. All my service had been with the British Army, in which there was a feeling that to be employed in a NATO environment or on attachment to other armies was to be cut off from the main stream of activity. There was, too, the fact that confidential reports were not accepted at face value.

The system in the British Army is that every officer is reported on, and graded, every year by his or her commanding officer. The report is then seen by two, or even three, superior officers, who can add their views if they wish to. An officer's grades will seldom always be the same, obviously — it depends on aptitude in a particular job, on personality clashes, on personal circumstances at the time (domestic problems may affect work) but as time passes a picture builds up; he or she is generally below-average, average, above-average, excellent, even outstanding. The grades follow the typical Gaussian curve: not many at each end and — theoretically — the majority in the middle. There is a tendency, however, for the average to creep up so that most officers are rated above-average, primarily because they see their reports and COs have to look them in the eye when they do. (RAF officers, for instance, do not see theirs.) But if the selection and training procedures are as they should be then, let's face it, the majority of officers should be very good at their jobs. Perhaps the gradings should read Not so good, Good, Very Good, etc.

When serving with other forces officers are likely to get inflated reports, partly because the initiators, unaware of national systems, do not like to under-grade but also because in some armies — the American, for instance — nearly all officers are graded Outstanding. For this reason reports initiated by non-British officers tend to be discounted, which before a crucial promotion can be detrimental to an officer's career. (Reports, too, can be the occasion for humour. 'I would hesitate to breed from this officer,' was one renowned comment, written by a cavalry lieutenant-colonel about one of his less favoured captains. 'Geared low, pedals hard,' a succinct summing-up of an officer's character that builds an instant mental picture and needs no elaboration — almost as descriptive as 'This officer goes through life pushing doors marked 'Pull'.' I know the feeling. And ... 'The only reason anyone would follow this major is out of sheer, idle curiosity ...')

Apart from a background awareness of

these factors I was also woefully ignorant about what AFCENT actually did. I soon found out.

The forces were commanded by a four-star German soldier (a point that most people in this country were unaware of: that the British soldiers in the Army of the Rhine were under the command of a German.) With the break-up of the Warsaw Pact the organisation of the Central Region has now changed, but when I was there the C-in-C (Cincent) commanded Allied Air Forces Central Europe (which consisted of the 2nd and 4th Allied Tactical Air Forces) and the Northern and Central Army Groups.

Cincent had a four-star British airman as his deputy. Northag was under command of a British soldier (also C-in-C BAOR) and Centag was commanded by an American (also C-in-C of the American land forces in Europe.) Each of them commanded four Army Corps, starting at the top, in Northag, with the 1st Netherlands Corps, then the 1st German, the 1st British and the 1st Belgian; and, in Centag, the 5th US, the 3rd German, the 7th US and the 2nd German Corps. In the beginning AFCENT was at Fontainbleu and was commanded by a French soldier, the first being a seven-star general — Marshal of France — by the name of Juin, a tough-looking hombre if ever there was one. The third (or maybe it was the fourth) ended up in jail because he became involved, after leaving AFCENT, in the Algérie-Français, anti-de Gaulle business. Then de Gaulle took France out of the military element of NATO — they remained involved politically — and the job was given to a German, for the simple reason that they provided most of the soldiers. After being in limbo for ten years, by 1974 the German army was fielding thirty-six brigades on German soil compared to the British contribution of six. The Americans already provided the Supreme Allied Commander, whose deputy was British; it was inevitable, and right, that a German would get command of AFCENT.

When I went there Ernst Ferber was the Commander-in-Chief, a gnarled-looking man with that Hun caste of features typified by Conrad Adenauer. (The word Hun is not used in any pejorative sense: the Huns, a tribe from eastern Asia, invaded what is now Germany in the 4th and 5th Centuries, leaving behind a legacy of a particular type of German physiognomy that carries traces of Mongol features; high cheek bones, deep-set and slightly slanting eyes.) Ferber's deputy was Air Chief Marshal Sir Lewis Hodges, a nice man who had had a somewhat hairy war, amongst other things landing Allied agents behind the lines in Lysander aircraft.

The next most senior officer, the Chief of Staff, was a Dutchman by the name of van Ardenne, a big, burly man with a dominant personality and an outstanding wife, a very attractive and well-dressed woman. The 'ranking' American was an air force major-general by the name of Patillo: I never found out what his first name was — he was always referred to as the 'dee-oh-eye', meaning the Deputy Chief of Staff for Operations and Intelligence. He had flown Mustangs in the Second World War, Sabre jets in Korea, F-111s in Vietnam — and had a lot of medals to prove it! One day, during a boring conference I began to count them; he had 34 different ribbons and on them a progression of little stars: gold ones for each second, third and fourth award of the medal, silver ones indicating that five had been earned. Adding up all the ribbons and stars his total of awards came to 58. (The Americans, like the Russians, tend to tear the ass out of it when dishing out the gravy. There were British colonels in AFCENT with two or three medals, and lieutenant-colonels who sported one — or even none. In NATO eyes that meant they had seen no action, when in fact the post-war British soldier could have served in Malaya, the Dutch East Indies, Cyprus, Suez, Borneo, Aden and Northern Ireland and ended up with just two ribbons to show for it.)

Patillo sure was one helluvan airman, but he was not one helluva D.O.I. As I was passing his office one day a very depressed looking British lieutenant-colonel came out of it. 'What's the matter, John?' I asked. 'That man's driving me crazy,' he replied: 'He's already changed this paper I've written five times and when I took it in to him again just now he said: 'I don't know what it is I want, but it sure as hell ain't that' '.

I worked for a Belgian airman, Major-General Magain, who was a nice little man but out of his depth, and an American brigadier-general who stood about six feet five in his socks — which I presume he did morning and night — and looked like a polar bear. Lynn Hoskins had difficulty with the written word and was not exactly at ease with the spoken one either. To assist him over those hurdles he had a phone on his desk connected directly to the Pentagon in Washington: any decision of any substance was referred there for approval. To slow things up even more, under the cumbersome American system that operated in AFCENT any letter going out of the headquarters had to be signed by a one-star general, a brigadier, resulting in the holders of that rank becoming inundated with a lot of trivia.

I had working for me a Dutch army lieutenant-colonel, a German army lieutenant-colonel and two American majors, one in the army, the other in the air force. When the time came to write a report on one of the majors I rated him highly but added what I thought was a helpful comment about how he could improve his performance. Within hours, I had an urgent phone call from his superior officer in the U.S. hierarchy: 'Peter,' he said, 'this report is going to kill Andy stone dead. You just gotta remove this comment.' I did. I had no wish to kill Andy stone dead; he was a nice guy whose wife had been a Rockette dancer in Radio City Music Hall in New York — which seemed highly unlikely, looking at her: she was demure and shy, maybe because she had been Born Again.

The Dutchman, Albert Brakel, was half Indonesian but looked completely Oriental. He was married to a blonde Dutch woman, Fenneke, and they had seven children, who ranged in looks from dark-skinned, black-haired to fair-skinned, ash-blonde. All of them were pleasant to know; Albert was also admirable. He was wise, hard-working, totally reliable and had a quiet self-possession that I have never encountered in anyone else to a similar degree. I concluded that this must have been attributable to the racial mixture of common-sensical Dutch and inscrutable Easterner, plus what he had been through during the war.

The German, Fritz Schaefer, a pleasant, helpful man, was one of the first group of post-war officers to be commissioned. He and his contemporaries were efficient, well-trained courteous and single-minded. Traces of old German attitudes remained in them, for example, however well they knew each other, they were never on Christian-name terms. The Schaefer children were brought up to treat strangers with the acme of politeness: the boy, always immaculately dressed, would bow when shaking hands, the girl would slip a little curtsey — and smile.

The Schaefers came from a village called Waldek, which stands high above the Edersee. Before I met them I had been there and walked around its 15th Century castle, seat of the Graf von Waldeck, and looked down from its high battlements across the great, shimmering, lake. In one of its towers there is an oubliette, a dungeon with only one entrance, in the ceiling. Looking down through it I saw an iron ball and chain to which prisoners had been shackled. The ball had ground a groove deep into the stone where men had dragged it around for months on end — or even years, perhaps, though it is difficult to see how they could have survived the German winters without any form of heating.

The staff in the headquarters were dedicated, hard-working and professional, and had a surprising degree of unity of purpose. Whatever strengths the Soviets derived from controlling a dragooned, indoctrinated and censored population, who were obliged to tolerate immense expenditure on armed forces at the cost of a better standard of living for themselves, there could never have been in the Warsaw Pact the same extent of voluntary enthusiasm that was to be found in the military element of NATO. Our weakness lay in achieving unanimity amongst the governments of the nations that supplied the troops. It was one thing to propose, another to dispose. Internationally, the problem mirrored the difficulties encountered between our own armed forces and the Treasury.

Not long after my arrival I was asked to attend a memorial service in Roermond. I went in full uniform (with Sam Browne belt and sword) and found myself at the equivalent of one of our Armistice Day parades, only this time it was in remembrance of Dutch resistance fighters who had died in the war. For me it was a strange dichotomy: to be en rapport with German and Dutch officers at work and during our leisure time and yet be reminded of the brutal way in which the Germans had behaved in the Netherlands during the war. The Nazis treated the Dutch more harshly than any other western nation they conquered. Most of them fought the Nazis tooth and nail — though it has to be said that some of them formed a division of the German army — and suffered the consequences. In contrast, the Norwegians were considered to be Nordic blood-brothers, and fared better.

Earlier in this book I wrote that I have ambivalent feelings about Armistice Day parades. Some of them stem directly from my attendance at that Dutch ceremony. For how long are we going to perpetuate national hatreds by reminding ourselves each year of the cause of those hatreds? A hundred years? Two hundred? Three hundred? It is no lack of respect for those who died out of patriotism to suggest that one day it will have to stop. Times change. Old enmities must be forgotten, old injuries forgiven. The problems facing humanity are too great for their resolution to be delayed by out-dated sentiment.

★ ★ ★

My most memorable work moments in Brunssum were the exercises. Every so often we would 'go to war' and enact the scenario of Armageddon: a build-up of tension due to political and/or economic pressures, followed by a Warpact advance into western Europe, spearheaded by the twenty-one Soviet Divisions in East Germany and supported by more than three thousand front-line aircraft — with, in the background, the land and air forces of the Warsaw Pact. And the sixty Soviet divisions behind them. For days, we would work in the CROC, the Central Region Operations Centre, doing round-the-clock shifts and becoming totally disoriented as to time; emerging in daylight, expecting supper when it was breakfast-time, or darkness when the sun was shining. This added to the general feeling of unreality brought on by watching the red arrows marching steadily westwards, hour by hour, over the huge map on the war-room wall; seeing them crunching over first Brunswick then Hannover then Herford, and on down the autobahn I knew so well towards the Ruhr. The 3rd Guards Army, the 14th Motor Rifle Division, the 23rd Tank Division, the 35th . . . , all backed up by chemical and nuclear weapons. Mushroom shapes would sprout on the map as Minden, Osnabruck, Wesel, Arnhem, Cologne disappeared off the face of the earth in a blinding flash of light; green splodges of colour indicated where thousands of soldiers and civilians were writhing and twitching under a cloud of nerve gas. They were always defensive battles we fought; an offensive into Warpact territory was never part of the scenario.

The Colonel (Operations) was a calm, confident, tall British officer by the name of Paul Freeland. At five minutes past eight o'clock each morning, after the weather report had been summarily given for the benefit of the aviators, he would take the stage and General Ferber would lean across the balcony of his dais, smile and say, with great courtesy, 'Good morning, colonel,' in response to the greeting Paul gave him prior to beginning his briefing. The old German artillery officer, with his Iron Cross, who had fought the British at Monte Casino, had a rapport with the British infantry colonel who was still a boy when Ferber was caught up in Hitler's war.

For a few days this scene would be repeated. Then, in time, as the enemy forces neared the Rhine, nuclear release would be ordered. Our planes would fly into East Germany, Poland and Russia, our intercontinental ballistic missiles would arc over the northern hemisphere — passing Soviet planes and missiles going westwards. Then someone would pull the plug and declare Exend. We would get up, stretch, pack up our pens and files of data and gratefully emerge into the real world.

And yet, that play-acting WAS the real world. It was more important than anything else that was happening anywhere else — the economy of nations, the welfare of their populations, their personal relationships — for if statesmen miscalculated then the world would end in a matter of days. War was poised, ready to be triggered. Preparing for it demanded the attention of hundreds of thousands of people on both sides of the Iron Curtain. The far greater majority of the millions on each side went about their lives unaware of what was being planned, and at what dire cost, to preserve their political ideology. Better Marx than Mayhem, better Dead than Red? Nevertheless, it was the determination of the West to block communist expansionism that in the end brought about the breakup of the penal Soviet system by pricing it out of the business: the cost of modern weaponry became so great that their tottering economy could not keep pace. It was sheer pragmatism, not a change of heart, that brought glasnost. In the end the hard men of the Kremlin got it wrong and the people who had, for the most part grudgingly, trusted in them lost not only the standard of living taken from them for decades but the whole justification for having lost it. And the West, too, was a loser. How much better might the world have been if the billions spent on the cold war had been utilised in other ways?

Not long ago, at the end of 1991, I spoke on behalf of an organisation called Peace Through NATO to a group of Sixth Form students at a local Comprehensive school. I had been asked to provide counter-arguments to those that would be put forward by a representative of the Campaign for Nuclear Disarmament. On the day, she suggested that, as there was now no threat from the Soviet Union, we should disarm completely. I countered that the situation was more confused and dangerous than it had ever been while the stand-off existed between East and West, and that this was not the time to roll over and wag our tails. I told the young people about the CROC, and that nearly all the weapons that had been deployed by the Soviets in those days still existed — tens of thousands of them, now under no centralised control. It was a very lively debate, in which the majority, strangely enough as far as I was concerned, were anti-CND. At the end of it all, after questions had been answered and we were breaking up, a nice lad came up to me and said: 'Did we ever win?' 'No,' I replied, 'we never won.' But then, nobody did.

★ ★ ★

Didcot, like Kineton, had been bad news. Brunssum turned out to be a welcome contrast. While there I lived alone, to begin with in the Officers' Club, run on American lines, later in a little flat in a village called Wijnansrade (Vinansrahder), about seven miles from Brunssum. At weekends I had lots of options as to where to go.

When the headquarters moved from Fontainbleu it went to a depressed area of Limburg where old coal mines had been closed down. (The headquarters is at the pit-head of one of the old workings.) Limburg province is a finger of Dutch land that

404

protrudes into Belgium and Germany — at one point it is possible to straddle all three countries. On one side is Aachen, on the other Liege. The Ardennes are an hour away, Brussels and Amsterdam an hour-and-a-half, Paris two.

Holland is a lovely little country, flat and green and studded with sparkling gems of red-brick towns and villages, all spick and span and neat. People eat well and take pride in an orderly and sane society. It is a pity that modern Holland has bred a lot of drug-cult citizens. It is having trouble finding the balance between the disciplined, Dutch-Reformed-Church background and the promiscuous, porn-oriented, free-expression trend of recent times. In The Hague, sex shops flagrantly flaunt their phalluses beside old churches that were there when Rembrandt walked the streets — perhaps thinking of similar gymnastics in bed with Saskia but at least having the good grace to keep his thoughts off his canvasses.

It was in the Mauritzhaus in The Hague that I saw the painting that has impressed me more than any other I have ever seen: the view of Delft painted by Vermeer; the one with lowering clouds casting a dark shadow over the waterfront, making the skyline of turrets and towers stand out in silhouette while, behind, the sky is blue, and sunshine warms the air. It is not a very big picture, about four feet by three, I suppose, but it completely dominates all the other master-pieces in the room. I stood in front of it with Albert Brakel and wondered if Vermeer had realised what he had achieved, or if he regarded it as just another effort that had not come up to his expectations — and worried whether people would notice that he had painted out a couple of figures in the foreground. In comparison, for me the Mona Lisa is smiling because she is wondering what all the fuss is about.

During the same trip, a conference to discuss the logistics of getting tens of thousands of tons of logistic re-supply on to the Continent prior to war, the team went aboard a small ship and cruised along the waterfronts of Rotterdam. The sight of vast container ships towering above us, the cranes roosting on the docks like grey flamingoes on the edge of a lake, the sheer size of the enterprise, amazed me. As did Lynn Hoskin's reply when I asked him if he had tried one of the fine restaurants in the Hague the night before: 'Aw heck no, we found a McDarnalds and had a burger.' Everyone to their taste, but what a wasted opportunity, eh?

★ ★ ★

'You're an ammunition man,' a British colonel said to me one day. 'Want to see some interesting stuff?' It transpired that two American sergeants on the base were World War Two buffs who had made a surprising find in the Ardennes. The colonel and I went there one Sunday morning.

Not far from Malmedy and about twenty miles from Bastoigne, a bit off the beaten track but near to a minor public road, we found a forest of tall old pines, amongst which were the remains of an American battalion defensive position. We walked around and identified the headquarters dug-out, the company command posts, the platoon fox-holes. There were bullets everywhere, and ammunition clips; whole hand grenades and the remains of rifles and steel helmets; even, on the lip of a crumbling fox-hole, an old, rusty field cooker. And scattered human bones. I picked up shins and arms and pieces of feet and fingers, looked for skulls but could not find any. It was quite unbelievable.

Standing looking down a slope the road dipped, then turned away into the trees. The sleepy-eyed soldiers in that position must have been standing in their slits looking down

407

the road when German tanks came straight at them, just before Christmas 1944. There must have been a short, sharp fire-fight and then the weight of armour in von Rundstedt's last fling, the final spasm of the Nazi war machine, threw them back violently. The Americans pulled out without even having time to retrieve their dead, let alone their equipment. The whole place must have been blanketed with deep snow, then, after the battle moved on, more snow fell through a long winter. It was many months before the thaw came. When it did, foxes pulled the human remains apart, gnawed them and scattered them around. They, and all the military paraphernalia, settled into the loam and slowly bleached and rusted as the seasons passed. Why nobody had found them before is inexplicable.

The next day my friend went into the Belgian liaison officer's room and dumped a bag full of bones and bits on his desk. Soon after that, a Belgian army squad began to clean up the mess, which brought on a hue and cry in the local press. Why had this happened? Who was to blame?

Not very far away from the scene of that little battle there are two big American cemeteries, at Henri-Chapelle and Margraton. The recipients of the Congressional

Medal of Honor have their names picked out in gold on their headstones. Maybe some of the men defending that position earned that medal but there was nobody left alive to recount their deeds. I hope the bones we found under the pines have joined those of their comrades.

★   ★   ★

General Ferber's Personal Assistant was a German colonel by the name of Franz Wiesner. One day he asked me if I would be so good as to take his wife and daughter to Munich, where they lived, on my way to the NATO School at Oberammergau, where I was to attend a course. I did so with pleasure and began a friendship which bore surprising fruit.

Wiesner asked me to his house for supper one evening. When I arrived I found that the only other guest was to be the general. It was his last night in the army; he had already handed over command, his wife had already left for Bavaria. I found myself sharing a fine meal, served by Inge and Sabine, who did not sit down with us, and drinking fine wine, while Ferber reminisced. Now and then he reproved Franz when he lapsed into German. 'Speak English for the colonel, Herr Wiesner, if you please.' I feel privileged to have been there that night, but sorry my German was not good enough to have been able to spare them the need to speak in a foreign language.

Ferber's successor was General Doctor Karl Schnell, an appropriate name for a fast-moving German officer. He was meticulously thorough and had an acute brain. I am sure no-one could have delved more deeply into the intricacies of the strategy and tactics of the Central Region of NATO than he. For instance, he did a detailed terrain study of every one of his eight Corps areas, getting to know all brigade and even some battalion positions. His was a cooler personality than Ferber's but in both of them I had complete confidence. Schnell subsequently became a minister in the Ministry of Defence in Bonn, where one day I went to attend a conference chaired by General Sir John Mogg, who was by then Deputy Supreme Allied Commander. On my return to AFCENT I heard with disbelief that Franz Wiesner had been sacked and had already left the headquarters. It seems that, tactlessly, he had repeatedly told Schnell how his predecessor would have done things; did it so often that eventually the general felt he could no longer work with him. It was a pity. Franz had been selected for the command of a brigade in the Mountain Division, which appointment was delayed for a year or two.

That episode was mirrored by another in the American Zone when ComCentag sacked one of his Corps commanders on the spot during a visit: he too was out, bag and baggage, within twenty-four hours and on his way back to the USA. His C-in-C had objected to the man's attitude towards officers in other armies. As might be expected, news of that event travelled with the speed of light through the whole of the NATO command. It certainly sharpened people's awareness of the frailty of their careers, though in the British Army it would be quite inconceivable for a three-star general to be peremptorily fired like that — except in wartime, when other considerations apply. I think that, rightly, the view would be taken that if a man has achieved that sort of eminence he must have earned it along the way. But it was typical of the American way of doing things: generally they are lax but if someone steps over the line they get ninety-nine years in the brig. Or they are wired up to three thousand volts.

Some years later I lectured at the American Army Staff College at Fort Leavenworth, next to which is sited the biggest federal prison in the United States. Part of it is the military jail, in which officers are incarcerated along

411

with soldiers. We at least insist that law-breaking officers who are given terms of imprisonment lose their commissions and leave the army before beginning their sentence.

★　★　★

On a bitter winter's day en route to Heidelburg in a staff car driven by a German lance-corporal Albert Brakel and I chanced upon the scene of a road accident. A woman in her thirties had skidded on black ice and been hit hard by an oncoming car. She was sitting dead at the wheel, almost unmarked, when I opened the door a few moments after it happened.

We were starting to move away from the car when Albert saw a movement under the tumbled back-seat cushion. It was her little daughter, aged about nine. Because the doors were smashed and twisted it took a while to extract her. As always, Albert was calm and positive. As I fussed around with the ignition and a fire extinguisher Albert put the unconscious child on the ground out of sight of her dead mother, straightened her broken leg, soothed her as she regained conscious-ness and waited beside her until she was lifted into an ambulance. Albert had been a

412

prisoner of the Japanese for three years, working on the Burma-Siam railway. Once, during a night-watch in the CROC, I asked him about it.

He was twenty-two when he was captured, he said, and was marched off wearing a khaki drill shirt, shorts, stockings and boots. When he was finally released all he had left was the tattered remains of the shorts. He had no possessions with him at all except a mosquito net, and that he guarded with his life.

'How did you sleep?' I asked. 'On a bamboo mat,' he replied.

'What did you eat?'

'Rice. But every night, on a roster, men went out into the jungle in search of fruit, nuts and edible roots with which to augment the diet for everyone.'

'Why did the Japanese allow you to leave the camp?' I wondered.

'Where could we go? There was nothing but jungle for five hundred miles. They knew there was nowhere for us to go.'

'Did many of you die?'

'If you were over forty you died, otherwise most of us lived.'

'How could you live, with nothing except a handful of rice to eat every day and a mat to lie on at night?'

413

'What more do you need?' Albert asked me.

He could speak Dutch, Indonesian, German and French — and, of course, English — with fluency, and during international conferences would amaze me by switching from one to the other without pause. Most of the Dutch people I met spoke three, sometimes four, languages. The British and the Americans, almost without exception, spoke only one.

Another friend I made in Brunssum was Ernst Petersen, a German lieutenant-colonel who had been captured by the Russians in 1945, in the very last days of the war. The Soviet armour had lunged past on its way to Berlin, leaving the 1st German Division isolated on the Baltic coast north-east of the capital. After it fell the Russians turned their attention to mopping-up, and in order to avoid further fighting offered the Germans the right to march out of their defensive positions carrying their arms. They agreed, provided officers and soldiers were not separated, but as soon as they handed over their weapons, they were. Petersen also was twenty-two at the time, and was released seven years later only because he had contracted tuberculosis. Most of the men of his division whom he left behind in the

414

Russian camps never came out of them.

When he told me his story I commented that it must have been terrible to have spent the most sexually potent years of his life deprived of all female contact. 'We never thought about sex,' he replied: 'All we thought about was food. We had no sexual urge because we were always nearly starving. The only people with a sexual urge were the cooks, who sometimes managed to have sex with Russian women who worked in the camp kitchens. Other people had no strength, and never thought about it. All we dreamed of was food . . .

'We had no paper either. Paper was like gold. If a man found a scrap of paper he would write menus on it with the stub of a pencil or a burnt twig. The things he dreamed of — gravies, roasts, dumplings, sauces, puddings. We hardly ever thought about our families: we thought they must have given us up for dead long before — our wives and girls. We lived one day at a time, dreaming about all the food we would eat when we got out, making lists, comparing notes.'

Ernst had a bad fall from a horse one day and broke an upper arm in five places. I visited him for weeks as he lay with a steel pin in the elbow and the arm wired up above his head, a position that seemingly would drive most people mad. He remained cheerful, and eventually made a good recovery. A third friend was made under strange circumstances.

His name was Oberst Oberst. (Sounds like a character in Catch 22, doesn't it, oberst being the German for 'colonel'. Colonel colonel? But it was real.) On my very first exercise, around four a.m. on this mighty long night, this American lieutenant-colonel came up to my desk and hovered there. I could see him thinking Goddam Limey Colonel; he had that look on his face. He asked me a question very rudely. I replied, and he gave me a surly answer. I was not in the mood. I blasted him out of earshot, but from that day forward, strangely enough, we were good friends. It turned out that Oberst had been born a German and had been in the Hitler Youth — most young men were, it was the done thing to be in those days because of what we would now call peer pressure. During the war he had fought with the German army, but after it, had emigrated to the USA. In due course, on becoming an American citizen he had joined their army, and here he was, back in Europe. He had a young, all-American wife, and no doubt has now settled down back in the good ole USA.

I had tried to join the American army too, in my young days. Looking back, it was an extraordinary thing to do but growing up in the war it had seemed to my innocent mind that we were all interchangeable. Maybe, one day, that will be the case, but it's a long way off, I fear. I had a reply from the Commanding General in Europe, Lucius D. Clay, telling me that I was an alien, but thanks all the same! I was very affronted. Me, an alien?

Two remarks made by German officers stay in my mind, one of them regarding the North African campaign. I mentioned it once to Harry Marx — a strange name for a German colonel — and he said, rather testily, 'Oh, you British are always talking about it! To us it was nothing, just a little side show. We had only a handful of divisions there: on the Russian front we had a hundred.'

The second was made by an air force lieutenant-colonel in a wine bar in Oberammergau. He was employed on Taceval, the inspection and evaluation of NATO airfields. I said something to the effect that the East Germans seemed to be hard-line communists. He gave me a sideways look, smiled and said, 'You have to realise, Colonel Peter, that it is the German nature to do everything one hundred per cent: be a Nazi, be a communist, be a capitalist. It doesn't much matter which.'

The only time I ever had an angry reaction about something I said was when I told a group of Europeans that Britain was not part of the Continent of Europe. To me, as to many people in this country, the channel had always partitioned us off, mentally as well as physically. They just did not see it that way and were furious. On reflection, I know they were right. It is like the Armistice Parades. We all sink or swim together, and old enmities and ideas must be forgotten.

Two instances of national pride:

After a conference with six or seven French officers who came from the French Corps stationed near Freiburg, during lunch and in a pause in the conversation I said to the man sitting next to me, 'This is the twenty-fifth anniversary of the fall of Dien Bien Phu.' He froze, and so did all his companions. There was dead silence for several moments before conversation began again. A British officer would have made a wry comment, or begun to talk about the campaign, which is what I had hoped would happen, but to them it was an open wound. (And still is, as I found to my cost recently, when my biography of General Vo Nguyen Giap, the man who beat them at Dien Bien Phu, was published in Paris: they didn't want to know.) The second was also concerned with Vietnam.

It happened that there was a big official function in the Officers' Club on the night that it was announced in Washington that the USA was withdrawing from South Vietnam. We were all there in our mess kit, the men in blues and reds and golds, the women high-coifed and sparkling in long dresses. That night and for the rest of my time in Brunssum most of the American officers resolutely avoided a single mention of that war. The exception was Bill Pinner, who told me he had flown hundreds of missions there. 'Yeah, hundreds. We had sensors, an' we dropped them right along the Ho Chi Minh trail. Those things could hear a man's footsteps. They were all tied in to computers so we noo just how many people an' trucks were goin' up an' down that trail, an' where. Ah flew up an' down beside it naght after naght, takin' a drink every forty minutes from one of the big tanker birds flyin' up there at thirty-thousand feet. Then Ah'd go in an' zap the trucks. Man, we musta busted a thousand trucks that year.'

'A thousand trucks, Bill? That's a hell of a lot of trucks.'

'Nah, Peter. A thousand wasn't a lot. Jeez, they had ten thousand trucks.'

That, to me, just about sums up the

Vietnam War. That and another story.

'We had a lot of technology out there. Too much, maybe. There was a big deepo ten miles by ten, packed with equipment. Trouble was, no-one noo where anythin' was. The people kept registrin' non-availabilities an' the people stateside kept raght on sendin' them more, which got heaped on top of the pile. An' still they couldn't find anythin'. An' still it kept coming, an' bein' put on top of the pile.'

In the end, the North Vietnamese got the lot, when they finally took over Saigon in April 1975.

Another time, a bit maudlin after a few Southern Comforts Bill asked: 'Wanna know wha Ah never got promoted, Peter? Ah'll tell you wha. My brigadier-general, he had a Vietnamese girl friend. Ah put a sensor right under his bed. He didn't like that.'

He may not have liked that or my friend but Ah sure did. He gave Simon and me a marvellous Thanksgiving dinner he had cooked all by himself because Kathy was stateside looking after her ailing Ma — black-eyed peas, turkey and cranberry sauce, the lot. And a fantastic dish made of layers of oysters sandwiched between layers of crackers (water biscuits) eight deep and cooked slowly in an oven-proof dish. Man, Ah aint never tasted anythin' like it.

Simon, who was eighteen, visited me quite often, often unexpectedly. We had some good times together, went to Amsterdam once and stayed in the posh Marriott hotel. Once, the whole family went to Oberammergau where we rented an apartment in the NATO School — the commandant of which had a pet rabbit called Harvey that he took for a walk after breakfast every morning. I met a lot of other memorable characters in AFCENT. There was a very tough, hard-bitten looking French general with rows of medals who sat biting his nails down to the quick, holding the fingers of one hand hard against his teeth with the other, nibbling and tearing at his nails. There was an American colonel who had a Queeg of the Caine Mutiny-type tick: he rolled his West Point ring up and off his middle finger and then in turn down and up all the other fingers of his left hand, doing this with the thumb; then he would transfer the ring to his other hand and do it all over again. And again. And again. Unconsciously, while talking all the time or making a note or two with a pen clutched in the spare hand. Both, I fancy, would have cracked up if we had ever gone to war.

There was another 'bird' colonel (they wear a sort of splattered eagle as a shoulder badge to denote full colonel rank) with a very lived-in face who told me that he went home to Arizona every year without fail and with a bunch of buddies took off into the mountains on horseback, just like the pioneers of old. They slept out under the stars, roughing it but delighting in being away from female company for a while, no doubt being henpecked, as many American males are. Everything they needed was carried on a pack horse or two. Everything? 'Yeah, well, every three days a heelo brings in the ice and the beer.'

Lynn Hoskin's wife, Beverly, was a pretty woman from Georgia with an enormous beam. 'Aw, shoot,' she would say when the bingo line did not come out for her in the officers' club: 'D'ya-all see that, Lynn?' One evening I went to the Hoskins to meet his cousin, an opera singer. I said he was big. Well, she was gigantic, and had a voice to match. A very big lady, all round, she was, with bright red hair. After supper she gave us a snatch of Brunhilde. She stood there like a Valkyrie, took a deep breath and let rip. Her fantastic voice, which could, and did, fill the hall at Bayreuth, made the chandeliers (yes, they had chandeliers) tremble and the glasses rattle on the table. I sat there with a smile frozen on my face trying desperately not to go into hysterics and cause an international incident. Another time when I had to bite my lip was during the presentation of a medal by Hoskins to one of his colonels, Andy K Jordan the Third. Andy's wife was Korean, Yung Hee, and she stood there demurely while Hoskins droned on about what an outstanding career Andy had had and what an outstanding contribution he had made to the work of AFCENT. It was all taken so very seriously, the three of them standing in front of the Stars and Stripes, with me in the background, an honoured guest. No band, though.

I tended not to take such things seriously, or the fact that people said the CIA had an active contingent in AFCENT, but after one particular incident came to the conclusion that the CIA, unlike the fairies at the bottom of the garden, really does exist. It came about like this:

I was sitting alone at dinner one evening when Yung Hee trotted over to my table, all excited. She was sharp, and a marvellous Bridge player. She and Andy had living with them the daughter of one of her sisters, whom they had adopted. Peanut, they called her; she was thirteen and skinny, wore glasses and was very shy, but when she played the piano, well, that was something else, as they say.

'Conglatulations, Peter,' she said: 'Hear you gonna be one-star.' I stared at her. 'Nonsense, Yung Hee,' I said, 'No way.'

'True!' she said insistently, touching my arm. 'Go on! You mean tell me you don't know? You kiddin'.' She gave a little snort. 'You just not 'llowed to say. I very pleased. Blirriant!' she said. 'Conglatulations.' And she trotted off back to her husband.

I don't suppose there are many officers who heard of their promotion to the rank of brigadier from the Korean wife of an American colonel, but that's how it was.

When I had finished eating I joined them. They were sitting with another colonel, a nice man by the name of Ralph Kretzner, and his wife. When I asked where they had heard this rumour he said: 'Aw, it's right, for sure, Peter. An' what's more, I know where you're goin'. To Germany. To Bielefeld.' It turned out he was right, but I did not hear about it officially for several weeks.

When that news came through Cincent was furious and wrote to no-one in particular in the Ministry of Defence, Whitehall, London: 'I strongly object to this officer being moved until he has done a full tour of duty.' Signed FERBER, General, German Army.

I understand that this epistle rattled around for a few days while people figured out what to do with it. Then the Military Secretary wrote a placating letter. In fact I did not go to my new job for another nine months, in June 1976.

★　★　★

Before leaving Brunssum I paid another visit to Aachen. Standing beside Charlemagne's throne — plain, square blocks of white marble — I looked down from the gallery in which it stands into the well of the lovely octagonal cathedral he built there around the year 800 AD. I imagined him listening to the chanting of the monks, his long blonde hair falling to his shoulders. He was a big man, six feet two in height in the days when people were pygmies. He had piercing blue eyes, so it is said, and in his youth had been strikingly good-looking — though no face could be as handsome as that of the solid gold, gem-studded 'death mask' that stands in a glass case in a room behind the cathedral.

It was a harsh, cold night and a strong wind buffeted the cathedral. Beside him the flame on a chunky candle, spiked on to a tall, twisted, iron stand, guttered in a draught, almost died, then steadied and grew tall again. He shivered, pulled at the furs around his shoulders and stamped his feet in their thick-soled boots. Below the balcony on which he sat the priests were going about their business. Too slowly for his liking. Fussily. Trying to please him. It was his own fault for insisting that they got it right.

He picked up his Bible and slowly turned the beautifully-illuminated parchment pages but the lettering was difficult to see and he could not understand some of the words. Impatiently, he shut the book again with a thump that echoed in the high roof. Though he did not want to admit it, it seemed as if he would never learn to read properly — and still less to write. He had tried, off and on, but something had always happened to prevent him from continuing with his studies: a sudden journey to this place or that, another war to fight, mostly against the Saxons, curse them, in those desolate places where they lived. Stunted people crouching under stunted, wind-bent trees. So stupid they never knew when they were beaten! He pulled at his beard and grunted, and a priest standing beside him holding a wavering taper looked around, startled. Wax dripped onto the floor. He glared at the man, who hurriedly turned away.

Sheepskins were piled into his hard-edged, square throne. He wriggled down into them and tugged again at his otter-fur cape but try as he might, he could not get warm. Suddenly, he felt very tired. Perhaps he was ailing? Was he? No, not he! A mug of mulled wine to drink and a big plate of food would soon set him right. He coughed, and chomped his jaws, feeling with his tongue the gaps in his gums where teeth had been wrenched out when they rotted and ached. A short agony had relieved a long pain . . .

Why must these clerics go on so, he complained to himself? God knew that they were here in the cathedral, didn't He? Knew they had left the warmth of their fires to come and speak to Him! Wasn't that enough?

There was no warmth here, though! He glared at the dead brazier and gave it a shove with his foot. Iron scraped on the stone floor and Rotrada, his best-loved daughter, turned and looked up at him. She smiled shyly and then bent her head again over clasped hands. Beyond her were his other daughters, and beyond them his rascally son Pepin. A pig-headed, lewd youth he was. And hunch-backed, what was more! His fingers tightened in anger on the arms of the throne. He would send him to a monas-tery, that's what he would do! That would bring the puppy to heel. A few years of lone devotions would dry the sap in him. Prum! That would be a good place. Miles from anywhere. In the Eifel. He looked away from Pepin, on whom his eyes had never lingered, and lovingly at Rotrada.

A beautiful girl, she was: blue-eyed, soft skinned, warm and gentle. Her long blonde hair, plaited almost to her waist, was thick, like a golden rope. She wanted to marry, but the man was not good enough for her. And besides, he could not bear to think of her leaving his side; of not seeing her every day. Perhaps he should let her take the boy as her lover, here, in the palace. She was only human, and he understood the human urge well enough; had felt it surge ten thousand times . . . Four wives he had had, and many, many women. And only God knew how many children. He would keep the count! His eyes misted dreamily, but then he pulled himself together: such thoughts were not for this place.

He was amazed by what he had achieved, with God's help. His lands stretched from the Atlantic shores to the Danube and the Black Sea; from the bitter north to the gentle south. Brittany escaped him, and some of the winter lands, but apart from those desolate places the whole world was his. There were other places, clearly there were, the Holy Land for one, but the real world was his, by God's grace, and he was slowly bringing God's word to it. In the many places he had conquered monasteries had been built and monks were preaching.

Gersvinda . . . She was a Saxon. He could see her now, shaking with fear when the prisoners were brought before him. She would not look up when he ordered her to, and on an impulse had told his men to bring her to him that night. He was glad he had spared her, but others he had not. Boys who were taller than a sword had been shortened by a head . . .

His kick at the iron bucket had stirred its embers. It was giving off more heat, and at last his feet were beginning to feel warm. He settled more deeply into his furs, the chanted beauty of the litany relaxing him. Through the leaded windows he could see snowflakes whirling; drifting down or slantwise. Even upwards, now and then. Puzzled, he wondered about that . . .

He had had a long day, hunting in the thick forests around Aachen. A hard day riding a fine horse over rock-hard earth, the breath from horses and riders hanging in the air like swirling, vanishing plumes of smoke, his hands which held the reins stiff with cold. Ermine he had caught, as well as better game. He took hold of a black tail on the white trimming of his robe, rolling it between thumb and fingers. Then, suddenly, his arms and legs felt like lead, his head nodded forward on his chest, his left hand loosened its hold on the Bible. He breathed heavily and dreamed.

Over a period of forty-six years Charlemagne master-minded fifty-three military campaigns, most of which were intended to bring Christianity to pagan Europe but some of which were necessary to maintain his power. When he died at the age of seventy-five — a mighty age in those times for a mighty man — he controlled almost the whole of what is now Europe, from the Danube to the

Atlantic, from Denmark to northern Spain and northern Italy. It is a tragedy that only one of his sons outlived him; not the rake-hell Pepin, whom he had banished to a monastery and who might have been a strong leader, but the gentle muddler Louis the Pious. Quite soon the empire broke up into small kingdoms and principalities ruled over by ignorant men who, generation after generation, century after century, passed their time in useless and bloody disputes.

In a way Charlemagne, Carolus Magnus, was the first commander of the Central Region.

It is one of the greatest Ifs in history. What would have happened if he had ensured the succession in the hands of a man as strong and wise as he.

He never conquered the Brits, though.

12

Last Post

In my previous tours of duty in Germany I had often visited the Corps headquarters. It was housed in what had once been a German army barracks (as was much of the British Army of the Rhine) on the main road that leads into the town off the autobahn. I had also visited people who lived in the so-called Music Alley, in roads named after German composers. I was allocated a house in Joseph Haydn Strasse, but I was to be unaccompanied there too, for a lot of the time. Unfortunately, Sybil and I had become used to being apart and were now living distant lives — with no acrimony but no craving to be together, either. She visited me occasionally but most of the time she was at home in Sevenoaks. (Not long after I left Bielefeld a colonel was shot dead by the IRA a few houses further down the road.)

My job in 1st British Corps was to be in charge of the Ordnance supply organisation, which consisted of about sixty units ranging in size from two men and a dog to a battalion of five hundred men. Together, they were responsible for supplying the four Armoured Divisions and Corps troops — more than thirty thousand men — with ammunition, petrol, vehicles, food, stores and spare parts; and for looking after the contents of the scores of barracks and the sixteen thousand married quarters in which the soldiers and their families lived.

I had eight lieutenant-colonels — four of them called Mike — under my command and it was interesting to compare their abilities, personalities and characters. It is character that counts in the end. The overheated zealot, however superficially efficient he may be, is a pain in the neck and makes work. The man who tries hard, fluffs the occasional trick but knows that he has done so, is prepared to admit it — instead of trying to bluff it out — learns from his mistakes, and smiles withal, is a pearl. One such was Mike Robinson who, several months after I had arrived in the Corps, attended a guest night on his birthday, went home, felt unwell, went to the Medical Centre, was sent back to his house to get his 'small kit' so as to be ready for admittance to the British Military Hospital at Rinteln and when he got there dropped dead of a heart attack at the feet of the doctor who had come to see what was wrong with him. I missed him a lot, and his little boy, who called me Paddington because, like the bear, I had come from Peru.

The four divisional headquarters were at Verden, Soest, Lubbeke and Herford. Their brigade headquarters were scattered around the North German Plain; in Minden, Osnabruck, Munster, Detmold and so on. The one that had been in Catterick when I was in Lubbeke, the 6th — then commanded by 'Wobbly' Scott-Barrett, a big, breezy ex-Scots Guardsman — was back where it should have been all along, in Germany. My job was to see that my many units were functioning efficiently, and to do it I had constantly to travel; in a helicopter if one was available or up and down that bleeding autobahn in a staff car if one was not. (It and the others did bleed, quite often. I have seen some terrible accidents on autobahns. Once, on a Sunday afternoon, when I went with the family to Munster where the art college there had undertaken to cast the clay figure of Sybil I had made, we ran into dense fog that lay in a blanket about twenty feet deep. Through a sudden gap in it I saw a column of black smoke rising high into the sky. I guessed what it might be, but fortunately it was on the other side of the road. As we approached, we could see that several cars had crashed and were on fire. I could not stop without probably causing another accident on our side of the road, nor do anything more than flash my lights in warning as cars went past us at speed on the other side of the road and smashed into the pile already burning there. It was a nightmare situation.) Travelling was a major part of my life, and as had happened in the Cross Keys 2nd Division, we frequently left barracks and took to the woods and villages.

Soon after my arrival there was a particularly big exercise code-named Spearpoint. (The 1st British Corps tac sign is a spearpoint.) Eighteen thousand troops were deployed, about eight thousand vehicles and also elements of the 2nd (US) Division, who acted as enemy. I was much impressed by the panache of these soldiers as they rolled over the countryside near the great castle of Marienberg, one-time seat of the Elector of Hannover, ancestor of the lady I was working for. In their tanks, camouflaged differently from ours, standing up in the turrets chewing gum and waving, they reminded me of the GIs in their General Grants that had rolled through Helsby in the early 1940s when I was a boy, en route from Liverpool to the south of England and eventually, some of them, as far as the Elbe.

Exercise Spearpoint was intended to validate the concept of a restructured Corps in which the brigade level of command — something that had evolved over centuries — was done away with and replaced by smaller divisional headquarters that controlled bigger battle-groups. There were few people who thought it was a good idea but it had been accepted for trial by the Army Board because it would have saved a few hundred men and avoided yet another cut in the army's order of battle — and another propaganda battle to 'Save the Argylls,' or whoever. Sure enough, it did not work: the divisions could not control the battle-groups effectively without the brigade level of command — something, incidentally, that had already been proved by the Americans when they experimented with what they called the Pentomic Division. In the end our organisation reverted to what it had been for a long time. Yet again money had been wasted because the government had to accede to cuts in expenditure demanded by the Treasury, and laid some of them on the Defence vote. But it wasn't their fault, was it? The fault lay in the national characteristic of skiving on the shop floor and milking the system by management: of unproductive time on one side and long 'business' lunches, company cars and lavish expense accounts on the other.

Flying over the battlefield, as I did every day during 'Spearpoint,' I came as near as I ever would to seeing what the Third World War in Europe would have been like if it had ever come. Fighter/ground-attack aircraft whistled past me to put in simulated strikes on the enemy. Tanks rolled out of woods to engage in a fire-fight with other tanks hull-down on a defended ridge; tank tracks criss-crossed the autumn fields, leaving a complex spirograph pattern in the mud — loops and whorls and overlapping circles similar to those I had seen twenty years before when flying over the Libyan desert. 175mm heavy guns, their trails split and splayed out, roosted on the edge of woods. If you knew where to look, you could spot the muzzles of self-propelled 105mm and 155mm guns poking up out of clearings in the woods, and the pointed snouts of Lance missiles. Sappers were building a bridge in the shadow of Marienberg. I have a cine-film clip of me standing on one side of my Landrover — on the front bumper of which is a red plate with a single silver star — with, on the other side, Lance-Corporal Sam Snodgrass, my driver, an ex-miner from County Durham, a grand, cheerful fellow. He was married to an American girl and soon left the army to go and work in the American zone of Germany.

During the exercise Prince Philip visited the control headquarters. When we were introduced I was astonished to find that his hand was a hard, leathery, horny mit. From riding, and playing polo, I suppose.

A propos Lance missiles, when I had been responsible for overseeing their acceptance into service in the British army our liaison officer in the United States told me that there were no special safety features envisaged for them since the Americans believed 'their engineering was done to such fine tolerances that there was no danger of anything going wrong.' I told him to go back and insist that unless special tools and safety equipment were designed we would not buy the missiles (not that it was in my gift, but making the threat was the point). In due course the safety measures were produced, but I have since wondered if that same attitude had anything to do with the tragic malfunctioning of NASA's space exploration rockets a few years later. From reading the reports it seems it did.

★　★　★

As with seeing those American tanks, another loop closed for me when I went to visit the CO of 50th Missile Regiment in Menden. Standing in his office surrounded by photographs of previous commanding officers I told him I had a long association with the regiment. 'Not as long as mine, I bet, Brigadier,' he said confidently: 'I have served in it in every rank from second-lieutenant to lieutenant-colonel.' I couldn't resist it. 'I was a troop commander in the regiment in the 1950s,' I told him, 'and then Assistant Adjutant. And my brother was captured with it in Tobruk in 1942.'

Mike's Bar, named after General Sir Michael West, an early, very distinguished Corps Commander who was fond of social life, was the place in which VIPs were entertained to lunch by the Corps Commander and his brigadiers. On one occasion Robert Brown, the then Under Secretary of State for the Army, was the VIP. Seeing him standing alone while Sir Richard Worsley, the commander, fetched him a drink I walked over to keep him company. For want of something to say I told him that I had once worked for one of the members of the Army Board, of which he was now the head. He looked sideways at me, sniffed and said: 'All I get from t'Army Board is a loada crap.' Which only goes to show that years of association with the old Labour movement broadened the vocabulary and sharpened the wit. Later that afternoon, during a briefing in the War Room, Brown asked the Corps Commander, ' 'Ow many divisions do you 'ave 'ere in Germany? Is it three or four? I can never remember.' Fred Mulley, his boss, the Secretary of State for Defence, had clearly not made a good job of briefing Brown. Or then again, maybe he didn't know, either.

★   ★   ★

I was still writing. Stopping the Clock, an account of post-war terrorist bomb disposal operations, had been published in July 1977, and I had now begun a novel about the Anglo-French intervention in Suez in 1956. To me, since that debacle marked the beginning of the end for this country as a major world power, it seemed a suitable subject with which to begin a quartet of books charting our decline and fall.

After a few months I came to an impasse: I needed a first-hand account of the parachute assault on Egypt in 1966. The problem was that any officers who had been there must now either have left the service or be very senior indeed, and difficult to get at; any soldiers would have left the army or been commissioned. In the Training Centre at Sennelager one evening I walked into the bar in the mess to find it packed with officers of the 2nd Battalion of the Parachute Regiment, down from Berlin to do field exercises. I looked around for a likely lad, went over to him and said: 'Do you know anyone who dropped at Gamil on 5th November 1966?' 'Yes,' he answered, 'I did'. It turned out he had been a corporal in the 3rd Battalion then and was now the quartermaster of the 2nd. We had a few drinks together and I got the details I needed. Serendipity, they call it.

★ ★ ★

When I was a young officer I had to have my appendix out in Warrington hospital. I had pneumonia again in 1962, and in 1963 had to have a hernia repaired in the Military Hospital at Catterick after ripping my stomach muscles while carting sand for a sandpit for the boys in a wheelbarrow. Seven years later, fool that I was, I again damaged myself lifting a heavy suitcase onto the roof-rack of our car outside the Royal George hotel in Perth. In consequence, I put in train a long series of surgical encounters of a dread kind: between 1971 and 1974 I submitted three times to starvings, shavings, tranquilisings, dimly-seen spacemen in rubber boots who had gleaming eyes, the sudden onset of darkness and a roaring in the ears after counting to eight — then waking up with a lot of pain in the region of a vital area.

Usually, it is not difficult to repair an inguinal hernia but for some reason my flesh proved to be a great challenge to the surgeons who operated. Twice, they made a cock-up of it, and once the man in rubber boots was in the benefit-of-the-doubt category. The only good side-effect of the operations was that I twice went to Osbourne House in the Isle of Wight to recuperate from them.

Osbourne was built by Prince Albert and was Queen Victoria's favourite home. Overlooking the Solent, it is a lovely place with small royal apartments, which include the fantastic Durbar Room in which she received visiting Indian princes and rajahs. Adjoining it is a substantial administrative block in which her courtiers lived and worked — for years on end, for after Albert's death she hardly ever left the place, as a result becoming very unpopular with the general public. (Forty years on her reign had become known as Sixty Glorious Years.) The block was given by her son to the nation as a convalescent home for officers of the Armed Forces, but after World War II it was also opened to the Civil Service.

I met some fascinating people there and sat totally enthralled as they spoke. They were living history on its last legs: grand old men speaking of distant battles, brave old men who knew death was just around the corner. On one occasion there was an admiral (Burgess) there who had commanded the Home Fleet during the Second World War, he could recount in detail exactly what it was like to have been a midshipman on a cruiser during the battle of Jutland but got lost in the corridors in his wheel chair trying to remember where the loo was. There was also an ancient colonel with a young wife who had just had a pacemaker fitted.

At dinner one evening retired Rear-Admiral Rudd, the House Governor, a little Irishman from Dublin, mentioned that he had recently been in the naval hospital at Haslar. When I told him I hoped they had sorted out the problem he shook his head and said, matter-of-factly: 'Oh no, it's cancer of the prostate. There's no question of sorting it out. It's inoperable. Terminal. Talking about operations . . . ' He then told me a story about HMS *Warspite*.

During the battle of Jutland when the helm

was put hard over, the rudder locked — something to do with the design of the keel and the swell that was running at the time. Escorting destroyers had to make a run for it as the big ship turned in a great circle. In the Second World War, when Rudd was the medical officer on board, as she steamed down the Libyan coast to bombard the German headquarters in a hotel on the sea front at Tripoli ('where I spent my honeymoon, as a matter of fact,' he said) he was urgently summoned from the bridge to deal with a man who had acute appendicitis. 'I was just about to make my incision, had the scalpel poised, when the Stukas came over and the captain ordered hard-a-starboard. The rudder locked again, and the ship heeled right over. I've never removed an appendix so fast in all my life,' he chuckled: 'Six minutes flat! And that included the time it took to get the poor fella up off the floor, where he'd landed when the ship rolled, and put him back on the operating table.' He paused. 'She was a lovely ship, the *Warspite* . . . You know, when she was being taken to the breaker's yard she went aground in Sennen Cove. She didn't want to die like that, you see. She wanted to go with a bit of dignity.' So did he, I am sure.

months? I don't know. However long it was it became clear to him that the only way out of their dilemma was for him to leave her and return to his family, friends and way of life. He could not bear to do so and on a sunny summer's day, while walking together in a field looking down over the sparkling sea, he shot her dead, and then himself. She was still in her teens. Simon, Alex and I found them lying, side by side, in the graveyard of a little church at Landet, on the island of Tassinge. It is such a tragic and poignant story, yet their death lifted them into legend: they epitomised one human being's capacity to love another. And for them there was no time for disillusionment or the blunting of feelings; for pain or for growing old.

★   ★   ★

Prum is a little town in the Eiffel. In it there is a twin-towered basilica church — one that contains the bones of a saint — built in the year 722. In its ancient, calm stillness, wearing camouflaged combat uniform and boots, I stood in the shadows and watched two nuns praying. They wore a black coif, held in place by a white silken band embroidered with small red crosses. In the porch there is a board that lists the names of all the abbots. Pepin, the son of Charlemagne, was the third. Just outside the town there is a small Soldaten Cemetery in which there are sixty-nine graves. The occupants all died in September 1944, middle-aged or very young; I saw the graves of men in their late forties and early fifties, and one of a boy of fifteen. And the resting places of several seventeen-year-olds. It was about thirty miles away and three months later that those Americans left their bones in the Ardennes.

★　★　★

Braunlage is a small spa town in the Hartz Mountains, not far from Goslar. Legend has it that witches inhabit the great pine woods that cover the mountains. The shops are full of toys: witches on broomsticks, long-haired, big-eyed trolls. Braunlage was on the border between east and west Germany, almost on The Wall.

I drove a mile or so out of the town, escorted by a man from whom I had asked directions, and there it was. Like the Great Wall of China it marched along a swathe cut in the trees on the hill to my left, down along the valley in front of me, then straight through the trees and out of sight up another hill on my right. Wire in front of pillboxes, then a war-dog run (like our pi-dog Bonny in Cyprus, they were kept on a running lead), then more wire, then mines and automatic shotguns; then dragon's-teeth concrete anti-tank blocks, then more wire. All of it covered with aimed fire by soldiers in the pillboxes. It was there not to keep us out but to keep the East Germans in. Six hundred miles of it. What a chronic, shocking waste of money, apart from anything else.

★　★　★

Carnival. In 1978 I went to the carnival parade in Dusseldorf. It and Cologne, Mainz and Frankfort vie with each other to produce the most imaginative, the most startling, the most outrageous, the most colourful pageants. I watched for hours as floats went by and bands marched. It was dreamland. There were people in weird masks everywhere; girls with almost nothing on in the biting wind, waving, laughing; girls kissing strangers; people awash in alcohol but benign and affable, embracing each other, all smiles. Balloons, bunting, beer and bratwurst. It was Corpus Christi in Arequipa all over again, only more so. But hilariously bacchanalian, not devout. And played fortissimo. One hundred per cent . . .

After years of abortive attempts to sew me together the stitches kept popping out. I was told I would have to have yet another operation or be medically downgraded and lose my job. The crisis brought about by this news made me think deeply about my future and eventually I decided to leave the army, five years earlier than I had to. For many reasons the decision warranted a lot of heart-searching — my way of life, my pay, my pension, my prospects, all of them would have been much better had I stayed — but I had an itch I could not scratch; felt I should be writing, not doing what I had been doing for the last thirty years. My sons, aged twenty-one and nineteen, could now look after themselves, I thought (selfishly).

In 1977 Sybil and I journeyed again to Berlin, this time to stay with friends we had made when we lived next to them in Albert Schweitzer Strasse in Lubbecke. Roy Redgrave had taken over from the suddenly deceased Roger Chandler — as is often the case in life, one man's misfortune is another's blessing. Roy, from The Blues and Royals, had won an MC in the war and under a veneer of gentle good manners is a sharp, imaginative and determined man who speaks

450

several languages. He is related on one side to a princely Romanian family, the Ghikas (John Ghika, in the Irish Guards, had been on the same Camberley course as I, and would one day rise to high rank), and on the other to the acting family. Roy was now GOC Berlin, and we stayed with him and his wife Valery in the Villa Lemm, a late 19th Century mansion built by a businessman who made a fortune out of shoe polish by hiding a silver Mark in every hundred tins. The house was taken over by the Army at the end of the war and remained the GOC's residence until the mid-Nineties, when the British pulled out of Berlin.

One ice-cold morning I flew in a helicopter along a length of the Berlin wall, over Spandau prison and Hess' exercise yard, in which he was plodding along with his hands in his pockets, over the Kurfurstendamm and the Tiergarten, and then I hovered above the Brandenburg Gate looking into the snow-covered east. It's like that all the way to Moscow and beyond, I thought: grey and bleak, humourless and arid. (Not true, of course: people are much the same the world over, regardless of the political regime imposed on them, which can bind them to a greater or lesser degree.) When we landed my feet were so cold I could not feel them as I walked away from under the whooshing rotor blades.

Once or twice we drove in Roy's enormous, bulletproof Daimler with the Union Jack fluttering on one side of the bonnet and the GOC's pennant on the other. I was a very long way indeed in time and circumstances from 1946; from the callow youth wearing a Utility suit and carrying a cardboard attaché case who had joined the army in Carlisle.

* * *

I was lunched out of the mess in Bielefeld on my fiftieth birthday by a representative group of the officers of Headquarters 1st British Corps. It pleased me that sitting at the long table were men from almost every regiment in the British Army: cavalry, infantry, artillery, engineers; signallers, logisticians, a chaplain, a doctor . . . Every eventuality could have been catered for! They gave me an excellent lunch and the statuette of a soldier, suitably inscribed, and in return I broached a few bottles of champagne to mark the half century. Soon after that I was dined out by my own corps — and as a special treat allowed to conduct the band . . .

It happened that 1st (BR) Corps headquarters were in the field on my last day in uniform. That pleased me, too. I left my active life in the army on a summer's day when we were deployed in yet another of those long-suffering German villages. Cam-nets were draped over the vehicles, radios crackled, bees buzzed around hollyhock and lupins, German children strolled around hand in hand, chattering and pointing at the weapons of the soldiers on guard duty. Military Policemen in red hats stood at the crossroads. A helicopter sat knee-deep in clover in the centre of a field basking in the sunshine. In the office-trucks young officers marked maps with chinagraph pencils, drawing in the tac sign of this regiment, that battalion, the other squadron . . . and updated the latest position of the FEBA, the Forward Edge of the Battle Area — the front line, beyond which were the big red arrows . . .

I said goodbye to my successor, got into my staff car, waved a return salute to big Don McColl, a major on my staff, and then drove off down the road.

I felt ill at ease. I had cut the umbilical cord. Or, to put it more accurately, I felt like a deep-sea diver whose airline has just been severed by a swordfish. I had done what I had always been told not to do in the army — I had volunteered. Of my own free will I had left my friends and cast myself into the turbulent, uncaring waters of civilian life.

Well, as the sergeant had said when I was a recruit, 'You'll have nobody to blame but yourself if things go wrong, lad.'

★ ★ ★

In the army one is taught to end a written paper in a specified way. There should be a concise summary of the contents so that a busy general will get the point without reading the whole paper. There should be conclusions, and recommendations as to future action. Well, of course this is not a military paper. For one thing, at a hundred thousand words it is very much longer than any military paper ever written, except perhaps the operation order for the invasion of Normandy in 1944. For another, does anyone want to know my conclusions?

The answer to that is yes, I do, if for no other reason than to put things into perspective. Lessons must have been learned. As to recommendations, draw your own conclusions.

So here goes. Family life, my life, Life.

★ ★ ★

I could have been more fortunate with my parents but I could have been a lot less. I regret that they bickered a lot, because in practice I was an only child and got the brunt of it. I regret that their many worries dominated my life and became my worries. On the credit side, I am grateful that they cared so much for my welfare and did so much for me with so little. That they always made me feel good about myself and never belittled me even when imposing an awareness of right and wrong. I was not ignored or disliked, as some children are, did not suffer because they were selfish. Anything but. No, on balance, I was fortunate.

★ ★ ★

As to women, I have never been able to make up my mind. I love being with a pretty, vivacious woman but am off-put by bossy ones who must out-man a man if they reach positions of authority. Big, butch women terrify me, silly ones irritate me: the sort who haven't the faintest idea how things work and don't want to know. But I am easily moved emotionally when I see women achieving things that nature never intended them for physically; like the lovely, tiny, intensely feminine Claire Francis, who took on everything that storm and tempest and isolation could throw at her and triumphed.

Over the years women have given me more anguish than anything else in my whole life, but having said that, the act of love with a loved and loving woman must surely be the ultimate experience — and I have been fortunate to have had that too, in good measure.

* * *

So far I have lived in fifty-three different places — made my home, slept, eaten, passed my days — in fifty-three barracks or houses. No wonder I feel no affinity to any one place, always feel that yet another move is imminent. But on the credit side I have lived in or visited twenty-six countries, all over the world, and that is a marvellous bonus. It is nothing to boast about, it's just the way it turned out, but I was fortunate. Now, I have a home in Bristol, a fine city with a wealth of history.

* * *

I have witnessed many changes in my lifetime, though less than my father did. At the turn of the century when he was a young man Britain was the most powerful nation in the world. His was a time of national pride. Lions lived in the jungle and Longleat was the home of a distinguished marquis and not a circus presided over by a clown. He began life in the time of horse-drawn transport, steam engines, outside toilets, gas-light and coal fires — and no bathrooms. Of tuppenny post and no telephones. By the time Andrew died man was in Space, though a fat lot of good that will do him.

★   ★   ★

On the day I was born you could buy an Austin 12 for £255 and a ten-bedroom house in eight acres for £4,000. Stay in the Hotel Metropole in Bexhill-on-Sea for three guineas a week and send a letter for only tuppence-halfpenny. Now, a letter costs five shillings by first-class mail, and £5 notes are wrinkled confetti. In my time we have gone from cat's-whisker radios to digital camcorders, from biplanes to Concorde, from Model-Ts to Lamborghinis. From cold bedrooms and drafty windows to central heating and double-glazing. (And from chords to cacophony, from singing to wild shrieks that pass for music. From the

Post-Impressionists to heaven alone knows what: to names that will fade even faster than the acrylic paints they use.)

* * *

I first flew in an Anson, a twin-engined bus, from the RAF station at Wellesbourne Mountford in Warwickshire, as a change from wading around knee deep in mud fixing detonators to explosives. Since then I have flown a lot — in big jets, small planes, helicopters; even, once, in a glider. I love small planes and helicopters but don't care much for commercial flights. They are so boring by comparison. And, my dear, the food! I have owned seventeen cars, which I suppose is very few compared to some people: a man I knew a few years ago had owned more than sixty. By now, he must have reached the ton. When he went out alone his wife never knew what he was going to come back in. But at least he came back: perhaps it was the cars that kept him from going spare.

* * *

It bothers me that these days this country is not a very happy place to live in. Despite the fact that our population is at the peak of present day human development and comfort nothing is ever right, nobody is admirable, envy and back-biting abound. What a Pity.

★   ★   ★

God? Ah, well now, there's a question for you. As Voltaire said, if He did not exist it would be necessary to invent Him. As Pascal said, it would be unwise to bet that He did not exist. Yet even that witticism carries in it the implied threat of punishment. Is God, then, a martinet sergeant-major wielding the big stick?

Will Hindus, Christians, Moslems, Jews, Buddhists and the rest ever take a deep breath and admit there is no-one out there waiting to strike them down and blight their crops, to condemn them to eternal fire or a worse incarnation in the next life if they do not so as their priests tell them? I doubt it. Man needs the comfort of religion; cannot accept unending death and must have immortality to look forward to — though why, beats me: he's always complaining about how bad life is.

Having given religion a lot of thought over the years I have come to the simple conclusion that people should do their best for others and acknowledge their faith without rancour, whatever it may be, for at root they are all based on morality.

I have been pretty immoral myself, from time to time, but the moral bit is important. Some people say that government has no business preaching morality, but if Christianity means nothing to most people in this country, with more of us going to football matches than attending matins, then who is going to give the lead if not government? As everyone knows, example is the best form of leadership.

★ ★ ★

Had I not been conscripted it is impossible to say what I would be doing now — except that I would not be writing this book.

I certainly do not regret that I spent most of my life in the army, among people I could respect. The Army has maintained standards of right conduct that went out of fashion in civilian life decades ago. How long this can continue I do not know; in time, the lowering of standards in the population from which it is recruited can only result in the lowering of standards in the army.

★ ★ ★

The single dominating political factor during my life was that the Soviet Union was the open, avowed enemy. Men on both sides, West and East, devoted whole careers to organisations whose raison d'être was preparation for a war that never came. In 1986 I went to a reunion dinner of the Joint Services Staff College, at Greenwich, where it had moved from Latimer. After dinner I remarked to Dennis Healey, a guest of honour, that the British Army of the Rhine had been in Germany for forty years; how much longer did he think it would be there? 'Another forty years,' quoth he, instantly. But within two years the Iron Curtain had been torn down. It was predictable, though nobody predicted it. East Berlin 1953, Hungary 1956, Prague 1968, Warsaw 1981 . . . It was only a matter of time. No punitive regime endures.

★   ★   ★

And a last word?

The thing that strikes me most forcibly when trying to sum up, to find the key to the whole baffling, often depressing but neverthe-less astonishingly stimulating fact of being alive, is the certainty that because our basic genetic structures are all the same, all living things are related. We are one creation. And we are immortal: no living thing ever dies, because the combination of atoms that made it exist disperse again and become something else; almost certainly, in time, parts of other living creatures. Our body cells contain atomic particles which in their time have been many things — people and animals, plants and chemicals, earth and sea and sky. And even stars.

★　★　★

It is said that the best wine is drunk last. I would like to think that that is so, and that the best is yet to come, but somehow I doubt it.

Meanwhile, I have a few mementos to remind me of the way we were. A piece of carved Roman marble from the sea at Salamis. The fossil of a sea creature six-million years old blown out of the clay in Warwickshire. A silver snuff box containing a few grains of soil from Agincourt, and another with bloodstained earth from Dien Bien Phu that I brought back from Hanoi. A piece of Blue John marble given to me by a Derbyshire staff-sergeant when I left the army, and an American kidney-shaped mess tin I picked up near Malmedy.

It has a bullet hole right through the centre

of the bottom of it, as if its owner was warming his cold hands around it on a frosty morning and taking a sip of hot coffee when another mother's son did what the conventions of the time required him to do and, good marksman that he was, put an end to warmth and drinking and light and everything else.

We do hope that you have enjoyed reading this large print book.

Did you know that all of our titles are available for purchase?

We publish a wide range of high quality large print books including:
Romances, Mysteries, Classics
General Fiction
Non Fiction and Westerns

Special interest titles available in large print are:
The Little Oxford Dictionary
Music Book
Song Book
Hymn Book
Service Book

Also available from us courtesy of Oxford University Press:
Young Readers' Dictionary
(large print edition)
Young Readers' Thesaurus
(large print edition)

For further information or a free brochure, please contact us at:
Ulverscroft Large Print Books Ltd.,
The Green, Bradgate Road, Anstey,
Leicester, LE7 7FU, England.
Tel: (00 44) 0116 236 4325
Fax: (00 44) 0116 234 0205